INDIAN MAID

Spur lay on his back, then leaned up on his elbows a moment to check his mare. She was moving around as if something were bothering her.

Suddenly something flashed in front of his eyes and he felt the cold steel of a knife blade pressing against his throat. Spur tensed; the knife was poised to slash across his windpipe. He was totally at the mercy of his unknown assailant.

MONTANA MINX

The intruder squirmed into the room over the sill, landing on his hands on the floor two feet below the opening. He brought in his feet and stared at the bed. As silently as death his hand brought up a six-inch knife and he held it like a sabre. Clearly the man had used a knife before. He checked the door, then moved on silent feet toward the bed.

He thrust the first time with all the power of his body behind it, striking what he thought was a broad back. The knife went in and he pulled it out and jabbed it twice more into the dummy on the bed. Spur shot him in the right leg and kicked the knife from his hand.

Other Spur Double Editions:

GOLD TOWN GAL/RED ROCK REDHEAD
SAVAGE SISTERS/HANG SPUR McCOY!

SPUR DOUBLE:

INDIAN MAID

MONTANA MINX

DIRK FLETCHER

LEISURE BOOKS NEW YORK CITY

A LEISURE BOOK®

December 2006

Published by

Dorchester Publishing Co., Inc.
200 Madison Avenue
New York, NY 10016

Indian Maid copyright © 1984 by Dirk Fletcher
Montana Minx copyright © 1984 by Dirk Fletcher

ISBN 0-8439-2856-5

Visit us on the web at www.dorchesterpub.com.

INDIAN MAID

CHAPTER ONE

May 12, 1870—Northwestern Nebraska.

(Everyone on the East coast was talking about the marvels of the Atlantic City Boardwalk finished in June of 1870. Most of the panic caused by the attempt to corner the gold market in September of 1869 had faded. The first Negro U.S. Congressman, J. R. Rainey, was sworn into office. Philadelphia was the scene of a motion picture showing, animated photographic picture projection before a theatre audience. In that same year, the first U.S. Weather Bureau was authorized and the first trademark registered by the government. This was the year the donkey was first used as a symbol for the Democratic party in a cartoon in New York City. The first Japanese legation was established in Washington D.C. and an ambassador arrived. General Phil Sheridan had taken command of the enormous army Division of Missouri. It covered twelve states and three territories,

*more than a million square miles of land and con-
tained some 192,000 settlers. There were seventy-
six established army posts and some 17,000 army
regulars under General Sheridan's command.
And Spur McCoy was riding from Sidney,
Nebraska north to Camp Sheridan near the
Dakota Territory line.)*

Spur McCoy sat on his bay behind a light screening
of cottonwood brush as he watched the approaching
riders with a growing sense of dread: he had been
correct. The ponies had no saddles, and the party
consisted of two Indians and a white woman who
had been tied to her mount.

Spur slid to the ground silently, pulling the sturdy, reliable Spencer repeating carbine from the scabbard. The carbine was only 43 inches long but could
fire seven shots as fast as a man could work the trigger guard lever and cock the hammer. The big .56
caliber round was a little short on distance and stopping power, but at close range it could tear off a
man's head, white or Indian.

Spur ran quickly to the fringe of rocks thirty
yards from the gully. The trio continued along the
dry creek as Spur figured they would. They were
moving south and west through this hot and
unusually dry day in May. They would follow the
water course well past his position.

Both Indian braves rode as if half sleeping. Their
heads hung down, one hand holding the rawhide
hackamore around their ponies' heads as they
swayed from time to time on the horses' backs.

The woman wore no hat and had been stripped to
the waist, her only garment a green gingham skirt.

Her breasts jolted with each step of the pony which had been tethered to the warrior's horse in front. As the trio came closer Spur could see that the woman had been in the sun too long. Her face, shoulders and breasts were badly sunburned, and he could see tears streaking her dust-covered face. Spur knew about Indians' treatment of white women. He made sure there was a round in the Spencer's chamber, then cocked the carbine and rested it over the rock. Spur had no qualms about "fair play" or warning the savages. They were kidnapping the woman; she was tied and a captive. It was his duty to rescue her any way he could.

Spur waited until the trio was exactly opposite him, less than fifty feet away, and at a place where the braves would have few places to hide. He sighted in with the Spencer. He had checked this weapon for accuracy the day before against a giant cottonwood, firing at a carved X. It had fired a hair high and to the right at 100 yards.

Spur sighted down on the first Indian's head, aiming slightly above his ear and to the left. He squeezed slowly and when the Spencer fired, the bullet tore through the redskin's ear, exploding out his forehead, splattering brain matter, bone chips, and blood and gore all over the dusty trail. The dead Indian jolted from the saddle and sprawled in the dust. His horse stopped.

Spur pulled back on the trigger guard at once, cocked the carbine and swung the muzzle to the second Indian. In the three seconds the movements took Spur, the remaining Indian had tumbled off his horse on the side away from Spur and raced toward a pile of rocks using his horse as a shield. Spur fired twice more, and saw one round slam through the Indian's leg and send him tumbling, but by then the savage was protected by the rocks where there was plenty of cover to hide his retreat.

Spur looked at the woman. She sat on the horse, and started at the sound of his weapon, shaking her head in numb surprise. Her horse had shied away at the smell of death, then quieted, glad to stand still for any reason.

Spur left his concealment and ran to the woman, cut the rawhide binding her to the horse and helped her down. He led her to the shade of the cotton-woods, and gave her a drink from his canteen.

For a moment he wondered if she were out of her mind. She sat there nude to the waist and either not conscious of the fact or not disturbed whatsoever by it, he couldn't tell which. Her long blonde hair was tangled and dirty, her shoulders, back, breasts, stomach and face all burned a bright angry red, but not blistered by the relentless May Nebraska sun. He guessed she had not been a captive for very long. Spur pulled open the carpet bag on his pack horse, took out one of his lightweight cotton shirts and found a large kerchief. He laid them in front of the woman who stared at them, then looked up at him without a word.

She had the largest, most interesting eyes he had ever seen. They were light brown, with flecks of gold, and so wide and wondering that she looked like a lost fawn. Her oval face was unmarked by time or toil and he guessed she was no more than twenty-three. She was a foot shorter than Spur, and couldn't weigh a hundred pounds. Her breasts were

8

full and high with small budlike nipples centered in dark pink areolas.

"Oh, my," she said at last, her voice strained, but pleasant. She glanced up at him with a kind of bewildered gaiety. "It's so hot out today, I'm just totally bemused."

"Yes, Ma'am, it certainly is hot. I brought a shirt for you."

She stared at the shirt, took it when he gave it to her, but made no effort to put it on. Spur slid the shirt around her shoulders, helped her push her arms into the sleeves and rolled up the cuffs so her hands showed. He waited another moment, then, since she seemed incapable of helping herself, buttoned the front. McCoy folded the kerchief into a triangle and fastened it over her head, tying it under her chin. He realized she was barefoot, a standard Indian tactic for captives so they wouldn't try to run away.

She watched him, her face working, as though she were waking from a deep sleep.

"Thank you," she said slowly as if searching for words.

"You're welcome." He waited a moment, then gave her another drink from his canteen, making sure she didn't take too much. She looked down at the shirt she wore and a smile touched her lips, then faded away.

"Would they have killed me?" she asked in a voice so devoid of emotion that it made Spur uneasy.

"Yes—later."

"Oh, I see, after they. . . ."

"We should be moving away from here. There

could be more Indians about."

"No," she said positively. "They were alone, a raiding party. Sioux. I saw them kill a rancher and his wife."

Spur had heard about the fighting qualities of the Sioux, fierce plains Indians who were battling to save their homeland. He'd heard they were, next to the Apaches, the most fierce fighters.

"Are you from the army at Camp Sheridan?"

She didn't answer for a moment, then she raised huge brown eyes filled with tears.

"I was . . . once."

"How long have you been with the Indians?"

"Two days. I can't ever go back to Camp Sheridan."

"Of course you can. That's where I'm headed. It can't be more than a day's ride north."

"I can't go back!" She looked down at the shirt again. "Oh. . . ." She stared at him. "This must be your shirt. I must have been. . . . Yes—they made me take off my blouse and chemise. I . . ." Tears flooded her eyes again.

"I understand. My name is Colonel Spur McCoy. I'm with the Quartermaster Corps, requisition and supply. I'm out here on a survey. Are you—is your husband in the army?"

She wiped away the tears. "Yes, at Camp Sheridan. That's why I can't go back."

"You can go back with me." Spur smiled and pointed to the north. "We really should be moving. Can you ride? We'll ride double on my bay. She's sturdy and you don't look like you weigh that much."

The sun went under a cloud and he saw her getting

herself emotionally ready for what lay ahead. He knew why she felt she couldn't go back. She had been captured by Indians, most surely violated several times in those two days. The other wives would shun her. If she were an officer's wife her husband would be in an intolerable situation and undoubtedly would ask for a transfer. If he were an enlisted man, it might be easier, but the women would be more outwardly vicious.

Spur found two pair of heavy socks and used them to make temporary footgear for her, then helped her mount the bay and they rode away. At first she barely touched him, riding behind, then at last she put her arms around him and sobbed against his back.

"I'm sorry," she said once, her voice breaking.

Spur turned to look at her swollen, red, beautiful eyes.

"Ma'am, you've been through an ordeal in hell that no one should have to withstand, and you've survived. I reckon you're strong enough to stand up to those cats back at the camp. You're alive, and not injured, that's the important part."

She held him tightly a moment with her arms, her head still resting against his back. "I wish other men thought the way you do," she whispered, then she sobbed again. Spur could think of nothing to say to make her feel better.

All afternoon the sun came in and out from behind the clouds, and the day cooled. There was a hint of rain in the air. About five o'clock Spur selected a sheltered spot near a small stream, a thicket of willow and a few wild mulberry bushes and some wild plum. He stopped in the shade.

11

"I'm not sure how much farther it is to Camp Sheridan. If it's all right with you, we'll make camp here and let you rest up before going on in tomorrow."

"Another night to account for," she said softly.

"You don't have to account for anything to anyone," Spur said, angry but not at her. "Your husband will be overjoyed to have you back safe and well."

She laughed bitterly and it so surprised Spur that he turned and gawked at her. She stopped and took a long deep breath.

"You don't know my husband. And you *certainly* don't know army wives." Her attitude changed then; seemingly her resolve strengthened and her spirits rose.

"Yes, Colonel McCoy, let's stop here. It will be a blessing to be able to sleep without being tied up."

They halted and Spur unpacked his light camping outfit, a small two-man army tent four feet high at the center, three army blankets, and his mess gear. He set up the tent and spread out two of the army blankets as a ground cover, and told her the tent was hers. Then he started a fire before dusk closed in, and cooked some of his provisions. First he fried the rest of his bacon, then sliced fresh potatoes into the drippings and mixed in diced onions.

Spur boiled coffee and sliced a loaf of brown bread from his pack. The woman had stayed in the tent while he cooked. Only when he told her the food was ready did she come out. He had provided her with a basin of water, soap, comb and a towel and she had made an attempt to look presentable. Now her face was scrubbed and her hair clean and combed.

12

She came out of the tent with the tails of his long shirt tied in a knot in front. All the buttons but one were fastened below her chin. She sat down on the log and watched Spur.

"Colonell McCoy, my name is Janet Casselberry— Mrs. Robert First Lieutenant Casselberry."

Spur gave a short bow and handed her a tin plate with half the fried potatoes, onions and bacon. "It's a pleasure to meet you, Mrs. Casselberry. I'm sure your husband will be proud of you for showing so much courage."

She nodded. "I'm sorry I was so . . . so vague when you rescued me. I think I was a little out of my mind with the heat, the terror, the rage, and the shock of seeing that Indian's head shatter just in front of me." She looked up and in the firelight her eyes were even more beautiful. "I went a little crazy. I didn't even realize that I was—uncovered." She looked away, blushing. "I thank you for saving my life, at least what is left of it. I realize this isn't a worthy show of gratitude, but that will come later when I am in a better position."

"Mrs. Casselberry, your life is just beginning. You'll always remember this episode, but you will outlive it and defeat it, and be happy and fulfilled. Don't decide anything right now. Wait until we get back to the camp. If your husband doesn't welcome you with open arms, I'll have the scoundrel horse-whipped and then courtmartialed."

Janet smiled at him. It was a delicately beautiful smile. "Colonel, I know you're trying to bolster my spirits. I appreciate that. I'm also intelligent enough to know you can't possibly influence or courtmartial my lieutenant. But I thank you for the thought. Now, where did you learn to make such delicious fried potatoes?" Her plate was empty and the two large slices of bread had vanished as well.

"When did you eat last?" he asked her.

"Eat? I can't remember." She stood and he was surprised at her quickness. "I'll do the dishes. Is there any sand to use to wash things?"

He brought some sand in a pan of water and she washed the plates clean, then the skillet and helped him put them away. They sat beside the small fire not talking, just watching the coals, Spur thinking how glad he was to be out in the wilds again, to smell the crisp air, to hear the cry of the night creatures.

She peered at him a moment, then threw some twigs on the fire so it blazed up and she could see his face plainly.

"Colonel McCoy, I hope you won't try and make the people back at Camp Sheridan accept me. I know how they will react, almost exactly what they will do. It's the army. We were stationed at another army post where a woman was rescued from the Indians. She had been gone almost a year. At last she escaped and was found by a surveying crew. She wasn't army, but she stayed at the fort for two months.

"At first the women only gossiped about her. Everyone said she was used by all the braves in the tribe. Then the story was that she was the prize for the best warrior and was passed from brave to brave. At last they said she was claimed by the second chief as his second wife. Then the women began asking her about what it was like—ah—er . . .

14

you know . . . being with a savage. It got so whenever she came outside she was pounced on by the women and asked embarrassingly outrageous questions. She was never invited to dinner, or to the officers' dances, or to any socials. Two months after she arrived at the post she put a gun to her head and killed herself. I *know* what it's going to be like."

"But with you it's different. You *are* army."

"Yes, and an officer's wife, which will make it twice as bad for me." Her eyes held him and he knew it was true. He had rescued her, only to take her back into another hell.

A short time later they let the fire die down and Spur told her goodnight. He tied the flaps on the tent after she went inside.

"Good night, Colonel, and thank you," she said through the canvas.

"You're entirely welcome, Mrs. Casselberry."

Spur lay down on his blanket, with his favorite Merwin & Hurlburt .44 loaded, cocked and lying under his right hand. The night was warm. He could see the moon edging past some clouds and filtering faint light through the trees. Crickets began chirping as the fire went out; soon the night birds called and Spur dozed, knowing that the world was once again at peace.

Something touched his shoulder. His hand closed around the six-gun and he sat up suddenly, the .44 aiming at the dark, shadowy figure bending over him.

"Colonel! It's me!" Janet Casselberry whispered.

"Oh, sorry." He let the hammer down gently on the loaded chamber. "Are you all right?"

"No. The tent is so stuffy, hot. I've brought out the blankets. Would it bother you if I slept out here?"

"No bother at all."

She nodded and put her blankets beside his. Janet Casselberry looked at him sternly. "I'm not meaning in any way that I want to get intimate . . ."

"I understand."

She smiled into the darkness. "Yes. Yes, Colonel, I really think you do." She lay down, stretched out and turned on her side. They both were still fully clothed. She squirmed a moment, then reached a hand out and touched his shoulder.

"Just so I know you're there," she said. Her voice went softer so he had to strain to hear her. "I was so frightened those two days—I'm still frightened. I don't want to be alone."

He didn't reply. A moment later she sighed, then almost at once she was breathing deeply, evenly. Janet was sleeping. Spur dozed and woke, dozed again and when he woke the next time, Janet Casselberry was curled against him, her arm over his chest, her head cuddled on his shoulder, as she slept soundly.

Spur wondered about her, worried about what kind of man her husband might be, and at last drifted off to sleep.

CHAPTER TWO

Fragments of daylight on the eastern horizon awakened Spur several hours later. He opened his eyes without moving, aware of a soft, curved body next to his. Blonde hair tickled his cheek, making him smile. The woman lay half on her side, half against him, her arm over his chest gripping his far side, her legs pressed against his.

Carefully he moved her arm and edged away from her. She slept on. He slid across the blanket, covered her shoulders with one of her blankets and got to his feet quietly. She'd need all the rest she could get to prepare for the hard day coming.

Spur found wood and silently built a cooking fire, then made coffee.

Spur McCoy was thirty-two years old, over six feet tall, and carried two hundred pounds sleekly. He had sandy red hair, a full moustache and mutton chop sideburns. He had strong hands, was an excellent horseman, and a crack shot with derringer, six-gun or rifle. He looked back at the sleeping woman.

She would be off his hands soon and someone else's problem.

For a moment he thought about his assignment. "An inspection survey," he had told her. In a way it was true. And he had once been in the army, though not as a colonel. He had made captain during the Civil War before Lee surrendered. After two years in the army he'd gone to Washington as an aide to Senator Arthur B. Walton, a longtime family friend. In 1865, Charles Spur McCoy was appointed one of the first U.S. Secret Service Agents. Since the Secret Service was the only federal law enforcement agency in existence, it handled a wide range of problems, most of them far removed from the original task of preventing the circulation of counterfeit currency.

He had served six months in the Washington Secret Service office, then was transferred to head the base in St. Louis and handle all problems west of the Mississippi. Spur had been chosen from twenty men for the position because of his excellent marksmanship. He also was the best horseman in the group.

Spur pushed more sticks into the fire. If his Harvard professors could see him now they would be amused. This certainly wasn't the future he had planned. His father was a well-known merchant in New York City and Spur had gone to Harvard as a matter of course, graduating in the class of 1858. Now here he was in the middle of the western Nebraska wilderness heading for an army camp near the Black Hills in Dakota territory. Indians in that area had been acquiring more and more rifles, and the army commander in Chicago wanted to find out their source of supply and have that source eliminated.

William Wood, Spur's Agency director in Washington, had given the assignment to Gen. Wil Halleck, who had passed it on to Spur; since it fell within his jurisdiction.

Spur had taken the train to Sidney, Nebraska, then picked up some gear and headed on horseback nearly 150 miles north to his target.

"You should have wakened me." The sharp, accusing voice cut through his thoughts, and Spur looked over to see Janet sitting up in the blankets. Her blonde hair was rumpled and she still looked half asleep. Two of the buttons on the shirt had come undone during the night and the swell of one breast was tantalizingly revealed. She looked so vulnerable, so alone and appealing that Spur had to stifle a surge of desire.

"Good morning. I figured the rest would do you good."

"For my coming ordeal no doubt?" She stood, briskly fastened the two shirt buttons then knelt down and began straightening and folding the blankets. "Aren't you in a rush to get started?"

"No."

"Oh?" It surprised her. She sat back on her heels and looked at him. "Well, I am. I want to get it over with. I want to find out what Neil is going to say to me. The suspense is driving me mad!"

Spur grinned. "Anything you say. Coffee?" She nodded and hurried toward him. He could see her breasts bouncing under the shirt and he remembered how beautiful they had been unemcumbered, swaying and swinging free, naked and sunburned . . .

Spur shook his head to clear it and poured a cup of coffee for her. Her fingers touched his as she took it and she glanced up at him quickly, then away.

"Thank you, Colonel."

"My pleasure, Ma'am."

He tried to make small talk about the army post, but she was anxious to be moving. They packed up and she let him help her up on the back of his bay, then he swung up. The pack horse was tethered to his saddle and trailed behind with a slack line.

"Have you any idea how much farther it is to the camp?" he asked her.

She stared around, frowning, and when they came to a slight rise, she murmured, "Yes, I remember that bluff over there. If we angle toward it, we should come to the White River. From here I'd say the camp is upstream about fifteen miles more."

"Thanks. I could use you as my scout."

"I'd probably get us lost."

She put her hands on his shoulders now. Spur found her touch a little unsettling because he kept remembering her large, sunburned breasts and the way they bounced and swung when she walked. Spur grinned ruefully and kicked the bay into motion. Her arms stole around his waist and he heard her give a small sigh.

By noon they could see the army post nestled beside the White River, an odd collection of log structures chinked with a mixture of mud, sand and lime. There was no outer wall, no palisade to hide behind. The buildings were built against one another in a rough square. As they came closer, Spur saw that the two largest buildings were made of adobe blocks. Like most army buildings of the day, these had been built with whatever materials were close at hand.

When they were barely a mile from the camp, a rider approached them from an angle. The trooper was obviously a lookout of some kind, keeping an eye peeled for anyone who happened to approach the area.

The trooper in his blue uniform and low crowned brown campaign hat rode up, stared at the riders for an astonished moment and saluted.

"Mrs. Casselberry, Ma'am! Glory! We never expected to see you again, Ma'am!"

"Corporal Jeffers, isn't it? I'm quite all right, as you can see. But please don't spread the word. I want my arrival to be a surprise. You may return to your post."

"Yes, Ma'am."

"This is Colonel McCoy, Corporal. He'll be staying at Camp Sheridan for a time."

The corporal stiffened and saluted. Spur returned the salute.

"At ease, Corporal. You're excused to return to your post."

"Yes sir!" the corporal said, saluted again, pulled his horse around and rode hard away from them.

Janet tensed and he felt it. "We better go now, quickly, Colonel McCoy, or I might just get off this horse and start running the other way. My bravado is starting to desert me."

Spur turned and looked her in the eye. "Janet Casselberry, you suffered at the hands of the Sioux and you got away. Those biddies at the camp are not going to be half as tough. Remember that, and you'll do just fine."

A half hour later they created a sensation when they rode through a gate in the fence near the sutler's store. Women streamed from a dozen houses and rushed up to greet Janet, escorting her into her own house. Spur continued to the commanding officer's quarters and tied up his horses.

One room of the commander's residence was partitioned off to form an office. In this separate "office" he conducted the business of the camp.

Spur was asked by a sergeant to wait a moment while the trooper went through a door into the residence section. He came back a moment later with a tall, thin man whose uniform hung on him like rags on a fencepost. Black, thinning hair barely covered an oversized head that seemed too large and heavy for the slender neck. The man's eyes were piercing and black. He made no pretense of cordiality and offered no welcome.

"Colonel? Colonel? I made no request for any kind of a damn survey! What do you mean, survey? Where are your papers?"

Spur picked up a leather case and opened it, handing the lieutenant colonel a sheaf of formal army orders, instructions, and a carte blanche that permitted the bearer to do virtually anything on the post that wasn't overtly seditious or mutinous.

"Yeah, seen this trash before. Killing the goddamned Indians is our job, not mollycoddling some paper shuffler from Washington!" The camp commander sat in a chair behind his desk and peered balefully at Spur who had seated himself in the only other chair in the room.

"I seen this kind of orders during the war. Wrote

up a few myself. Always did it this way when I sent in a horsewhipping spy to get to the bottom of some trouble in an outfit. Ain't no trouble here. No sir, young feller. Don't care if you *are* a full colonel, I got the years and experience on you. Hell, don't matter none! You just keep outa my way, don't make trouble, and I won't give you any problems."

Spur stood and walked to the desk, frowning down at the older man, who looked up with a touch of impatience.

"Colonel, thank you for introducing yourself. You sound like a man who doesn't really want to stay in the army, or stay in command of this facility. Now what is your name, your permanent rank, and your official mission in this god-forsaken rat's nest?"

The man behind the desk snapped to attention.

"Sir! My name is Ezekiel Underhill. Permanent rank of Major. Brevet Lieutenant Colonel March 1869. Sir! My mission at this post is to render all possible aid to settlers, to maintain the peace with the indignous Indian population, and to follow those army orders issued to me by The Division of Missouri, General Phil Sheridan, commanding."

"In that case, Colonel, you're doing a damn poor job!"

Lt. Colonel Underhill's face turned red and he started to say something but Spur cut him off with a quick gesture.

"I usually don't use my rank, Underhill. I'd rather work incognito. But in this case I can and I will, if you force me to."

Colonel Underhill's eyes blazed but his voice was steady.

"Yes, sir. I understand, sir."

"I hope you do. I'll need quarters, a mount on call, and I don't want an aide trailing me around."

"Yes, sir."

"I'll want to meet all of your officers as soon as possible. Do you have a central mess?"

"No, sir, but we have a social and card party scheduled for tonight, eight sharp. You're welcome to attend."

"Thank you, Colonel Underhill. You're more than kind. Now, if you'll have someone show me to my quarters and provide some hot water, I could use a bath."

An hour later Spur McCoy had finished scrubbing his long body and washing the trail dust out of his hair. He was just about to get out of the tub, when the rear door to his quarters opened and the rounded backside of a woman pushed through the door.

"Don't pay me no attention, Colonel. I'm Molly what is sent over to do up your bed." As she finished speaking, she turned and saw Spur sitting folded up in the oval galvanized wash tub and she giggled. "Lordy, lordy, lordy, now that's what I calls one big tall chunk of mankind!" She dropped the sheets she carried and picked up his towel.

"Now, I wash backs too. Your back all scrubbed clean?"

"Sorry to say it is, Molly."

She laughed and walked around the tub, looking admiringly at his genitals. "My, my! Now *that* is a big one, and I bet he can get one hell of a lot bigger."

Spur chuckled. "No bet, Molly."

"Colonel, I got me this little itch. I mean, if you could help me I'd be ever so grateful."

"Itch?"

Molly unbuttoned the top of her blouse and a moment later flipped out a big breast. Molly was decidedly buxom, with short brown hair, a happy chunk who was proud of her rounded figure and billowing breasts. Spur stood, took the towel from her hands and dried himself. She watched in surprised delight as he dried his crotch first and his manhood came up stiff and ready.

"Lord love a duck, I think Mr. Dick there likes me tittie!"

"He loves both of them," Spur said and took three long steps to the rear door and locked it. Molly hurried to the front door and bolted it, then met him by the bed.

"Molly, little darling, do you have another bouncer like that one?" Spur moved his hand around her exposed breast, caressing it gently. It was as large as half a watermelon.

"Hot damn!" Molly said softly. "This is gonna be fun!"

She ran ahead of him to the bed, flopped on it, and spread-eagled herself on the blanket.

Spur sat down on the edge of the bed and she lifted up beside him and reached for his ramrod hard stiff.

"Lordy, lordy, what a prick!" She touched it reverently, then her hand wrapped around and she stroked him twice. Molly bent and kissed the very tip of the purple head and Spur felt a stabbing jolt of desire throughout his body. He pulled her up and took off her blouse and a thin chemise. Both breasts billowed out and Spur groaned in delight as he pushed his face between them, kissing them in turn,

25

working around until he found a heavy brown nipple which he kissed and then nibbled until Molly yelped with pleasure.

"My, my, you *are* an eager fella! I love it! I bet you could just chew my titties off if you wanted to. But I've got places even better!" She wiggled out of her skirt and two petticoats and lay there, round and frankly fat and loving it. She laughed. "Hey, bet you ain't never fucked a real fat girl before. Shit, we're *fun*. We got to be. More bounce to the ounce and we shake like jelly. We have the padding to make your ride more fun." She nodded. "Yeah, I can see you just ain't never fucked a fat girl. Don't worry, time comes, I'll pee a little bit to give you a good target." She set off in shrieking laughter and he put his hand over her mouth to quiet the sound.

"Oh, yeah, I ain't home now." She bounced up and sat beside him again, then grabbed his heavy scrotum and brushed his big balls together tenderly. "Oh, yeah, I got to see what these sweethearts produce. About six times a night I'd say. Christ, wouldn't *that* be a ride!"

She played with him and stroked him a few more times. "Lordy, am I going to eat you! Gonna get down and spread your legs and kiss your big balls, then I'm gonna get each one in my mouth and chew them until you go wild. I can make a fella come just chewing on his nuts, you know that? True. You'll love every hour of it." She laughed. "Course, I can't stay no hour. Got to be back in about twenty minutes. You a quick performer?"

She turned and went down on his staff, gulping more of it in her mouth than Spur thought possible, then began a rhythmical bobbing of her head that soon produced urgent results. Spur caught her head and pulled her up.

"Now, darlin'," he said, "we better make it now or it ain't got time to happen." She spread herself out on the bed and lifted her knees. Spur knew exactly what to do next. A moment later they were locked together and she pushed her legs higher on his sides but couldn't lock them on top.

Spur's steam pressure had been building since the moment she had pushed in through the back door of his room and turned around. Now he stroked quickly and before he knew it the magic trigger tripped and he was off on a mission of no return. A moment later, it was over. and he lay on top of her panting as if he would never get enough oxygen back into his depleted system.

She hugged him tightly, not letting him lift away when he attempted to.

"Lordy, but you were good! I had my own party and you didn't even feel me, you was way out there in the sky somewhere. I even talked to you, but nothing would make you hear. You is something, Colonel. Damn! You're really a wild one."

Spur moved away and sat up. She might be a good source of information. He'd try a little gentle questioning.

"Molly, you know this camp. What do you think about Colonel Underhill? Is he a good soldier?"

"Shit, no! He's half crazy. He goes on tears now and then and the men don't know what he wants or how they should do something. He changes his ass for his nose more times than you can piss in a circle. He's just plain crazy, but nobody can get him relieved. Major Rutherford—Vern. Now *there* is a good

27

man. He's fair and honest, fucking good soldier, but he's stuck under Underhill. Damn shame. One of these days this camp is gonna blow sky high, and when things come down, Underhill won't be here. He's an Injun hater like all officers. Christ, us enlisted can get along with or without the savages. Figure they got a right to live too, and this is their land we're on. But they pulled back into the hills, and now pretty soon orders will come to push them back farther. Been happening for a hundred and fifty years now, longer than that I guess."

She sat up and began collecting her clothes. "Christ, I got to get moving. Got two more beds to make up. I work the Bachelor Officers' Quarters. Get paid three dollars a fucking week for it, so me and my man make out fine." She grinned in reply to Spur's unanswered question. "Naw, hell, he don't mind my fucking around a little. Just so I don't bring home none of them diseases. He's been to Alaska. Says the Eskimoes got it right, fucking a cunt can't hurt it none, just makes it better." She laughed. "So far I think them Eskies is right!"

She dressed quickly, picked up the sheets she had dropped and hurried out the back door.

Spur dressed in clean clothes, civilian blue shirt and pants and a wide belt with a silver buckle. He was looking forward to the bachelor officers' mess call at five o'clock.

CHAPTER THREE

The Officers' Mess was adjacent to the kitchen, on
the far side from the enlisted men's messhall, but
much smaller. Most of the officers had family with
them, since this was not designated as a dangerous
or hardship post. Only five officers ate at the mess
that night, plus one civilian who was introduced as
an army scout, on the army payroll but due soon to
come to the end of his contract.

The highest ranking man there was Captain
Grove, the camp adjutant. He was a quiet little
man, barely five-feet two, who had little to say and
did not enter into the round of jokes. The most talk-
ative was the most recent arrival, Lt. Omer Imhoff,
who had been at the camp for six months. He was a
newly commissioned officer, fresh out of West
Point, and had waited only three months for a post.
Most freshly graduated second lieutenants from
West Point had up to a year's wait before they received their actual commission and were appointed
to an army post or camp.

"Of course I was damn lucky to get this spot. I'd have taken anything. But this senator in Washington said he could get me a post if I would contribute a hundred dollars to his campaign fund. What the hell, I borrowed the money from my mother, paid him and here I am."

Imhoff was solidly built, about five-feet ten, and probably weighed over two hundred pounds. But there was no obvious flab; he looked all muscle and willing to use it. He was blond, with a fair moustache and a short trimmed beard of a slightly darker shade. He was the most friendly of the group. Everyone knew who Spur was and why he was there —the quartermaster survey story.

"How did you get to be a colonel so fast in Quartermaster?" Lt. Imhoff asked.

"I must know that same senator you do, Lieutenant," Spur shot back. Everyone laughed.

"Are we still at a standstill on cleaning out the savages in the Black Hills?" one of the officers asked.

"You must realize I don't get into the operational side of the decision making," Spur began. "But from what I hear the official position is that we have a treaty with the Sioux. Unless they break it we are honor bound to respect their lands."

"But when the murdering bastards break out and kill and loot our settlers and farmers and then run back into the Sioux lands, we can't go in after them?" another officer demanded.

"Well, now, gentlemen, the army has always been rather firm about that. A hostile is a hostile, and if he's broken the law or a treaty, the army usually goes in and gets him."

"Yeah, the only safe Indian is a scalped Indian," Imhoff said.

Captain Grove shook his head. "I heard it the only good Indian is a dead one."

"At least old two-gun Sheridan is going to have his way with the Military Division of the Missouri," Imhoff said. "Ten will get you a hundred that we're on full-scale hunt-down-and-kill Indian missions by the end of the year. General Sheridan is sitting back there in Omaha dancing with every pretty skirt he sees and wishing he could be out here killing Indians."

Lt. Wes Pauley grinned and pounded the table with his fist. "Yes, and it's about time! I've seen enough innocent settlers killed, and wagon trains wiped out! I just don't believe in molly-coddling these savages. The only way we'll have peace with them is to grind them down and wipe them out if necessary." Lt. Pauley was slight and was never seen without his service revolver. He had mouse-brown hair and a straggling moustache; otherwise he was clean shaven.

The main course came at last and the men settled down to eating.

Spur sat beside the only other civilian at the table, who said he was Buffalo Kane, the post scout. He was long haired, with a full beard, both unkempt, and wore a fringed buckskin shirt that Spur knew was far too hot for the weather; but he evidently refused to part with it. He had on regulation blue pants and army boots. Spur had felt Buffalo Kane stiffen when Lt. Pauley talked about wiping out all Indians. But when Spur looked over at him, the scout was working on a slab of roast beef with a vengeance, cutting and eating, and lifting his laden fork to his mouth with his left hand.

The talk turned to the army, about other commands, other posts, and when the dessert of deep-dish wild plum pie was gone, the men began drifting away. When Spur said good night to the others, they reminded him about the card party and social at eight o'clock.

"Then you'll have a chance to meet some of the illustrious ladies of the post," Lt. Imhoff said. He laughed. "Of course some of the most important females won't be there because they're only wives of enlisted men. But some of the officers here think those ladies have abundant charms!" The officers all laughed and the men ambled away into the dusk.

Outside, the scout called to Spur.

"Colonel, could I talk to you a bit?"

Spur nodded and they leaned against the wall of the sutler's store which was closed and dark.

"I got to talk to you, Colonel," Buffalo Kane said earnestly. "I got me something that's eating my guts to pieces and it's gettin' worse and worse. Nobody in camp will listen to me. My contract is up in a month, and I got to settle it quick."

Spur nodded, wishing he could light up one of his favorite crooked black cigars, but they were all in his quarters.

"Just what is this problem, Kane?"

"My family, sir. While I was on a patrol up near the Black Hills, somebody murdered my whole family, my wife and my two sons. The boys was only three and four. Just butchered them. And nobody will help me find out who did it. But I got my suspicions, and I think the murderers are right here at Camp.''

Spur had been listening with half an ear, still evaluating the officers he had met, but now his interest quickened.

"My wife, Walking Fawn, was only twenty. She was Cheyenne—that's why we weren't allowed to live here at the camp. I built a nice little place two miles downstream. Not fancy, but Walking Fawn thought it was beautiful. I been a scout a long time, Colonel. I know the army, but I never thought they would do this to me.''

"You sure it was the army, Mr. Kane?''

"Hell, yes! I'm a scout, a tracker. I put the whole thing together from what I found out there. I came home two days after they were killed. There had been six men, all on army mounts. One man held the horses. They set up in three spots around the shanty. I picked up sixty brass casings at those three spots. They were having target practice, and I won't rest easy in my mind until I see the guilty ones hung, especially the officer who led the patrol. I know who was out with me, and the other officers here. But you got to help me. They stick together like molasses and glue.''

"You went to Colonel Underhill?''

"Shit! He threw me out of his office. Said he wouldn't have signed me on as a scout if'n he knew I was a squaw man.''

"Major Rutherford?''

"Good man, should be commanding here. He said he can't do anything without the approval of the colonel, and that crazy man is an all-out Indian hater.

33

You just got to help me out somehow!"

"You have any solid proof, Kane?"

"You bet. I found some of my wife's jewelry in the sutler's store. I got his signed paper that says it was sold to him by two soldiers, but he says he don't remember which ones. They was needing some drinking money. And they sold the brooch and pendant and a piece of pounded gold two days after my family was killed." Kane rubbed his rough hand across angry, wet eyes. "You got to help me, Colonel, 'fore I go plumb crazy myself! Don't matter much what happens to me, long as I get at least one of them. The men wouldn't of done it unless an officer ordered them to. Hell, one or two of the men had been down and seen my boys."

"The normal course would be to register a complaint through regular channels. . . ."

"Hell, Colonel, you know that wouldn't work. Anyway, I'm not Army. I don't got to go through no damn channels." He stared up at Spur for a few seconds. "Damn, I don't think you're spit-and-polish either. You can twist some tails, get some action going. Christ, tell old Underhill you know the Inspector General is coming this direction. That might shake him off his damn stubborn stool."

"How long had your family been living here?"

"Almost six months. Most of the men and officers knew all about me and my family. Someplaces things gets touchy, but I thought it was all simmered down here."

"You have this all written out, Kane? I'll need to know the date they were killed, when you went on the patrol, the officers and men with you on the patrol, and which officers were left in camp."

34

"I . . . I don't write none too good, Colonel. But I got it all writ out by a friend."

Spur said he would look it over and returned to his quarters, where he put on his uniform. He wouldn't wear it much, but he wanted to get off on the right foot with the ladies. In the course of the evening he would meet all the officers on the post. The odds were that the rifles were being supplied to the Indians through this very camp. If so, that would mean an officer would be needed to make the contacts on both sides. Spur would evaluate and check out each officer on the post.

An hour later Spur was on his way to the social at Colonel Underhill's quarters when someone called to him. An officer in full dress uniform hurried up and saluted. Spur returned the salute. He had not met this young lieutenant before.

"Colonel, sir. If I could delay you for a moment there is an urgent matter we must discuss."

In the flickering light of a lamp on a post, Spur could see the rugged, stern, almost angry expression on the young officer's face.

"That might be arranged, Lieutenant, if you will have the courtesy to identify yourself and state your problem."

"Sorry, sir. First Lieutenant Casselberry, Company B. It's about my wife, sir."

Spur nodded and studied the man in the lamplight. He was about two inches under six feet, stocky, clean-shaven, and his face was set in a scowl. His dark eyes were angry, his brow furrowed.

"Yes—Mrs. Casselberry. I hope you welcomed her back warmly. She was a bit concerned."

"I did *not* welcome her back, sir. My relations

with my wife are a private affair, a personal matter, not a subject for casual speculation."

"You're quite right if you go by the book. But the woman was as terrified of you and coming back to the fort as she was of the Indians."

"There were no Indians, Colonel."

"I beg your pardon, Lieutenant? Didn't she tell you?"

"She did. I've ordered her to change her story. *There were no Indians.*"

Spur stared at the officer, unable to believe his ears. At last he nodded. "You're afraid if it is whispered around that she was captured by Indians, it will adversely affect her reputation on this post."

"Sir, I *know* what it would do. I've seen it happen before. That's why I made her carry a hide-out gun. She says she used up all four rounds shooting at the Indians."

"And you would rather that she had . . ."

"Yes, quite right, Colonel. I had ordered her to save the last bullet for herself, if all else failed. I even showed her where to hold the gun, just over her right ear."

Spur shook his head incredulously. "I'm not sure anyone will swallow some trumped-up story, Lieutenant. I suppose you've told her to say that she became lost, disoriented perhaps, and walked the wrong way while picking—what, crabapples? Then, amazingly enough, I found her, untouched and pure as the driven snow."

"Yes, that's close enough, sir."

"But what about *my* story, Lieutenant?"

"Sir, it's my private affair. It seems to me the only way out of an intensely embarrassing situation.

You must see it my way. After all, Colonel, we are both Army."

Spur's first impulse was to lash out and knock the man into the dust beside the sutler's store. Instead, he stared at the blank, tense, stern face of the officer.

"Yes, Lieutenant, we *are* both Army. And every army man I know treats his wife with the utmost respect, consideration, love and tenderness. What does Mrs. Casselberry say about this plan of yours?"

"It doesn't matter what she thinks or says, sir. I am in command of my own household."

"Your most important command is of one wife."

"Yes, sir, if the colonel wishes to put it that way."

"How does she feel about your plan, Lieutenant?"

The young officer hesitated, stared at Spur with controlled anger for a moment, then scowled. "She doesn't like it. Although she knows how the women on the post would treat her, what the other officers would subject me to, she still says we should tell the truth."

"Which is?"

"She was picking choke cherries, strayed too far along the river and was grabbed by a pair of Sioux hunters who obviously didn't know they were so close to any army post. You came upon her the following morning. She swears they didn't touch her, just made her ride stripped to the waist. But if the women find out she was captured by the Sioux. . . . You know what that would mean, Colonel. You know what these army wives can do to a woman with a taint of *any* kind."

"And it might affect your career as well. Isn't

that what's bothering you most, Lieutenant? Are you West Point?"

"Yes, of course."

"Christ! We should burn that place down!"

"Sir!"

Spur's angry glare bored into the younger man. "You know what bothers me the most, Casselberry? Your attitude toward this whole thing. You haven't once mentioned the suffering your wife has been through. You haven't worried about how she is bearing up under it. You haven't been *concerned* about your wife. What you're really worried about is your career."

"Sir, if this gets out, my wife would never be able to hold up her head on any army post. Everyone would say that she had been defiled by the Indians. The women would cackle and gossip and the officers would all ostracize both her and me. I would never be trusted again. Don't you *understand?* This is a frontier post. We fight Indians here. Our womenfolk are instructed, are *ordered* never to allow themselves to be captured alive. Janet knew what to do."

"And now, since she had the audacity and the gall to get rescued and did *not* kill herself, you are outraged."

The man's face froze into a harsh, angry stare. "If the colonel says so, sir."

"Damn, haven't you learned anything since you got out of the Point?"

"Sir, all I'm asking you to do is support me when I tell how you found Janet wandering in the plains along the river. She lost her way, that's all. No harm done. It isn't much to ask."

"Lieutenant, which is more important to you,

your army career or the well-being of your wife?"

"My. . . . Sir, I'm really not sure, not now. But I don't *need* to make a choice between them." He paused and came to rigid attention. "Sir, this is a most difficult favor to ask of a superior officer. It is extremely hard for me. I would appreciate the colonel's answer."

"I'll think about it, Lieutenant Casselberry. If it comes up tonight, you make your explanations, and by then I'll have decided what to do. I'll either support you—or totally ruin your army career. You're dismissed, Lieutenant."

Casselberry shivered, saluted, did an about face and stamped away.

When Spur moved on toward the lieutenant colonel's quarters, he met two more officers and joined them. They all introduced themselves. At the commander's house a receiving line was established with Spur beside Mrs. Underhill, who turned out to be a short, round lady in a pink gown with light blue trim, and an elaborate hairdo with her curls piled on her head and spilling downward. Spur assumed it was the latest style. Her name, it turned out, was Grace.

"Colonel McCoy, we're all so thrilled how you rescued that poor Janet Casselberry. Found her wandering along the river and all. We're so proud of you! It's just pure chance that some roving band of Indians didn't find her first. You know of course what *they* would have done!"

By the time the receiving line was through, eighteen officers and twelve women had come through and chatted with Spur. He had a first impression of each of the officers, and would get a list later with

39

the assignment of each man and any personal information Major Rutherford might be able to come up with.

Soon the card games began. Two couples were playing whist and several more engaged in a game new to Spur called bezique, in which the queen of spades and the jack of diamonds made a large count. Three games of four-handed, serious poker began. Spur drifted from one table to another, and at last settled into a poker game with Major Rutherford. No one was allowed to lose more than five dollars.

"New money, men—the colonel is anxious to make a good impression by losing his stakes quickly," Major Rutherford said. "And since he's a redhead too, watch out for him." Four other officers at the table laughed. The sixth person seated there smiled and twin dimples dented her cheeks. Spur had met her earlier; Felicia Jones, daughter of the camp doctor, Captain Hiram Jones.

Felicia was shuffling the cards. She nodded. "Yes, Colonel, I *do* know how to play poker, and I usually win. I am an excellent bluffer and also I draw marvelous cards, so try your luck. This game will be draw poker, jacks or better to open. The ante is twenty cents. Everyone in?"

Spur smiled, tossed two reds into the pot from the stack of chips he had received for his five dollars, and waited for his cards.

He was sitting beside Major Rutherford, and liked the man at once. He seemed to be a reasonable, calm, efficient man who was at the same time attuned to the needs of his position and the men and officers who served under him. It was completely opposite to the impression Spur had received from Colonel Underhill.

Spur discarded to a pair of eights, bought his cards for a dime and folded. Felicia shot him an approving glance. She won the pot with three kings, and passed the deal along. She looked at Spur again and smiled, then shifted her gaze. She was a delightfully pretty girl, with a flair for dressing well, and from what he had seen so far, a bright, outgoing personality. But if he wanted more than a smile from her, Spur knew he would have to made the advances.

He played poker automatically, trying to remember each face and name at the table. It wasn't his best talent. He concentrated on a few of the men, trying to block out the women for the moment.

Lt. Casselberry had arrived slightly late, apologizing to Mrs. Underhill, who waved him away. He did not seem to be popular with the other officers who were polite, but a bit distant. Spur's secondary impression of him reinforced the previous one: he was a professional soldier, dedicated to the army, good at what he did but as cold and stiff as a military saber. Would he sell army rifles to the Indians? Spur didn't know, not yet.

Among the eighteen officers present, Spur could find no obvious candidate for a suspect. Perhaps any one of them could turn traitor, given the right situation, or a pressing need. But the Army was so righteously anti-Indian that it must be a strange kind of man who would help arm the savages who he would later have to fight. It was grotesque in a way, and Spur wondered if he were dealing with a man who had lost his mind. At the very least, the

41

traitor's understanding of right and wrong must be seriously confused.

The card games broke up promptly at ten o'clock and the dancing began. Felicia Jones played the violin, two men strummed guitars and another played a brightly decorated accordion. The carpet was rolled up and the dancing began. During every other dance set, Spur noticed that Felicia Jones was dancing rather than playing, with a multitude of different partners. Twice he spotted Lt. Omer Imhoff guiding her around. She was the most popular girl in the group, the only unmarried one as far as he knew, and the young bucks were constantly cutting in on each other.

Spur danced with the colonel's lady, and then wandered over and watched the band. In the middle of one number, Felicia smiled, put down her fiddle and came up beside him.

"Could I have the honor of this dance?" she asked with a mischievous smile.

"I would be delighted," Spur said. "In Washington D.C., it's becoming positively fashionable for ladies to ask the gentlemen to dance."

He rested one hand lightly on her waist, took her right hand in his and spun her away in a waltz. She made a contented sound deep in her throat, almost a purr.

"You are an excellent dancer, Colonel McCoy, the best on the post."

"If I'm doing well, it's only because I'm inspired by such a beautiful lady, who is also such an exquisite dancer," Spur said gallantly. He was pleased to see a slight blush tinge her cheeks.

"Thank you," she said, shyly, her bravado suddenly deserting her. "I hope you don't think that I was too forward. The officers' wives are going to be gossiping about me all week!"

"And well they should. They are jealous of the marvelous way you dance. I've waltzed with some of them, and most don't know their right foot from their left."

Felicia laughed. "Goodness, please don't tell *them* that!" The dance ended and Spur took her back to the chair where she had left her instrument.

"Thank you for the dance, Miss Jones, it was delightful."

She bowed slightly, smiled and turned away.

Spur walked across the room and sat at a table near Major Rutherford. Their host had supplied sipping whiskey and most of the men cut it with branch water, but Major Rutherford took his straight in a shot glass. Spur mentioned that he would like to look over the personnel files the next day and the major nodded.

"Yes, I expected you would ask. We have a good group of men here. There are a few I would rather send back to Omaha, but that happens in any command." He watched Spur closely for a moment. "Colonel, have we met before? I served in Washington D.C. for a short time right after the war."

"I was still pushing cavalry in Texas at that time, Major." Spur paused and lowered his voice. "Major, is there some kind of a problem here with your commanding officer?"

Major Rutherford took a long breath, then looked up. "I have not found sufficient justification for anything approaching the evidence needed to relieve anyone of command. All of us have a few little

43

quirks—Zeke just has a few more than most. But as far as going any further, I wouldn't want any part of it, not right now."

"Thanks, Major, forget I mentioned it."

"Gladly."

Lt. Casselberry sat down on the other side of the major and caught his attention.

"Sir, I just wanted to report that my wife is fine, no worse for her experience. It was as we feared. She became lost and disoriented and simply walked the wrong way along the river. She went away from the post instead of toward it. She had discovered her mistake and was on the way back when Colonel Mc-Coy overtook her and gave her a ride to camp. Sir, I hope this will put to rest any of the rumors that I've heard about her being captured by Indians."

Major Rutherford nodded his head. "Good, Casselberry, good. I know how relieved you must be. Our scouting patrols must have missed her somehow. Give her my best wishes and tell her we hope she will feel well enough to come to our social next week."

"I'm sure she will, sir," Casselberry said. He nodded curtly at the two officers and stared at Spur for a long moment before he turned and walked away.

"Good man, that Casselberry," Major Rutherford said. "But he takes himself too seriously. You'd think he had to wade in and wipe out every Indian in all the Nations singlehanded. Glad you found his wife. She's a charmer and one of the smartest women on the post."

"It was pure chance that I ran into her, Major, pure chance," said Spur calmly.

Around midnight the party began breaking up.

Colonel Underhill withdrew early complaining of a bad cold. He wasn't missed. Spur was getting a definite feel for the command and some of the men who ran it. Major Rutherford seemed to hold the whole post together as the executive officer. Spur hadn't found a chance to talk to the major about the scout's problem. It was the kind of situation that could cause trouble for the whole post. Spur could see no immediate connection between the slaughter of the scout's family and the rifles, but he was keeping that option open. Buffalo Kane would be an ideal liaison between the army and the Indians. And the scout had an intense hatred for the officers on the post. He would think more about that.

Felicia Jones came by with her father, a balding captain with a paunch that showed he was a garrison soldier. Spur bet the man hadn't sat a horse in ten years. Felicia smiled.

"It was good to meet you, Colonel McCoy. We don't get many visitors here at Camp Sheridan, especially ones who can waltz so well. Will you be staying with us for long? The ladies are hoping that you will."

"I'm not rightly sure, Miss Jones. I hope so, just so I can have another dance with you."

She smiled over her shoulder at him as her father led her out the door.

Spur paid his respects to Mrs. Underhill, then walked out with Major Rutherford. They talked about the Black Hills Indian situation, then parted at the major's quarters. Spur was thinking more about the smile on Felicia's pretty face than he was about anything else, and consequently his guard was down. He came around the corner of the store and was heading for his bachelor quarters when a rifle fired fifty yards ahead of him and splinters exploded from the boards next to his head.

Spur dropped flat on the ground in half a second and crawled backwards to the protection of the sutler's building. The rifle boomed again and Spur felt the impact as the bullet smashed into the dirt beside him. He had just rounded the corner of the store when the third round slammed past.

Spur peered around the edge of the building. Who in the hell was shooting at him, and why?

CHAPTER FOUR

Spur did not have his six-gun with him as he took another quick look around the corner of the sutler's store, then pulled back. He had no idea who had taken the shots at him. He listened. There was no outcry from the guards. Perhaps it was normal for rifle shots to punctuate the midnight calm at this army post, but he doubted it. A door slammed somewhere ahead and a light flickered on down the line of log houses. It was time to investigate.

Spur came around the corner in a crouch, running hard. He made it to the opposite building which was set twenty feet from the store. As quietly as possible, Spur edged to the far corner of the officers' quarters and looked around.

Nothing. The soft moonlight let him see plainly along the rear side of the row of attached quarters. No one was there in the fifty yard length of the line of buildings. He took two steps around the quarters and stopped. At his feet something glinted in the pale light. He bent down and found the brass casings of rifle bullets. He searched until he had found all three, then hurried back to his room. Spur struck a stinker and lit a lamp, then bolted the door and moved away from the window. He checked the shell casings and frowned. They were not standard army issue, he was sure of that. He would examine them in much more detail in the morning.

Suspects for the bushwhacking were hard to figure. The one possibility that immediately sprung to mind was Casselberry. The young lieutenant was obsessed with his army career, and Spur presented what could turn into a roadblock to that officer's future. It would take an extremely dedicated, even fanatical man to go to such lengths to forward his career.

Who else? The gun runner to the Indians was the second best suspect, whoever he was. But how would he know Spur's real mission so quickly? He had confided the true facts to no one. A leak of information from St. Louis or Washington D.C. was extremely unlikely. Perhaps the traitor was a thorough and cautious man, thinking a murdered colonel now would be better than the chance of exposure later.

Spur yawned. A real bed looked good to him. He enjoyed the nights on the trail but the ground was getting harder each time he slept out. He double checked the bolt on the front door, saw there was none on the back, and locked it with a simple skeleton-type key and wedged a wooden chair under the handle. If anyone tried to get in it would make a racket and alert him.

The secret agent stripped down to his underwear and slid into bed. The warm Nebraska weather meant he would need only a sheet. He stretched out, thought for a moment about the day's events and knew that he had made a good start. The brass shell casings could be a big break for him. In two minutes he was sleeping.

Later, Spur had no idea how long it had been, he awakened, listened, and knew that the chair at the rear door was scraping as it moved. He was on his feet in a second, the big Merwin and Hurlburt .44 in his right hand as he moved silently on bare feet to the door. Spur waited until the door was pushed from the outside again, then flipped the chair away.

The person in the hall, fell forward into the room as the door swung inward. Spur dropped on top of the figure, pinning it to the floor. There was a shocked moment of total silence and no struggling at all.

"Oh, my goodness, hello," a softly familiar woman's voice said.

"Felicia?" Spur said, amazement showing in his voice. But he didn't move. Now he recognized the soft contours of a woman's body. "What are you doing breaking into my room?"

"Spur McCoy, I'll be glad to tell you. First, let me up, then put a blanket over your front window and light a lamp."

He grinned in the darkness. "Now that seems perfectly reasonable." Spur pulled a blanket from the bed, hung it over the small window that overlooked the parade grounds and then lit the lamp. He put on the chimney and turned up the wick, then looked at her. She wore a robe that brushed the floor and was buttoned tightly at her throat.

Spur felt no embarrassment standing there in his

underwear as she smiled at him.

"Well, Colonel McCoy, I see you were in bed after all. I had to stop by to tell you how much I enjoyed our dance tonight. But now I feel suddenly over-dressed."

She unbuttoned the robe and let it fall open. Felicia wore only a white, frilly chemise underneath, which stopped just below her crotch and on top revealed the delicious curving swell of both lovely breasts. Her legs were finely formed, slender, her waist narrowed delightfully, and now her face beamed with a combination of pride and desire. "I thought you might want to see what *I* wore to bed."

She let the robe slip to the floor and stood there waiting. A moment later she ran to him, her arms clasped around his back tightly as she pressed her body firmly against his.

Spur picked her up and carried her to his bed, lay her down gently, then leaned over and kissed her quivering lips. She pushed up to meet him and held the embrace as long as he did. When they parted she sighed and smiled.

"Oh, yes! I have been dreaming about how it would be to kiss you ever since we first met."

"And how was it?"

"Delicious! How about another?"

He kissed her again, and this time her lips parted. His tongue darted inside and she moaned in plea-sure. Then they began a brief skirmish of teasing tongues, and at last she gracefully conceded defeat. Already she was breathing faster. Spur left her for a moment, went to the back door and locked it again, then pushed the chair firmly under the handle.

"So we won't be disturbed," he said kissing her

nose, then finding her mouth again. As they kissed, one of her hands trailed down his shoulder to his thigh. Spur felt the most intense jolt of desire he had ever known exploding inside him, and he crushed her lips, as his hand moved to the fabric covering her breasts.

"Yes! Darling Spur, yes, touch me there! Oh, yes, fantastic, marvelous. Oh, just like that—don't stop —yes, I just love it!"

He caressed her breasts while she moaned in absolute pleasure, then gently lifted the short hem of the chemise, exposing her thick black thatch, tiny waist and full breasts.

She lifted her arms docilely and he pulled the chemise over her head, then looked down at her. She was perfectly formed, with generous hips and a slender waist. Spur raised her up to a sitting position and her breasts brushed against his chest.

"So beautiful!" Spur said. He bent and kissed each rosy nipple and as he did, she climaxed. Her whole body trembled and she held on to him, her nails sinking into his back as the ecstatic vibrations traveled through her frame, bringing from her small, intense cries of tormented pleasure and marvelously delicious quivering.

"Oh, my goodness!" she said softly. "I've never done that so quickly. You are the most marvelous lover in the whole world!"

"Sweetheart, we haven't even *started* yet!" Spur kissed her breasts again, nibbling on her nipples, turning them hard and pulsating and Felicia cried out sharply and climaxed again. She clung to him, then rolled over on the bed so she was on top of him. He felt her whole body vibrating in a series of delightful spasms. When at last she collapsed against him, resting her head on his chest, he asked, "Do you break into men's bedrooms often?"

"No—only once before, but I couldn't stand the thought of not being able to make love to you."

"When I played at your poker table and danced with you, I decided you were so shy I would have to make the first move if I were going to get to kiss you."

"That's exactly what I wanted you to think, because then those gossipy old biddies would think the same thing, and I'd be safe. You don't *know* what they can do. We're a closed society here. In a town, there is always the town drunk or the fallen woman to talk about. Here, all we have is each other. And the competition gets vicious. I'm so relieved that Janet Casselberry *wasn't* captured by the Indians. The old cats would have driven her out of her mind within a month, and her husband would no doubt have shot himself. It happened once that way in Texas where we were stationed."

One of her hands had been worming its way between their bodies as she spoke, and now it closed around Spur's erection. "Oh, my! Such a big boy, but I know what to do to bring him down a notch, to turn him into a long, soft worm." She rolled off and lay beside him, but kept her handhold and slowly stroked his manhood, then moved lower and gently massaged his scrotum and its heavy orbs.

"Oh, my goodness! I think we have a long, long night ahead of us. My guess is at least five times. What do you think, Spur?"

"At *least* five, I would think, pretty lady."

She bent over him then and began licking him, his

face, his ears, then down his neck to his chest where she licked and nibbled at his nipples.

"Just relax, big man. I won't hurt you. Felicia never has hurt any man she's made love to yet."

Spur lay there, relaxed and enjoying it. He marveled that this outwardly prim and proper girl could keep her intense sexuality so controlled and hidden on the small army post.

Her questing mouth moved lower and Spur felt her tongue tantalizing his long shaft. He started to stop her, then steeled himself and waited. Her tongue caressed his pulsating erection slowly, with a teasing perfection that soon left Spur gasping. Her lips toyed with the purpled head of his cock until Spur sputtered with frustration, then relaxed as he felt her hot mouth envelop it and her head began a steady bobbing up and down. His hips picked up the beat and worked against her. He lifted his head and was surprised to see how much of his shaft she had sucked into her mouth. He must be half way down her throat!

In spite of his session with Molly that afternoon, it didn't take Spur long to build up a wildly frantic head of steam. His hips bucked harder. He moaned and felt her hand slip around the base of his shaft so he wouldn't choke her.

To his surprise she began to hum a tune and it set him on fire. He moaned in pure animal lust, heard himself shout aloud as he erupted into the container of her mouth and then cry out again before he dropped flat on the bed, exhaustion smothering him like blankets, as Felicia licked him clean and then snuggled beside him.

"You were tremendous!" she said softly in his ear.

"Absolutely amazing! Let's make love every night you're in Camp Sheridan!"

He put his arm around her and hugged her naked body against his as he rested, still gasping for breath, hoping that he wouldn't die from the magnificient exertion of his climax.

As he recovered, they talked. He discovered she had been the housekeeper for her doctor father for the past four years, ever since her mother had died of the Texas fever. She told him that at first it had been fun; suddenly she was a woman with the duties of a housekeeper and even managing the household funds.

"But now I'm getting restless and tense. I want to get away from the army, to see San Francisco, and New York and Boston! Have you ever been to Boston?" She kept on talking without giving him a chance to answer. "I want to be rich. I won't settle for anything less. And someday I will be!"

As they both rested she toyed with the thick red hair on Spur's chest.

"I know I'll be rich because I like men, and I can please them. Why, right now I bet you'd do lots of things for me if I really wanted you to." She guided his hand to her breasts. "Now, Spur, honey baby, wouldn't you do good things for me?"

"Not for at least one hour," he said, then, changing the subject abruptly, "I had a little run-in with Lieutenant Casselberry earlier today. What do you know about him?"

"Not much. He's a spit and polish type, does everything by the book, all army. I swear he was born with those lieutenant's bars on! He'll probably be a general someday, but I still don't like him. I

54

guess you have to be something of a son-of-a-bitch to become a general." She giggled. "You jumped when I said those bad words, do you know that? I know worse ones. Want to hear me?"

"No," Spur said and reached his hand between her legs. She spread them at once and purred.

"*Now* you're going to do nice things for me, I just know that you are."

His hand slid up the inside of one thigh to the furry swatch, then down the other thigh and she tensed. When his fingers rubbed her mound, Felicia trembled.

"I don't know why it is, but I just *love* it when you touch me there. It's marvelous!"

His hand moved lower and his fingers expertly found her clitoris, rubbing with a gentle, insistent rhythm. She began crying softly. Tears trickled down her cheeks and her fingernails dug into his shoulders, then clawed down.

"Darling, I'm sorry," she gasped, patting his shoulder. Then she kissed him so hard his lips felt bruised, and all the time she continued to cry.

"I just can't help it. I feel so glorious, so beautiful that I could die. Have you ever felt that way?" She wiped tears from her eyes and moaned in gentle rapture. Her hips had started moving gently against his finger which found the hard node and played it like a mandolin.

Before he realized it she climaxed again. This time it was more physical. Her voice soared and wailed, then she jolted from side to side until he could hardly keep his finger in place and at last she jumped away from him and stood on the floor, pumping her hips at him in the air a dozen times, then fell back on the bed moaning softly.

"Now! Now you big cock, Spur. Now! I want you to shove it up into me so far I scream! Push it into me damnit, right now!"

She lay on her stomach on the bed and Spur went between her legs, lifted her hips, sliding past the brown rosebud of her anus to the pinkness of her slit. He probed carefully, then wedged in and a little at a time worked into her to his roots.

"Goodness, but that is fine!" she said. She crooned a small song as he settled in, then she looked over her shoulder at him.

"You just going to rest in there all night? Get something moving. How about a little action?"

Spur caught her under her hips and lifted her as he went to his knees, and holding her half in the air he pounded into her in a grinding, driving motion that kept Felicia moaning and yelping in the pleasure-pain of it. Spur knew it wouldn't take long. Rockets were going off and the red glare of their brilliance, the lightning-like streaks of passion slammed through him. He knew she was climaxing again as he did but he couldn't hear or see much of her reaction because of his own overpowering surges.

He let her down gently to the bed and lay on top of her, and she purred, "Yes, yes! Just crush me, I love it!" She laughed. "And this is what all those teachers and those old biddies who said they were my friends kept warning me against! 'Don't let a man have his way with you. Keep your skirts down. Never let a boy touch your breasts.' What a bunch of hypocrites! They were getting screwed every night and they didn't want me to know how good it was. I bet they were afraid I'd get their husbands interested." She was silent for a moment. "Hey, big Spur McCoy. What are you thinking about?"

"Right now?"

"Yes, right now."

"About you, how delicious you are. Wondering how long you can play around this way before you get pregnant. And wondering what you'll do if you get in the family way."

"Goodness gracious, don't even think about that! I'm having too much fun to worry. Anyway, I'll know quickly if I'm in the family way, and then I'll pick out the best man I can find and make him think he made me pregnant and I'll marry him. It just depends where I'm living then. If I'm in San Francisco it'll be harder—although I hear they are still short on women out there. I think I'll go next month."

She squirmed under him and he lifted away from her. She turned over at once.

"Hold me," she said.

"Yes." His arms went around her, and their bare torsos met, her breasts crushed against his chest.

"Good. I love being held this way. I guess . . . I guess I just love men!"

Spur laughed. "I'm damn glad of that!" He paused. "Shouldn't you be getting back?"

"No. When my father goes to sleep it takes a cannon shot to wake him. Anyway I live just two doors down." She wiggled in his arms, then settled down again. "I'm hungry." She pushed away from him, jumped off the bed and found her long robe on the floor. A moment later she had put it on and pulled the chair away from the door.

"I know you don't have any food in here. I'll slip back to our quarters and get some things. Don't go away, and *don't* get dressed. You promised me *six* times. You're going to have to prove it."

She was gone a moment later and Spur sat on the bed chuckling.

She was a delight, cute as a bouncing puppy, as sexy as a fancy lady and as unpredictable as a fresh-roped wild colt. She could also be a good source of information about the men in the officer corps, if he didn't push it too hard.

Before he had her evaluated completely, she was back. She carried a bottle of wine, a sack of crackers and a wedge of yellow cheese.

"Cheese and crackers in bed with some fairly good wine to wash it down."

He reached for the cork and began to loosen it. She produced two wine glasses and began slicing the cheese. He had a bite of the cheese and nodded. It was so sharp it seemed to slice his throat on the way down. Spur curved his hand around her naked side and captured one of her soft breasts. She pointed the knife at him.

"Still eager, I see. You give me another hour or two and I'm going to turn that cock of yours into a skinny little worm that won't have the strength to lift his head."

By four A.M. on Spur's Waterbury, the secret agent realized that Felicia had been right in her prediction.

"I told you!" she said and laughed. "Now it's time I get home. I'd better take all the evidence." She smiled. "You're good for a girl—but you already know that. Gentle, tender. Now, when can we get together again? This is Thursday. How about Saturday night? I'll invite you to our house for supper, then after you and father chat a while you can leave and I'll see you here after the doctor has his nightly nip and falls to sleep."

"Nothing I'd love better, Felicia, but I might not be on the post by then." He saw the pout forming on her mouth, and kissed it away.

"Tell you what. Let's call it a date, and if I can't come, I'll let you know early."

"You better come, Spur." She smiled and touched his limp penis. "I just *love* what that big lad down there does to me. You try. Please try, Spur."

He laughed gently, helped her into her robe and piled all of the remains of their midnight snack into her arms.

"I'll try," Spur said. No doubt about it, he would more than try.

CHAPTER FIVE

Buffalo Kane had walked directly back to his quarters after talking to the new colonel. He was vaguely pleased. There was a feeling he couldn't quite pin down that this tall, strong individual was not the usual run of the army man. There was something about him that bred confidence.

Kane walked into his room, silently thanked the servant who had cleaned up his quarters the same as she had the officers', and flopped on the bed at the far side of the room. He found the half-full bottle of scotch whiskey near the front leg of the bed, picked it up, and stared at it a moment. Old John Barleycorn was his favorite companion these days. He hadn't done any work since his family was murdered, had done nothing but try to find out who had led that patrol. The enlisted men wouldn't even talk to him now, and the officers never had except on official business. They had told him he had to cut his hair and cut his beard. He'd told them all to go to hell. He had a scouting contract, and there wasn't a single word in it about how he wore his hair or his clothes. He tipped the bottle again, welcoming the raw whiskey as it sped down his throat and spread a warm glow throughout his body.

Walking Fawn! Kane blinked back hot tears as he thought of her. He'd been married to a white woman once, in Texas. He'd gone out on a scouting mission with the 5th Cavalry, and when he came back, his pretty young wife had left with a drummer who had been selling goods to the sutler's store. He never saw her again.

Kane blinked, wiped the wetness away from his eyes, and lifted the bottle.

He had found Walking Fawn after an army raid on an Indian village. She had seen her parents killed, her whole tribe nearly wiped out. Kane saw her escape into a patch of woods and waited until the company had left, then went in on foot and found her huddled against a tree, sobbing. She had been only sixteen years old, but he had used the few words he knew of Cheyenne and convinced her he meant her no harm. She went with him and they set up a crude camp half a day's ride from his post. Those had been the good times. Walking Fawn had been a proud Cheyenne, and made him remember it, but she was also eager to learn. He taught her English and she had picked it up quickly, eagerly. Their first son was born a year later, a healthy boy Buffalo had promptly named Karl after his father.

Buffalo would never forget the first time the men and officers on the post in Kansas learned that he had an Indian wife living off the post. The officers had selected the biggest, meanest enlisted man in

61

camp to call Kane out. Kane remembered it as if it were yesterday.

"Hey, squaw man!" Corporal Larson bellowed. "Get your sneaky ass out here. I'm gonna shove your asshole right out your mouth 'fore I'm done with you."

Kane had been in the sutler's store getting some chewing tobacco, and had been hurried outside by the merchant, who didn't want the upcoming fight to take place on his premises.

Buffalo stepped into the blazing Kansas sun blinking, and Larson attacked him from the shadows. Larson was over six feet, as wide as a pair of plow handles, and loved to fight dirty. He caught the still-squinting Buffalo and drove him backwards into the street, ramming him into the dirt and slamming on top of him with his 230 pounds of muscle. With a quickness that surprised the big man, Buffalo squirted out of his arms and leaped to his feet. He kicked his assailant in the ribs and again in the shoulder before Larson could get up.

"Gonn' kill your ass!" Larson roared. He came off the ground in a charging crouch and swung a massive fist at Buffalo. But the target wasn't there when the fist sailed through the air. Instead, Kane slammed down his own fist as hard as he could against Larson's wrist. The force of the blow snapped the wrist bone with a sound that could be heard halfway across the parade ground.

Larson screeched in pain. Anger and fear, mixed with a new respect for the squaw man, filled his eyes, then he unleashed a string of profanity ending with a scream for someone to go get the doctor.

"Lucky son-of-a-bitch!" Larson screamed at

Kane. "Wait until the wrist gets healed. I'll kill you with my bare hands!"

Buffalo Kane laughed at the corporal where he sat in the dust.

"Like hell you will, Larson. You'll never fight as well again. You'll always be afraid somebody else might get 'lucky' like I did. And you'll never lay a hand on me again, Larson, 'cause if you do, I'll cut your balls off!" Buffalo Kane turned and walked to the stables, took a horse and went home to his family. Nobody, enlisted man nor officer, bothered him about his Indian family after that.

Kane shivered, just remembering Kansas. But this was Nebraska, it was a different post, and his family was dead. He lifted the bottle and drained the last of the whiskey. Two hours of steady drinking and the booze hadn't affected him. Goddamnit, he couldn't even get drunk!

Kane remembered that first summer with Walking Fawn. She was such a little thing, barely four feet ten inches tall, and as slender as a willow shoot. He had never known any person as alert, as sensitive to nature as she had been.

Once they were walking through a patch of hardwood trees. She stopped and motioned for him to wait. She stayed quiet for a minute, then pointed ahead and to the left. A doe with a spotted fawn walked into view, the mother grazing, the youngster prancing around her. The pair nibbled on some leaves, and the fawn tried to nurse but the doe brushed him away and they moved on into the deeper woods.

Walking Fawn turned and smiled radiantly at

Kane. He reached down, picked her up and hugged her. She frowned and pretended that she didn't like it, but at last she put her arms around his neck and softly kissed his cheek.

In most of their camps near the various army posts she could find most of their food from the land. She snared rabbits, dug roots and picked berries, and if there were fish, she knew how to catch them in small reed or willow mesh traps.

Little by little she had taught Buffalo how to live with nature, to accept both the bounty and the harsh laws of the natural world, instead of trying to bludgeon the land into subservience to the needs of man.

It was Walking Frawn who named him Buffalo. She later told him that first day that she thought he was a man-buffalo come to rescue her from the pony soldiers. From then on he discarded his given name and used Buffalo.

This small, tough, Indian girl, had given him so much. She had brought to his life form, design and purpose. He was looking forward to the time when he could find a small plot of arable ground and settle down to being a kind of a farmer—maybe raise a few head of cattle, sell some, grow their own food. He would raise his two boys to know better than he had.

That was his dream, but it had been shattered that afternoon more than a month before by the fusillade from six Spencer repeating carbines. There weren't a lot of Spencers in the army, but a few dozen 1860 Spencers were around.

He knew the weapon well. It was a .52 caliber using number 56 Spencer rim-fire cartridges and had a twenty-two inch round barrel with three rifled grooves. Its total length was thirty-nine inches and it weighed a little over eight pounds, had blade front sight and sliding leaf rear sight. All the metal was blued except the receiver which was case-hardened in mottled colors.

Kane could imagine the troopers that fatal day with their Spencers. The picture came to him once more of his two sons playing outside the hut near the big cottonwood tree. The rifles fired again and again, cutting down the two children, then the big bullets ripping into Walking Fawn's soft flesh as she screamed and raced outside to help her sons.

He saw the rifles firing and firing.

And Buffalo's family died.

In less than three minutes they were all dead. Then the troopers had left, quickly. One set of hoof-prints showed that one rider had moved around the bodies. At least they had not been further violated.

Buffalo Kane stared at the empty bottle, then threw it across the room where it broke against the rough wall and fell into pieces to the floor.

Somebody was going to pay.

Somebody was going to admit to the crime, and then Buffalo Kane was going to shoot that bastard six times, make him suffer as much as possible, damn well make him know *why* he was dying.

Damn sure!

Drunk, Goddamn finally got drunk. Buffalo tried to get his clothes off. Had a bed, didn't have to sleep like a trail drive cowhand . . . Take off his clothes . . . At least his boots. Man slept better . . . slept better with his . . .

A moment later Buffalo Kane's head fell to one side, his mouth sagged open and he snored.

Kane dreamed as he did every night. This time he arrived just in time. He set up the Gatling gun and wiped out the patrol before the men could get off the first shot. He saved the lieutenant, and marched him up to the commanding general's office in Omaha and made him confess that he had tried to kill Kane's family. The general had ripped the indicators of rank from the officer's uniform and spit on him. Then ceremoniously, the general had taken out his pearl-handled .44 and shot the faceless officer in the head.

Kane moaned as he rolled in the bed, but no matter how he tried, he still couldn't see the face of the dead officer. Who was he? Who was the murderer who had killed Buffalo Kane's family?

CHAPTER SIX

The morning after his marathon with Felicia Jones, Spur woke with a groan and sat up slowly. She had drained him within a pair of deep breaths of all his energy. But it had been worth it. What a feisty, sexy little fireball! It was five-thirty, and he shaved and trimmed his moustache. He washed the sleep from his face and did two dozen quick pushups, then a hundred jumping jacks and washed down his face, head and bare torso.

That morning he put on a regulation dark blue army shirt, and lighter blue pants. Then he pulled on slightly worn army boots and a tan, wide-brimmed low-crowned army campaign hat. To complete the effect he tied a yellow kerchief around his throat, buckled on an issue cartridge belt and slid his big .44 into the holster. It was the only uniform he had with him. His full colonel's eagles gleamed in silver on his shoulder epaulets.

He had breakfast with the officers, dining well on eggs fresh from the sutler's chickens, hashbrowns and onions and half a dozen large hotcakes and syrup. He talked with several of the officers he had met, then went directly to the camp commander's office.

Colonel Underhill had recovered from his malaise of last night and sat behind his desk, his thin face puzzled over some problem sketched in front of him on a pad of paper. He noticed Spur come in, glanced up and saw the twin eagles, and eased to his feet.

"Good morning, Colonel McCoy."

"Good morning, Colonel. I need to have a short conference with you this morning. Last night someone tried to kill me."

Colonel Underhill's head snapped up and he stared Spur in the eye. "Then it's true. You aren't here on some survey. I've heard the junior officers say you're a spy for Phil Sheridan."

"General Sheridan doesn't even know I'm here, Colonel. My orders come from much higher up than that." Spur sat down in the chair across the desk, and the camp commander waited until he was settled, then sat himself.

"Colonel Underhill, I must insist that what I'm about to tell you must remain in the strictest of confidence."

"Naturally, sir. I understand."

"Your casualty figures for the past three months are interesting, Colonel. You show thirteen troopers killed and forty-seven wounded. But the important part is that all these casualties but one were caused by rifle fire. As I'm sure you know, most of the army's casualties from Indians are caused by arrows. Most of our fights are against bows and arrows, not against rifles. Do you know how this happened to several of your patrols in your section?"

"No, sir. It's been worrying me."

"The problem is getting worse. Indians in this sector are somehow acquiring large numbers of rifles and ammunition. My job, Colonel Underhill, is to find the supply route, snuff it out and locate whoever is supplying the weapons."

"I've heard of civilians trading guns to the Indians for all sorts of goods—even gold."

"That isn't the case here, Colonel. There are no civilians in this area who could barter with the Sioux. My instructions are to take a careful look at some far west army establishments in this sector and determine if any of the rifles falling into Indian hands are coming directly or indirectly from army supplies."

Colonel Underhill leaped to his feet. "Sir!" he thundered. "That's an insult! Are you accusing me or any of my men of trading with the enemy? Accusing me of *treason?*" Underhill's face had flushed. He was breathing so heavily he almost panted. His eyes were wild, furious, darting glances at Spur, then around the room.

Spur crossed his legs and leaned back in the chair.

"Sit down, Colonel. I'm not accusing you or your men of anything. What I am saying is that it is highly probable that the savages have somehow obtained army rifles and ammunition from this post or some other, and it is my job to find out what supply route is used and to stop it."

"Goddamn you! You are implying that me or my men are selling rifles to the enemy! In my own office you're accusing me of treason! I don't have to stand for that!" He marched around the room, his arms

69

flailing the air, his face dark red now, his eyes wary, one hand near the sabre that hung on his belt. He picked up a chair from the far side of the room and threw it at the wall. A leg broke off the chair and it crashed to the floor.

"I don't have to put up with this! I'll send word to Phil today that you're a disgrace to the uniform. I don't care what your higher authority says. I've served my country for almost thirty years!"

He stormed to the door and opened it, looked out onto the parade grounds. For a moment the colonel shivered, pulling himself together, then he staightened his shoulders and closed the door gently. When he turned around his complexion had returned to normal, his eyes were placid and his breathing was even, quiet.

"Now, Colonel McCoy, you say you're here to investigate those stolen army rifles. Good thinking. We have lost a few recently. Not a lot—one or two here, one there. A rifle missing from the stack in the barracks. Supply reports another gone from the armory. Nothing you can trace or pin down. Good thinking. Perhaps there *has* been some kind of a traitor right here at Camp Sheridan. You probably will want to consider Camp Robinson, Fort Fetterman and Camp Brown as well."

Spur nodded, completely astonished. The colonel had exploded before Spur's eyes into a raging maniac, then within a few seconds had reverted to a logical, reasonable individual. There was something definitely wrong here.

"Fine, Colonel. I wanted you to know exactly why I am here. As far as the men are concerned, I am still conducting a survey for the Quartermaster Corps.

This is something they can understand, and we won't scare off anyone who might have some connection with a larger conspiracy, if there is one. And if we're successful, Colonel, we should be able to reduce your casualty figures a great deal. At least we can cut off the supply source of the ammunition. Rifles are relatively benign without cartridges."

Colonel Underhill chuckled. "Quite right, Colonel, absolutely right. Oh, could I ask your authorization again for this job."

Spur smiled. "As I told you, the commanding general of the Quartermaster Corps."

Colonel Underhill nodded. "I understand. Some things I get to know, and some I don't. Anything I can do for you, just let me know."

Underhill's uniform hung on him like it was draped over a picket fence. His smile was more sincere now but looked out of place on his large head that slanted slightly forward.

Spur McCoy went out the door into the harsh Nebraska sunshine and a wind that sent grit stinging against his cheeks.

Next stop on Spur's agenda was the supply room, the supply sergeant. There must be one—or whatever he was called now. Spur had been away from the army for several years and knew some things had changed.

The supply and equipment storage area was at the center of the five administrative buildings. It was one story and made of bricks. Just inside the door sat a barrel-chested corporal, clean shaven and totally bald. Bushy eyebrows shaded small eyes that looked reasonably intelligent. He snapped to attention and saluted.

"Colonel, sir. Corporal Kramer."

Spur returned to salute and the corporal stood stiffly at attention.

"At ease, Corporal Kramer. You probably know why I'm here—the survey." Spur looked at him closely. Kramer was an old time soldier who had found light duty. He had learned the army system and benefited from it, and had mastered the art of army politics. It was a wonder he was only a corporal.

Spur dug into his pocket and took out the three shell casings he had picked up the previous night.

"A small problem for you, Corporal. A friend gave me these shell casings and wants me to find some ammunition for him. He says it's army issue, only most posts don't have any. Can you help me? He didn't even tell me what kind of a weapon takes these rounds."

Corporal Kramer took the brass casings and scowled at them a moment. "Sir, I think you're in luck. You're right, that ain't one of our usual rounds. Looks like what we used to use in the old 1860 Henry repeating rifle. Near ten thousand of them were made. Lots were lost during the War when the Yankees used them." He turned over the cartridge and looked at the base.

"Yep, look here, Colonel. See that 'H' stamped on there? That's for B. Tyler Henry who invented that weapon. The Rebs used to say the Henry was the damned Yankee rifle that a body could load on Sunday and fire all week. Had a tubular magazine under the barrel that held twelve rounds. It's a .44 caliber, of course. You want me to see if we'uns got any rounds? Must be two or three Henrys still in camp."

"Yes, Corporal. If you don't have any, I'd like the names of the men who have the weapons. Perhaps I could persuade them to sell me a few cartridges."

"No problem, Colonel. Give me an hour or so to check and I'll have some rounds for you and the names."

"Thank you, Corporal. Now, about this survey. How many spare rifles and carbines do you keep in stock?"

"Spares? Damn, sir, don't know right off. Got some in I haven't checked out yet. Boxes. Then we have three or four that need some repair work." He paused. "I can get you the figures, sir, but that's going to take a little longer."

"No rush, Corporal. By noon will be fine. I'll also want a list of all rifles and carbines by serial number and which man they have been assigned to."

The corporal raised his eyebrows. "That's going to take some doing, sir, but I'll try to have it by this afternoon."

"Fine, Corporal. Have the lists delivered to me at my quarters." Spur turned and left, pondering what the corporal had told him. Three Henry repeating rifles in camp, and one of them had been used in his bushwhacking. That should make them easy to find.

Spur heard a volley of shots and moved quickly to a vantage point. He found a company of men firing at a stationary target. Each trooper was given twenty rounds and was scored on his efforts at the large bull's-eye target 50 yards away. Spur watched for a while and kept his eye open for a Henry repeater but didn't see any.

He checked his Waterbury and found he had time to make a walking tour of camp before checking

73

back with Corporal Kramer. When at last he returned to the armory, the corporal had some answers for
him. There were thirty-four spare carbines and rifles
in operating condition and twelve that needed
repair.

"But there are five missing, sir," Kramer said in a
rush. "I don't know for the life of me where they got
to. They ain't signed out to anyone, and they ain't
here!"

"Put that in your report to me, soldier. I want the
type weapons and the serial numbers. Right now!"

"Yes, sir! I swear I don't know what happened.
Nobody checks out rifles and carbines except me.
No chance they could just be lost. Some son-of-a-
bitch *stole* them from me! I'm gonna have somebody's hide."

"So am I, Corporal. So am I. Now show me where
you keep the weapons."

The enlisted man led Spur into the storeroom,
down an aisle and to the back wall where the rifle
rack held the weapons. They had a chain through
the trigger guards and were padlocked on each end.
One of the rifles was four feet long. Spur looked at it
and pointed.

"Is that one of your Henry repeating rifles?"

"Yes, sir. Here are the names of the troopers who
have the other two. Some of the platoon leaders like
to have one long gun along for longer range sharp-
shooting."

Spur took the piece of paper and put it in his
pocket. "Finish that report with the serial numbers
and get it to my quarters, Corporal." He turned and
walked out of the supply room.

It was time for Spur to go to the commander's

quarters for the noon meal. Grace Underhill had invited him during the dance the preceding evening. As he walked, he thought about the camp commander again. The man certainly had a variety of personalities. He had been cold, irritated, angry when Spur first arrived, then had turned into a raging maniac when Spur suggested the rifles the Indians were using were army issue. But seconds later he had changed again into a relatively normal man, eager to please a superior officer, and to get at the root of the problem. Underhill could develop into a definite threat to Spur's mission.

Spur returned a few salutes and then walked into the commander's office. A sergeant at the side desk braced at attention and reported that Col. McCoy could go into the living quarters. The sergeant knocked, then opened the door for Spur.

Grace Underhill met him with a firm handshake. She wore what he guessed was her best dress, light blue and covered with bows and ruffles.

"Colonel, you don't know how exciting it is having you here!" she bubbled. "We get so few visitors that we must make a fuss over them. Ezekiel is polishing his boots—he'll be right here. I told him he had to be on his best behavior."

Someone came through a door behind them and Spur turned. He caught his breath and he knew his eyes widened. Her skin was a light dusky tan shade and her dark hair was braided on each side and hung to her waist. She was obviously and proudly Indian, but Spur had no idea of what tribe. She was dressed neatly and attractively in rose-colored flowered calico. Her face was round, her features softly etched, with almond shaped eyes, a small, pert nose, parted lips that glistened as if she had just licked them, and a strong chin that now lifted a little as her glance found his and locked on it.

Mrs. Underhill turned. "Yes, Chitsa, I'm glad you decided to come have dinner with us. I *told* you Colonel McCoy is not like most of the officers. I sensed that right away. Colonel McCoy, this is my ward, Chitsa. She is like my own daughter since I never had any children of my own. She has been with us now for almost fifteen years. Chitsa, this is Colonel Spur McCoy."

The girl took in a quick breath and bowed her head an inch, then straightened and looked up. She was tiny, under five feet tall, Spur guessed, with the slender but voluptuous body of a woman. He decided she must be nearly twenty years old.

"I understand, Colonel McCoy, that you do not favor slaughtering every Indian you see just because she has red skin."

Spur laughed and saw that she was not offended. "You are quite correct. But just as there are vicious, unprincipled cowardly, and rebellious white men and women, I assume the same is true of the Negro, the German, the Japanese, the Eskimo and the Indian. It is only those whom I would find objectionable."

"You see, Chitsa? I told you he was cultured and sophisticated, and could keep up with your book learning. Gracious, this poor girl has had nobody but me to talk to for so long, but she reads so many books. We tote around more books than you could shake a dead rattlesnake at, and she reads most of the day."

"Now, Grace, that's not entirely true. At the last

camp, I used to play our neighbor's piano."

"Yes, dear, and I wish we had one for you here. When we go back to Washington, we'll be sure to get one. Oh, here is Ezekiel now. Let's go in to dinner."

Colonel Underhill was in his work blues, the same uniform that Spur wore. They moved into a dining room Spur had not seen the previous night. To his surprise it was rather luxurious. A thick carpet covered the floor and the single window was draped with heavy curtains which let in the light but kept out most of the heat. Framed pictures adorned the papered walls and a cherrywood dining table set for four stood in the center. Matching cherrywood chairs had artfully stitched needle work seats.

Grace indicated where each should sit. Spur quickly took Chitsa's chair and held it for her, then sat at her right between the ladies.

"I trust the colonel has had a productive morning?" Underhill began.

"Hush, Ezekiel!" Grace cut in quickly. "We are not going to talk army. We get quite enough of that. I was hoping that Colonel McCoy could tell us something of what's happening in Washington. Is General Grant really going to double the size of the army? You know, Ezekiel was a brevet major general during the War. My, those were the days! We were in Washington for most of the War, did he tell you that? We miss the good things civilization can provide. Out here, we feel, cut off, stranded."

"Mrs. Underhill, I doubt very much that President Grant will be able to expand the army. We're at peace, and most of our citizens have bad memories of the Civil War. And remember, President Grant is just getting started. He has a lot to learn about Washington politics. It will take him at least a year to get many of his programs underway."

They went on talking for an hour as they ate roast pheasant with crabapple jelly, assorted vegetables, and tarts. It seemed like an unusual lunch, but Spur decided that was the way Mrs. Underhill had planned it.

Several times Spur noticed Chitsa watching him, a shy smile on her softly pretty face. She did a lot of the talking, and Colonel Underhill was plainly disturbed by her vivacity.

When the women were about to retire, Chitsa came up to him and paused a moment, then smiled. "I want to remember one army officer who does not hate all Indians on sight," she said. Then she smiled. "You actually think of us as human beings, which is a great step forward." She laughed. "I bet your general doesn't know about this!" She took his hand and shook it solemnly. "Thank you again." Then she turned and left. Spur felt a strange tingle of excitement when she touched him, and now as he watched her leave, her shoulders squared, her head held high, he was determined to see her again as soon as circumstances permitted.

CHAPTER SEVEN

Lt. Casselberry took his noon meal in his quarters. The officers' mess had butchered a steer from the camp herd last night and everyone had steak or ground meat. He cut into his steak, saw the rich, red blood seep out and smiled, then put a large bite into his mouth.

"I hope it's cooked right, Neil. I did it just the way you said."

Janet Casselberry had combed her hair carefully and tied it with a ribbon so it fell down her back in a golden stream. She had scrubbed her face until it glowed and put just a touch of rouge on her lips. She was wearing a checked gingham dress that was just a little tight and showed off her breasts and small waist. She sat across from him, nibbling at her steak.

"Yes, Jan, yes it's good. It's been a long time since I've had steak. Damn good!"

"Neil, after you eat, could we have time for a talk?

I've been so miserable these past two days. We have to get this straightened out."

"There is nothing to discuss," Neil said, his voice turning cold. "We simply watch the reaction of the men and more importantly, of the officers' wives. After you pass that test, we'll talk. If they figure out what actually happened, I will ask for a transfer as quickly as possible. Then we'll discuss our future."

"Neil, I need you! I've never asked you this before . . . but would you, right now, come into the bedroom, and make me feel needed and whole again?"

"*What?* It's not your place to suggest . . . I'm shocked, Janet."

She stood and moved behind him, bent and put her arms around him. "Neil, for God's sake, I need you to make love to me!"

He turned and saw that she had unbuttoned her bodice. Both full, pink-tipped breasts swung gently in front of his face.

"Oh, damn!" He stood and had to stop himself from caressing her breasts. "Janet, I'm as confused as you are. I don't know for sure if those Indians raped you or not. You might have been sleeping, or unconscious, or . . ."

"I told you, they were afraid once they saw the camp—they were rushing away. They never did a thing but make me take my blouse and chemise off."

"Oh, God how I wish I could believe that!" His hand curved around one of her breasts, then he groaned and pulled away. He ran for the front door, grabbing his hat and sabre as he went, tears stinging his eyes. Just outside the door he stopped, turned and went back inside.

"Janet, I'm sorry. I just can't . . . can't trust myself to love you, not yet. *I must be sure.* I know—I have your word, but a man must sometimes have more than that. We must be sure of the people here, then I'll know for sure."

He ran to her, caressed and kissed her naked breasts, then stood and wiped tears from his eyes. "In another week or two we should know. It won't be very long. Try to understand what this is doing to *me.* You were half of my life, half of my dreams, and now this ugly . . . those savages . . . It's just almost more than I can bear!" He wiped his eyes again, straightened his sabre and walked out the door, closing it gently.

Janet locked the door and ran sobbing into her bedroom. For a moment she touched her breasts, remembering his caress, the touch of his lips. The tears came then, floods of them. She wanted him so much! She needed him to make her feel like a woman again! Her hand rubbed her nipples. It felt so good! It wasn't his hand, but it was a caress. She thought back, remembering their wedding night, and slowly she began to smile. Her hand rubbed harder now, and her other hand pulled up her long skirt and deftly wormed inside her cotton drawers. This is wrong! she told herself. But I need it so badly, she answered, and her hand explored downward until it found her soft nest, already damp with desire. Janet touched it and her body quivered as she moaned softly and pretended that it was her wedding night . . .

After his noon meal, Spur made the rounds of the

barracks, the mess, the stables, justifying his protective cover of making a survey. He had a pad of paper on which he jotted down notes, and at times even looked interested. He ate supper at the officers' mess and then checked over the list of names, weapons and the records of the two enlisted men who had the Henry repeating rifles. Nothing seemed to make sense from the list, or the group of missing rifles. Wearily he decided to get to bed early and perhaps make up for some of the sleep he had missed the night before.

As Spur lowered the light in his desk lamp, a solitary rider galloped out the far gate and rode toward the river. The horse was an army mount, and an army man sat there, riding easily. There was no hesitation. The rider knew exactly where he was going and how to get there.

He rode with skill, and from time to time the moonlight glinted off gold bars on his shoulders. The rider was an officer. Ten minutes away from the camp, he came to a ford over the White River and crossed, letting the horse walk. On the far side, the officer turned and rode upstream, away from the camp and deeper into Indian territory.

A mile upstream he stopped, checking the tie-downs on a long blanket-covered package behind his saddle. When he was satisfied with the lashings, he crooked one leg on the saddle and built himself a cigarette. The tobacco filled the trough in the white cigarette paper and he put the sack of makings in his pocket, then rolled the paper between his fingers so it formed a thin tube. He expertly licked the flap and sealed it, then looked at it in the faint light. A little lumpy, but it would have to do. A stinker flared and he lit it, put his foot back in the stirrup and rode upstream again, heading in a southwesterly direction.

After another half hour of slow riding along the river bank, he came to a lightning-struck cottonwood that was now little more than a jagged, two-forked snag towering over a bend in the White. He got off his mount, tied her to a small tree and pulled down the blanket-wrapped package.

The officer sat against the base of the tree, rolled another cigarette and lit it openly, then smoked as he listened to the night sounds of the prairie. It was all totally foreign to him, but he would make it work *for* him, not against him. He would turn *everything* into an advantage for himself.

He sat there for fifteen minutes, and then had a feeling that someone else was nearby. A few seconds later the feeling became a certainty when an arrow whispered through the air and thunked into the dead cottonwood tree two feet over his head.

The army officer didn't move. He smiled, knowing that his contact was coming, and that the final negotiations would go forward as planned.

After another five minutes he heard a horse and soon an Indian pony came into view over the slight rise. An Indian wearing a beaded headband, loin cloth and moccasins rode the pony. The Indian carried something as he slid off the pony. He tied the animal to a bush, then walked up and squatted a few feet from the officer.

"You bring?" the Indian asked.

"Damn right. Did *you* bring?"

The Indian held out a rawhide sack closed at the top with a drawstring. It was eight inches long and heavy.

The officer pulled his bundle forward, untied the leather thongs from it and rolled out two army rifles and a carbine. In a small square box were two hundred cartridges.

The Indian nodded and handed the heavy rawhide bag to the officer who undid the rawhide and laces and looked inside. He poured some of the chunks into his hands, then struck a stinker match to check.

He grunted, evidently satisfied.

"Yeah, some of it looks right. But remember, just the squaw clay. That's all we want. Not the other rocks. Understand that? Just squaw clay."

The Indian nodded. "Bang, bang?" he said, indicating the weapons.

The next ten minutes were spent showing the brave exactly how the cartridges went into the rifles, and how they were fired. When he was through with the instruction, the officer removed the ammunition and had the Indian load each weapon, then fire and reload. With each round the brave became more excited.

"Many, many!" the brave said when he had the package wrapped up again and ready to travel.

"Fifty, you understand. Fifty."

The Indian shook his head. The officer held up both his hands with fingers extended. "Ten," he said. He then closed his fists and opened them again saying "twenty," and worked up to fifty. At last the brave understood.

"For fifty rifles, you must bring me two powder kegs filled with squaw clay. The kegs will be at this spot tomorrow night. You come pick them up."

It took another ten minutes to get the arrangements straight for the sale. At last the Indian nodded, clutched the rifles and leaped on his pony. He galloped off into the night without a backward glance.

"Uppity son-of-a-bitch!" the army man said, then hefted his sack, tucked it inside his shirt and rode for the camp.

As he approached Camp Sheridan, the officer slid off his mount and watched. He gave a poor imitation of a night hawk's cry, but there was no answering call. A half hour later the officer tried the call again, and this time the guard near the rear entrance to the camp responded with the same call. The officer mounted, rode through the gate and quickly put his horse in a stall at the back of the stable.

The guard who let the officer in watched the man ride inside. He didn't have the slightest idea what the lieutenant was doing out there in the dark, but that was his affair. The trooper would get a two-dollar gold piece tomorrow—that was all he was interested in, and all he needed to know. The less he knew, the less anyone could make him tell.

CHAPTER EIGHT

Spur McCoy kept no notes on current assignments, but he did keep a kind of report diary. He noted each day where he was and generally what he was doing. He had just finished a two-line report on the day and put the pad and pencil away when a knock sounded on his door. He went to the front and opened it, but saw no one. He closed it and bolted it, then heard the knock again.

This time he went to the rear door and opened it. He fully expected to see Felicia Jones. Instead, he found a tentative and slightly embarrassed Janet Casselberry. She looked both ways along the darkened buildings.

"Colonel, could I talk to you a moment?"

"Yes, of course, come in." Spur opened the door and she entered quickly.

"Thank you. I didn't want anyone to see me come in. You know—it would look bad, somebody might talk."

He nodded. She wore a simple dress in some cotton fabric that fit snugly around her breasts and covered her from neck to floor.

"I . . . I just wanted to thank you again." She looked up, her pretty eyes pleading with him. She blinked the tears from her eyes. "Oh, Colonel, I simply don't know what to do! My husband is still so hostile about everything." She covered her face with her hands. "Sorry—I'm doing this very badly. I should never have come this way." She tried to dry her tears with her sleeve. Then she squared her shoulders and faced Spur. "Colonel, I'm a woman of my word. I told you I would thank you more appropriately later. Now I want to do that. But I . . . I have nothing of value to offer you . . ." She stopped and started for the door. "I'm simply no good at this!" Suddenly she stamped her foot, turned and marched back to him, standing so close that her breasts touched his chest. She looked up defiantly. "Colonel, the only thing I can offer is myself—to express my gratitude." She put her arms around his back and pressed hard against him, resting her cheek on his shoulder. "Neil even sleeps on the couch, he won't touch me. If you would help *me*, Colonel, I would be ever so grateful." She pulled his head down so she could kiss his lips and he felt her tongue against his mouth.

"Colonel, I've only made love to one man in my whole life, but now I *need* someone. I'm willing to . . ."

"Janet, I talked with your husband. I know how he feels. You don't have to do this. In a week or two it will be all settled down and he'll be loving you again—in every way."

"I tried to tell myself that. But this noon I tried to

87

seduce him. I couldn't. It made me think. . . . made me think I'm old, and homely and ugly and no man will have me. I know it's not logical, that it's silly— still . . ."

She looked up at him and he bent and kissed her lips. This time his were open as well. Her tongue darted into his mouth and she gave a little sigh. When the long kiss ended she moved her hands to her throat and unfastened one button. Then she looked up shyly.

"Would you . . . do you want to help me take this off?"

"Janet, you mustn't do this. You are a beautiful young lady. You're so pretty, with all that long blonde hair and those big brown eyes, that any man on the post would give a month's pay to help you undress just to look at you. You have a marvelous figure, your breasts are fantastic, your waist is so small and your hips . . . Are you sure you don't want to wait out that two weeks?" Spur wondered if he could wait another two minutes.

In response, she caught one of his hands and held it over one of her full breasts.

"Spur, please love me," she whispered.

His hands worked as if of their own volition, as he caressed her.

"Spur, you don't know how fine that feels! Just to know that a man is a little bit interested . . ."

"Janet, never, never question your appeal to the opposite sex again. Shall I show you exactly *how* interested I am?" He took one of her hands and pushed it down between their bodies to his fly where a large bulge had developed.

"Oh, thank God," she said. She left her hand there, rubbing him tenderly.

He opened the rest of the buttons on her bodice and at once it was apparent she wore nothing underneath. Her soft breasts were unconfined and his hands devoured them. Her nipples surged upward, pink and hot in their surrounding seas of softer pink areolas. He bent and kissed each nipple and Janet shivered.

"Nice, so nice!" When his head came up she kissed his lips.

Spur picked her up and carried her to the army bed and put her down gently. He kissed both her breasts, then her open mouth, and she sighed contentedly.

"Hey, I thought *you* were going to seduce *me*," he said jokingly.

She smiled ruefully. "I don't have much experience."

"Try—I'll cooperate," Spur assured her.

She smiled in that soft, enigmatic way, and slid off the bed. Quickly she lifted off her dress, then pushed down two petticoats and a pair of white drawers and stood before him beautifully naked.

"Marvelous!" Spur said. "Now get to work." He sat on the bed and played with her breasts as she started undressing him. At last he helped her, sucking one of her nipples as he did so. She made a little noise in her throat as she pulled down his trousers and then the short underwear.

"Oh!" she gasped as she saw his erection. "I've never seen anything so huge! Can I touch it?"

"You better!"

She caught his penis in her hand, marveling at its size and heat.

"I think it might *burn* me!" she said, excitement in her words. Then she pushed Spur flat on his back and straddled him, sitting on his belly and leaning forward so one breast dangled over his lips. Spur chuckled, caught it in his mouth and sucked. As he did, he felt her climaxing. It was short and sharp, a double jolt that contorted her face and brought a series of small sharp yelps. Then it was done and she smiled tremulously.

She let him suck on both breasts, then moved forward until her fuzzy swatch was close to his face.

"Eat me!" she said with surprising command in her voice.

Spur lifted his head as she moved forward and pushed his face into her crotch, his tongue reaching for her heartland, touching it, digging into the soft petals and plunging inside.

Janet gave a piercing wail and fell back on the bed, her whole body quivering in a gigantic climax. The wail turned into moans of delight until the last of the tremors stopped and she tapered off into a soft, cooing rest.

At last she lay on her stomach, propped her chin under her hands and stared at him. "I didn't think a man would really *do* that. It was incredible. Can I travel with you and be your pet?" she teased, then crawled over him and kissed his throbbing manhood. "Since I'm seducing you, I want to be on top. I've never been on top before."

Spur lay on his back, spread his legs and laced his fingers together behind his head. "I'm all yours, Janet. Do with me what you will."

She giggled, went to her hands and knees and bent taking his cock in her mouth and licking it tenderly.

Then she hovered over him on her knees, positioned herself again and then leaned forward and lowered herself onto his shaft. Spur felt a surge of emotion as he slowly slid into her. She was panting, and then she groaned as he felt himself drive into her. She leaned forward, her knees still bent, and kissed his lips.

She began rocking back and forth, riding him like a spring stallion, making more little moves and creating delicious friction unlike anything Spur had ever experienced.

"Wonderful!" she moaned once, then he saw her eyes glaze and her breath come in a surging gasp as she began trembling violently. She fell on top of him, shattered by the ecstasy within her.

She pushed up from him and he saw sweat beading her forehead. "Oh, Spur, it's never, never, *never* been so marvelous! Good, but never like that. You are wonderful . . . Oh—how selfish of me! It was *your* turn—I forgot all about you. You feel so huge inside me. Let's see if we can do nice things for you."

She pushed upward until she was sitting, his cock, still inside her. She leaned backward until Spur groaned, then began to weave forward and back, and to lift up and down in wildly erotic movements that tore Spur apart. He knew he couldn't stand it much longer. Another series of the rotations and he knew the time had come. He thrust up at her and lifted her into the air. His hips gave one last powerful thrust and he collapsed. She lowered herself on top of him, cushioning her breasts on his chest and kissing away the sweat from his forehead as Spur lay there panting, gulping in a torrent of air to revive his drained body.

All at once she wanted to talk. She began pouring out all of her troubles to him. Spur could barely listen, drained as he was, but he tried to follow it.

" . . . So I told him that of course I loved him and I wanted him, and I took my dress off and tried to entice him, but he ran out the door and I was so crushed that I had to go lie down. Then I did a sinful thing. I mean, I touched myself . . . down below . . . I rubbed and rubbed and it felt so good. I know I shouldn't have, but I was so crushed and so furious with Neil. Do you ever do that?"

"Do what?" asked Spur groggily.

"You know, *pretend* you're with someone."

"Everyone does, don't worry about it," he told her.

"Everyone? Even at *my* age?"

"And even much older than you." He put his arms around her. "How come you were able to come to my room? Where's your husband?" He realized he should have asked this before.

"He's on guard duty. Watch officer tonight."

"Oh. Then you can stay all night?"

"I never thought about it. Do you want me to?"

"You are a silly woman." He kissed both her breasts. "Yes, please stay."

And she did. Just before three in the morning, she got out of bed. Spur stood beside her and kissed her lips, then her nose and both eyes.

"Janet, you are a marvelous, beautiful woman. You make love deliciously, and any man alive would *kill* to spend one hour in bed with you. This unpleasantness will die down. Go back home and give Neil a little more time."

Janet giggled, reached down and patted his limp manhood. "I hope we didn't kill it."

"His nickname is Lazarus—he can rise from the dead." She laughed and he kissed her once more, then helped her put on her dress. She slipped out the back door into the night. Spur sighed and locked up after her. He stumbled back to bed and went to sleep at once. He didn't get up for breakfast. At 5:30 he awoke as usual, but turned over and went back to sleep. A man had to have some sleep, after all.

When Spur got up shortly before ten that morning, he wasn't sure what his next step was to be. He had been waiting for the bushwhacker to try again. He would follow up on the owners of the rifles. Both were enlisted men so that might make it easier to get the officer. There had to be an officer involved. He dressed in his uniform and walked around the post. Just before noon he was at the south end of camp where the rifle range had been set up. A different company was using it today. Lt. Omer Imhoff was the range officer. He barged up and down the line barking out orders as though he had been in the army for thirty years. Spur was surprised to see Lt. Casselberry there and discovered it was his company. Even though Neil had been on duty all night, he had come out with his troops.

Spur stood with the two officers for a moment, just in time to hear what must have been the final thrust of a series of teasing remarks.

"Casselberry, I hear you're going to need a papoose board in another nine months for your new family."

The words were said jokingly, but underneath Spur recognized in Imhoff a real dislike, a need to wound.

Lt. Neil Casselberry exploded. He charged across the space between them and thundered a fist into the surprised Imhoff, who staggered backward. Casselberry was all over him, slamming one solid punch after another into Imhoff's face until the big officer crumbled into the dust.

"Nobody talks that way about my wife, you bastard!" Casselberry roared. He punctuated the remark with a solid kick at Imhoff's belly. "You say anything like that again and I'll kill you, believe me, Imhoff, I'll kill you!" He kicked the man again.

By that time Spur was running toward them. The troopers on the line stopped firing, and turned to watch the fight. Any fight was a treat, but one between officers was a rarity, something to write home about. Before Spur got there Imhoff bellowed, "You fucking idiot, it was a *joke!*"

"Nobody jokes about my wife!" Casselberry roared and kicked Imhoff a glancing blow on the side of his head. The big officer rolled over and lay still. Casselberry was aiming another kick when Spur charged into him, caught him around the chest and drove him away. Spur slapped Casselberry twice and the junior officer shook his head, his eyes still glazed with hatred.

"Casselberry, sit down, right there, and don't move until I order you to. Do you understand me?" Spur snapped.

Casselberry shook his head again, and the mists dissolved. He looked up and nodded. "Yes, sir."

Spur hurried back to Lt. Imhoff. A sergeant had turned him over and lifted his head out of the dirt. He was conscious, blinking and groaning. Spur knelt beside him.

"Good morning, Lieutenant. What's your name?"

"Name . . . name . . ." Imhoff mumbled. "Yeah, I've got a name. I even know your name . . . Jones, old Doctor Jones."

Spur told the sergeant to keep the officer down and sent for the doctor. He stood and looked at the forty men who had clustered around. Spur picked out another sergeant and told him to take the men back to their barracks. The party was over.

By the time the doctor arrived, only the four men remained.

Casselberry sat throwing small pebbles at a bush. The scowl on his face seemed formed in stone. Spur watched the doctor look over the line officer, then went and sat beside Casselberry.

"Had Imhoff been talking like that before I came?" Spur asked.

"For an hour, sir. I just got to the point where I couldn't stand it."

"That's no reason to stomp a man to death."

"I know. I went out of my head for a moment."

"Put that in your report. I'm sure there will be some kind of an inquiry. It all depends how badly you shook up Imhoff's brains."

They watched the doctor get Imhoff to his feet and walk him toward the small dispensary.

"At least I didn't kill him," Casselberry said.

"An incident like this isn't going to help disperse any rumors about your wife, you must know that. If you want to help her and your career, put a capper on your temper. Now you had better carry on with your normal duties."

"Yes, sir. Thank you, sir." Lt. Casselberry stood and marched back toward his company area.

Buffalo Kane sat in the shade of the last barracks near the south end of camp. He had been watching the target practice and had seen the two officers fight. It wasn't much of a fight, he decided. That Lt. Casselberry had got in a surprise punch, and then waded in like a bare knuckle champion and knocked Imoff on his ass.

Kane kept whittling on a twisted cottonwood root as Lt. Casselberry strode past. The young officer was in trouble. From the looks of things, Casselberry had lost his temper. Temper. That made Buffalo think. Temper and anger. Anger at the Indians, all Indians. It fit. Casselberry was known to be a spit-and-polish, by-the-book officer. That kind always wants to impress his fellow officers and his superiors. Wiping out an Indian family might just help do it. Buffalo Kane went on whittling what looked like a wooden knife. He didn't even look up as Casselberry walked by, but he was thinking, could Lt. Neil Casselberry be his man?

CHAPTER NINE

Spur McCoy was hungry for dinner that noon. He noticed that Lt. Imhoff wasn't there. That whole business could get nasty depending how Major Rutherford handled it. No, the major would understand the situation, and since Imhoff was the bigger man physically, he wouldn't want it on the official record that he had been beaten up by Casselberry. The outfall there would feed the rumor mongers. Janet would suffer in the long run.

The dinner was one long conversation about the fight that morning. Everyone in camp knew exactly what had happened and why. Most of them were cheering Lt. Casselberry.

"That Imhoff can be a real pain in the butt," Lt. Pauley said. "I've had a run-in or two with him. But, hell, he's young. Give him five years out here and he'll shape up."

"If he lives that long," Captain Grove, the adjutant, said.

No one asked Spur specifically what had happened, and for that he was thankful. Rank had certain privileges, even if the eagles were only flying temporarily.

After the meal Spur talked to the sergeant major and found out where the two men were who had the Henry rifles. One was on stable duty and the second was on a day-long patrol that had left just before dawn.

Spur found the first soldier, Private Hargrove. The young man was tall and lean, had a Texas accent and had been in the army for only two months. He was petrified to be talking to an officer, let alone a full colonel. All he could do was stare at the eagles. Spur wasn't about to tell him to relax and throw away a free advantage.

"Soldier, this is a part of my survey of this camp. One thing we're interested in is the Henry repeating rifle. The commissioner is interested in standardizing our arms. We want everyone to have the same make and caliber of rifle or carbine so it will make it easier on supply, and better tactically in the field. Do you think the Henry repeating rifle should be considered as the standard army weapon?"

"Uh, nope. I surely don't, Colonel."

"Why?"

"Well this 'un weapon of mine, say. It's nigh four feet long. No way to carry it comfortable on a horse. Scabbard too damn short, can't carry it across the saddle. Hail, 'bout the only thing a body can do is carry the damn thing in the crook of your arm. Fine for a couple miles, but forty miles a day and beans don't cut hay, Colonel."

"Is it accurate? Can you hit anything with it?"

"Hail, yes, sir. Got me the best shot in my company. 'Course I done some shooting down home. But my Henry will outshoot any of them other army rifles. Onlyest trouble is a body got to get the blamed thing to where you aim to use it."

"Do you have your weapon with you, Private Hargrove?"

"No, sir. Back at the barracks."

"Go back to your barracks and give your Henry to Corporal Kramer at supply. I need to inspect it. He'll issue you a temporary weapon."

"Now?"

"Right now, Private!"

Spur watched the gangling youth running for his barracks. Spur intended to eject some rounds from the two weapons and see if the extractor marks on the brass matched. A weapons expert in St. Louis said each extractor left a mark that was unique, and that any casing could be mated up with the gun it was fired from.

Spur went to the barracks where the second soldier with the Henry bunked. The barracks was a showplace, with neat bunks along each long wall. It was a spacious building with a high ceiling, windows every ten feet, and the bunks all had thick mattresses and blankets. In front of each bunk was a footlocker. A stove every twenty feet down the center provided heat. Three circular rifle racks stood in the center aisle with the polished weapons at the ready. A barracks orderly on duty tripped and almost fell when he saw the colonel, quickly got up and saluted.

"Soldier, which bunk belongs to Private Vuylsteke?"

"The middle ... down in ... Can I show you, sir?"

Spur nodded and the soldier tripped again but this

time kept his feet under him. Vuylsteke's bunk was the eighth one in from the end.

"He's on a patrol, I assume. Did he take his Henry rifle?"

"Don't know, sir—oh, no sir, he didn't take it. It's the long one in the rifle rack."

"Bring it here, Private."

The man ran for the rack, opened it and took out the long repeating rifle. He brought it back and gave it to the officer.

"I need to inspect this weapon, soldier. I'll give you a temporary receipt for it. If Vuylsteke needs another weapon he can sign out for one at the supply room." Spur handed the bewildered trooper a slip of paper with a short note and McCoy's signature.

Ten minutes later Spur was on the rifle range with Corporal Balder and the three Henry rifles. Spur fired three rounds from the first weapon and put a slip of paper with the cartridge cases with the serial number of the weapon. He put the brass and the paper in one pocket, then fired the other two rifles. Back in the supply room he laid out the brass with the slips of paper and compared them with cartridges from the bushwhacker's weapon. Spur used the largest magnifying glass he could find on post, and compared the scratches on the casings made by the extractor. Each was distinctive. Not even all three from the unknown gun matched each other, but there was a certain pattern they followed.

He studied each cartridge casing separately. Vuylsteke's gun could not possibly have fired the rounds. The next weapon was from the stable hand. Anyone could have stolen the Henry, used it and put it back. But the second set of brass did not meet the test. He checked the rifle that had been in the supply room. To Spur's surprise its cartridge cases matched the rounds exactly.

Whoever fired at him had taken the Henry from the supply room, used it, cleaned it and put it back before it was missed. Could it have been Corporal Kramer? Not likely.

He was back to step one of his journey, without a solid clue to work on. He kept going over the factors. Stolen army guns were turning up in Sioux hands; the raid on Buffalo Kane's shack and the murder of his family; the bushwhacking done by someone the first day he had arrived. Something else niggled at his mind—then he had it. The hammered gold trinket that belonged to Walking Fawn and had shown up later in the sutler's store bartered for some drinks.

Spur didn't know if any of it tied together. He wasn't even sure that the rifles were coming from this installation. But the fact that there were five rifles missing, gave him his only strong lead to this camp. He needed more facts, more hard intelligence about both sides of the trade. Which Indians were in on this?

Corporal Kramer stood at the door to the room where Spur had compared the casings.

"Corporal, could I talk with you a minute?" Spur asked.

The supply man came in and closed the door.

"This is all confidential, Kramer. I don't want anyone to know I've been comparing shell casings and extractor marks. This is just between us. It's important. Also, I need to know who has access to the supply room nights when you're not here."

"The Officer of the Guard has all the keys. I guess he could get in."

"Thank you, Corporal. If you would return these two weapons to the men I would appreciate it."

"Yes, sir!"

Spur walked slowly as he left the supply room and headed across the compound toward camp headquarters. The idea had come a few hours ago, and now it seemed more realistic. He had to get into the Black Hills. He had to watch the Indians, to see what they were up to. Nice work if you could do it without getting scalped.

He pushed into the outer office and was ushered into Colonel Underhill's quarters. The colonel was smoking a cigar, and Spur fished a crooked black one from his pocket and lit it.

"Underhill, I've got a problem. There is no chance I can identify the man who tried to shoot me. I need more information. As I understand it, the hostiles attack and retreat into the Black Hills. I've got to go in there and see what I can find out. I'm trying to solve this puzzle with only half the pieces."

Underhill took a long drag on his stogie, and blew the smoke halfway across the room. "Ordinarily I'd say what you suggest was suicide. But lately most of the Sioux have quieted down. We get a lot of Teton Sioux and Yankton Sioux around here, depending where the best hunting is. We haven't had any real trouble in two or three weeks. Might just be in between some tribal meets or pow-wows of some kind. I'll give you three good men and if you travel at night and stay hid during the day, you should make it."

"No men. I'll go alone. I can hide my trail and myself easier that way. I've been in Indian territory before, Colonel. All I'll need are some supplies and some weapons. I'd also like a dozen sticks of dynamite and caps and fuses. Never can tell when they might come in handy. Oh, I'd like a pound of six-penny nails too, and some kind of sticky tape."

Colonel Underhill stared at Spur for a minute, then nodded. "You're welcome to all the supplies you want. But I'd appreciate it if you'd leave me a signed statement that you're going in alone, that I offered you an escort, and why you're going in. It might be handy to have when the board of inquiry arrives just in case you don't come back from the Black Hills."

Spur shrugged. "No problem. I'll have it ready before I go. Might as well get started today, get used to traveling at night."

Spur turned and walked out of the room and directly to the stables where he checked out the bay he had been riding. She was sleek and well fed, had been brushed down daily and exercised.

Back at his quarters he sorted through the equipment he had brought along. Most of it he rejected as too heavy. He would have no pack horse, just his own mount with saddle bags and a sack of food and gear. He selected carefully. Then he went to supply and drew a second pistol, a Remington new model army revolver and fifty rounds for it. At the mess hall he took exactly what he figured he would need for the six day ride including beans, coffee, two loaves of bread and some salt beef. At last he put in four tins of beef and a can of peaches. Two meals a day would be more than enough. He had everything put in a snap-top canvas bag. He then went to the ammunition magazine to pick up the dynamite and chose six sticks that looked stable, carefully cut them in half with his knife and fused each one with a six-inch fuse. He would put the blasting caps on later. Out here you never knew when a hand bomb like these would come in handy.

Back at his quarters, Spur had his mount brought around and watched as two men loaded on his provisions. It was nearly three in the afternoon. He would have plenty of time to move well away from the camp before nightfall. Then he could practice his night travel. It had been some time.

Colonel Underhill stood on the porch of his headquarters and watched as Spur rode over and gave him a sealed envelope.

"This is what you wanted, Colonel. I promise that you won't need it. I'll be back in seven days, unless I find something worthwhile. Then it may take me two days longer."

"Good luck—you're going to need it."

Spur waved and rode out the front gate and angled north. He crossed the White River and using a hand compass headed for a butte on the skyline that he should be able to identify for two hours after the sun went down. He rode at a gentle canter for the first two miles, then let the bay slow to a walk. Once he turned and watched the trail behind him. There was no reason that Underhill would send a patrol to follow him, but a man in his condition wasn't very reliable. Spur watched his backtrail for ten minutes from the far side of a rise, but could detect no movement.

Spur rode through a seemingly endless grassland, cut here and there by rivers and gullies. But the flatness of the Great Plains was both exciting and deadly. He angled a little more to the west to take advantage of a long valley leading to some low bluffs on the skyline.

It was dark before he reached the bluffs. Spur spotted a clump of willow and scrub with one cottonwood at the edge of the valley where some wet-weather feeder stream evidently came in. A half hour later he eased into the area, checked it thoroughly for any visiting Sioux hunters, and then relaxed. The Sioux must all be in their favorite hunting grounds to the north and west. He wouldn't worry about Indians for another two days.

Spur loose-tied his bay, fed her a quart of oats and let her drink at the tiny stream. Then he made camp. It was what he called a fast camp. McCoy took from the supply sack only what he needed, left the horse saddled and the sack in place, and only loosened the cinch strap. He could be in the saddle and moving within a minute of any sign of trouble.

Spur spread out his two blankets and searched the dry stream bed for some small, dry sticks. They would make a nearly smokeless fire for his coffee. He didn't mind missing a meal or two now and then, but coffee was a necessity. He made the fire and brewed his java in a tin can and at once put out the fire.

Spur sat back, letting the blackness close in on him again. He noticed a star or two through the thin canopy of leaves overhead. He hadn't seen a settler's cabin all day. He was out beyond the limits of the Nebraska pioneers. In fact he wasn't sure if he had crossed the line into Dakota Territory. The chances of finding friendly faces in the Dakotas were even smaller. He might not see anyone but Indians until he got back to the fort.

Spur lay on his blankets on his back, then leaned up on his elbow a moment to check his bay. She was moving around as if something was bothering her.

Suddenly something flashed in front of his eyes and he felt the cold steel of a knife blade pressing against his throat. Spur tensed. The knife was poised to slash across his windpipe. He was totally at the mercy of his unknown assailant.

CHAPTER TEN

McCoy felt the knife pressure on his throat increase. He had not heard a thing, nor seen a movement. All he could do was talk.

"Hold on now, whoever you are. Don't do anything sudden or rash. I can't reach my weapon. If you can understand English, I hope you realize I'm not coming here to hurt anyone."

Spur felt movement behind him, and heard a soft sound that wasn't a word.

"Listen, I'm just passing through. I won't harm your lands. I'm not a scout for the army. I come in peace."

As quickly as it came, the knife was removed from his throat and he heard a laugh behind him, high bubbling feminine laughter that trailed off as he sat up and spun around, his hand clawing for the M & H 44 at his side.

"Colonel McCoy, you won't need your weapon. I won't hurt you—I came to help you."

He couldn't see through the murky darkness but

he recognized the voice. Spur relaxed and now it was his turn to laugh.

"Chitsa, welcome to Dakota Territory."

"We can have a campfire if you like. There isn't a Sioux within twenty miles of us."

"Why are you here, Chitsa?"

"I told you, to help you. If I let you go into the Black Hills alone, you will be caught, tortured and killed. I don't want that to happen." She paused. "Wait a moment, I'll relight the fire, and if your grounds are still good, could we brew another cup? I'm very fond of coffee."

Spur turned and lay forward on his blankets as he watched the small dark shadow moving near where his fire had been. Sooner than he expected the fire blazed up. Chitsa brought more wood and built it up so it lighted the small campsite.

Chitsa sat in front of him on the ground and he saw that she wore a one piece doeskin Indian dress tied at the waist with a leather thong, and moccasins. She smiled at him.

"Do not try to send me back. You are going into dangerous areas. It is a foolish journey, but I can't sit by and let you die. It would be a great waste. We can ride out another day, camp in a place I know where there is sweet water, many berries and some wild fruit and rabbits. We can talk and I'll show you how Indians live, work, and play."

"No, Chitsa. I have a job to do, and it must be done."

"Then I must go with you. What exactly are you trying to find out on this fool's mission?"

Spur laughed and she smiled. "You have a delicate way with words, Chitsa. I may just tie you up and leave you beside a tall tree until I return."

"You would have to catch me first. And remember how I slipped up on you even when you were quietly listening. I am an Indian, Spur. I can take you places so the Sioux will never know we have been there. But I must know what you wish to discover."

He told her his mission, then, quickly and simply. Her eyes grew cold, and her fists tightened.

"I am an Indian, but I have been educated by white men. I am a woman in two camps. I detest whoever is selling the rifles to the Sioux. Although they are not my tribe, they will die like buffalo being driven over a cliff. I will help you find out what you need to know."

Spur thought about it. She could be a tremendous asset in the next few days—and a great temptation. He decided to avoid that issue for now.

"Chitsa, if you come with me it may help. I need to find out which group of Sioux are buying the guns and I need to know who among them has contact with the insider at Camp Sheridan. I also need to know what schedule or method of payment has been made."

She thought about it, her round face serious now, her almond-shaped eyes showing worried. "Most of what you seek will be impossible to find out. But we can learn some of it. We must be cautious. After tomorrow we will travel only at night, and we must not light a fire once we reach the land of the Sioux."

"A question. At lunch the other day you looked like a fashionable, civilized young lady. How have you kept your worlds intact? Have you learned Indian skills so you could be comfortable in both camps?"

109

She smiled at him. "Grace Underhill said I had been with them for fifteen years. She exaggerates. It's been ten years. I am now twenty-one. I had eleven years to learn Indian ways. My tribe was the Shawnee and we learned to live with the white man quickly, but still we never abandoned our Indian heritage.

"Even now I get restless. Grace knows it and pretends it doesn't happen. I go out into the prairie, and live as the Indians do. I am sometimes gone for a day, sometimes a week. One summer I stayed away for a month, and Grace was ill with worry when I went back. I can live off the land. I can provide my own food and clothing if necessary."

"Remarkable. So you think my mission is stupid and that we should go back?"

"You should have consulted me before you planned it. We may be able to find out some things you need to know. Yes, it will be productive to continue."

"How? Do you have a horse?"

"Of course. Your bay sniffed her out—that's what almost gave me away."

"Now there is one other matter," Spur said, staring at her. The loose fitting garment totally hid her figure, but he had a powerful imagination.

"Spur McCoy, I'm just as interested in that 'other matter' as you are. But first we must see what information we can find to stop the sale of the rifles. That is much more important. Then we will discuss my virginity, and how and when you will instruct me in making love for the first time."

Spur sat back, astonishment washing over him.

"How did you know that was what I was talking about?"

"I am woman, and an Indian. I could tell. There is an old Shawnee custom that allows any Indian girl unmarried by the time she is eighteen to choose the man who will pierce her maidenhead. The selected male does not have the right to refuse—and usually he does not wish to refuse."

"Is that a real custom, or have you created it especially for your own situation?"

"If I could create plots like that, Mr. McCoy, I would be a great novelist or write plays to rival Shakespeare."

"You just might be good at it! But you're right about one thing. If we're risking our lives out here, we better not worry about anything else until we get back."

"From now until then, I will be your sister, your guide, your scout and your advisor. If I need to bathe in a stream, you will stand guard and look the other way, and you will not intrude on my privacy. Now we should sleep. We will make much better time tomorrow than you did today. Do you realize that you had to backtrack twice today to get around bluffs you could have avoided?"

She stood gracefully, vanished out of the firelight for a few minutes and returned with her horse, an Indian Pinto pony with an army saddle, complete with .44 pistol and carbine in the boot. She took down a blanket roll and spread it beside his. Then she scooped dirt onto the fire with her hands and lay down on top of her blankets. Within minutes she was sleeping, lying on her back, with one hand across her stomach and the other above her head.

Spur watched her in the pale, filtered moonlight. She was his sister. She was also a combination of Indian and white that would surely get her in trouble sooner or later. San Francisco would be a good place for her. She'd be a sensation . . . He shook his head. Sleep—what he needed was sleep. He drifted off and dreamed of finding a secret cache of rifles in boxes, but when he opened the boxes, the rifles turned into rattlesnakes and began striking at him.

He woke once, saw that Chitsa was still sleeping soundly, and dozed off again.

Spur awoke at 5:30 as usual. As soon as he sat up, Chitsa was awake and on her feet. Before he got up off the blanket she had the fire going and had started frying bacon and making flapjacks from her own supplies.

"This is the last civilized food for you," she said. "The eggs are from camp, in honor of your bravery —and foolhardiness. Eat this in good health."

Spur thought he knew all about camping and life on the trail, but in the next ten minutes the small Indian girl showed him that he was a total neophyte. She had everything packed and the horses ready to go before he had the sleep out of his eyes. She wore the same doeskin dress and rode her pony astride. She led the way, made a sudden turn to the left following the valley and headed for a cliff he was sure they would never be able to climb.

He asked her about it and she only smiled. Just as they came to it, Spur spotted a pass. While not more than two hundred feet high, going around the bluffs would have caused them a five mile detour.

"You do good scout work," Spur said.

"This is nothing. I know this country like my bedroom. I've been into the Black Hills twice while I have been here. Neither time did I let the Sioux know I was there. If they found me, they would take me prisoner."

By noon of the first full day they had passed Lone Butte and Spur could see a tower ahead that Chitsa said the Indians called Hay Canyon Butte. Several times that morning she had stopped, dismounted and stared into the distance, turning her head to catch the wind and testing the scents in the air. The last time she nodded and smiled.

"Come, we must hurry, I want to show you something."

They rode hard up a slight draw to a continuation of the monotonous plains. At the top she held up her hand to stop and they walked the horses cautiously so they could see over the waving grass.

Spur caught his breath. "Magnificent! I've never seen a better herd. But what are they doing here?"

Ahead of them on a gentle, rolling downslope were more than a hundred head of buffalo. The bulls stood nearly six feet tall, huge shaggy, angry-eyed creatures with short pointed horns and now almost bare hindquarters due to the summer shedding. A dozen or so bulls patroled the outer limits of the herd and the cows and spring calves grazed inside.

"You knew they were here," Spur said.

"Yes, of course. I'm Indian."

"You smelled them on the wind?"

"Partly. My senses are not sharpened yet. It usually takes me two or three days. Then I could have scented them from five miles away. These were less than a mile."

"But they are *downwind* from us."

"Yes. It is more than the scent, there is a *presence* with the buffalo. So many Indians rely totally upon them for their life. They use the meat, the hide, the horns, even the hooves. No part of a bison goes to waste in an Indian camp. We make buffalo robes when the big creatures have their full winter coat of long shaggy hair and the dense wooly undercoat. We make our teepees from the hides. We preserve the meat, dry it, pound it into pemmican. Many of the Plains Indians also worship the buffalo."

She frowned. "We must go."

"Why?"

"We go now because wherever there are this many buffalo at this time of year, there surely are Indians, scouts at least to keep track of the herd. It is the right number for a medium-sized camp of Sioux to attack. Here they would start grass fires and drive the buffalo over the cliff. It's the easiest way for the braves to kill the beasts. Some of the big bulls weigh more than 2200 pounds. Even the cows can weigh 1200 pounds."

She turned her horse and rode at right angles to the herd, which did not see them, and soon they were into a draw that led in the direction they needed to go.

He came abreast of her. "It's a little unusual to see that many buffalo together this time of year," she said. "We're right in the middle of the calving season. Usually they wander around in bands of eight or ten with their newborn calves. Come August it will be breeding or 'running' season and the males become restless. Fights between the bulls

114

is common and the small bands merge into giant herds that often go as high as five thousand. The bellowing and bawling of that many buffalo keeps everyone awake for miles around."

"And the Sioux live off the buffalo which means we need to get away from them," Spur said. "Makes sense."

They stopped near sunset. There had been no noon break, and Spur figured they had covered over forty miles. Chitsa picked out the campsite, a dense growth of willow and chokecherry bordering a small trickle of a stream. Behind the willow a sandstone cliff rose thirty feet.

"Not even an Indian could sneak up on us here," she said.

Chitsa decided that they could risk a small fire for coffee, but only if she gathered the materials. She prowled the almost dry stream bed for half an hour and came back with her hands full of dry sticks. She showed him how to find branches that had been weathered, soaked and dried for years until they had most of the sap drained out of them. She prepared everything, then lit the fire and Spur soon watched the coffee boil over the smokeless flames.

"After any smoke gets through the willow leaves, it will be washed nearly clean," she said. "Even the best Sioux hunter would need to be within 200 yards of us to smell this smoke."

They had coffee, some slabs of cheese with the bread he had brought and he opened a tin of the beef. She heated it on the coals of the fire and then built up the fire enough to boil more coffee.

"We won't eat this well for several days," she warned him.

It soon grew dark and they let the fire die down and go out. Spur watched her in the moonlight. She was like a wraith, a ghost dancer, and at the same time more educated than most white women. She was truly Woman of Two Camps. She had put up her long twin braids in a bun at the back of her neck so they would be out of the way. The soft doeskin dress clung to her now, showing the swell of her breasts.

She turned and found him staring and she smiled. "Not yet, Colonel. Remember that must wait until after we spy on the mighty Sioux." There was a smile wreathing her face as she went on, "Now, which of Shakespeare's plays were his greatest? Would you say *King Lear, Macbeth* or perhaps *Hamlet?*"

She watched him and Spur chuckled. "You caught me. But as far as the bard goes, I have no favorite, although *The Merchant of Venice* does hold a warm spot in my heart."

"I might have known." She smiled. "Now, Colonel, if the beast in you is corraled, we should be sleeping. When midnight comes we'll be up and moving again until dawn. We travel only at night from now on. Do you trust my scouting?"

"So far, fine. I'll wait until we're back before I give a final evaluation. If we don't both get back alive, you fail."

"Sleep time, Colonel."

Spur woke promptly at midnight as he had instructed his mental alarm clock to do, but Chitsa was already up and had both horses ready.

An hour later Spur was amazed at the way the small Indian girl maneuvered her mount through

116

the Dakota plains, and how well she kept them on a northwesterly route. They made good time and he figured they had covered another twenty miles as it began to get light. They entered a small valley with a heavy stand of cottonwoods and got inside the woods just as the first streaks of dawn tinged the eastern sky.

Once beneath the trees, Chitsa stopped her mount and sat motionless, signalling Spur to do the same.

She pointed ahead and Spur listened. A murmur of voices came through the morning stillness. Chitsa slid off her mount, handed the reins to Spur and vanished into the woods without a sound. They had agreed that any chance happening of a Sioux war party or even a two or three-man hunting group meant they had to dissolve. If they were seen they would be hunted down and killed. If they saw the Indians first they would attempt to stay unobserved. Now his scout and new friend was walking toward the Indian camp.

She was back in less than a minute, holding up two fingers, and drawing an imaginary bow. Two hunters. Spur slid off his bay, pulled out his Spencer repeater and made sure a round was in the chamber and the safety off. They both held the muzzles of their mounts so the sensitive nostrils would not pick up the scent of the Indian horses and reveal their presence.

As they stood there waiting for the Sioux to leave and continue their hunt, one Indian rode past the cottonwood brush and directly into them. The Sioux carried his bow in his right hand, ready for any game. When he saw the two horses, he notched an arrow and had it half drawn when Spur fired the

117

Spencer. The slug caught the rider in the throat and tore out half his windpipe and a section of his spinal column. The dead brave jolted backward off the horse which kept going, pounding past them.

Even before the rifle shot sound had started echoing, Chitsa was running toward the camp they had just left. Spur ran with her, crashing through the brush while she moved soundlessly. The girl stopped behind a tree. He halted behind a cottonwood and looked toward where he figured the camp should be. Spur saw nothing but more brush. Then something moved. He watched again. To the right, away from the camp, the movement came once more and he made out the form of a lurking Indian, drawing a bow. The arrow was aimed at Chitsa.

Without aiming, Spur jerked the Spencer around and fired the long gun from his hip. The Indian screamed in pain and fury, slammed against a tree and slid downward, dead by the time he hit the ground.

The shot's crashing roar faded slowly, and when it was gone, so was Chitsa. He saw her a moment later twenty feet ahead, then farther toward the camp. Spur followed her cautiously, making sure no more redskins lurked in the brush. He remembered her two fingers, but there might be another Indian or two away from camp.

Five minutes later he came from in back of a huge cottonwood and saw the remains of a small cooking fire. Over it lay a rabbit on a spit. One Indian pony stepped nervously where it had been ground-tied.

Chitsa returned to the camp and stared at Spur for several seconds. Then she walked up to him, loosened the tie at her waist and pulled the doeskin dress over her head. She folded it and knelt on it in front of Spur. He was amazed at the perfection of her body. Her breasts were small, darkly nippled and with almost no areolas. Her waist was narrow and the black fur at her crotch was luxuriant.

"Most honored one," she said softly, her eyes downcast in respect. "Most skillful and brave one who has this day saved my life, I humbly submit to your every wish. All previous agreements are canceled." She looked up at him in admiration. "I was truly a dead woman. I saw death in the eyes of the Sioux at the same time your bullet struck him. It was my own death I saw. My life now belongs to you, Colonel McCoy. I am yours in body and mind. Each waking minute of my life from now until I die will be at your service, since I no longer have a life of my own to live."

She stood and put her arms around him, pressing close. "I am yours to command. The hunting party was only two. One was rushing somewhere, perhaps with a message about the herd of buffalo. The other came when your shot alerted him. We are safe for now. No other Sioux warriors are in this area."

Spur bent and kissed her cheek.

"My little sister is still my little sister. Now dress quickly and let's find out if the rabbit is cooked."

A flash of relief covered her face for a second, then she turned, pulled on the dress, tied the belt and checked the rabbit. She built up the fire with dry twigs and by the time Spur had brought up their horses, the meat was cooked.

They ate it hungrily, licking the bones clean, then washing their hands in the small stream.

"We must not stay here," she said. "The spirits of

119

the two Sioux warriors will not let us rest."

They mounted and rode to the northern edge of the brush, and she studied the scene.

"The valley goes north and east. It will be an hour's ride to that green spot by the bluff. We should be unseen this early."

Spur watched her small round face critically.

"You say 'shouldn't,' but what if we are? What if a larger hunting party is coming? What if a lone warrior spots us and spreads the word?"

"Then we will ride like the wind, use our rifles and our pistols and when the night comes we will hide ourselves and escape. We *shall* return from this patrol. I know. I saw it in the stars last night." She frowned. "I am Indian—I can read the sign."

"But you are afraid of two dead Sioux."

A frown touched her face. "Do not joke about the spirits. I will go now. Either go with me or stay here —it's up to you."

CHAPTER ELEVEN

Spur let the Indian maiden ride a hundred yards alone. She never looked back. Then he dug his heels into the bay and caught up to Chitsa, riding alongside. She urged her horse faster and they cantered the two miles to the spot below the bluff and checked the woods carefully. There were no overnight visitors there ahead of them.

"You knew I'd come with you."

"Of course. You're a logical man. And right now you need what I know, you need me to help you. I'll need you later. I'll need you then very much." She was serious as she said it, then turned away and picked out the best spot to hide the horses. They took their sleeping blankets and nestled down in some thick brush toward the back of the woodsy area. Spur stretched out and she put her blankets beside him, rolled toward him and snuggled against his side.

"Now we sleep," she said and closed her eyes.

Spur woke up around noon. He felt the girl move

beside him. She had one arm thrown over his chest, then she smiled in her sleep and turned the other way. Spur stood and checked the area. The horses were still where they had been tied, and quiet. He went to the edge of the trees but saw no movement in the long valley.

When he lay down on the blankets her head searched for him, found his shoulder and she smiled, moved closer to him and returned to her deep sleep.

Spur woke again at five that afternoon. Chitsa was not beside him. He checked the horses and she was not there. A twinge of fear touched him. He went to the stream and found her kneeling beside it. She had shed her dress and was washing. He stopped, embarrassed, afraid of offending her.

"It's all right, Colonel. Don't be shy—you and I have no secrets. Bathing is good for the body." She had spoken without turning around and he saw only her brown back where she knelt. Now she stood and turned. She was naked, holding a small cloth at her face, drying it. Her light tan skin glowed and she was the most naturally beautiful woman he had ever seen. Her small breasts bounced slightly as she bent and pulled on white cotton drawers, then a pair of brown men's pants she had cut down to fit. Over this she put the doeskin Indian dress.

"The trousers make it much easier to ride on the saddle," she explained. "Are you ready to eat?"

He had not seen nor smelled her fire, but it glowed red with coals as she led him to it. The can of coffee boiled gently and there were slabs of bread spread with crabapple jelly. As they ate and drank the strong coffee, he caught her attention.

"Chitsa, you weren't serious about that slave-for-life story you gave me, were you?"

"Of course I meant it. I am Indian!" There was pride and a touch of anger in her voice.

"Well, uh. . . . We're going to have to talk about that. You see, slavery has been abolished. It's against the law."

"I will be a love slave, that's different."

"We'll talk about that back at Camp Sheridan," said Spur, feeling distinctly uncomfortable.

"I will not be able to be your sister much longer, either. I have these feelings when I touch you, even when I'm sleeping."

"Later. It will be dark soon. How far are we from the Black Hills?" he asked.

"We have been in them for half a day. The section we are heading for is another day's ride north. But there could be camps of Sioux hunters anywhere through this area. We must be cautious."

Ten minutes later it was dark and they were moving out of the patch of woods and into the valley. They angled past a mountain on the left and moved up another valley, went to the ridgeline and there Chitsa stopped and looked to the north.

"Smell the smoke?" she asked.

Spur shook his head.

"Four or five miles ahead. A big campfire. Probably a hunting party roasting buffalo steaks and skinning the kill. Let's go have a look."

He started to stop her but shrugged. Any Sioux he saw might provide information, especially if he had rifles. He followed her, watching how straight she sat on the horse, and he wondered what it would be like to make love to her. Young, tender and un-tried. She would be an exciting experience, he knew, and he was starting to look forward to it—but not yet, not while the threat of a Sioux tomahawk loom-ed over them.

An hour later they had left their horses and faded from one tree to the next as they worked their way up a hill concealed by its welcome growth of young pine toward the Indian camp.

After another hundred yards, Chitsa lay down on her stomach and crawled the last fifteen feet to the brow of the ridge. Below them a huge campfire blaz-ed, sending sparks and smoke high into the air and lighting up the gully like noontime.

To one side, squaws worked skinning out two huge buffalo. They quartered one animal, lay the slabs on the skins and cut them into portions for the various family units, then some squaws joined the braves around the fire. Someone had a bottle of fire-water. It went the rounds. The braves grew more boisterous. A rifle shot slammed through the peace-ful silence, and Spur turned his head quickly to find the shooter. The man stood to one side, his posture showing the effects of the strong drink. Two braves grabbed the man, grabbed the weapon away from him and pushed him back to the circle around the fire.

"Twelve braves, a small band," Chitsa said. "They killed two bison, probably with the rifle. They butchered them where they fell, and made their camp here. They will treat the skins, dry the meat, eat until they almost burst, and then move on to wherever they were headed when their scout

124

found the buffalo. Everything stops when buffalo are sighted during hunting season."

Spur listened. He wished he had brought a better pair of binoculars. With the army issue, he was able to pick up some details of the rifle, but not enough. It was either an old Sharps, or a Spencer repeater. Either one would be deadly in the hands of an Indian who had taken the time to learn to use it. More and more Indian chiefs now wanted rifles. The "fire-sticks" at first were laughed at because they belch-ed their fire so slowly. A tomahawk could be swung forty dozen times while a soldier reloaded the old muskets once with ball and powder. Cartridge rifles were better.

"How long will they stay here?" Spur asked.

"It depends how much whiskey they have. The squaws will be finished with their duties in three or four days, depending how thin they cut the meat to dry, and some of the braves will be drunk for three or four days."

"Do you see any more rifles?"

"Yes—the brave at the center of the group around the fire. He could be some kind of sub-chief."

Spur turned his glasses there. The Indian was holding a Sharps, a powerful long-range weapon that came in several calibers and was highly accur-ate. Two rifles, two buffalo. He wondered how many settlers those same guns had killed.

Chitsa motioned him to move back and when they were safely into the woods she touched his arm.

"We should be leaving this place. I have bad feel-ings about it. No sign, but some evil thing is here. I don't like it. The spirits are not pleased."

They walked to their horses, made a wide detour around the camp and pushed on north along a ridge-line that kept moving higher and higher. Just after two in the morning by Spur's Waterbury pocket watch, they stopped.

"We can't go much farther before I have a chance to look around in the daylight. So tell me exactly what you want to see," she said.

"I want to find two or three camps, maybe an abandoned campsite. I want to learn if every band has guns, or only a few. And I want to see if there is any move toward making war on the whites."

"That is possible. Now we will sleep and in the morning I'll find some villages we can spy on."

They found a small ravine clogged with young pine trees, a dozen larger ones and a smattering of brush that would hide the horses. The end of the canyon sloped up into a rock wall and below it the brush was thick. Chitsa hummed a little tune as she spread out the blankets, then took one and using pointed sticks turned the blanket into a wall masking them from the downstream side. She took a candle from her supplies and lit it. It made a surprisingly strong light after the darkness. She sat on the blanket.

"Now, Spur McCoy. Now I want you to make love to me." She smiled at his expression. "Yes, we are safe here. The Sioux are not making war. Hunters do not roam this land at night, and no travelers would come past this area. Even if they were, it would be only blind luck for one to stumble on us. I have waited many, many summers for this moment. Please help me."

Spur sat beside her, reached down and kissed her

cheek, then turned her pretty face and kissed her trembling lips. Gone was her sense of control, her sureness. Now she was on uncharted waters.

Chitsa made a small mewing sound in her throat. Her hand came up and touched his cheek, then she parted her lips and let his tongue probe inside. His arms came around her and she whimpered softly, her small hands clinging to his shirtfront as the kiss continued. When it ended she smiled up at him in the candle glow.

"Kissing. Yes, I like kissing. Especially that kind. Could we try it again?"

Her arms went around him this time and she held him tightly. He let her tongue explore this time and she made the small sounds again. He broke off the kiss and leaned away so he could touch her breast through the soft doeskin. She looked up at him in wonder.

"Yes, I *want* you to touch me there. I've never thought about it before, but it's a very pleasant sensation."

Both his hands cupped her breasts and he caressed them gently, then he slid one hand under her dress and upward to her left breast. When his hand touched her bare flesh, she sighed, "Yes, yes! That is nice. I heard two women talk about it once. Yes, it feels delicious. May I take this off?"

He helped her lift the doeskin over her head and he marveled again at her small round breasts and their dark nipples. He touched them again, playing with them, watching her reaction of surprise, then acceptance, and saw her desire building.

"Breasts are the most beautiful part of a woman, did you know that, Chitsa? So perfectly round, so symmetrical, so delightfully tipped, and so good tasting!"

He bent and kissed one of her breasts and she jumped in surprise. Her glance darted to his face and then her expression mellowed. He kissed her breast again, then licked her nipple and she sighed.

"That's nice, Spur, so nice."

He licked her again and then nibbled at her dark nipple which had sprung up almost doubling its size.

"Suddenly the night air is quite warm," she said, smiling mischievously at him.

Spur finished with one breast and moved to the other one, where his ministrations brought a low moan from Chitsa.

"Spur—beautiful man—I hope you're not in a rush. I would like you to nibble on me that way for an hour."

"We have better things to do," he said, taking off his boots, and sliding down his pants. He pulled off his shirt and smiled at her. She was tense, pensive, but Spur kissed away her doubts, and then slid off his underpants.

"Great Spirits!" she said, staring at his erection. "Huge—it's so big—I never dreamed . . . You don't mean that huge thing is supposed to go inside . . ." She stopped, her hand over her mouth.

Spur moved closer, picked up her other hand and moved it to his thigh. "Go ahead, look at me. Touch me, nothing down there will break. Go ahead."

Her expression changed and she was like a little girl with a new toy. She touched him, grasped his manhood, bent it back and forth, then moved lower to Spur's heavy scrotum and the forest of reddish hair.

She looked up. "I'm not hurting him?"

Spur chuckled. "Lazarus doesn't mind at all. You're going to be very good friends with him."

She moved Spur around, inspecting him thoroughly, but was most fascinated by his penis.

Chitsa still wore her trousers. Spur reached for the buttons on the fly, but she moved his hands up to her breasts and leaned over to be kissed. Spur did, rubbing her breasts harder now as his tongue drove deeply into her mouth. As he kissed her, he pushed her down gently on her back, and moved his mouth to one breast, then unbuttoned her trousers as she moaned softly beneath him.

When the fasteners were open, he pulled the pants off, then put his hand on the white material of the drawers and worked downward.

"Are you seducing me?" she asked, interested.

He kissed her, then put his hand on her crotch and felt a wet place through the thin cotton material. She gasped with delight and when he ended the kiss, he smiled.

"Of course I'm seducing you, which only means a little persuasion. The next time you won't need so much persuasion, and after that *you'll* probably be seducing *me!*"

She nodded and his mouth went back to her breast and his hand rubbed the damp spot. She moaned again and he sat up and put his fingers under the tops of her cotton drawers. She held his hands.

"Are you sure there will be room? I mean, he's so *large.*"

"Yes, sweet little Chitsa, there will be room, and it will be so delightful you'll want to stay this way all night." He bent and kissed her fingers. She let go of his hands and he pulled the fabric down slowly. For each inch he moved the white cloth, he kissed her hips and then her little belly, going around her thick black thatch, and kissed the cloth down her legs until the drawers came off her feet.

Her legs were tightly together. Spur put his hand on her fur and kissed her lips until she purred. Then his finger explored until he found the wet spot. He worked farther to find her tiny hard node and swiftly he rubbed it back and forth. Four times was all it took before Chitsa cried out in surprise as her body trembled with a short sharp series of vibrations that left her gasping.

When she recovered he kissed her gently. "That, small Indian Maiden, was a climax—your body giving you a thrill of the preliminaries to making love. It's even better during lovemaking. Did you like it?"

"Oh, yes, do it again!"

He did.

"So marvelous! So wonderful! Why didn't those women tell me how glorious that feels! Oh, no *wonder* they didn't tell me." She kissed him. "Now, what's next?"

He took her hand and closed it around his erection.

She shivered. "I *still* don't see how it's going to fit."

Spur kissed her, then spread her legs and moved his hand down and found her slit. He edged a finger into the wet, slippery place and Chitsa murmured with pleasure. He spread her juices around the outer lips, kissed her again, then knelt between her spread thighs.

"This is the most wonderful part," he said. He used his hand to coat the purpled head of his cock with saliva, then angled down and touched her sensitive outer lips with his staff.

She shivered. "Will it hurt?"

"It will feel so marvelous you'll not remember anything else."

He probed gently, was sure he was positioned, then increased the pressure a little at a time until he felt her muscles relax and he drove forward.

Chitsa yelped with a sudden, harsh pain. Then it was over and she realized that she was a woman—no longer an Indian maid—and tears filled her eyes as she moved her hips to meet his thrusts with a pleasure, a warmth, a womanly understanding that she had never known before. Total joy and possessiveness flowed from her and she was determined never to leave this man's side. She would be with him and be his woman forever and ever!

Spur let himself go. He felt primitive, like a male animal in final union with the female. He rooted and soared, he pounded forward into her slender form listening to the contented sounds she made as she accepted his plunging. He sensed her feet rising until her legs were in the air over his back and he powered again and again into her until sweat beaded his forehead. Spur erupted inside her five, six, then seven times in ecstatic spasms.

He lowered himself toward her then and kissed her lips gently.

"Oh, that was *beautiful!*" Chitsa said. "I've never felt so wanted, so needed, so loved!"

He shook his head, hearing her words but not quite sure what she was saying. He blinked, saw her

131

face below him and bent and kissed her again, then eased down on her for just a moment. Her arms wrapped around him and pulled him lower. He let only part of his weight rest on her, and she smiled at him and nodded.

"Yes, I want you on top of me! I'll come with you —I'll go anywhere you want me to. After we find out about the rifles, and discover who is selling them, then I'll come with you to whatever army post you are assigned to. All I have to pack is my books."

Spur's mind unfroze and he recognized the meaning of her words. He tried to move gently away but she held him, still gasping after his exertion.

Chitsa listened to him and grinned. "You really got your steam boilers heated up! Did I do all right? I mean, I heard some of the women talking about 'satisfying' a man. Is that what I did? Did I satisfy you?"

He laughed, bent and kissed her and then pulled himself up, lifting away from her and sitting on the blanket beside her.

"Yes, small Indian maiden, you satisfied me. What about you? Were all those summers of waiting worth it?"

"Oh, yes! Yes! I loved it. The little hurt at first was over so fast, and then everything was perfect. Marvelous, wonderful, a feeling like nothing I've ever experienced before! Can we do it again?"

Spur chuckled. "The male of the species can't do it a dozen times in a row like you girls can. I need a little more time to recharge my energy."

"An hour?"

He nodded. "An hour will be fine."

She sat up suddenly and looked at his crotch. "I

want to see him all relaxed and soft. He *does* get soft, doesn't he? You couldn't ride around all day with that hard thing in your pants."

She found his penis and watched for a minute, then her curiosity satisfied, she turned.

"I'm hungry."

"Making love affects some people that way. But maybe we should get some sleep."

"First we'll eat the last of the cheese and some bread and then we'll make love again, and *then* we'll get some sleep," said Chitsa firmly.

CHAPTER TWELVE

They both woke up at dawn. She reached up and kissed him. Her naked body slid half on top of him and her nipples tickled his chest.

"I wish we had time to make love again, right now, but we have to be moving." She sat up, pulled up her white drawers, then shook her head and took them off. She put on her doeskin dress, tied the rawhide and then touched her hair.

"It is too long and too clean. I must look like a Sioux squaw if they see me." She picked handfuls of dirt and rubbed it into her hair and into the braid, then rubbed more of the dirt on her face, arms and legs. She dug into her supplies and brought out a forked stick and a stained, dirty rawhide bag.

"I will be just another squaw digging for roots and searching for berries. Even the mighty Sioux braves like more to eat than bison meat."

"Your horse?"

"No. Indian women are not permitted to ride horses. The horse is the prize and the privilege of the brave. And you said slavery was outlawed!"

She ate the rest of the bread and some of the cold canned meat, then looked at the hills. "I'll go first to the ridgeline and see where I need to go and how I can get there. I'll stay in the pine timber as much as possible. And I won't be more than two or three miles away. You stay here and keep quiet and invisible. There shouldn't be anyone coming through here. The main trail leads well around this area. I should be back before noon."

Spur nodded and sat on the blanket cleaning his pistols. He worked on the Spencer repeating rifle as well, and soon had all three in perfect order. Chitsa had faded from the camp so silently that he didn't know when she left. She had taken down the blanket tent—it might attract attention.

He went to the horses, found a place he could walk them to water without being seen and let them drink, then ground-tied them in a hidden spot where they could find some graze. He would feed them the rest of the oats as soon as Chitsa came back.

Spur had wanted to go with her, but he realized she was right. Indian country was her element, not his. If he had blundered in here alone, it was possible that he might not have returned. That would have pleased Colonel Underhill.

With nothing to do, Spur grew restless. He checked the camp again. It was practically impossible to identify the area from even a few feet away. The heavier pine cover helped. It was a relief to move from the plains into the gentle foothills, then deeper into the Black Hills themselves. The sturdy pine trees began scrubby and short, then lifted taller and taller until in this place many were two feet thick and a hundred feet high.

Spur worked his way up the side of the ridge, staying undercover in the heavy growth. At the top he could see out both sides, including the valley they had come up last night, and another smaller valley. He checked both carefully for any movement. Nothing at all showed in the larger valley, but in the other one across the ridge he saw motion near the far end. Using his binoculars, Spur made out a small band of buffalo—one huge bull, five or six cows and several calves grazing peacefully.

Suddenly below him in the valley, a pair of horses bolted from the tree cover and raced across the grasslands. Spur felt a moment of panic, swung the glasses to the animals and saw that both were wild horses, a big black which might at one time have been an army mount, and a smaller Indian-type pony. Both were free and racing across the meadow just for the enjoyment of it.

Once more Spur quartered the valleys, searching for any sign of Indians. He found none, rolled on his back and had a half hour nap, then went below to the campsite.

Chitsa came back an hour later. She had stopped at the stream and scrubbed herself, and washed out her long black hair. She had combed it with her fingers, letting it dry in the sun. Chitsa slipped out of her doeskin dress and walked to Spur, all glistening, clean and lovely.

She knelt beside him and leaned over him. Spur caught one breast and kissed it. She purred in her throat and pushed him flat on his back.

"Please, darling Spur, make love to me right now!" she whispered.

Twice they made gentle love on the soft grass in the mountain meadow. Only afterwards did she tell him what she had found.

"Two miles from here is a good sized Sioux village. It looks like a hunting camp, and I'd say it's about ready to move. We can get there under cover all the way. No one will spot us. Everyone is working hard. The women are taking down dried buffalo strips, the braves are making arrows and feathering old ones, getting ready for another hunt. We can leave here just after midday and get there quickly. I did see one rifle."

"A hunting camp, not a war camp?"

"No, not with women and children, and pack horses to carry back the buffalo meat."

They had a quick lunch of cold canned meat and berries that she had found, then packed up and moved out. Chitsa led the way, and both walked their horses. Spur carried the repeating Spencer in his right hand with a round in the chamber ready to fire.

They wound up the valley in the edge of the timber, went over the crest and down the other side, then over two more ridges and left the horses in some dense timber. They moved slower going up the last ridge. Chitsa said the camp was just over the top.

They edged into some small pines growing on the ridgeline and could see the camp below. There was one tipi, and a fire. Spur guessed there were about thirty men and women working around the camp. The women were now packing dried buffalo meat in bundles made from buffalo hide.

To one side Spur saw the glint of sun off metal and found a tall Indian with a wide strip of hair running down the center of his scalp and wearing blue Cavalry pants. He was demonstrating how to load and fire the rifle. Spur studied the weapon through his binoculars. It was a Sharps single shot carbine. There were thousands of them still in use by the army. It probably was an army weapon, perhaps belonging to the same trooper who had worn the pants the brave now wore.

The carbine fired below, and Spur jumped as did most of the Indians in the camp. The brave laughed. He went through the process again, instructing another brave how to pull down and forward the trigger guard lever to eject the used round. He then showed the brave how to load in a cartridge and push the trigger guard back in position.

The teacher made his student go over the routine five times, then helped him to aim and fire. From the way the Indian demonstrated the technique of holding and firing the weapon, Spur knew he must have been an army scout or had been around army weapons training. This one Indian at least was looking for a fight. He and Chitsa watched as four different braves took their basic training with the carbine. Spur wondered how much ammunition they had.

They pulled back from the skyline of the ridge.

"You said it looks like they're moving out," said Spur.

"Yes. The squaws are packing up, loading everything. In Indian society, the women do *all* the work. The men only lie around and brag, make babies, hunt and go to war." She was laughing, then sobered. "I'd guess this camp will be broken up within an hour and they will move on to another buf-

'alo hunt. They don't have the big tipis, the pottery. This is just a hunting camp."

They moved back to the top and watched. Six more braves went through rifle training, and now it was obvious to Spur that they had only one Sharps. There was no war paint, no dancing. The braves were getting in some instruction as the squaws got ready to move. Some of the braves worked on hunting equipment. Two older men sat chipping spear points out of large slabs of obsidian. They used a hard rock and struck the obsidian a sharp blow with a hammer-like rock which chipped a flake off the obsidian. By chipping away at the right spot, the craftsman could fashion a sturdy, sharp spear point with a flange at the end for tying to the spear end.

Two more braves worked at fastening feathers onto their arrows.

The Indian horses were kept in a rope corral farther up the ravine. Now, one by one, horses were brought up and big baskets made of buffalo hide were fitted over the mounts' sides and filled with meat, tools and camp goods.

Within an hour the camp was struck. Only the fire pit showed that anyone had been living there. The big tipi had been taken down and formed into a travois pulled by two horses. It was piled with lighter goods, freshly scraped buffalo hides, and carried one old woman who evidently couldn't walk.

When Chitsa saw it she stared in wonder.

"Who could she be?" Spur asked.

"I don't know," Chitsa said. "Strange, unusual. In most Indian societies, when the old can no longer produce and work for the good of the tribe, they are sent away. They simply walk into the desert or the

139

mountains or the plains and when they get exhausted, they lie down and die. There is no heroics, no charity, and no compassion. This old woman must be someone important."

"The chief's mother?"

A look of knowing scorn shaded her pretty face. "Of course not! The chief's mother would be the first to know that she was not contributing. She would build a small fire in front of her tipi or lodge, welcome all of her friends around and talk of the wonderful days when they were young. When the fire went out, the talking would stop. The old woman would get to her feet and walk away to die. Her name would never be spoken again."

They watched the last brave mount and ride away and saw one squaw go over the camp carefully to find anything left behind. Then she, the squaws and the children walked single file behind the procession of Indian ponies as they wound into the valley and around a bend.

Chitsa jumped up and ran, following them, keeping them in sight but remaining hidden herself. Spur followed her. At a vantage point half a mile away, they watched the little band working its way slowly across the valley and toward the far slope. When the tribe was far enough away, Chitsa said they would not come back, so the two observers retraced their steps and went down to the campsite.

Spur found the spot where the men had fired the rifle and picked up two of the brass casings. They were .50 caliber. He pushed them in his pocket.

Chitsa prowled the camp. She found a knife, but the point was broken off. Under some brush she found a small buffalo skin bag and inside a good knife with a four-inch blade. She smiled and kept both.

Spur could find nothing else to help him. He went to the place where the large tipi had been. The grass was matted down where the floor of the tipi had been laid, but he found nothing of interest. He prowled the outer rim of the tipi location. Something caught his eye in the trampled down grass. Spur bent and picked it up. In his hand he held a piece of gold. It looked as if it had been melted down and cast in a round form of some kind, then hammered. The shape of a flying bird had been delicately carved into the soft squaw clay. He showed it to Chitsa.

"Squaw clay," Chitsa said. "The chief's squaw is going to be furious with herself for losing it." Chitsa turned it over in her hand. "The art work is very good."

"You know that's gold?"

"Yes. Some of the squaws in the Black Hills find gold and melt it down in a hot fire and form it in wooden molds. Then they pound it and shape it and carve it to form trinkets. The braves say the soft metal is not good for anything. They want steel for their knives and tomahawk blades."

"You know what happened in California in Forty-Nine?"

"Sutter's Mill—the gold rush. Yes. It sent millions of people rushing to California."

"You know what a gold rush would do to the Black Hills? What would happen to the miners who tried to come in here?"

"The first thousand would be slaughtered by the angry Sioux. Then the army would move in and slaughter the Sioux. But for that to happen there would have to be massive amounts of gold in the Black Hills. I don't think there is that much. The stories I've heard is that the squaw clay is hard to find, except for the *Rio del Oro.*"

"Spanish?" Spur asked, surprised. "River of gold. What's a Spanish name doing up here?"

"Some Spanish missionary came here more than a hundred years ago, that's the story I've heard. It isn't a big river and the gold stretch isn't that long. That's all I know. The story may be just somebody's creative imagination. But there *is* gold in the Black Hills."

"And the more people who hear about it, the more trouble we're going to have with the Sioux. Damn!"

"It's there, Spur. And one of these days there *will* be a gold rush. Nothing we do will stop it or slow it down. We'd better get back under cover."

They went into the woods and Spur stared again at the carved piece of gold. He hefted it in his hand. Three, maybe four ounces. It was worth over a hundred dollars! Millions of workers in the East toiled six months to make a hundred dollars. He slipped the gold into his pocket and they moved deeper into the woods.

"I'd like to see one more Indian camp. Are there any close around?"

Chitsa shook her head, her long black hair flying freely.

"Not that I saw. I could take another scouting mission."

They came to a small cleared place in the woods on their way back to their horses. Spur was still trying to decide if he had seen enough.

"*Eiiiiiiiiiiiyaaaaaaaaaaaaaa!*"

The sudden Indian war cry lanced through the trees and into Spur's consciousness as two Indians on horses charged out of the brush twenty yards ahead of them. Both had bows and arrows and were drawing them for the kill.

"No guns!" Chitsa screeched.

Spur knew instantly what she meant. A gunshot now would bring every brave in the hunting party racing back here. Chitsa and Spur both darted behind big pine trees before the braves could loose their arrows.

Spur held the long gun. No rifle shots. What now? He would shoot as a last resort, he decided. It was obvious the Indians were charging ahead. He could hear the hooves pounding in the rocky soil. Spur took a chance and peered around the tree. Both braves were continuing their charge straight at the trees where Chitsa and Spur hid. Spur's mind raced. What in hell was he supposed to do now?

CHAPTER THIRTEEN

In the ten seconds he had left before the two mounted Sioux braves were upon them, Spur looked at
Chitsa and saw she had drawn the big knife. She
held it in her right hand high over her head behind
the tree.

He *did* have a weapon. Spur turned the Spencer
around, holding it by the barrel, and lifted it. It
would make a deadly club.

The riders were almost upon them. His timing
would have to be perfect. No time to take a look. He
would strike when he first saw the muzzle of the
first horse coming past the tree.

The snorting flaring nostrils suddenly appeared
and Spur swung the Spencer downward. He was
slightly early—the heavy butt of the Spencer came
down just in front of the brave's head, but the forward motion of the horse slammed the Indian's
throat into the heavy wooden stock, jolting his head
backward. Spur heard a sharp crack like the breaking of a dry stick. The Sioux brave's head rolled to

one side, his eyes blank and staring, the drawn bow falling from his hand. He slid sideways on his mount, tumbled toward Spur and fell to the ground a dozen feet beyond, his arms against another pine tree and the pony running like a fleet mule deer through the woods.

The Indian didn't move. Spur looked at the tree Chitsa had hidden behind. He had heard no sound, but now Spur saw that the other Sioux brave had gotten off his horse. One hand held a long slash on his side where blood drained through his fingers. In his other hand he held a knife and advanced on Chitsa, deadly fury in his every movement.

Spur wanted to shoot the savage in the heart, but he knew he couldn't. He drew back the Spencer and shouted, running toward the brave. The Indian never looked back, concentrating on his primary target.

Spur got to the Indian from the side, and swung the Spencer. It slammed into the Indian's side, breaking his ribs and driving him to the ground on his stomach.

Before he could get up, Chitsa darted in, dove on the Sioux's back and her right hand brought the knife across the brave's throat. In one desperate move the red man turned over and Chitsa stared at the slash across his throat. Blood spurted from both arteries as the Sioux's arms dropped to his side. His eyes rolled upward and his head turned to the side.

Spur lifted Chitsa from the corpse, picked her up and hurried with her into the deeper timber. He expected to hear her start crying, but she didn't. Spur put her down next to a large pine, and sat beside her.

Chitsa stared straight ahead, eyes unblinking,

face in total repose as if she were sleeping.

"Chitsa," he said softly. "Chitsa, you did what you had to do. He was trying to kill you. He could have sent you on a journey to the hereafter right now."

She didn't move. He had seen the same thing happen in the war—the sudden shock of killing or seeing a friend die or sometimes being wounded. Spur slapped her, a sharp, stinging blow on the cheek which turned her head around.

"No!" Her voice came with sudden anger. "Don't hit me!"

Spur looked at her again and saw her eyes moving. She took a deep breath and sighed. Then a tear seeped from the corner of her eye and then another and a moment later she leaned into his arms, sobbing her heart out.

She was still crying five minutes later, and Spur lifted her and carried her toward the horses. Soon she pushed away and indicated she wanted to walk. He let her down but held firmly to her hand.

"Chitsa, you did only what you knew you must. You were right. The Sioux would have killed you like stepping on a bug."

"But. . . . but there were two of us! It was not fair!"

"It was not fair for them to attack us with arrows when we had none. Did that stop *them?*"

"No." Her response was barely loud enough to hear.

"We are alive, Chitsa, that is the most important thing. To be dead and absolutely right might be satisfying to posterity, but it certainly isn't much fun."

She didn't respond.

"Chitsa, how long before the braves will be missed?"

"What?"

"How long before those two Sioux will be missed and someone goes looking for them?"

"If they were a day hunting party, it would be several hours. If they were scouts, an hour or two. If they were on a long range hunt it might be days."

"Then we must head back, right now, as quickly as we can. Is there cover for us to move back south?"

"I think so."

"We have to know for sure. Chitsa, is there cover?"

She looked at him, her face changing from despair to a degree of hope. "Yes—I can find enough. It will be dark in three hours. We must find the horses and start now and travel all night. You must feed the horses the oats the first chance you get. They will need all of their strength. We will canter for half an hour, then walk them for an hour, and canter again." She nodded. "Yes, both are strong and deep chested, they can stand that pace for at least ten hours. Then we will be out of the greatest danger."

He lifted her up and kissed her, holding her tightly. "You are a marvel, pretty little Indian maid. Any other woman I know in this situation would have screamed, dissolved in tears and hysterics and been dead within seconds. That would have given the other brave time to sight in on me as I finished his partner, and I would be heading for Heaven myself. You are magnificent!" He kissed her again. She kissed him back, then squirmed in his strong arms.

"Quickly now, quickly! We must travel."

147

They found the horses where they had been tied, and rode at a gallop for the first quarter mile, slowed to a walk for ten minutes through the timber at the edges of the valley, then went over the ridge and re-traced part of their route.

It was just past midnight when Spur called a halt. He figured they had traveled almost thirty miles. The tall timber was behind them, and they were into the grasslands again. There would be little cover during the daylight, so they would have to be careful.

They ate his can of sliced peaches, and the last of the tinned beef. Then they pushed on for four more hours before they found a good hiding spot for the day.

Chitsa was so tired she could barely sit her saddle. He helped her dismount, spread the blankets for her and watched while she fell into a deep sleep at once.

Spur pondered their trip. So far he had discovered enough to make it worth while. There was no way he could determine who among the redmen was contacting the Camp. A 24-hour watch on the post might turn up someone leaving to make contact with a renegade, but even that might not be productive.

Twice that night Chitsa woke up screaming. Spur held her, quieted her, talked gently to her until the fear vanished and she slept soundly once more.

It was almost eight in the morning when Spur awoke. They had planned on staying there for the rest of the day, but something urged Spur to change the decision.

Chitsa had not awakened yet. At ten that morning he kissed her eyes and then her lips and her arms

148

came around him. She sat up quickly, saw him and smiled. Then she shivered.

"I had the most terrible dreams. It was awful. Why didn't you wake me sooner?"

"You needed the sleep. The dreams will pass. You'll gradually forget about it."

"No, never! I killed a human being—another Indian!"

"He was also trying to kill you."

"Yes, that's what I keep telling myself, but it doesn't help much." She stood up, then walked to the front of the wooded area and studied the plains.

When she came back she nodded. "You want to move on, right?"

He said he did.

"We're well out of the Black Hills now. Our chances of running into any Sioux are very slim." They built a fire, made coffee and, after finishing the last of the second cup, mounted up and rode.

They covered nearly fifty miles that day, fed the horses oats and settled down for a good sleep.

Chitsa rolled over toward him. "When we get back to the Camp it will be impossible for us to be together. Could you love me once more?"

They made love twice softly, with much tenderness, then went to sleep in each other's arms.

Late the next night they reached Camp Sheridan. As they had arranged, Spur went in alone. She would stay in the woods along the river for two more days, then come back alone.

Spur let a trooper take care of his horse and reported directly to the commanding officer's quarters. Colonel Underhill had been reading a book and slammed it shut when Spur came in.

"Thunder, man! Couldn't it wait until morning? It's almost ten o'clock!"

"And I could be coming in to tell you five-thousand Sioux are on the warpath. Would that be important?"

Col. Underhill looked up, his eyes alive. "The bastards are finally going to turn and fight, are they?"

"No, Colonel, the Sioux are *not* on the warpath. But they *are* learning how to use the rifles they have been getting. I watched for half an hour as one brave wearing cavalry pants taught every other brave in his camp how to load and fire a Sharps carbine."

"I hope you shot the bastard where he stood!"

"If I had, Colonel, I wouldn't have made it back alive to tell you this. My report will show that the Sioux are hunting right now, laying in their winter's food supply. They continue to object strongly to any whites invading their home territory. And it is my determination that they are preparing their braves to use the rifles they hope to get soon."

"So we must take four hundred men and go through the hills and kill every Indian we can find!" Col. Underhill said, his eyes flashing, his breath coming fast. "We can have two hundred men ready in six hours. We'll move out at noon tomorrow!"

"Colonel, you don't have any orders authorizing you to undertake any such campaign. That has to come straight from headquarters."

"Hell, we'll do it anyway! An officer's got to use some initiative to get along in this man's army."

"You go in there, and I'll have you courtmartialed."

"Bastard!"

"Colonel, have you thought of retiring? I don't think you're in good enough health to command this camp."

Colonel Underhill began laughing. He slapped his sides and roared for two minutes, then he was on his feet and his .44 revolver was pointed at Spur's chest.

"Soldier, you say anything like that again, and I'll shoot you dead where you sit! No brag. I'll kill you! I'm the best damn commander in Nebraska, Omaha included. Told them that. Told Phil Sheridan that. What the fuck does he know? Damn skirt chaser, regular cock hound, the son-of-a-bitch!"

Spur started to stand.

"Don't move, Colonel! Hate to have to shoot you down with you in the prime of life. Got to get my damned birds. My eagles. Got to! Damn brother-in-law got his last year. He'll make general if the bastard lives long enough." Colonel Underhill sat down, waving the six-gun at the ceiling.

Spur decided a sudden change of subject might bring the colonel out of his sudden disorientation.

"Colonel, did I tell you about the herd of buffalo I saw? One bunch was as near as across the parade grounds. Two or three huge bulls, a few cows and some calves as frisky as puppies."

"Buffalo?" Colonel Underhill turned and looked at Spur. "Aren't many buffalo around the camp here."

"No sir. I was up toward the Black Hills. Lots of them up there. But I never ran into a large herd."

The colonel looked at Spur, suddenly interested. "Yes—your trip into the Black Hills. I warned you it would be dangerous. Tell me, Colonel, just how did it go?"

Spur went through what he had said before. "So, Colonel, I think we should keep an extra tight inventory control on all rifles and carbines on the post, and make sure every man has only the weapon he signed out for."

"Yes, yes, fine idea, Colonel McCoy. I'll get a sergeant on that first thing tomorrow. If you think there's anything else we should do, you be sure to let me know." He saw the pistol in his hand, broke it open and Spur saw it was unloaded. He sighted through the bore. "I was about to clean this. Should keep a side arm as clean and well-oiled as possible."

Spur agreed, and after a few more words, took his leave. He was still worried about the colonel, but there was nothing he could do, not yet.

CHAPTER FOURTEEN

Buffalo Kane was waiting for Spur when he left the commander's office. The scout fell into step beside Spur and grinned foolishly in the soft light of the half moon.

"Evening. Heard you was back. Got a minute?"

Spur knew Kane had been drinking, but the man did have a problem.

"Sure, Kane." Spur looked at him expectantly.

Kane motioned toward the two chairs sitting outside the sutler's store. They sat down and Kane leaned forward.

"Remember I told you I was hunting the killers of my family? Well, I think I found them—at least one of the bastards. Sort of like you to come with me and see what you think."

"I assume you're going through the proper army channels."

Kane laughed. "Damn right I am! Hail, colonel, I'm still under contract with the fucking army. Another twenty days. I got to go through channels or I get my butt reamed out, right?"

"Quite true, Kane."

"Well, why don't we wander down there then, and I'll let you give me your sayso."

"Where?"

"Down by the back gate."

"Seems like a strange place for a courtmartial."

"Well, we ain't quite at that stage yet. Just got some evidence I want you to take a quick gander at."

"Fine, let's go. It's been a long day for me."

They walked past the barracks to the stables. Behind the stables, Kane drew his .44 and held it on Spur.

"Now, Colonel, just keep walking. We go out the back gate and down to the river. Most nigh a quarter of a mile but I'd bet my ass you can walk that far even without an army mule under your bottom."

"Kane, you don't need the weapon. You want me to go down there, I'll go."

"Right, Colonel. Right. And you're a fucking bird colonel and I'm a lousy almost-run-out-of-the-army scout all 'cause I had an Indian family. Yeah. Now let's go. I'll kinda have my old .44 down beside my leg here, Colonel, so we don't 'tract no attention, but she's there and she's ready to shoot. Let's walk."

They went out the gate, past the guard who merely waved at Kane and paid no attention to Spur.

It was a short walk and they soon came to the water, turned left downstream for a hundred feet to a big elm tree.

Spur saw the rope looped over a large branch and hanging down. It cut a path across the moon. When Spur followed it down, he found a man standing on a wooden box. The man's hands were tied behind him, and the rope was fastened around his neck. Spur was not surprised to see an authentic hangman's knot tied around the man's throat.

"Kane, if this is some kind of a joke . . ."

"Ask *him*, Colonel. It sure as shit ain't no joke! Go on, ask him. That's the son-of-a-bitch who murdered my wife and my two sons!"

"Kane, listen to reason a moment," the man on the box said. Spur recognized the voice. It was Lt. Casselberry.

"Shut up, you killer!" Kane shouted. "You'll get your chance to defend yourself. We got us a judge and jury now. Colonel McCoy wil listen to the evidence, give the verdict and then I'll kick that box out from under you and watch you hang! Only you got to know *why*. The *why* is because you killed my family!"

Kane's voice soared upward at the end until he was screaming.

Spur walked up to Casselberry.

"Lieutenant, have you entered a plea to the court?"

"Yes, sir. Not guilty."

"Thank you. Mr. Prosecutor, you may begin. What evidence do you have to support your charges?"

"A lot, your honor. I come home on the afternoon of April 2, 1870, from a patrol and found my wife, Walking Fawn, and my two sons killed by regulation army rounds. The brass was all over the place. The bastards didn't give them a chance!"

"Mr. Kane, no opinion allowed. Just state the facts."

"Yeah. My wife had a gold medallion—I found the gold myself and pounded it into a circle and fixed it up. She loved it. It was stole and turned up later at the sutler's store. Two troopers turned it in for some beer. It was my wife's. I bought it back. The troopers said Lt. Casselberry sold it to them for ten dollars."

"Mr. Kane, are you prepared to bring those two troopers to this court to testify?"

"Your honor—Colonel—one of them deserted last week, and the other was killed about three weeks ago on a patrol. They can't testify."

"What other evidence do you have, Mr. Kane?"

"There was just one set of horseshoe prints around my place that day. Just one bastard rode in to loot the cabin and look at the bodies. One horseshoe had the tip broken off on the left front hoof, same as the horse that Lt. Casselberry still rides. He done it, plain as the sunshine in the morning."

"Is that your evidence, Mr. Kane?"

"Shitpot full should be enough, your honor!"

"Thank you, Mr. Kane. Now for the defense. I assume you will be representing yourself, Lt. Casselberry."

"Yes, damnit! Can we get this charade over with? Colonel, I have never seen that gold piece before. I did not sell anything even resembling it to any enlisted man. If I had the gold I would have kept it and exchanged it for its true value of something over a hundred dollars. Secondly, yes, my horse had a broken shoe. I noticed it just this morning and had it changed today. Mr. Kane happened to see the farrier at work, which gave him his idea for these trumped-up charges."

"Your testimony is taken under consideration, Lieutenant. Is there anything else?"

"Yes, Colonel. The raid on the Kane family was made the afternoon of April 1, as close as our people could tell. We investigated, but could come to no conclusions other than that it appeared that some army unit or army personnel had indeed gunned down Mr. Kane's family. On that day, April 1, I was on patrol with twenty men of B company. We were searching for a missing Conestoga wagon and a party of four civilians. We found them, all deceased and the wagon burned. We returned the afternoon of April 2, arriving at camp at about three o'clock. The scout on our patrol was Buffalo Kane."

Spur turned toward where the scout had been standing, but he was no longer there. He spoke into the darkness. "Mr. Kane, we have some contradictory testimony here. Would you tell the court for the record, who the officers were on the patrol you were on which ended April 2?"

"No!" a voice said from behind Spur. "There sure as hell wasn't no bastard called Casselberry on it, that's for damn sure. Check with Major Rutherford. He's got the records." Kane's voice went high and wild again.

"Mr. Kane, are you ready for the court's decision?"

"Hell yes, and I'm ready to kick that box out!"

"Mr. Kane, I've heard all the evidence, examined what is reasonable and practical. I have weighed the contradictory evidence and have come to my decision. Are you prepared to accept the verdict of this court?"

"Yeah, yeah, get on with it."

"I, Colonel Spur McCoy, United States Army, presiding at this special courtmartial, do find and declare the accused, one Lt. Neil Casselberry, innocent of the charge of killing . . ."

Spur never got the sentence finished. Buffalo Kane burst out of the darkness, dove at the wooden box holding Lt. Casselberry and slammed into it with his shoulder.

Spur dug out his .44 to go for Kane, but he was too late. He saw the box tilt and start to slant outward. He could see the slack tightening in the rope over the tree limb; he knew the fall would be enough to snap Lt. Casselberry's neck. Spur was too far away to catch him. His .44 came up and he fired, pointing his weapon at the rope over the limb. Four times he shot, faster than he ever had before, and the second round caught the rope in the center, snapping two of the three strands.

When the box toppled, an immediate strain went on the rope and the remaining strand was not enough to take the increasing weight of Lt. Casselberry's body. When he came to the end of the stretch, the last strand over the limb broke and Neil Casselberry hit the riverbank on his feet and tumbled to his knees. The hangman's noose did not break the officer's neck. All it did was put a minor rope burn around his throat.

Spur got to Casselberry quickly, cut the ropes off his wrists and lifted the noose away from his neck.

For a moment Lt. Casselberry couldn't speak. He had come within one .44 slug of meeting his maker and he knew it. He stared at Spur, then at the frayed end of the rope. Then looked down at Buffalo Kane and realized that the scout had passed out.

"Are you all right, Casselberry?" Spur asked.

"Yes, sir. But I got the shit scared out of me. Jesus!"

"He had himself convinced you were the guilty man," Spur said. "I'm glad I got back when I did."

"He would have waited. I've been standing on that box for two hours, and he's been drinking for two days. He'll sleep it off. When he gets sober he won't remember a thing about any of this."

"There was an official investigation about Kane's family?"

"Yes. Shall we go back? My wife will be worried."

They turned walking toward camp.

"Major Rutherford was incensed by the killings. Underhill thought it was a joke. The major called in every officer who wasn't on my patrol and questioned him. He thought he had it narrowed down to three men, but when he called the troopers to testify with total immunity, not a man came in."

"Did Rutherford hit it too hard?"

"That was the talk around the officers' side. The E.M. were afraid they would get burned right along with the officers, even though they had no choice but to follow the officer's orders."

"Who were the three men the major narrowed it down to?"

"He wouldn't say."

"The guilty man had to have been on some kind of patrol or training outside the camp that day."

"All three were. I narrowed it down myself. It had to be either Lt. Wes Pauley, Lt. Omer Imhoff or a man who transferred out a week ago, Lt. Dabler. He was a patsy, a by-the-book soldier. He wasn't cut out for murder."

"Does Buffalo Kane know this?"

"He will tomorrow. When he sobers up and gets rid of his hangover I'm going to tell him. What he *doesn't* know almost got me hanged."

They walked to the stables.

"If you had to pick one of the two suspects, which one would you choose?"

"Imhoff every time. But then I don't like the son-of-a-bitch, so my vote doesn't count." The young officer hesitated. "Colonel, I know I said some things I shouldn't have when we first talked. I was almost out of my head with worry. Things have been easing off a bit here now—about my wife."

Spur nodded. "Good. I'm glad to hear it. The army needs conscientious and honest young officers."

"Thank you, sir. I . . . What happened tonight was so unbelievable that I can hardly conceive of it. This fantasy with Buffalo Kane—I'm embarrassed about how he caught me. He said he had something to show me down by the stables I'd be interested in, and once we got there he pulled his pistol and marched me out the gate and down to the tree. He was wild drunk then, and I figured he'd just as soon shoot me as hang me. Hanging sounded slower. I talked him into a trial with you as the judge. He had the rope and the box and everything ready. I didn't get scared until he put me on that damn wobbly box and tied off the rope tight.

"Colonel, that hour alone down there in the dark is about as scared as I ever want to get. What I'm saying is, you saved my life tonight. I don't know how one man thanks another for something like that. But anyway, thanks for my life. I appreciate it."

"Casselberry, that's what colonels are made for.

160

Just see that Buffalo Kane knows about his choice being down to two. He only has three weeks left."

Lt. Neil Casselberry said he'd take care of it in the morning, snapped a West Point perfect salute which Spur returned, and the young officer walked off toward his quarters.

Spur watched him go for a moment, then turned toward his own room. He had not felt so sore, tired and washed out in a long time. The idea that he might have to make the ride back into the Black Hills soon was not exciting.

He found his room all cleaned and ready for him. There was fresh fruit in a bowl on the dresser and clean sheets on the bed. He imagined Molly had fixed it all for him. Right then he wanted nothing more than to test out the sheets. But he did wonder how long the army would continue the "laundress" system. Someone in his superior understanding had decreed that each army camp and installation would have one laundress for each nineteen-and-a-half enlisted men. The women who did the laundry were usually the wives of enlisted men, though the army actually discouraged the marriage of the troopers. Any enlisted man who wanted to get married had to get permission from his commanding officer. If there were too many laundresses on a post, the permission was denied.

Spur forgot about Molly, forgot about gold and forgot about missing army rifles. He barred the front door, put a solid chair under the back one and locked it, then undressed and slid into bed and immediately fell asleep.

CHAPTER FIFTEEN

The same night Spur arrived at Camp Sheridan, a tired, still slightly awed Indian girl changed her mind about propriety and slipped into the camp and into her room in the Underhill quarters through her open window, as she always did after her outings.

She brushed her long hair, braided it carefully in one long plait falling down her back, and went to bed. She tried to figure which day it was. Each day there was some social function for the officers' wives. Tomorrow was Monday or Tuesday. Or was it Wednesday? She would have to put in an appearance, no matter what day it was. For just a moment she thought about the man she had killed. She would never forget the look in his eyes as he died. She wondered if she would sleep.

She did, dropping off at once. She did not have any bad dreams.

The next morning Chitsa helped Grace Underhill prepare breakfast as usual. Chitsa said she'd had a wonderful time in the open, watching the animals sleeping under the night sky, living as she had as a child. Grace had made a habit of not prying, but she did wonder. She made absolutely no connection between the time Chitsa was gone and Colonel McCoy's absence. She wasn't even aware that Spur was back in camp.

The women's meeting that day was in the Colonel's parlor, and the ladies would gather for tatting, embroidery, point lace, crocheting and knitting. There was usually one of the women who could instruct them all in one of the types of needlework.

Janet Casselberry came in precisely on time, ten o'clock. She didn't want to come too late or too early. It was the first of the social affairs she had attended since her return. She wore her prettiest dress, and her long blonde hair was freshly washed and knotted demurely at the back of her head. She smiled so hard her cheeks hurt, and took Grace Underhill's hand.

"Grace, I just had to come today. I'm feeling fine, none the worse for wear. I was scared spitless out there in the wilds, but it turned out fine after all. That nice Colonel McCoy came along and like a perfect gentleman brought me straight back to camp. I know I'm the luckiest person in the world not to have met any Indians. I must have been born under a lucky star!"

Grace Underhill beamed. She was so glad to see Janet, and to see her looking so well. Obviously the rumors she'd heard were all nonsense. She beamed and put Janet beside her for the tatting lesson they would have that day. Six more women arrived promptly. Two of them sniffed and moved away from Janet, but the others smiled and said hello and treated her much as usual.

Chitsa came in quietly and sat to one side, her nimble fingers flying as she worked on tatting some squares for an armchair. Some of the women nodded, the rest ignored her. She was, after all, only an Indian.

When all the ladies were assembled, nine today, Janet cleared her throat and they all looked at her expectantly.

"Ladies, I haven't seen you for several days. I've been resting. I had quite an experience, and I'll certainly *never* get lost again. I simply turned the wrong way and before I realized it, the night had closed in and I was totally turned around. I found some trees and I sat up most of the night, but at last I nodded off toward sunrise. Then I got my bearings and began walking, but somehow I became confused by the trees and the river and I went the wrong way again.

"But with my lucky star watching over me, I did not meet up with any of the Sioux hunting parties that sometimes come close to camp. Then Colonel McCoy found me and gave me a ride back to camp. He was a perfect gentleman, naturally, and I'm ever so thankful he did find me."

A pale young woman in her twenties sniffed. "That is unusual, Janet, dear. My Willy says there always are a few Sioux hunters upstream on the White. Says it would be an absolute *miracle* if any woman could be out there two whole days and not be caught by some Sioux hunting party."

"Willy wasn't there, Mrs. Crowder," Janet said sweetly.

Sitting beside Mrs. Crowder was Milicent Orlando. She was known as the camp's biggest gossip,

164

and was always willing to invent a few embellishments as she passed on a tale.

"Janet, dear, we all are just terrified of something like that happening to us. And you know we *are* curious. I can't think of anything worse than to have an Indian capture me. Just *thinking* about it must have been awful! I mean, those savages—to have them touch me, and tear at my clothes, then to throw me down in the grass and . . . well, you know. I just don't . . . "

"Stop it!" a voice shouted. Everyone looked up at the sound and found Chitsa glaring at them. "The two of you should be thrown out of this house and horsewhipped! You are cruel and insulting! You are snide, insinuating and gossips and tellers of tall tales. I don't like either one of you!

"If this were my house, neither Mrs. Crowder or Mrs. Orlando would be invited back. If Janet says she became lost and was found by the colonel, I believe her. Most everyone in this camp does! If it weren't for a pair of tattling busybodies with nothing better to do than make up stories, the whole thing would have been forgotten days ago!" Chitsa ran and knelt in front of Grace Underhill. "I apologize if I have embarrassed you in your own house. I will go. I'm not sure I can live with whites anymore. I never could if they were all like those two." She rose, moved over to Janet, bent down and kissed both her cheeks. Janet reached out and hugged her. Then Chitsa marched out the front door and walked toward the river.

In the room Chitsa had just left, the ladies sat in shocked silence. Never before had Chitsa said a half dozen words at their socials. She had been there watching with her black eyes, absorbing every word.

Grace Underhill took a deep breath. "Ladies, Chitsa as you just heard, has strong opinions and a definite mind of her own. She is a guest in my house, as are all of you, but I do apologize if she has hurt anyone's feelings. We are a small society here. We must strive to be friends and to get along with each other.

"Chitsa is a sensitive person, shy and quiet. She is Indian, a Shawnee from southern Ohio. She was naturally upset about all that talk about bad Indians. She's been with us for almost fifteen years, but sometimes I don't really know her. She spends a lot of time with her books."

"She's beautiful," one of the ladies said. "What I wouldn't give to have long luxurious hair like that!"

There were some murmurs of approval.

Janet Casselberry sat in a soft glow. She didn't dare to look at anyone, but she was sure it was over. Now there would be no more gossip about her, no stories. Neil could relax.

"You say Chitsa reads a lot?" another woman said. "Goodness, she sounds so *educated*. She sounds like one of those college educated girls. I am impressed."

Two more of the ladies remarked about Chitsa's intelligence, her evident book learning.

Then Mrs. Grove, the instructor of tatting, got them busy on their work.

The session was over early so the ladies could get home and fix their men's noon meal. Janet bustled around her small kitchen, humming, slicing bread baked fresh that morning, knowing it was all over, realizing that one small Indian girl had waded in vhere she could not go and had slain the giant!

She was humming when Neil came in after his drill. He was tired and dusty. She brought a pan of cool water and washed off his face and arms. Then she told him about Chitsa.

"She was just magnificent! She stood up to those biddies as I could never do."

Lt. Casselberry smiled. "The women will tell their husbands and that should end the whole thing." He reached over and kissed her. "Hey, pretty girl. Would you mind if we skipped the food and I nibbled on you instead?"

"I was hoping you would say that!" She unbuttoned his shirt and kissed her way down his hard, muscled stomach.

Casselberry groaned with desire. "Keep right on kissing," he murmured. She looked up, kissed his lips and forced her tongue into his mouth, pressing her body eagerly against his.

"Darling, that sounds like such a delightful idea. I'll kiss you all over, and then you can nibble me to pieces!"

He lifted his brows. "I never knew you wanted me to—that you would let me."

He led her to the bedroom then, and they enjoyed each other so much Lt. Casselberry was a half hour late getting back to his troop for its weekly inspection. He didn't mind the delay in the least. His men wondered what had happened. It was the easiest and most casual inspection they had undergone in months.

CHAPTER SIXTEEN

That same morning Spur McCoy sat in Major Rutherford's office talking about the murder of the Kane family.

"I swear to you, McCoy, there would be nothing I'd like more than to find that officer and see him shot. Whichever man it was knew damn well that those people were protected. All my suspects had been in camp long enough to know that. It was simply blood lust."

"And there's nothing you can do now?"

"Not without some evidence. We think our officer corps is a tight little unit. Hell, we can't hold a torch to those enlisted men. There must be forty, maybe sixty men out there who know *exactly* what happened that day. But their code won't let them talk. I must have come down too hard on the whole thing. No one will come forward now."

A sergeant came into the room.

"Sir, you said to let you know about the patrol. It will be formed up at noon. The twenty men have eaten and will be ready for the four day march. The normal supply train should be met about halfway here, south of Box Butte somewhere. The supplies will be off loaded from the train at Sidney, and put on our re-supply wagons which are already at the station."

"Very good, Sergeant. Lt. Imhoff has volunteered for the mission. He'll be leading it. Our scout is ill and can't make the trip. Issue a hundred and forty rounds per man. There shouldn't be any trouble riding due south."

The sergeant saluted and left the room.

"Regular re-supply?" Spur asked.

Major Rutherford nodded, looked away and stood up. "Dammit, I guess I can tell you. There also is a shipment of fifty new rifles on this load. With the trouble we've been having about missing rifles, I'm a little edgy."

If the local rifle smuggler knew about this shipment, it would be an ideal time to steal more weapons for the Indians. Only how do you fight off a twenty-man patrol? Kill them all? Not likely. It would make more sense to meet the wagons a day and a half out. It was at least a three day ride. Spur had just done it. He made up his mind in a hurry.

"Sir, I'd like to ride along with that escort."

"Why, Colonel?"

"Rifles, fifty of them. That's a big prize for some rampaging Sioux. And then Imhoff is leading it. Isn't he one of your prime suspects in the Kane massacre?"

"Who told you that?"

"A friend. Did you know that Buffalo Kane almost hanged Lt. Casselberry last night?"

"I heard. Thanks for your help." The major thought for a minute. "You really want to go on this supply run?"

"Yes."

"Fine. I couldn't stop you if I wanted to, but I don't want to. Watch yourself. I have a bad feeling about this."

An hour later Spur was at the head of the cavalry column beside Lt. Imhoff. Major Rutherford had given the young officer instructions; if they ran into any kind of action, or were attacked, Colonel McCoy was the commanding officer. Imhoff shrugged, nodded and they moved out.

A few wives came to the rear gate to see them off, then the double column stretched out over the prairie as they moved at a lope toward the south. Spur couldn't decide why he had chosen to come on the patrol. A hunch, he supposed as the miles melted away beneath the horses' hooves. A strong hunch that something was going to go wrong. Nothing he could pin down. He'd been following hunches all his life.

The second day at dusk, they hadn't met the wagons. Imhoff sent out scouts to watch for dust just before dark, but they came back and reported seeing no sign of the dust trail or any movement for at least ten miles ahead.

Imhoff didn't seem worried. "Hell, they could have missed the course, gone up another valley. Might have had a late start. They can't make more than twelve, fifteen miles a day with those heavy wagons. They started five days ago. That should put them somewhere about halfway. But who knows? They might have lost some time with broken axles, anything. This ain't exactly the Washington D.C. turnpike they got to travel down here."

Spur nodded. He didn't like it, but there wasn't much he could do. The logic was sound. But there seemed to be something else there, some undercurrent. Then he had it. The superior grin that touched Imhoff's lips now and then. Was it only when he thought he wasn't being watched?

As he lay on his blanket that night, Spur did some figuring. Five days traveling at twelve miles a day would be sixty miles. If the escort had come out a day and a half at forty miles a day, that was also sixty miles. The whole trip should be one hundred twenty miles. Something was wrong. Spur slid out of his blankets at midnight, took his Spencer repeating rifle and his rounds of ammunition and packed up his horse. He told the guard he would be gone for a while on a scouting mission and rode to the highest promontory he could find.

Two miles away from the sleeping camp he came to a knoll and stared south. He could see no fires, no lights, no sign of white man nor Indian. He stared to the west with the same result. A sound came to him faintly, but then faded. It came again and Spur turned to hear it better.

Rifle shots!

He listened again to be sure. There was no mistaking the sound. It came from the east, at least five miles away.

Spur rode down the slope and across the prairie as fast as was safe. A canter devoured the miles, chewing them up and spitting them behind him. It took him over half an hour to cover what he guessed was five miles, where he found another small ridge and rode to the top of it. Now he could hear the rifle fire clearly. It came in single rounds, then two or three, but not a sustained fight.

Spur turned again to catch the direction. More easterly. He rode until he could hear the rifle shots over the creak of his saddle and the rushing wind of his ride. Another slight rise showed ahead. He rode up it and looked below.

A siege.

Even though most Indians didn't usually fight at night, there was some kind of attack going on below.

He spotted more than a dozen fires burning in a rough circle outside a ring of six covered army wagons. The horses were inside the circle. Evidently the commander had used the fires to keep the Indians from sneaking up in the darkness and overrunning his defenses.

The whole tableau was five hundred yards away. Spur checked the surrounding area but could find no Indian campfires. They were either on the line or resting, perhaps keeping a dozen men around the wagons to keep the defenders awake and on the alert.

Spur began moving down the slope. He would go two hundred yards, leave his horse and pick out a defensive position where he could also give support to the surrounded troopers below. There was little he could do until daylight. At sunup the Sioux would probably make their attack. It was a wonder the wagons had not been captured already. Evidently there were some good soldiers down there who had a little luck on their side.

As he waited for dawn, Spur prepared his firing

position. He moved two rocks on top of the boulder he crouched behind. The slabs gave him a good firing slot and added protection. From his view of the blackness below, there seemed to be more cover on this side, so the majority of the hostiles should be below him, with their backs exposed.

Spur speculated on how the two army units could have missed one another so far. Either the supply wagons were much too far east or the escort was too far west—perhaps a little of each. But as Spur thought about it he remembered wondering two or three times where some of the landmarks were he had seen on the ride up to the fort. Maybe Lt. Imhoff had deliberately taken them by a route designed to miss the wagon train.

Spur dozed, but the first double rifle shot he had heard in some time drifted up to him and he was awake. Dawn was creeping over the eastern horizon. Spur studied the landscape below.

He could see more than a dozen bronzed bodies below behind rocks and trees, looking at the wagons. Now he could make out blue clad men under the wagons, behind boxes and a makeshift wall.

Time to go to work, Spur told himself and sighted in on the closest warrior. He triggered the round, saw the Indian below jolt with the force of the bullet and then lie still. He levered the trigger guard down, slamming another round into the Spencer and moved his aim to his next target and fired again. He killed or badly wounded five Sioux warriors before they found the blue smoke of his powder and returned fire. He heard a cheer from the wagon train, and renewed firing from the men there.

Below he could hear an Indian yelling in the quiet

of dawn, then the shapes were up and moving forward in an all-out assault. More than a dozen rifles pinned down the soldiers as their comrades ran forward. It was a surprising show of military discipline not often seen among Indian fighters. The rifles below crashed and Spur began picking off the Indians in the lead. He soon was firing single shots, not wanting to take time to load another tube. The first of the Indians had thrown flaming torches on two of the wagons, and the fighting became hand-to-hand at that point. Spur aimed his weapon at another section where the Indians had not yet reached the wagons and sent two more into their own private happy hunting ground. Spur saw the Indians concentrating on one wagon. They killed three soldiers defending it, and began rolling it away from the others, using a slight downgrade. Spur shot one man holding up the tongue, but the wagon kept rolling. As it cleared the circle of immediate fighting, the Indians swept away with it, pushing it, guiding it dians swept away with it, pushing it, guiding it down the slope until it stopped some five hundred yards below. The soldiers around the other wagons ceased firing.

The Indians brought up horses and pulled the wagon away, sending a final volley of shots at the soldiers.

Spur fired a dozen times at the Indians, hitting two at the increased range, then watched as they hitched the wagon to the Indian ponies and towed it away. Spur was about to stand up and shout to the soldiers below when a rifle round struck his rock. He bent low again.

He sensed rather than saw the figure as it hurtled over the side of his makeshift fort, a gleaming knife in hand. Spur had no time to aim the Spencer. He reversed it in a vicious butt stroke. The metal base plate on the stock caught the Sioux brave under the chin and drove inward, crushing his windpipe, bursting the jugular vein and slamming him over the rock. As he fell, Spur reversed his rifle and shot the warrior in the head, exploding one eye and driving lead through his brain.

Someone shouted something from below. He listened.

"One more!" The words came through faintly. Spur slid down behind the rock and waited, his ears alert, every muscle tensed. A rock scraped to his left. Spur swung the rifle that way, jolted upward to look, then dropped back down. He had seen a brown leg extending from a rock six feet away. Spur worked the Spencer lever and loaded another round by feel, watching the top of his rock. He lifted up again quickly, the Spencer ready. The Indian had picked that exact time to take a look. Spur fired by reflex, aimed by dead reckoning, and the big Spencer blew off the top of the Indian's head.

There was a short cheer from below. Spur looked over the rock.

"Any more?" Spur bellowed toward the wagons.

"No more," came the reply.

Spur stood cautiously, ran back to where he had left his horse and rode down to the wounded supply train.

A sergeant came to meet him, snapped a salute and then grimaced. His left arm was in a sling.

"Sergeant Edwards reporting, sir."

"Edwards, looks like you were caught. How many casualties?"

175

"Six dead, sir, including Lieutenant Wilson. Four wounded, including Captain Robert Casemore, a replacement line officer."

"They got the wagon with the rifles in it?"

"Yes sir, and half the ammunition, almost twenty thousand rounds. How did they know we were coming?"

"I don't know, Sergeant. Your escort missed you by about ten miles. The Sioux won't be back, they got what they came for. See what you can do about making the wounded comfortable and cleaning up here. I'll go bring the escort and get you back on the road."

"Thank you, sir. If you hadn't come, they would have killed every man here."

"Never any fun to have somebody punch holes in your backside. I'll be back, Sergeant."

Spur turned and rode up the hill. He had an idea that Imhoff would hold the escort exactly where it was until Spur got back. He was right. Spur quickly ordered the men to break camp and mount up.

"You found the supply train, sir? Some of our men said they heard shots to the east."

"Some of your men were right. Sioux attacked the supply train. It got badly cut up. Let's ride."

They made it to the supply wagons in twenty minutes, and Spur put a detail to work digging graves. He took the dead soldiers' personal effects, made sure that the six remaining wagons were fit for the trail, then had a squad cut two dead horses from the traces and pull them to one side. Two of the largest mounts were drafted to go into the harness. They complained but at last settled down. An hour after the escort arrived, the six remaining wagons

176

were on the move. One had the canvas burned off it, and a second was loaded with wounded. They rounded up the horses and had two spares which were tied to the last wagon. Spur put outriders on both sides, a three-man advance unit on the point and six men to the rear. The other troopers rode on each side of the wagons. At twelve miles a day, it would take them five days to get back to Camp Sheridan.

The wounded needed medical attention and Spur pushed the drivers so they made the trip in exactly five days. One of the wounded men died on the trip. The other three survived and Doc Jones patched them up.

Shortly after they arrived, Spur and Lt. Imhoff sat in Major Rutherford's office answering questions. The toughest one was why Imhoff had missed meeting the supply wagon.

"You should have had riders out forming a connecting link with the wagons from the first day. Why didn't you?" barked the major.

"The colonel didn't tell me to," Imhoff said.

"The colonel wasn't in charge of the escort, Imhoff, as you know. That was *your* responsibility."

"I didn't expect trouble. I planned on sending out scouts the last half of the second day. They went the wrong way."

"We also were eight miles west of the normal trail, Major." Spur said. "I just came up it last week."

"Is that true, Imhoff?"

"Not according to my reckoning, sir."

"Make out your report, Imhoff. I expect Colonel Underhill will want to have a long talk with you when he gets back."

"Where is he?" Spur asked.

"I'll tell you about that in a minute, Colonel. Any questions, Imhoff?"

"No, sir. I'll write the report."

The lieutenant did not salute as he left. He looked worried and Spur wondered why. His case would hold up—Spur had nothing on him but suspicion. When he closed the door, Major Rutherford frowned.

"We've been sending escorts to that train station for the three years I've been here. Nobody ever missed matching up before. Why this time, just when the Sioux were raiding the wagons? And how did the Indians know which wagon had the rifles in it?"

"Same questions I've been asking myself," Spur said. "Where is Colonel Underhill?"

"That may be a problem. This morning with no warning he came into my office spouting one garbled story after another. He was working himself up to something and I didn't know what. Then he showed me a set of orders. I didn't see the date on them at first. The last replacement we had brought them from Omaha about a month ago. Underhill was reading between and around the lines. The orders said something about *after* being attacked, and *when* attacked, and *if* attacked, the command held the responsibility for the protection of its own men, and the lives and property of all civilians within its zone of control. I thought I'd let him spout off and when he left, I relaxed.

"Then a half hour later I heard the bugle and he was at the head of a column of forty men, ready to ride. He told me I was in temporary command of the post and that he would come back when he had 'killed a hundred of those savages, those scum, those lice on the body of humankind, those Indians!' He rode off."

A knock sounded on the door and the sergeant looked in.

"He's here, sir."

"Sober?" asked the major.

"Nearly."

"Send him in."

The door opened fully and Buffalo Kane walked in, blinking at the light.

"Kane, are you sober?"

"Another five minutes of walking around and I will be. If you say I got to."

"I do." Rutherford frowned and shook his head. "I've heard you used to be a good tracker."

"Hail, Major I can still track! I can follow a cougar across a sheet of rock, I can trail a Chiricahua right into his water hole."

"Good. Can you follow a crazy colonel and forty troopers?"

"Drunk or sober, I can do that."

"Good. We leave in half an hour. Get your gear ready."

"Yes, sir, Major, sir."

When Kane left, Major Rutherford looked at Spur. "Colonel Underhill told me when he left six hours ago that he was going to ride until he found some fucking Indians and kill as many as he could. He said he was behind on his 'quota,' whatever the hell he thinks that means. You want to come along, or mind the fort until I get back?"

"Captain Jones can command. I want to change clothes and get some coffee and I'll be ready. Any idea which way he rode?"

"Straight into Sioux country, heading for the Black Hills."

"I hope we can catch him in time," Spur said.

CHAPTER SEVENTEEN

As the company of one hundred fifty men rode away from Camp Sheridan, it was four in the afternoon. They would have nearly four hours of light left. There would be little chance of tracking the troop in the dark, so they pushed their mounts into a canter and walk schedule that allowed them to move at an average of five miles an hour.

Spur knew why Major Rutherford had waited until he came back before going after his superior. To deny him his request for the troop would have been insubordination, and to counter that, Major Rutherford would have had to relieve his superior of his command. Such an extreme move could ruin two careers faster than a general courtmartial. Rutherford must not have been absolutely certain he could prove that the lives of forty men were at stake as a result of the rash and unwarranted move by the colonel.

But with Colonel McCoy along, Spur's superior rank could prevent the lieutenant colonel from continuing his charge, or doing anything else. Spur wished he could have been in Camp Sheridan when Underhill built up this fantasy. Or perhaps the colonel had waited until Spur was gone before he laid his plans.

There was no problem following the trail of the horses. They had been on an arrow-like course for the Black Hills since they began, often going over small hills instead of around them through regular passes and along river beds.

As the light faded, Spur asked Kane how far ahead the troops were.

"Hey, I ain't no Indian. But I'd say maybe four hours."

"Are they walking or moving faster?"

"Walking, good cavalry procedure."

"Can you track them at night?"

"In stages. You give me a good lantern and let me stay a ways ahead. No, make that two lanterns and a holder."

Spur whistled and a trooper rode up with two kerosene lanterns.

"I'm a damngoogled hogwashing son-of-a-bitch! You planned this," said Buffalo Kane.

"Seen it done before. The trooper is Private Johnson. Kick your butt into a gallop and get as far up that trail as you can and when it gets dark, leave Johnson on the trail with the lantern. We'll find him. You move up the trail as fast as you can, on foot or horseback—your choice. Keep Johnson in sight. When you get on the trail, and Johnson waves the lantern that we have his position, let Johnson catch up to you. Keep it moving that way. Take ten men with you and use them as a connecting file, dropping one off wherever necessary to keep in contact with the man behind him. Let's see how far we can get."

By eleven o'clock that night Kane was stumped. They had come to a section that showed a jumble of tracks. Kane waited for Spur to ride up.

"I'd say they had a minor skirmish here, sir. Say maybe ten to twelve hostiles with a chase. I can't rightly tell, but could be the patrol split up into five, maybe six groups chasing the redskins."

"Major Rutherford, any suggestions?" Spur asked.

"Let's make camp here and wait. Put twenty lookouts around camp and bed down. If we keep going all night, these men won't be much good for fighting come morning."

"Agreed, Major. Pass the word. Fires are permitted if the men want them. We're in force—we don't care if the Sioux know we are here. In fact it might be good if they know we're coming."

A half hour later thirty small cooking campfires dotted the valley as the men brewed coffee and ate hardtack and salt pork.

Spur routed the troops out of their blankets a half hour before sunrise and had them fed and ready to march with the first glimmer of light. He had sent out scouts during the night in five different compass headings north and northwest. The first came riding back ten minutes after they began moving north.

"Found them, sir! Or what's left of them. Small valley about five miles north and to the left. Looks like a medium-sized Sioux hunting camp. I heard the firing with daylight and lit out. Can't tell for sure what happened, but the colonel and his men are in the camp and there must be a hundred or more braves around them. I heard lots of rifle fire from the Indian positions."

"You're positive it's the colonel?"

"Yes, sir. I saw that big white horse he rides. No missing him. Looked like he had been wounded."

"Lead the way, Corporal. Major, bring the troops."

They rode.

Spur wished they could cover the whole distance at a gallop, with the bugler playing the attack call all the way. But the bugler was with the colonel, and the sturdy army mounts weren't made to travel so far at such speed. They cantered for the first mile, then sent out scouts to the area and moved along at a steady four-mile-an-hour pace. With luck, they should reach the area in a little less than an hour. If the Sioux kept up the dawn attack, Spur hoped the colonel could hold out. When Buffalo Kane told Spur they were a mile from the site of the fighting, Spur took a dozen of the best marksmen and rode ahead at a gallop. They would punish their horses for the mile and cut down the time of the first response. It might help.

At the scout's suggestion they came to the position along the ridge that the Indians held. They hobbled their exhausted horses and worked up to where they could see the trap. It had been neatly sprung by the attacking Sioux. The Indians held high ground on both sides of the hunting camp, and were systematically picking off the blue clad troopers below.

Spur positioned his twelve men on a line along the top and downward slope of the ridge, and at his command they began firing at the Indians on the near side. The first volley cut down ten of the Indians before they knew their backs were exposed. Then the men fired at will and within five minutes the hostiles on the near slope had retreated into the heavier growth timber and vanished over the side. Spur drew his men back on the downslope and bunched them along the ridge, expecting a flanking movement. It came almost immediately. Twenty Sioux stormed out of the woods. Most carried bows and arrows, but a few had rifles. Spur's well positioned men cut the charge to ribbons and drove back the survivors.

After another ten minutes the main body of troopers stormed down the valley and charged up both sides of the slopes, driving the overpowered and outnumbered redskins back into the woods.

By the time Spur had found his horse and ridden down to the former Indian camp, the situation was secure. He stared around at the destruction of the hunting camp. Bales of dried meat had been ripped open and scattered. The one tipi had been burned. He found more than a dozen bodies, half of them women and children.

Spur dismounted and strode up to Lt. Colonel Underhill who sat on a stump as an enlisted medical attendant dressed his wounded right arm. Spur motioned the enlisted man to stand back. He waved the others out of earshot and turned to Underhill, fury building on his face.

"Just what the hell do you think you're doing here, Underhill?" he thundered.

"Killing hostiles, as per my orders, Colonel."

"You have no orders to attack women and

children? You have no orders to attack peaceful hunting camps! You're a disgrace to the uniform you wear! If you weren't wounded, I'd knock you down and strip off your rank."

Underhill paled. "I was acting under orders. They came when you were gone. Major Rutherford saw them."

"That's why we came to save your stinking hide. How many men did you lose?"

"I . . . I don't know."

Spur called to a sergeant and told him to get a count of casualties for each of the units.

"Colonel, consider yourself under arrest until I can bring formal charges against you." Spur spun around and marched off, too angry to talk further. The sergeant brought him the casualty figures. Colonel Underhill's unit had lost eight dead and twelve wounded out of his forty-man group. Major Rutherford's troops had lost one dead and six wounded.

"We're still counting the Indian dead, sir. There are eighteen dead in the camp—eight women, four children and six braves."

"Was there another officer with the colonel?"

"Yes, sir, Lt. Pauley."

"Tell him I want a word with him."

Spur walked upstream a ways, found a rock and sat on it, staring into the rippling chattering water. Lt. Pauley came up shortly and saluted.

"Pauley, what the hell happened?"

"The colonel ordered us out, mostly my company and a few others. He said he wanted forty men. Said he could whip half the Sioux nation with forty good cavalrymen. So we marched. Almost at dusk, we ran into a band of about fifteen Sioux, some kind of hunting party. We attacked them. They scattered and we never drew blood. By the time we got back together, our scouts had located this camp. We attacked just at sundown and took the camp. Then as it got dark, more than a hundred Sioux surrounded us and started shooting rifles and arrows. We took casualties, but held off the Sioux until daylight when they resumed the attack. Shortly after that a friendly force appeared on our left flank and fired at the Indians, pushing them off the ridge. Then . . .''

"I know the rest of it. Did Colonel Underhill *order* you and your men to kill the women and children?''

"Yes, sir. He said the only good Indian was a dead Indian. He specifically told us to kill every Sioux we found."

"Thank you, Lieutenant. I'll want your sworn testimony after we get back to camp. Bring in your dead. We'll take them back to Camp Sheridan for burial. I want Underhill to take full responsibility for all these deaths."

It took them two hours to regroup, find all the horses, and to pull out of the camp. Spur ordered no looting, no more burning or destruction.

"These people were trying to lay in their winter's food supply," he told the troops. "What has been done here will take years to undo. In fact it may never heal over—it may fester for generations."

The march back to Camp Sheridan took the rest of the day. It was a tired, silent column of troops that rode into camp just before mess call that evening.

One point Spur wanted cleared up: were any of the rifles the Indians had been using missing army weapons? The serial numbers of the captured rifles had been carefully noted. His men had found twelve rifles in the hunting camp which had been used by the attacking force of Sioux who came after the camp had been taken. Spur summoned Cpl. Kramer with his list of rifles and carbine serial numbers.

Ten of the twelve weapons matched those lost, stolen or missing from the Camp armory.

"Two were from men listed as missing in action, six were the ones that simply vanished from the supply room, and the other two were still signed out by current troopers," the supply man reported.

Spur thanked him and sent him away.

Major Rutherford came in and gave Spur his report of the operation.

"Did I understand correctly what happened at that camp, Colonel? You put Colonel Underhill under arrest?"

"Yes. The record will show that it was for his own safety. He was delirious from his wound but still trying to lead his men. I'm sending him to Omaha on the first available wagon going to Sidney to the train. The colonel is suffering from disorientation due to his wound, and it has seriously affected his ability to command. We also have two badly wounded men, including Captain Casemore, who should be moved to a hospital. That will be part of our reasoning. After the colonel gets two days' rest, I want you to draw orders for him and send him to the hospital in Omaha. I'll sign them."

"But isn't that a little extreme?"

Spur looked sharply at Major Rutherford.

"Damn right! It was 'extreme' when he took forty men and slaughtered the Indians in that hunting camp. Before they died, those Sioux women and children were aware of exactly how 'extreme' the colonel could be. It was also extreme that this camp had to commit a hundred fifty men to go to his rescue. The dead troopers under his and my command also bear witness to how extreme the action was." Spur got up and paced the length of the major's office. "Hell, Rutherford, you *know* he isn't capable of command! When we get him back to Omaha, the medical men there will know it as well and pension him out. He'll be well taken care of for the rest of his life."

"And he'll be out of the way so he can't endanger any more of our men needlessly," the major admitted.

"Right. That leaves you in temporary command of this camp. I'll recommend that you be appointed to permanent camp commander. That also will look good on your record when you come up for promotion."

Major Rutherford's sergeant opened the door without knocking.

"Sirs, I think you better come with me. Buffalo Kane has just called out Lt. Pauley and is threatening to kill him!"

CHAPTER EIGHTEEN

Spur and Major Rutherford dashed outside and saw a crowd gathered around the officers' quarters. There was a lot of hooting and yelling but when the troopers saw the officers they quieted.

Kane stood with his legs spread, his right hand near the .44 on his hip. Twenty feet down the sun-baked company street stood Lt. Wes Pauley, still in his sweat-stained clothes from the ride. He was bare-headed and he stared hard at Kane. There was a cluster of men against the buildings and another crowd in the parade ground.

Spur touched Major Rutherford's shoulder, motioning him to let Spur handle the situation.

Fifty feet from Kane's back, Spur called out, "Kane, you have two weeks left on your army contract. Is he worth it?"

"Damn right, Colonel! This bastard led the patrol that gunned down my family. I heard some men talking on this last patrol. They said the cold-blooded son-of-a-bitch ordered them to shoot. He told them there was six Sioux warriors in the shack getting ready to attack. The men said Pauley knew all the time just my wife was inside. Then he used his own rifle and murdered my wife and my two sons while they watched. They'll testify if I have to smash it out of them."

"You're drunk again, Kane," Lt. Pauley said. "Everybody knows you make up stories when you get drunk."

"Trooper Wilson and Corporal Montgomery know what happened."

Spur saw Lt. Pauley look up quickly.

"They won't say a word. It's all a lie! Sure, both men go on patrols with me—they're from my company. You're just bluffing again, Kane, you drunken bum!"

Kane fired a round that went between Lt. Pauley's feet. The officer jumped, his hand darted to his weapon on his right hip, but then he stopped and held both his hands in the air.

"You shoot me now, Kane, and it will be murder. I'm not even reaching for my gun."

"You killed her, you son-of-a-bitch! You shot her down in cold blood and then you shot my boys. You don't deserve to live!"

"They were just *Indians* for Christ's sake, Kane! We're people. They were *Indians!*"

Kane fired again. His bullet creased the officer's pants leg, narrowly missing his boot. Pauley paled with anger and fright. He looked up and saw Spur and Major Rutherford.

"Major, make his listen to reason! Make this crazy man put down his pistol! I didn't know the squaw was in the goddamn shack. Then she come running out bleeding. Christ, she was just an *Indian!*"

"You bastard!" Kane shouted. "Draw like a man, or I'm going to shoot you down like the rattlesnake you are!"

Spur touched the major's sleeve and turned away. Both officers walked slowly away from the scene. They would swear they hadn't seen a thing.

"Major, no . . ." Pauley screamed.

"On *three*, Pauley, you murderer! One . . . two . . . three!" Kane drew and aimed his weapon, but Pauley kept his hands over his head. Kane sighted in carefully and fired. The round sliced through an inch of Lt. Pauley's leg.

"Now, damn you, Pauley, you got one more chance. Draw or I'll kill you with your hands in the air!"

Pauley staggered back from the blow of the slug, but kept his feet. Blood poured from the wound and he looked at it and snarled, "You're an animal, Kane. Colonel McCoy wants you. Look!"

Pauley pointed behind Kane and the second the scout turned his head, Pauley drew and fired in one swift move. But Kane had only pretended to look. He dove to his left, protected his weapon as he rolled and came up firing. His .44 snapped off three shots so fast they thundered like one round, and all three slammed into Lt. Pauley's chest as he tried to get off another shot. His gun fired, but the lines of communication between Wes Pauley's brain and his hand had been severed. The big gun swung down to the ground. It went off once as Pauley slammed backward, carried by the force of the three heavy slugs in his chest which dumped him on his back,

192

dead in the dusty street.

At the sound of the gunshot, Spur and Major Rutherford turned and walked back to the circle of men.

"It's all over, Kane," Spur called. "Lay down your gun. We'll have a hearing, but it will be a fair and honest one. Any enlisted men with evidence will testify, I'll guarantee that."

"It won't work, Colonel. I know the army. You officers will protect your own and I'll hang."

"I'll be running the show, and I promise you it will be fair," Spur assured him.

Kane stood up slowly. He tossed down his weapon which Spur realized was empty, and drew another six-gun from his belt, aiming it at McCoy across the space that separated them.

"Won't work, Colonel. I been there. I seen it all before. He was a fucking *officer!* We all know it. Better settle it right now."

Kane fired. The round hit the dirt between the two officers.

"Let's talk about this, Kane. You're not drunk now. You know what you're doing," Spur called.

Spur noticed that some men from the patrol hadn't been to their barracks yet and still had their rifles and pistols. Some raised their weapons now, looking at the officers.

Without warning Kane fired again. This round hit Major Rutherford in the leg, knocking him down. Before Spur could intervene, a dozen shots by the surrounding troopers blasted and Kane jolted again and again as the .45 rounds and heavier rifle slugs slammed into his body.

"Cease fire!" Spur bellowed and the deadly company street became quiet. Spur ran to Kane, who lay on his back, his neck and chest already a mass of blood. Kane blinked as Spur lifted his head out of the dirt.

"Thanks, Colonel," he whispered. "I got my man . . . Nothing else to live for . . . Got to see Walking Fawn and my boys." He winked, his face contorted with pain and he slumped against Spur, dead.

Spur pointed to the nearest trooper. "You! Run and get Doc Jones! *Move!*" Then he turned to the still gawking troops. "I want every man who fired his weapon to move over here and stand for inspection."

The men hesitated, then a group moved slowly to one side, grim-faced but confident. They had done nothing more than defend one of their officers. Nobody could fault them for that.

"The rest of you men are dismissed. Report to your barracks at once."

Spur watched the troopers leave, some pausing to stare at Buffalo Kane's bloody corpse.

Spur motioned to a sergeant to take down the names and units of the men who had fired, then dismissed them all. Doc Jones came walking up, looked at Kane first, grunted, then nodded at Major Rutherford who sat on the ground, in pain but not making a sound.

"Managed to get yourself shot up right here in camp, eh, Vern? Knew it would happen. You're too easy on the troops." The medic checked the leg wound, using a sharp little knife to slit his pants leg. "Yep, went in, decided to stay there," the doctor continued. "Legs don't like a chunk of lead. I got to dig it out. Got me some of that new-fangled chloroform—knock you out like a wooden mallet. You'll never feel a thing." The doctor called to two troopers to carry the major to the medical office.

Spur stood there a minute, looking down at Buffalo Kane's body. The will to live had vanished as soon as he had revenged his family's murder. Deep and abiding love was a powerful thing, to affect a man that way. The detail which was moving the bodies of the dead troopers to ready them for burial the next day, picked up the scout's body and took it away.

An hour later, Spur had eaten at the officers' table, and was sitting in his quarters. He was little farther along in nailing down the gunrunners than he had been a week ago. His only real suspect was all too obvious—no one in his right mind would arrange for the sale of the guns, then volunteer to lead the escort that rode out to ensure the weapons' safe delivery into Camp Sheridan.

Or would he? Would it seem to be so obvious as to be ludicrous, and therefore effective? Spur thought about it. There had been no connecting file to contact the other unit so the main parties could meet. No scouts had pointed the right direction. And the escort's route was eight miles off course.

The more he thought of it, the more plausible it became. Lt. Imhoff was a cocky bastard, just the kind to try to make a big deal any way he could. With all that gold in the Black Hills, the kind of payment was obvious, too. Yes, the personality fit. Imhoff had been in the army only a short time. He bragged about how he had bribed a senator to get a spot on active duty. Imhoff could be the man. But how to smoke him out?

If Imhoff had been stealing rifles from supply and selling them a few at a time to the Indians, he must have hidden the payment somewhere, perhaps in his quarters. He was unmarried and would have quarters similar to Spur's. An unofficial inspection of the officer's room might prove helpful. Spur looked down the housing chart he had been provided with the first day and found Imhoff's quarters. The newer men were farthest from the center of the camp. Imhoff was second to the end of the officers' units. Spur realized that the sun had set and his room was dark. Good.

He slipped out the back door and walked down to the next to last building. There was no light. Imhoff might have been asked out for dinner.

On the way back to his quarters, Spur went around to the front of the buildings and stopped at the dispensary. The lights were on and he heard voices behind a door. He opened it and found Doc Jones washing his hands. An enlisted man was wrapping a bandage around the major's thigh.

"Got the damn thing. Deep in there beside the bone. Thank God for chloroform. Would have taken six men to hold Vern down without it. A real Godsend," the doctor muttered.

"He'll be back on duty?" Spur asked.

"In a week he'll be walking. Vern is strong as an ox. No lasting damage, but he'll have one hell of a scar."

The major wasn't moving.

"He still unconscious?"

"Yep. Great, isn't it? He'll be coming around in five minutes or so. Right now I got to get to dinner.

Felicia is holding it for me and making polite conversation with that blowhard Imhoff. Never liked him too much. I got to wait until Vern comes back to his senses, then I'm gone."

"Thanks, Doc, you do good work." Spur left the hospital and walked back to his quarters. Again he went through the back door and to Lt. Imhoff's rear entrance. He knocked, got no response and tried the door. Locked. Spur used his key and was not surprised to find that it fit. There were only two types of long skeleton keys that fit the keyhole locks. He turned the key and stepped into the blackness of the room.

Spur barred the front door, then hung a blanket over the front window and lit a small candle. He started searching the most obvious hiding spots—under the bunk, in the bottom of a wooden foot locker. Finding nothing, he moved to the shelf in a small closet and then to a dresser. In the bottom drawer under a spare army blanket he found it. Three rawhide pouches. Spur opened one and looked inside. Gold, mostly in small jagged chunks. Not nuggets, long washed by a stream, or gold dust, but chunks! He pocketed three of the pieces of gold, put everything back exactly the way it had been, and removed the blanket from the window. He heard voices outside the door and, quickly unbolting it, hurried out the rear entrance. Just as he locked the back door, he heard the front one open.

Back in his room, Spur knew the evidence was circumstantial, but it was all he had, and for him it was enough. First he would have to force Imhoff to admit his complicity, then figure out how to get the rifles back. He would play it by ear. A hideout gun might come in handy. He took a small .22 caliber derringer, loaded it and pushed it down the inside of his boot. Now for a long talk with Lt. Imhoff.

As he walked the hundred yards to Imhoff's room, Spur decided it might be good strategy to lead Imhoff on, ask for a share of the gold. It might get an interesting reaction.

Spur would try the back door approach. He knocked on the panel and waited. Spur heard movement inside, and a few seconds later a voice called, "Yes, who is it?"

"A friend, Imhoff. I need to talk to you."

"McCoy? Colonel McCoy?"

"Easy, we don't need a lot of names shouted around."

"I was in bed. Just a minute—let me get my pants on."

After what Spur guessed were two minutes, the door unlocked and opened. Imhoff stared out. "It *is* you. What's so damned important it couldn't wait until morning?"

"I'll tell you inside. I feel exposed out here."

Imhoff grinned in the half light. "That sounds ominous. Come in, Colonel, come in."

One lamp burned in the room, but it was turned low. The bed was mussed, blankets turned back. Clothes lay around the room. Spur leaned against the back door, crossed his arms and stared at Imhoff.

"How long have you been in the army?"

"Counting West Point, four and a half years, sir."

"And right now you're thinking that I'm totally stupid, right? You're laughing behind my back every chance you get. Well, Imhoff, I'll say this.

You covered your tracks well, right up to volunteering for that escort. That was the dumb part. Damn, at first I didn't even consider you! Too obvious. But you counted on that. When is the final payment—tonight? I should have known that a bullshitter like you would be the one. Gladhander, life of the party, and about as amoral as they come. How much did you get for the first ten rifles, Imhoff? Maybe fifteen pounds of gold? Let's see—fifteen pounds at twenty dollars and sixty-seven cents an ounce is about five thousand dollars. Not bad for a start."

"Colonel, you're talking right out your asshole, you know that? I don't understand a word you're saying."

"What about the three rawhide sacks of gold in your bottom dresser drawer?"

Imhoff winced. His eyes narrowed and he brought a .44 pistol from behind his back.

"I'll be damned, you must be smarter than we figured. The escort did it, I guess. It was a risk I had to take. You see, I'm new here and nobody told me about the escort going out to meet the supply wagons. A minor slipup, but I covered it."

"You *thought* you covered it."

"They got the rifles, didn't they?"

"They did. And a lot of troopers are going to die because of those weapons and ammunition."

"But you're not in much of a position to do anything about it, are you, Colonel?"

"Depends how much you know about me. You think I'd come in here blind, bluffing, and without an ace in the hole?"

"What do you mean?"

"I've got a complete report on you, a sample of

the gold, the whole story spelled out. It's hidden deep in the camp files, but in a spot that would be first to be searched if anything 'unfortunate' happened to me. I've told one sergeant on base what to do if I wake up some morning and find myself dead."

"So you're covered. You're still dead. You wouldn't bet everything on that. You've got more."

"True, lots more. What it all boils down to, Lieutenant, is that I didn't get to be a colonel by following the book. I picked you out as a man a lot like me that first day. What I'm saying is, if you and I can strike the right bargain, we both could go on living, and we both could wind up so filthy rich we would never have to see the inside of any army post again."

"Partners? You joking? I've done all the work."

"But I'll be taking the big risk. I'll be covering for you officially. I'm the only one who can take suspicion off you and let you resign gracefully and not have U.S. government agents chasing you for the next sixty years."

"Hell, I don't know . . . I need some time."

Spur saw motion from the corner of his eye and turned. Felicia Jones lifted up from the space between the wall and the bed. She was naked. She sat casually on the edge of the bed, smiling.

"Colonel, I think you're exactly right. We *do* need someone on the inside. Come over here and sit beside me and let's discuss this situation on a more personal basis." She looked at Imhoff. "Omer, you go down and check out Colonel McCoy's quarters. See what you can find. He and I will confer here, and you *know* this is the kind of convincing I do best!"

CHAPTER NINETEEN

When Felicia was sure that Imhoff had left, she pulled Spur down beside her, then kissed him.

"Now sweet Spur, we're going to have a conference." She began undressing him. "First, I like the
idea of your joining us. We do need someone inside,
and I've been worried about your effect on us ever
since you came. You're too smart for our good. But a
three-way split on, say, a hundred thousand dollars
worth of gold isn't bad. We've got two powder kegs
of raw chunk gold coming, like that you saw in the
dresser. And when we get this we'll know where it is,
exactly. What would you say to going back in with a
twenty-man civilian guard and bringing out a
wagon-load of gold!"

Felicia had his shirt off and was unbuttoning his
fly. Spur couldn't stop the hot blood from rushing
into his crotch and his manhood stood up stiff and
ready. Felicia laughed softly, then grabbed him.

"Let's talk about the gold," Spur said.

She laughed and kissed his erection. "You must

be joking! The lady wants to be loved. She wants to lie down and have you pump her, and you're talking about gold?"

Spur looked at her lovely young body, so sleek, so smooth, breasts so round and full, so chalky white and throbbing as her nipples filled and lifted. Her flowing hair shading one pretty eye, teasing him. Spur reached out and touched her flat little belly and the thatch below, and he knew he wasn't going to talk about gold for a while.

"Oh, yes, now that's better, big Spur man. You can spur me anytime you want to!" She moved to her hands and knees on the bed and grinned at him. "Dinner time," she said and Spur growled and pushed his head under her and lay on his back, her delightful breast teasing him, dipping low enough for him to lick, then to suck a moment before lifting and the other one swinging in, moving in and out like a dance routine.

Spur reached to her crotch and found it wet and ready. His mouth sucked on her ripe hanging fruit as his finger found the small trigger just over her slit and he played the hard node back and forth like a guitar.

"Don't do that, I'm not ready yet. No! Oh, God but that feels delicious. Not yet, I want you inside me!" She crooned as she arched over him, losing her balance and falling on top of him, quivering for a full minute, until she tapered off and made soft purring sounds. She rested a minute, then was back on her knees.

"Christ, but you are good! Nobody makes me explode that way so quick. How do you do it?"

He laughed and bit her breasts and she urged him

202

on. His hand found her crotch again and she groaned.

"Your turn, sweetheart, your turn. You ever play doggie? Can you do the doggie?"

Spur sat up and moved behind her where she still crouched on her hands and knees. He positioned himself and then edged into her, making her cry out with joy.

"So different! God, but that feels different! What are you *doing* back there?" She looked over her shoulder, laughing in a delighted way that encouraged him to continue.

He pushed deeper until she had consumed him and then leaned over her back, caught one of her breasts in each hand and massaged them.

"If I was a queen, I would keep you around just to fuck me. You're so *good*. You know more good places and positions and more *wonderful* little tricks!"

Somebody knocked on the back door.

"No, Goddamnit!" she screeched. "Get out of here, Omer. Go diddle yourself somewhere. Come back in an hour."

Spur laughed. "What if that wasn't Omer?"

"Then the biddies will have lots to gossip about tomorrow. Shut up and fuck."

Spur did. There was something about this kneeling position that always made him feel like an animal in season. It was best for his fifth or sixth time, usually not the first, but there was no turning back now—not that he wanted to.

His mind exploded and his body followed, jolting forward, almost pushing Felicia flat. She was moaning and shuddering at the same time, crying out so loudly that he was sure she'd wake the entire camp.

Then both of them collapsed on the bed and neither could speak as they lay there panting. Ten minutes later they still lay side by side on the bed. His hand played with her breasts.

"What happened to the payoff for the rifles?" he asked.

"It's right on schedule. We meet our guide at a lightning-struck snag out on the river, and he takes us into Sioux country. We pick up the two kegs of gold packed on Indian ponies and ride out."

"Why do you need me?"

"Officially, you can grease the rough spots. I'll be going out on the next wagon to Sidney to catch the train. Father knows I'm leaving. He can get by. But Imhoff needs to resign with no suspicion."

"And that's where I come in. You want me to sell out my career for thirty thousand dollars?"

"That alone is a fortune. You must make eighty, maybe ninety-five dollars a month, maybe even a hundred. Thirty thousand dollars in twenty years' army pay! And this is just the beginning. You've heard of *Rio del Oro?*"

"Yes—a fantasy. Some Spanish padre's dream."

"No dream, reality! It exists in there somewhere —a stretch of stream that runs across solid gold. Not quartz or dust, but solid gold like you saw in those bags. Think what we could do with a *ton* of gold!"

"A lot of money, granted, but.... "

"Not a *lot* of money, a huge, unthinkable sum! It would be almost seven hundred thousand dollars! Just one run with a good wagon, a dozen dray horses and about twenty men for protection."

"Protection from the army or the Indians?"

"The army wouldn't even know we were around. The Indians might."

"I heard that Chief Crazy Eyes can bring together over three thousand Sioux warriors. How can we go in with twenty rifles?"

"In the first place, each man will have two Sharps 12-shot repeaters. That's twenty-four shots before reloading. And we go in during the worst weather we can find, preferably rain. We don't let any scout or lookout who sees us get back to the tribe."

"You'll be along?"

"Damn right! I've been practicing. I can use a rifle better than half the troopers in camp."

"Do we get a look at this river of gold at payoff time?"

"That's the plan. We get as close to it as we can, scout out a route, and judge what kind of alert system the Indians have around it. From what I hear, it's only about two hundred yards long, up in the hills somewhere. One small problem may be that the Sioux consider it to be hallowed ground, about as sacred as it can get except for the chief's burial cave. But the injuns won't even know we're in there. We'll slip in and out with a ton of pure gold, ready for market!"

"If this *Rio del Oro* is really there, how come nobody has charged in there before and taken the gold?"

"I'll spell it out for you. S-I-O-U-X. The big bad Sioux don't want anybody to know about it. But I've got me two specialists in fighting the Sioux. How can we go wrong?"

Spur pushed her breasts together, admiring her

cleavage.

"How can we go wrong? About a thousand ways. You've got a dozen things that have to mesh together *right*. The weather, the time, hunting parties, the buffalo. What about your own men? Twenty guards could mutiny and take over the wagon of gold, reward us with a bullet in the head and jump their wages from two hundred for the week's work into thirty thousand dollars each! An operation like this has a thousand problems."

"Look, you big idiot, I never said it would be easy. I said we can *do* it!"

She sat up and began pulling on her clothes which she gathered from the floor beside the bed. "I said we needed you, not that we couldn't get along without you. You could still have an accident and wind up stiff in a pine box by morning."

"And by noon both you and Imhoff would be in the guard house."

"I think that's a bluff." She stepped into a pair of ruffled drawers. Spur enjoyed watching her. When she finished, he dressed. He forgot and pushed his right foot into his boot. He had edged the derringer down there as he undressed so Felicia hadn't seen it. Now he pulled it out and put it in place again without her noticing.

She stood with her hands on her hips. The blouse pulled tightly across her breasts and Spur enjoyed the view.

"All right, I've decided. I want you to come along tonight on our payoff pickup. I don't like the three-way split, so we'll make it two way and lose Lt. Imhoff somewhere beyond Sioux country."

"That's probably what he's expecting by now," Spur said.

"We won't give him any reason to think that. I'll be mean and nasty to you the rest of the night and on the trip. It'll all be an act, of course. Then we take care of Imhoff when we're well out of Sioux country and don't need him anymore."

"And how do I know that you won't tell Imhoff the same thing about me?"

"Oh, no, sweet Spur. I'd never do that. You fuck too good!" She stood in front of him, went to her knees and kissed his fly and crotch a dozen times. "I love this big one too much to kill him, ever!"

Spur caught her by both arms and lifted her up.

"Sounds reasonable and logical to me. When do we leave?"

"Midnight. That will give us time to get in touch with our contact and to get well away from the fort before we're missed."

"What excuse do we give?"

"You'll leave a note on your door that you've discovered a possible location of the rifles, and will be back in a week. You're taking Lt. Imhoff with you. I'll tell Father I'm on a secret mission and he has to cover for me for the next week. Then I'll be back. He'll do it."

"You've thought it all out. What about supplies? We still need to eat."

She pulled two army storage bags out from under Lt. Imhoff's bed. "Filled with enough food to last us for a month. Even some tinned goods in there. We've been buying it a little at a time for a month."

"You *do* plan ahead. Let me go get into some

civilian clothes. I'd guess that's what we'll be wearing so we don't rile the Sioux any more than necessary?''

"Yes. And bring that Spencer with you. We shouldn't need it, but you never can tell about the Sioux. Come back here at midnight."

Spur ducked out the back door and walked quickly to his own quarters' rear entrance. It was open. Lt. Imhoff sat there with a six-gun in his hand and it was pointed right at Spur.

"What the hell you doing with my woman?" he snarled.

"Imhoff, that kind is everybody's woman. Don't waste your time with her. You're a bigger boy than that."

Imhoff scowled, swore, then jammed the pistol back in his belt.

"Shit, she spreads her legs for anybody. Hell, maybe you're right. When we get this gold, I'm riding out. I'll leave the bitch for good."

Spur nodded agreement. "I'm going along."

Imhoff nodded, some of his good humor returning. "Hell, it might come in handy to have another gun along on this run after all. I'm not a hundred percent convinced, but we'll play the hand and see what happens. Colonel, I still don't trust your ass. And, remember, when we're both in civilian clothes, them eagles on your shoulder don't mean shit!"

They left the post shortly after midnight. Spur and Imhoff had each carried one of the supply sacks to the stables. The guard there was given a two dollar gold piece and they packed up and took one extra saddled horse—for emergencies, they told the stable guard.

As arranged, Felicia met them outside the gate near the river. She wore a split riding skirt and Spur was not surprised to see her riding astride as she took command of the whole operation. It was going to be an interesting journey.

At the same jagged, dead cottonwood tree where Imhoff had met the Sioux warrior before, they waited. The brave rode up with two others and after a brief conversation conducted chiefly in sign language, the Indians led the way north. Spur watched Felicia eyeing the braves, wondering if she would try to lure them into her blankets before the trip was over. The braves did not even look at her.

Two days later they were in the foothills. Nothing eventful had happened on the trip. Felicia had remained in her own blankets, tired after each day's long ride. The morning of the third day found them high in the Black Hills. Spur memorized the route and noted that they had turned west early and then north. He estimated they were thirty miles from where he had seen the first hunting camp with Chitsa as his guide. He wondered where she was now. At last report, she had ridden into the Nebraska plains and no one had seen or heard from her since.

High on a ridge overlooking a gentle valley where the glistening trace of a small stream could be seen, the three Sioux braves stopped. With sign language, the Indians indicated the three whites should dismount and wait. Each of the braves carried a new Sharps carbine, the type that had been on the shipment from Omaha. The Sioux had apparently put their new weapons to use quickly.

"I don't like it," Imhoff said, staring at the backs

of the Sioux as they worked their way down a steep trail toward the valley below. "I say we follow the bastards and get the gold and leave."

"You say you want to get an arrow or a .52 caliber slug in your brain," Spur replied. "We're in Sioux territory. We play the game their way or they take away your chips and replace them with our own scalplocks."

"He's right, Omer, and you know it. So sit down and relax."

"I'll relax with you, pretty tit," Imhoff said.

Felicia scowled. "I don't like that kind of talk when I'm not in the mood. And I'm not." She forced a smile. "Omer, once we have the gold, and we're on our way out of here, all three of us will have a party."

"Hell, I'm not much on sharing," Imhoff grumbled. "Damn!"

They waited for one hour, then another. Spur was watching the progress of the horses below. They had moved to the center of the valley where the little stream widened somewhat. The braves stayed there for some time and then moved back up the hill, leading two pack animals. Imhoff lifted his binoculars.

"Damn, they're finally heading back."

"Look!" Spur said. The sun had moved to a point where it shone directly into the center of the small stream and the light bounced off in a direct reflection that was blinding.

"The *Rio del Oro*," Felicia breathed softly.

"God, it's got to be the damn gold stretch!" Imhoff shouted.

"Either that, or they put a lot of mirrors in the river bed to fool us," Felicia said.

"If that is holy ground down there, I'm surprised they let us come this far so we could see it," Spur said. "I'd bet they will have a show of force to remind us how strong the Sioux are in this area, and as a warning not to come back."

"Back, hell. I'm not leaving until I can walk on that gold river bottom!" Imhoff declared.

"Don't mention it to the Sioux," Spur shot back. "Look, I know more about the Sioux than both of you. We do exactly what they tell us. We take the gold and we get our asses out of here. Imhoff, if you want to come back later, that's up to you. But, I'll shoot you down on the spot if you turn and ride down that trail into the valley while the Sioux are watching."

"Hell, Colonel, don't get your eagles shitting all over your shoulder. I ain't that dumb. I don't want to taste those Sioux arrowheads or their Sharps lead. You worry about your own ass, and I'll take care of mine."

Spur ignored him and watched the pack animals coming slowly up the hill. It took the Indian pack ponies a half hour to come up the steep trail even when led by the Sioux braves. At the top, the Indian said something and motioned to the ex-army powder kegs. The tops had been broken out and they sat upright on the back of the pack horse, tied down on four sides. Spur estimated the kegs must weigh a hundred and fifty pounds each.

Imhoff went forward, checked out the gold, tried to lift the kegs to test their weight, then nodded.

"Looks fine to me, chief," Imhoff said to the Indian, then made some sign Spur had never seen before. The brave responded with other signs, and at last pointed into the valley, shook his head and held up both hands as if holding the whites back.

"Sure, chief. We understand. We won't set foot in the valley of the Great Spirit. Yeah, sure. Thanks for the gold. You ever want any more good Sharps carbines, you give me a smoke signal."

The Indians turned and trotted down the hill, never looking back.

"Let's get out of here," Spur said. He caught the rawhide lead rope of one of the pack ponies and mounted his bay. The others mounted as well and soon they were working their way south.

"You'll notice the Sioux did not give us an escort on the return trip," Spur observed.

"I wondered about that," Felicia admitted.

Imhoff handed the lead on his pack pony to Felicia.

"You two go on ahead, I'll catch up with you. I have to go have a look at that river of gold. I at least want to say I saw it, *touched* it."

"No!" Felicia shouted, her voice enraged. "You go back there and they'll find you and kill you. We're riding south!"

Imhoff rode up to her and glared down. "Little bitch, you don't have any hold over me anymore. I've got the gold, and I'll do any damn thing I want to." He wheeled and rode at a right angle to them, moving to a different spot along the ridge to make his descent into the valley.

Felicia drew the .44 from her saddle, but Spur's hand closed over it before she could fire.

"You fire one shot and half the Sioux nation will be down on us. There's not a hell of a lot we can do to stop him. Maybe it's all for the best. He wants his reward for selling guns to the Sioux. Maybe the Sioux themselves will provide it."

They rode south another mile, hid the horses in a ravine with heavy brush over and tied them well, then walked back up to the ridgeline.

Both wormed their way to the very top and peered down into the valley. Spur took out his binoculars and sectioned the lush green mile-long valley. At last he saw movement down the near side of the slope. It was Imhoff, moving slowly from tree to tree. Spur checked but saw no Indians in the area. He showed Felicia.

"The fool might just make it yet, if the Sioux believed that we would not go down there. But somehow I doubt that."

"The Sioux are learning the ways of the white man—trust no one," Felicia said.

All they could do was watch. She moved up beside him.

"I know I *said* we should let the Sioux have Imhoff, but I don't think I could have done it. Now he's made the move himself." She pressed against Spur and he put his arm around her.

"Have you ever seen a man die, Felicia?"

Her eyes widened and she shook her head.

"It's not pretty. All we can do is wait and see what happens. If they catch him, they will kill him, there is no doubt about that. The big question is, will they then come after us for letting him go back and violate their sacred lands?"

"You think the Sioux . . ."

"Yes, without doubt. They have acted as men of honor, fulfilling their bargain. Now if the white man does not keep his bargain, which includes not going

213

into the valley, then all bets are off. It's open war-
fare—kill or be killed. And the Sioux will have one
hell of an advantage."

"Maybe we should leave now?" she said.

"An extra ten minutes or half hour wouldn't matter. It will be better to know than to run scared and
wonder what happened to Imhoff."

"You're a gambler. What are the odds?"

"Of being caught down there? At least a thousand
to one, and not in Imhoff's favor. If he's seen and
caught, his chances of getting away are a million to
one. And it won't be pretty."

Spur used the binoculars again, checking the far
slope beyond the river. He winced, then, at last put
down the glasses. He turned Felicia's pretty face to
him and kissed her lips.

"Do you want to leave now?" he asked.

She frowned and watched him intently. "You saw
something! What did you see? Sioux?"

"The Sioux may be mighty warriors, but they
aren't in the same class with the Chiricahua Apache.
So far I've seen five Sioux warriors who are supposed to be hidden in the brush and grass. All of
them are moving slightly, just enough to give away
their position. If I can spot five, there may well be a
hundred. But five is plenty to cut Imhoff into buffalo jerky."

"My God! Let's warn him!"

Spur used the glasses again. Imhoff was at the
stream, jumping up and down, and probably
shouting with rapture, but Spur couldn't hear him.
Imhoff walked in the stream, then sat down on the
bottom which evidently was little more than a foot
under the surface.

A bullet slammed into the water beside Imhoff. He jumped up and ran for the bank where he had left his rifle. A dozen rounds struck on and around the rifle. Imhoff stood immobile.

A long, low wailing call echoed through the valley and the Sioux warriors stood. They had nearly circled the valley.

"My God, look at that!" Felicia said softly.

"I'd say about two hundred Sioux braves, all armed with rifle, bow and arrow or spear. Lt. Imhoff is in an unenviable situation."

"Don't joke about it!"

"There's nothing we can do to help him. Let's go."

"No, no! We must be sure."

They waited. The Indians closed in slowly, firing only at his rifle when he made a move toward it. He held his hands over his head, then suddenly went for his pistol and fired three times, wounding the closest Indian, but an arrow slashed through his right wrist and knocked the weapon from his hand. The braves closed in then and Imhoff faced them, laughing.

"Why haven't they ended it?" Felicia asked.

"A quick death is seldom the Indian way for a captive. We should leave."

"No!"

They watched as three braves ran from the woods with three long poles. Spur shook his head. He knew what was coming. The Sioux moved quickly then. The poles were arranged in a triangle and the tops tied together. Imhoff was tied by the feet and hung from the center of the poles. His hands were tied behind him.

"Why are they doing that?" Felicia asked.

Spur just shook his head.

A brave moved in with hands full of something. They couldn't see what it was for sure. Spur knew but wouldn't say. Soon a small trail of smoke arose as a fire began to burn.

When the light breeze was right they could hear Imhoff screaming, but still Felicia wouldn't leave.

"Burning him at the stake!" she asked. Spur saw that she was crying softly.

"No. Worse than that, much worse."

Felicia bit her lip. "I want to stay."

The fire at first was small. Lt. Imhoff's head was six feet from the fire. Gradually he was lowered by a strong rawhide rope until the fire made him squirm and shout.

Spur had heard that this execution ritual sometimes took as long as four hours, depending on the skill and patience of the Indian who kept the fire burning at precisely the correct level.

The valley was quiet except for Imhoff's tortured, wailing scream that came floating on the breeze now and then. His hair had burned away.

"Is he . . . is he dead yet?" Felicia asked, her face turned away.

"No. They make it last a long time." Spur had heard of the torture, of how the victim would scream and fight. His hair might burn off quickly and he would be in shock, but alive. His scalp would blister and then the rope would lower him another foot toward the flames. Soon the blood in his brain would boil. Blood vessels would rupture and the victim would die in a screaming intolerable white-hot agony of pain.

But the ceremony would still continue. The head

would continue to be lowered until at last the victim's skull would explode and the game would be over.

Spur used the binoculars again. Lt. Imhoff's head was black. Fluid ran from one ear. The rope slipped another two inches, moving his blackened skull closer to the searing heat.

Spur put the glasses away, picked up Felicia Jones and carried her down the hill toward their horses. They might have an hour's head start if they were lucky.

When they reached their mounts, Spur used his knife and cut the thongs holding the two powder kegs of gold, carried them to the base of a huge pine tree with two tops, and covered them with pine needles, branches and fallen limbs. He made it look as natural as possible.

Felicia sat staring at him in wonder.

"Our gold . . ." she whimpered.

"No gold. We're trying to save our scalps. Carrying that weight, the horses would never have a chance. Now we can ride the Indian ponies until they drop, then put the saddles back on our regular mounts and keep riding. With luck we can be ten miles away before the Sioux start pursuing us."

"We must take the gold . . ."

"We must save our hides!" He had taken her saddle off and now cinched it in place on the Indian pony. He tied the reins of her army mount to the saddle and boosted her up. His own mounts were ready and they rode, Spur in the lead, angling down the slope to the edge of the valley. It didn't matter who saw them now. He looked back and saw Felicia keeping up with him. She was a good rider and that

217

might make the difference. The Indian ponies were fast and sure-footed. Spur sent them galloping across the short valley, up the ridge and over it. Down the other side he let them rest at a fast walk, and when they reached the next valley, he spurred them back to a hard run. Spur figured fifteen miles for the tough little horses. Then they would refuse to run, having a natural instinct when to stop before they killed themselves.

Felicia pulled up beside him.

"Was he dead? Did you *see* Lt. Imhoff die?"

"Yes. His hair burned off his skull . . ."

Felicia turned away. "I'm coming back for the gold. Someday I'm coming back and I'll dig it up. I'll remember exactly where it is. I'm coming back."

Spur rode on silently, concentrating on finding the best route. He had consciously headed south, knowing that they had to work eastward as well, but that a southerly route should take them out of Sioux country faster.

They had been riding for two hours. The Indian ponies were exhausted. They rode up to the brow of a hill and when Spur looked over it he saw a large Sioux hunting camp. He reined back and held up a hand to stop Felicia.

"Trouble." He turned and they rode along the far side of the ridge for half a mile. When he looked over the ridge he found more of the camp. It must be a permanent village of some sort. Should they wait until night? The Indian mounts were winded.

Spur headed east again, moving into a small valley, running just inside the woods line, and noticing that the timber were thinning. Ahead there would be only prairie, grasslands with no means of concealment. Spur went to the top of the next ridge and looked below. More Indians. A sea of tipis spread out in a large valley with a sizable stream running through the center. They were in the middle of a Sioux encampment—some kind of a gathering, a powwow maybe.

Felicia came up on Spur's right. She was shaking. "Spur, look, an Indian!"

Spur drew his six-gun as he spun to his left. An Indian girl on a horse burst from some trees and rode straight for them. A glance at the girl's face made Spur smile and put his pistol away. Felicia was clawing for her weapon.

"No," Spur said firmly. "Felicia, you know Chitsa from Camp Sheridan."

"Oh. Can she help us?"

"Chitsa, how long have you been following us? Never mind, can you get us out of this trap?" Spur asked.

She smiled. "And hello to you too, Spur McCoy. Yes, I can get you out. Follow me, and be as quiet as possible."

For the next hour they rode cautiously, hid in brush, then rode like the wind through a valley and over another ridge. When they were on the down slope Chitsa pulled her Indian pony to a walk and motioned for Spur to ride beside her.

"To answer your first question, I have followed you since you left Camp Sheridan four days ago. I saw your meeting with the three Sioux braves, and I got close enough to see the *Rio del Oro*. But I was not foolish enough to let the Sioux see me as Lt. Imhoff did. May God rest his soul."

"Will the Sioux follow us?"

"Will the sun come up in the morning?"

"How far behind us are they?"

"Close enough for you to change horses. We'll be in the grasslands in a few more hours, when the army mount's stamina should be of good use."

"We have a chance then?"

"You saved your scalp when you left the gold. If you had brought it with you, you would both have been scalped two hours ago. Let's ride."

Near dusk that day they saw twenty Sioux horsemen that Chitsa said were the ones following them.

They rode all night, using the darkness to good advantage and when the sun came up they had less than a day's ride to make Camp Sheridan. Felicia, worn out, nearly fell out of her saddle twice. They stopped and Chitsa stood watch while the other two slept for a while, then she roused them and they rode hard for two hours, let the horses walk for an hour and rode hard again.

Just before darkness they rode into Camp Sheridan, and within minutes the entire population came out to welcome them.

CHAPTER TWENTY

Spur sat in the officers' mess, eating. He had never been so hungry, even though he hadn't thought about food during the past three days. It had been butchering day at Camp Sheridan and Spur finished his second two-pound steak with mashed potatoes, thick brown gravy and butter fried parsnips. At last he pushed the plate back.

Major Rutherford chuckled where he straddled a chair leaning on the back, his chin resting on his folded forearms.

Spur had filled him on most of the affair as he ate.

"So Imhoff was the gunrunner all along. I never thought he might be the one."

"Gold does strange things to men—and women."

"That presents a problem. Nobody else knows how involved Felicia was. If we don't charge her, it will blow over."

"She will be put on a train somewhere. She wants to get away from here, I understand."

"We'll work it out. Doc is crushed. He had no idea

she was so eager to leave. I've ordered a wagon to take Colonel Underhill and his family to Sidney, and thence to Omaha." Major Rutherford grinned. "I lied a little bit, cleaning up Underhill's record. And knowing Underhill, he'll make out all right. His wound isn't that bad but they'll figure out quickly that he is in no mental state to command."

"What about Imhoff?"

"I'll take my cue from you. You'll write a report. I'll include it with mine. I'd just as soon tell it like it happened. We don't owe Imhoff a thing."

Spur left the table and they walked down the line of officers' quarters.

"Let's take a detour," Spur said. They went to Lt. Imhoff's room and Spur used the Major's pass key. Inside they lit a lamp and Spur looked in the bottom dresser drawer. The three bags of gold were still there. He picked them up and blew out the lamp.

"Let's go to your office for a talk," Spur said.

A half hour later they had reached an agreement. There had never been such a thing as the *Rio del Oro*. The fifteen pounds of pure gold Spur carried did not exist. He would turn it over to the mint without a clue where it originated.

"If the gold story got out, you'd have five thousand miners in here before winter," Spur said. "And the Sioux would probably kill all of them. You don't have enough men to protect everyone. Let's hold off the Black Hills gold rush as long as we can."

"You actually didn't see this river of gold, then?"

"I saw a stream maybe fifteen feet wide, and a flash of sunlight off something in the water. But I didn't see a gold-lined stream bed. Imhoff did and you know what happened to him. Major, that about wraps me up here. Right now I better find my bunk before I fall asleep in your chair."

"You'll be moving out soon, Colonel?"

"Yes, I came here strictly to find the gunrunners and stop them. As you've no doubt figured out, that doesn't sound much like a regular army job, and it isn't. Those eagles of mine are what you might call temporary rank."

"And I imagine I'm not supposed to ask any questions," the major said.

"Ask, but I won't answer. Yes, I'll be leaving as soon as I get some sleep. Probably the day after tomorrow. How is Casselberry doing?"

"Both Casselberrys are doing fine. Janet has been totally accepted into society, and Neil is working his balls off with his company." Major Rutherford paused. "Just for my own information, Janet *had* been caught by the Sioux, hadn't she?"

"Yes. Two of them. One got away, one didn't."

"I figured that. Now why don't you get some shut-eye?"

Two days later Spur McCoy in civilian clothes mounted his bay in front of the Camp Sheridan headquarters. Felicia Jones would be on the wagon to Sidney within the week. She had been pointedly excluded from the camp's social activities. Chitsa would be going to Omaha with the Underhills. Spur shook the major's hand one last time, returned his salute and rode out the south gate on the wagon track through the prairie. It would be an easy ride, and Spur looked forward to it.

He was barely an hour away from the post when he heard hoofbeats behind him on the sod. He turn-

223

ed and saw someone riding hard toward him—a girl with long black braids flying behind her. She rode up until her leg touched his. Chitsa had on a white blouse and a pair of cut down army pants. She looked beautiful.

"I decided to go for a ride. Mind if I tag along with you? I'll meet the Underhills in Sidney."

"I'm delighted!" He leaned over and kissed her soft, parted lips. "I have a lot of thank-you's to say to you for saving my scalp."

"That's what good friends are for," she said softly.

He took her hand, suddenly wanting to touch her. Spur smiled and she smiled back. She would be his love slave for three whole days.

Spur McCoy, United States Secret Agent, knew he had the best job in the world. And for the next few days he and Chitsa would be on the trail together. They would camp early, make a fire, eat and then enjoy a love-filled night.

Spur grinned. Damn, this was the life!

MONTANA
MINX

Chapter One

July 22, 1873—East of Helena, Montana Territory.

(In January, 1873, the great Credit Mobilier scandal was investigated by Congress and the swindle unearthed shamed many of the builders of the transcontinental railroad. Ulysses S. Grant was in his second year of his second term as President of the United States, with William M. Evarts as his Secretary of State, Henry Wilson his Vice President, and William K. Belknap was Secretary of War. Grant had won the election for a second term with 3,587,070 votes, beating out the famous "Go west young man, go west," Horace Greeley, a Democrat who gathered 2,834,079. This was the year the earmuff was invented by Chester Greenwood. The first formal list of rules for a new sport called "football" were put together in New York City in 1873.)

The daily stage from Helena to High Prairie rolled along through the valley moving east and was now little less than an hour from its destination. The four passengers inside the sturdy but uncomfortable coach were hot and a fine sheen of dust had settled on everyone and everything.

The tall man who had slept most of the way was a drummer, his line of fine workingman's hand tools packed safely in his carpetbag in the boot. He was forty-two years old, had a thin face and a wife and three children in St. Louis. This was the end of his twice yearly swing through the "sticks" as he called the wilds of Montana. It had been a hard ride, and he admired the young woman who sat beside him. But he had said no more than a polite hello to her.

The woman was twenty-four, more starkly striking than pretty, slender and well dressed. She had slept part way leaning on a pillow she had brought against the side of the coach. She tugged at her dress which was sticking to her thighs. She was conscious of a drop of sweat rolling down her open necked dress and seeping into the line of cleavage just out of sight under the garment. Another hour and she would have a bath.

The seat opposite her held a matron of thirty-two and her ten-year-old son. The boy had been half out the window a dozen times and wanted to ride on top with the shotgun guard, but he had been told company regulations made that impossible. He was brown haired and full of energy. His mother leaned back and closed her eyes, hoping her husband would be at High Prairie to meet

6

her. He said the ranchhouse was ready to move into.

On the high seat at the front of the stage, George held the twelve reins in his practiced hands. He had been on this run for so long he knew every rock and rut. It hadn't rained for two months and the ruts were gone, filled in with sand and dirt and knocked flat by the pounding of twenty-four hooves a trip and the wide iron flat rims on the wooden spoked wheels.

They would be in town in less than an hour. The horses were in good shape. This was a quick easy run, the last day from Helena.

On the wooden bench beside him Will Manson checked the Spencer rifle he carried. He had only used it once on this run, and had driven off two attackers. He got a ten dollar bonus that day! It was as much as a whole week's pay and he had bought a new gold watch. He was just over fifty, and looking forward to quitting the guard job. Maybe next year. He squinted down the track of a roadway at the Peter's Creek crossing. It was a small ford that crossed to get on the right side before the river became so big downstream they couldn't ford it. The area was always green because of the springs that fed the little creek, and the downstream flow.

This had been a favorite spot for a quick stop on days when they were ahead of schedule. Today they would swing right through, since they all were anxious to get into town.

The coach drew closer to the ford. George peered into the darkness under the trees, shadowed despite the hot sun. He could see nothing. Almost never anything to see.

They were thirty yards from the trees. Will Manson pulled down on the team of six to ease them to a walk through the foot deep water of the stream when they came to it. Not that much water today, George figured as he looked at the stream.

The first shot cracked through the silent Montana air with the surprise of a lightning bolt on a cloudless day.

George knew it was a Sharps when he heard the sound almost at the same time that a mighty fist pounded into his upper chest and sprawled him back over the top of the coach. His shoulder wedged against the little railing and his left hand grabbed it to keep from tumbling to the ground.

By that time there were a dozen shots blasting into the soft summer day. George saw Will slap the reins down on the six horses to get back up to speed. But another volley of shots came followed by a voice.

"Hold it! Stop the stage or you're all dead. We've got rifles, repeating rifles!"

Will Manson had wanted to make a run for it with the stage. But he knew better. Company policy was to run only when he would have a good chance to outdistance one or two gunmen. He had no clue how many guns were in the darkness ahead. He eased the rig to a stop just as it entered the shade twenty yards this side of the water.

Two masked men rode out of the brush on one side and two more from the other side. All carried rifles and holstered six-guns. There was little he could tell by the horses. No brands showed, which wasn't unusual.

A tall, thin man with a high-crowned black hat and a red bandana kerchief over his nose and mouth rode up to the coach while the others trained their rifles on the stage.

"Down!" he ordered in a whining voice.

Will helped his wounded shotgun guard down to the ground. The shoulder was bleeding badly.

"Can I stop the bleeding?" Will asked the robber.

"Hell, if you can." The tall rider motioned his rifle toward the stage doors. "Everybody out! No problems, or you eat rifle slugs for supper. Get out of there!"

The drummer came first, handing the two women down. The little boy jumped out and walked up to the robber.

"You an outlaw?" the boy asked.

"Jason!" his mother blurted. "Get back over here by me."

The robber tipped the brim of his hat. "All right, ma'am. Lad is curious. I used to be that way." He looked down at the boy. "I guess you could say I'm an outlaw, kid. Now you help. You get the ladies' reticules and the

9

man's wallet and his watch and all the rings and bring them to me."

"Yes sir!" Jason said grinning. He ran to his mother, took her reticule and stopped in front of the younger woman. By the time he had the purses and wallet, the tall robber had stepped off his horse. Two men had worked over the stage and shouted a moment later when they found a strong box in the boot at the rear covered by a blanket and an old canvas.

The leader bent down to take the reticules. Without any warning Jason's hand darted out, grabbed the mask and pulled it down, revealing a lean jaw, a hard mouth and broken nose. A thin scar showed on the right cheek through a day's beard. The robber jerked the mask up again, but it was too late.

"Goddamn, you're Cain Haworth!" Will Manson shouted. "I see you all the time in Prairie City."

Cain jolted his face up and stared at Manson. The stage driver grabbed his hat and slammed it against his leg. Too late he realized. The mistake he had made.

"No, no, not so," Manson said trying to undo the damage. "Can't be Cain at all, don't look nothing like him. Some other jasper. Ain't never seen this man before in my life."

Cain dropped the purses and leveled his six-gun at the stage driver.

"That was a bad mistake, driver. A damn fatal mistake. You know what we got to do now, don't you?"

10

"Christ! Six of us? You can't do that. Swear to God nobody will have any idea who robbed us. Shit, you can't just shoot six people. Women . . . two of them are women and the kid!"

Cain pulled the trigger and a small black hole appeared in Manson's forehead and almost at the same time a gush of blood, bone fragments and brain tissue splattered the side of the stage coach behind him. The body bounced off the coach and crumpled to the ground.

"Damnit, no!" one of the mounted men shouted. "Think what you're doing!"

Cain turned. "I am. You ain't the one identified, so shut up your ugly mouth!"

He had turned away for a moment, but it was enough time for the wounded shotgun guard to grab a derringer from his boot and pull the trigger twice. Two .41 caliber slugs whistled past Cain and caught the rider behind him in the chest. He toppled from his horse dead as he hit the dirt of the trail.

Cain turned and screamed, then shot George in the chest four times with his six-gun. His eyes were glaring, furious. A streak of spittle drooled from the corner of his mouth. After he shot the man he ran to him and stomped his face into a mass of blood and smashed bones until the shotgun guard was unrecognizable.

He whirled on the passengers who were still lined up near the stage. The drummer shivered. He had never seen a man die before.

The mother clutched her son to her breast, looking away from it all, holding Jason's face toward the stream.

The attractive young woman took off her bonnet and let her long blonde hair billow out. She looked at Cain and nodded.

"You don't have to shoot me. I'm the one person here you can trust, even more than your gang. And I can prove it." As she talked she began unfastening the buttons on her blouse. Quickly she stripped it off, showing the straps of her chemise and the white garment itself that covered her to the waist. She pulled the tail out of her skirt and pulled the chemise over her head. She wore nothing under it.

Her breasts were full and lightly nippled in soft pink. The mounds were rounded and swung slightly outward. She smiled and dropped the chemise and walked toward Cain with a calculated slowness that made her hips grind invitingly.

"I get all the women I want in town," he said.

"Not like me. Give me a chance to show you."

Cain slowly reloaded his .44, this time putting in six bullets. "Why should I?"

"I'm a dance hall girl. A specialist. I do all the things the other girls won't do."

"Anything?" Cain said, his interest caught.

"Anything. Everything." She undid a button at her waist and the skirt dropped into the dust. A moment later she pulled down her petticoats, kicked them to the side of the road and stood naked in the glare of the noonday sun.

"My God, but you are beautiful!" Cain said softly. "Right here, in the middle of the god-damned road!" he shouted.

"Of course," she said and sat down, then lay in the dirt, her legs spread, her knees lifted. "Come on," she invited. "The first one is fast. The second time is always better. Then the third and fourth and fifth I'll make you scream with delight. I told you I'm a specialist."

One of the robbers came up, got off his horse and searched the drummer. He put his hands over the mother and her son to be sure they didn't have weapons. The woman slapped him, and he shrugged, making sure his mask stayed in place.

He strode toward Cain who stood over the girl, rubbing the bulge in his pants near his waist.

"We've got to get out of here!" the second robber said. "We have what we came for."

"Not all of it," Cain spat. "I want her, six different ways."

"We don't have time," the robber said. "We have to figure out what to do with Zack. We can't leave him here dead. What we going to do with Zack?"

Cain slapped him across the face.

"Shut up! Just shut up. One fucking

problem at a time. First this bitch."

He dropped on his knees in the dust between her legs and saw the swollen, red slash through the dusting of reddish crotch hair.

"You got yourself a deal, bitch. Hot and hard and fast. I'll make you cry for more!" Cain tore open his pants and went down between her legs jamming at her, and then with a cry he plunged into her, thrusting forward savagely. There was no feeling, no passion, only the raw edge of lust in his face as he pumped a dozen times and screeched as he climaxed.

In front of the stagecoach, the mother shielded Jason's eyes, but she watched, unable to pull her gaze from the pair writhing in the dust, the woman doing everything to satisfy the man.

The drummer beside her had his hand in his pocket and had turned toward the coach. He was making small sounds in his throat and the woman looked away from him. By the time the duet had played out in the dust, the third horseman came up and talked with the second. They kept the group covered and together put their dead robber friend back on the horse and tied his hands and feet together under its belly. The horse shied and pranced, not used to the strange position of the load, and nervous about the smell of death that clung to the area.

Cain sat back on his haunches, his shrunken penis already put away and his pants buttoned. He reached for his weapon, pushed the muzzle toward the girl's crotch and saw her crawl away in terror.

"Hell, I thought you were supposed to be something special," he said, the cocked six-gun tracking her.

"You promised! The third and fourth time, tonight! It will be fantastic then! No!"

Cain smiled, nodded, then his eyes glazed with ice, his jaw froze in place and a small tic pulsed below his left eye. For just a moment his lower lip quivered, then he shot her in the heart. The dance hall girl flopped backward into the dirt and the mother by the stage screamed.

Cain spun toward the hysterical woman. He was still on his knees.

"Shut up!" he shouted. "I can't stand women who scream that way!"

The woman fell to the ground, screaming again, holding her frightened son trying to protect him. Cain fired four times. All four shots hit the pair and they died without another sound.

The drummer looked at the grisly scene and bolted for the trees. Cain swore, fired once but missed. His pistol was dry. He grabbed his rifle, stood and aimed carefully. His third shot caught the salesman in the back and flung him to the ground, half in and half out of the stream.

"Make sure," Cain told one of the men with him.

"Not a chance," the man said. "You are

plumb crazy in the head. I don't even know you no more."

Cain snorted, walked toward the drummer who was trying to crawl from the stream. He shot him twice in the side of the head and walked back to the stage.

"You got the strongbox?" Cain asked.

"Yes, and it has the double eagles," the second robber said. "We split them here. Fifty each and you get Zack's share. I don't want any of his."

Cain nodded. "Fine. Any other problems?" As he spoke he turned and shot the stagecoach's lead horse in the head with his rifle. It screamed as only a wounded horse can and fell, dragging the other lead horse down. Cain then shot all six horses in the head making sure they were dead. Next he took out a packet of stinker matches and set the stage coach on fire.

The two men who had helped him make the robbery watched from their horses. The smaller of the two spoke.

"We're riding in to town, right down the road. We were in a hunting accident and Zack got shot. An accident, stupid, but he's dead. We thought you should know."

"Where am I going to be?"

"Not with us. You go back to your place or set up an alibi or whatever you want. From now on, I don't know you, never have known you. And don't swing that rifle this way or you are one dead crazy man!"

Cain took a deep breath and nodded. "Yeah, alibi. I'll watch the road and make sure this fire burns good, then I'll fix myself up with a good alibi for all day. Nobody seen us. Should be easy. All day alibi, you two sure as hell better do that too."

They nodded, took the lead line from Zack's mount and moved down the road at a four miles to the hour walk. They would be into High Prairie about three that afternoon.

It took Cain a half hour to feed the fire and make sure that most of the stage burned. He used the girl's blouse and clothes to help it burn, then threw in some pine limbs and pitch sticks. When he left he had a hundred double gold eagles in his saddlebags.

Not bad for a day's work. Two thousand dollars! He turned his roan down the road, then cut cross country heading for his father's Box H ranch. It would take too much time. He was west of town, his father's place was north. Town was closer. That's when he thought of Pauline at the Pink Petticoat Saloon. He could talk her into anything. She would be as good an alibi as he could get for today. If that didn't hold up, it wouldn't matter much anyway. Which meant he would be out on the road. But not yet. He had a lot of choices before that one.

Cain Haworth rode hard for town. It was about five miles, and if he pushed the horse he could go around the three riders in front of him and get there in a half hour or maybe

17

less. The horse wouldn't be much good, but what the hell, it was just a horse.

Cain shoved the rifle deep into the boot, raked his spurs down the roan's sides and jolted down the road at a hard gallop.

Chapter Two

Cain Haworth stood over the naked girl in the crib above the Pink Petticoat Saloon. She had one small bruise on her left breast, and sobbed as she nodded in agreement.

"Yes, yes! I'll say anything you tell me. I've been sick most of the day and haven't had any customers. I'll say you were here all day. Yes!"

Cain smiled. It helped to know where to hit a girl so she didn't bruise. He caught her breasts and petted them. Kissed them separately and then pushed her down on the bed. She was smaller than the girl from the stagecoach, her tits were tiny, her hips not so wide. He shook his head and stood.

Cain was tall and solid. In these days when the average man's height was five feet nine, Cain was half an inch under six feet. Broad shoulders and a narrow waist gave him a swaggering look as he walked with long strides. The scar stood out whitely now as color tinged his face.

"You just be damn sure you know what to say if I need you to say it. Now I got to go meet some folks coming into town." He ran his hand down her belly and to her crotch and probed for a minute. He laughed softly as she reacted.

"You stay ready, Pauline, good and ready. I'm still all jazzed up and I need about six more today, six different ways. You be thinking up some new positions."

Cain strode out of the room, down through the saloon and waved at Miss Claudine, who owned the saloon, the whores, the gambling hall, the whole shooting match. She had to be worth thousands.

In the street Cain slowed, meandered down Main toward the west looking for the two riders and a body. Then should be along soon. He had passed them two miles out of town.

Cain saw nobody coming down the road, so he leaned against the hardware store wall and rolled a smoke. Bull Durham in a sack. He'd been smoking since he was ten. If he put his mind to it he could roll a smoke with one hand.

The "weed" was half gone when he saw them coming. They rode faster as they hit the outskirts of the little town of High Prairie. It wasn't much of a place. Main Street ended in the road leading east and west. There were three blocks with businesses on both sides, and two blocks of houses behind them. That was the whole thing. The population sign at the west end said the town had 384 people, but that must be when everyone was in town on Saturday night.

Cain watched the little caravan pick up a following. The sheriff's office was in the basement of the courthouse along with the two jail cells. The courthouse stood in the center of town half a block back from the street with a lawn and a small park in front of it.

By the time the two riders and the corpse got to the courthouse there were thirty people, mostly men and kids following them.

The sheriff heard about the body and came out to the street to meet them.

Cain had wandered that way with the crowd and listened as his two friends swung down from their mounts.

"Who is your friend?" Sheriff Quigley asked. Quigley was duly elected in Whitewater county, and had a star to prove it. He was a short man, wearing a black suit and vest and a pure white, high crown hat. He did not wear spurs and rode a horse only when absolutely necessary. He preferred a light buggy.

Jim Darlow cut the body free and eased it to the boardwalk the county had built along the front of the park.

"Sheriff, this here is Zack Kinsey. Friend of mine. We was hunting and he was messing around with his forty-four and he shot himself. Wasn't nothing we could do for him."

The lawman looked at the other rider.

"You know me, Sheriff Quigley. I'm Roger

21

Olsen. That's what happened. We was looking for a buck up along Tinder Creek and Zack was trying to fast draw and dropped his iron and it went off. Shore wish the Doc had been there."

A small man in black suit and a black beard hurried up. He looked at the sheriff who nodded. The undertaker asked a pair of men to carry the corpse to his parlor and the sheriff motioned to the two riders.

"Come inside and we'll fill out some papers. Danged foolish thing to do, shoot yourself that way." He paused. "Didn't you boys get into some trouble a few months back?"

Darlow shrugged. "Nothing serious, Sheriff. Just a little fist fight about a card game. Happens to everybody."

The lawman nodded. "Your weapons been fired?"

"Sure, Sheriff. We been hunting." Darlow said it. "We had a shot at a big buck, but he got away. Then we were plinking at rabbits with our revolvers."

The sheriff said something that Cain couldn't hear and the three went into the sheriff's office. Cain smiled and relaxed his hand that had hung close to his .44. The damn sheriff was just plain stupid. He would believe anything. Almost anything.

Cain walked away as the crowd scattered, the excitement over. He wanted to stay in town for a good tussle with Pauline, but he had a feeling he should get back to the ranch. He might even work a few days just to get on the good side of his father. He never knew when his old man's help might be needed again.

Cain shivered as he thought about how the girl had looked sitting there in the dust of the road just before he shot her. As he pulled the trigger on her he had climaxed. The same thing happened when he shot the woman and the boy and then the drummer. Crazy! Wild! But he was really fucked out. He couldn't do any good with Pauline tonight anyway. He went to the livery and picked up a second horse he kept there to ride the four miles north to his father's ranch.

First thing he would do when he got back to the home place was hide the hundred gold eagles. He wouldn't spend any of them for a while. Gonna be old Billy Hell kicked up about this stage robbery. But they weren't going to find out who did it. Not a chance!

Chapter Three

Spur McCoy swung down from the stage coach and looked at the little town they called High Prairie. Not much, even by outback Montana standards, but it would have to do. And somewhere around here was a wanton, crazed killer. He had been in Helena on some other business when word came through about the massacre of the stage crew and passengers.

What brought Spur to the case was that this was the fifth robbery of the U.S. Mails on this same stage line within six months. The Postmaster General had screamed to President Grant after the fourth robbery, and Spur had been alerted to watch the situation. Now the Secret Service would spring into action. West of the Mississippi that meant Spur McCoy.

Spur walked across the street to the town's one hotel, the Plainsman, and registered. He got a second floor room with a view of main street.

Spur was a big man at six-two and two hundred pounds of iron hard muscles and bone. His dark brown hair had hints of red and he wore muttonchop sideburns that met his full moustache. Flinty green eyes stared at the world under thick brows. His favorite hat which he tossed on the bed in room 212 was a low crowned brown Stetson with a ring of Mexican silver coins around the band. For the trip he had worn denim pants, a blue shirt and a tan vest.

He unbuckled the wide leather gunbelt and draped it over the brass rail on the foot of the bed. In the leather rested his trusty Colt Peacemaker .45. It had a mother of pearl handle with a screaming eagle engraved on it, as well as more engraving on the barrel, cylinder and housing. He had taken it off an outlaw in New Mexico who no longer had any use for it. He found that the balance and fit suited him fine.

Spur McCoy was one of a small number of federal law enforcement officers who belonged to the United States Secret Service. The service was established by an act of Congress in 1865 with William P. Wood as its first and continuing chief. It began with the purpose of protecting U.S. currency from counterfeiting. Then as other problems came up, there were no other federal law officers, and the Secret Service gradually took on any law problems that could not be or was not being handled by local lawmen.

McCoy joined the service soon after the act was passed in 1865. He served for six months in Washington, D.C. before he was transferred to head the office in St. Louis where he became a force of one handling all problems west of the Mississippi. He found out he was chosen because he had been in the army and had won the service marksmanship contest. He was also the best horseman of the group.

He had just unbuttoned his vest and was wondering how he could arrange for a bath, when there was a knock on his door. Immediately a key unlocked it and a woman backed into the room carrying an armload of fresh linen. Once inside she pushed the door closed with her foot and then turned.

She was a pretty twenty-one, long red hair that flowed almost to her waist. Green eyes that sparked at him in a pert face with high cheekbones and a small nose and delicate chin. She dropped the linen by the door and put her hands on slender hips posing for him. She wore a tight white blouse and floor sweeping brown skirt.

"Mr. McCoy, is your room all right? If not, I'm here to fix it for you." She paused and grinned pointedly. "And to offer any other services which you might desire."

Spur smiled. He had been busy in Helena and had not had the company of a pretty girl for longer than he wanted to remember.

"Do you give baths?" he asked, his ruggedly handsome face breaking into a wide grin.

"Only if I get to have one too," she said.

"Good. How do we start?"

She popped the buttons open on her blouse and walked toward him. She was shorter than he was and reached up on tiptoe and pulled his face down and kissed his lips. Her blouse billowed open and her breasts peeked out. Spur's hand found one and she murmured in response. His hand rubbed the mound and he felt its heat singe his flesh.

"Do you want the bath before or after?" she asked, pulling her lips from his for a moment.

Spur picked her up and carried her to the bed. He put her down, spread her blouse and nuzzled her breasts, then kissed the heavy brown nipples.

"I think I want the bath in between somewhere."

She giggled and slipped the blouse off her shoulders and tossed it to the floor.

Spur moved to the door and braced the room's straight backed wooden chair under the doorknob. He pulled the blind down on the window and went back to the bed. She sat up, her breasts looking much larger now.

He sat down beside her. "What's your name?"

"Vivian. Call me Vi."

"Hi, Vi," he said and kissed her mouth. Spur felt her tremble. He came away. "You've made love before?"

"Oh, yes. I'm older than I look. Sometimes I see a man like you who just makes me melt. I want to run right up and undress in front of him. Is that bad?"

"Of course not. It could be dangerous for you, but not bad. It could get you in trouble."

"I can't get pregnant. I never will. I'm not right inside somehow. My husband threw me out. That was in Denver."

"I'm sorry."

"That was a year ago. I'm used to it now. He wanted six kids. He was a farmer. Needed boys, he said."

She unbuttoned Spur's shirt and ran her fingers through his thick mat of chest hair. "I adore a man with hair on his chest. I don't have any there."

"Good." He bent and kissed her breasts and she wailed, then her hips pumped and she pushed him down on the bed, her slender hips pounding a tattoo on him. Her cry came low and steady, like a call for more, a cry for something not possible. Tears welled out of her eyes, and she sniffled. She brought one of his hands up to her breasts.

In thirty seconds her sudden climax was over and she sat up, wiping the tears from her cheeks.

"My former husband hated that. Sometimes I get worked up and have to let it come out. Does that bother you?"

"No. I enjoy watching a woman have a climax. Do you really work here at the hotel?"

"Sure. That's why I have a pass key, and I get to use a room on the top floor unless we're all full, which ain't happened yet in a year."

Spur's hand moved to her breasts. He petted them and she purred like a kitten.

"Oh, Lord but that feels good! Just about the best feeling there is, I guess, for a woman. That is next to you being inside me, actually fucking." She looked up quickly. "My old man used to hit me whenver I said that word. You mind?"

"No."

She had his shirt unbuttoned and took it off. "This get you excited, my undressing you?"

"I was excited the minute you came into the room."

She smiled. He liked what it did to her face. She shook her shoulders and made her big breasts bounce and roll and jiggle. She watched him as she did it. "You like that?"

Spur bent and kissed both orbs. "There are men who like a girl's legs, and men who dote on a girl's breasts. Me, I'm a tit man."

Vi laughed. "Good. I can help out there. When I was growing up these things embarrassed me. And boys kept pawing at me and touching them. Now I'm glad I got big ones. God, would you kiss them again?"

Spur licked her nipples, then kissed them, and sucked half of one breast into his mouth. She gasped and then sighed and played with the long hair down his neck.

"That is soooooooo good! I love it!" She

pushed him away and stood. "Up here so I can take your pants off. I want to see your good stuff, too."

He stood and felt strange as she undid his belt and then opened his fly. She pulled down his pants and the short underwear he had on. His penis swung out like a big stick and she gasped, then giggled.

"Oh, yes! My goodness, such a big boy! We know just what to do to him to relieve that dangerous swelling!"

She pulled his boots off, then his pants and quickly stepped out of her skirt. She wore a pair of ladies drawers, tight at the waist, with loose legs that came to her knees. They were of white cloth with half a dozen pink ribbons on them. She lay down on the bed and held out her arms.

Vi was shivering.

He lay down beside her and held her in his arms. She rolled over until her body touched his all the way down, then she sighed.

"I still get worried," she said so quietly he could barely hear. "He rejected me so many times. I wanted him and he said it was useless, that I was useless, I should be a whore somewhere. I couldn't have kids so what good was I. Even now, when we're like this, I still worry. I mean . . . I mean . . . I wonder if you're going to laugh at me and send me away too."

"Your former husband wasn't a man. He didn't want a wife, he wanted a little bitch, he

30

wanted a country girl cow who he could breed every year for another free farm hand son. If I ever seen him I'll punch his eyes shut."

She snuggled closer to him. He could feel the heat of her body penetrating his own. She writhed against him and her hand found his erection. He petted her breasts and then kissed her, working his tongue into her mouth.

She sighed.

His hand worked lower to her drawers and slowly he rubbed along her leg, working higher.

"You don't actually have to seduce me, but it is nice," she said. She moved away from him, sat up and wiggled and slid the drawers off her hips and down her legs. She kicked them onto the floor and lifted up on her knees, her legs spread slightly.

"Here I am," she said.

A "V" of dark red hair clothed her crotch. Her hips were as sleek and slender as he had guessed.

"Come down here, I want you," Spur said, a husky wheeze filtering his words.

She yelped in delight and fell on top of him, then rolled over so he was on top.

"Darling, sweet man, please make love to me!"

Spur bent and sucked on each breast, then moved her hand to his erection and his own hand found her crotch.

31

She began talking, talking fast, not expecting any response. It was a defense mechanism Spur decided.

"I was a virgin when I married. Yes, I had been good, and careful, and lucky. Once one of my uncles came to the house when I was about sixteen and the folks were gone. He kept rubbing himself and started talking bad and told me what he was going to do for me. He would introduce me to the marvels of intercourse. I was frightened to death, but he was older and stronger than I was. He took his penis out of his pants and I almost fainted. I'd never seen one before. I hit him with a pan from the kitchen and ran next door to the neighbors."

Spur touched her crotch and she shivered. He delicately worked around her outer lips and she relaxed a little. Then he rubbed them and she sighed and whimpered in relief and delight.

"Oh, yes, darling. Yes, that's so good!"

He probed with one finger inside her and she screeched and climaxed again. He held his hand over her mouth as she yelled and bounced and humped for a solid minute before she tapered off.

Tears worked down her cheeks as she lifted up to kiss his lips. She lay down and stared at him.

"Oh, lord but you are tender! So thoughtful and loving. Why don't we just get married? Yes, for right now we are married and I don't need to hold back at all. Married! Yes and I can love you, and love you, and . . . fuck you!''

She began a steady stroking of his erection and he stopped her. She smiled.

"Just wondered if he was still loaded.''

Spur moved over her and she shook her head. She squirmed out from under him and got on her hands and knees. She pushed her hips up toward him, presenting her red love lips to him. Spur nodded and knelt behind her. The rear entry was quick and easy. She was more than ready.

As he penetrated her she wailed in pleasure. He couldn't get a hand over her mouth now. Half the guests in the hotel would know what was going on in room 212. Spur shrugged. There probably weren't that many registered.

He began moving slowly and she gripped him with hidden muscles on every stroke, and to his surprise was ''milking'' him. With that kind of encouragement it didn't take long to excite him.

Vi began to build before he did and soon she was shouting and wailing and moaning as if she were on fire. Soon she fell to the bed flat on her stomach and he went with her. The increased tightness drove his own desire to the exploding point and he planted his seed deep within her and then lay gently on top of her.

"You can squish me right into the mattress,'' she said. "I love the feeling.''

They lay there for ten minutes, then he got up and sat on the side of the bed. She sat up beside him, touching his chest with her hand, then stroking the side of his rugged jaw.

"You are simply perfect, Spur McCoy. Do you know that? There is nothing in the whole world like a good man! Nothing. I've known the other kind. When we get our clothes on after a while I will ask you to marry me. Why is it the man's place to do the asking? Not fair. A bath. Were you . . . us . . . we going to have a bath? I think so." She looked at him. Spur nodded.

"Yes, I know so. I better dress a little so I can get some bath water brought up. We do it right in our room here. No separate bathroom, which makes it nicer."

A half hour later Vi had made arrangements and a man brought a round wash tub and three buckets of hot water up to the room. He came back with a bucket of cold water and a big towel and a bar of soap.

"You first," Spur said, and Vi laughed and slid out of her skirt and blouse as he poured in two buckets of hot water and then half a bucket of cold.

Vi stepped in gingerly, then sat down and crossed her legs. She fit in the tub snugly. Spur began washing her and concentrated on her breasts. She laughed.

"Please don't wash them off. I'm going to need those tits to get you back to bed."

Spur laughed. "Sorry. I told you I'm a tit man."

He scrubbed her back, helped her wind her long red hair into a knot on top of her head so it wouldn't get wet. Soon it was his turn and they played for another fifteen minutes, adding the last of the hot water.

Vi washed his genitals carefully, then slowly she began to excite him. Minutes later he stood from the tub, grabbed her and walked her to the bed. They both tumbled on the sheets, wet and soapy and laughing.

They made love again, slowly, with all the tenderness and discovery of a wedding night. At last they lay on the sheets side by side, watching each other, talking softly, becoming more adult and more serious.

"I'm glad I broke in on you today," she said.

"I'm glad too."

"No, I mean because you are a good person. You didn't just use me, you let me participate, you let me enjoy the lovemaking too. I've never really had a chance to do that before."

They were silent a moment.

"You should have. Your husband should have helped."

"I know. Now, I know. I should go. There are a lot of beds to be made."

"Will you get in trouble?"

"No. The owner of the hotel understands. He doesn't bother me. But he expects me to go see him every Saturday night in his rooms."

"Oh. I could have a word with him."

"No. It's practical. I get by. I'll find someone who wants to take care of me. I've been here less than a year."

"Vi, I hope you find someone. I really do. You deserve something better than these one night flings."

Tears crept into her eyes. Vi blinked. "Thank you." She dressed slowly. Spur watched. When she was dressed he stroked her breasts through the material, then kissed her gently and led her to the door.

"Good bye, nice man," she said.

Spur dressed, checked the time by the Waterbury watch on a leather thong in his pocket. Almost due for supper. He dressed in fresh clothes, another pair of denims, blue shirt and his soft leather vest, then went downstairs to the dining room and had supper as soon as the place opened. He needed a good meal on his stomach because he planned to tour the saloons tonight on a fact finding trip. He wanted to be ready to do some drinking.

Chapter Four

Spur McCoy lifted his first lukewarm beer at the Silver Dollar Saloon. He sat at the bar and listened. He heard a little talk about the robbery and the murders, but the story was a week old by then. He stood near the poker and faro tables listening, but again heard nothing to help. Generally saloons were the best spots in town for the local gossip. Not this one.

He went by the sheriff's office and jail, but a deputy said the head man was home. He'd be in the office by eight the next morning unless something happened tonight and he was needed. Spur thanked the young man and hit another bar.

The Naked Lady saloon produced little more than the first one. He did learn that the two biggest ranchers in the area were the Box H and the Lazy L. Both were good sized operations with 20 to 30 hands. The rest of the ranches, about a dozen, were small and usually fighting the larger ones over one thing or another.

A notice tacked on a wall outside the next saloon advertised that the great Tom Ashworth and his traveling thespians would be in town the following month to present the greatest play in the English language, *Hamlet* by the bard himself, William Shakespeare.

The Secret Service man smiled, imagining the reception Hamlet's soliloquy would get from the raw and rought ranchers and townsmen. The actors would be lucky to get out of town alive.

It made him think back. He could have stayed in Washington with the service. That was more the life Spur had been used to. He had been born in New York City and went to Harvard in Boston graduating with the class of 1858. His father was a well known merchant and importer in New York City, and after college, Spur went to work for him. Then the war came and Spur joined the army with a commission as a second lieutenant, and advanced to a captain's rank before Lee surrendered. After two years in the army he was called to Washington, D.C. by Senator Arthur B. Walton, a long time friend of the family. He served as an aide to the senator for almost two years. Perhaps he should have stayed in Washington and the exciting life of high level politics.

He shrugged. He was contented. The life out here in the West was exciting and there was always something different happening. He saw the Last Chance saloon across the street where a drunk was being hustled to the boardwalk and pitched into the dust beside a wagon. Maybe there would be some action there.

Five dance hall girls circulated among the tables, accepting the pats and pinches with little more than a wince and bringing drinks when customers ordered them. All five were tired and no longer young. It seemed to be a slack night.

Spur ordered a beer in a mug and worked on it slowly as he absorbed the local culture. Again he learned almost nothing. It had been a long day, and the bouncing in a stage always left him bruised and exhausted.

Vi hadn't helped his energy level with her ministrations. He left the saloon, by-passed the last drinking and gambling establishment, the Pink Petticoat, and decided he could investigate that one the next day. He would get a good night's sleep and talk to the sheriff bright and early.

When he got back to the hotel room nobody was inside waiting for him. No pretty girl knocked on his door. Nobody shot at him through the window. He put the chair under the door knob again and went to sleep. The bed was a cross between a rock and a lumpy pine log, but at last he slept.

After a quick breakfast of ham and eggs and coffee, Spur went to call on the sheriff. Thurgood Quigley was not Spur's idea of the right kind of a sheriff for a town like this one. He sat in the office as the sheriff finished his breakfast at his desk. Spur had told the sheriff his connections, his authority, and asked the sheriff for total cooperation.

"Most impressive, Mr. McCoy. Your credentials. I've never met a Secret Service man before. Never even knew there were any. About the stage robberies. You said five of them. Quite right. I have it all on file. Mail taken and never found. Some important documents from what various townspeople have said. I trained as a lawyer, did I tell you that?"

"Yes, Sheriff, you did. Do you have any kind of a file on these robberies at all? Any suspects? Have you questioned anyone?"

"No. No clues. That's not my long suit, Mr. McCoy. But you get me a case in court and we'll win it every time!"

Spur looked out the window. "What you're telling me is that you have done nothing about a series of five robberies, the last of which resulted in six murders, including two women and a small boy?"

"Oh, I've asked questions." The small man in the black suit, black tie and black vest shifted in his chair. "It is just that I have no suspects."

"Have any other acts of violence taken place in the past week? Anyone shot, any houses burned down, any vigilante hangings?"

"I should say not! Nothing like that. We're a law abiding town." He paused. "Just that one hunter who shot himself when he dropped his revolver. Ridiculous little episode. Like I say, we're a small cow town trying to keep things pasted together. Times are getting hard. Banks having a tough time. One man I know in Chicago predicts we're going into a depression. He says it could last for five years."

"That's about when we'll solve this case. Do you have time to ride out to the scene of the crime with me?"

"Yes. When?"

"Right now. Let's go."

"Oh, well, I'll have to get my buggy hitched up."

Spur frowned. "You can't ride a horse?"

"Not when I can ride a buggy. Much easier on the back and kidneys. I'll meet you out front of the livery stable in five minutes."

An hour later Spur and the sheriff walked around the scene of the ambush and slaughter. Spur kicked several rifle casings from the dust in the road. Spencer repeating rifle casings. He pocketed them.

The charred remains of the stage had been dragged off the road and down a little slope by a team of horses. Near the same area lay the remains of the six horses. Parts of them had been torn off by predators and vultures. The exposed flesh was putrid and crawling with maggots. The stench was overpowering.

The sheriff left his rig and walked toward the remains.

"This coach has been deliberately burned," Spur said. "Not just torched and left. It's been tended, so more of it would burn. Why, Sheriff?"

"No idea, Mr. McCoy."

"And the horses were all shot in the head with rifle bullets. Why, Sheriff?"

"I don't know. Nor do I know why the robbers killed all six persons on the stage."

Spur nodded thinking out loud. "The shotgun guard and even the driver could have been shot in the ambush. But why the passengers? If the shotgun guard was killed in the first•attack, and the driver or one of the passengers identified one of the robbers, that could have been enough."

"Could they have been killed so they couldn't identify the robbers?" the sheriff asked.

"Possibly. It's the only reason I can see. You said one of the women was naked when found?"

"Yes, and the undertaker said she had been sexually attacked, raped."

"Well, now. It seems you know quite a little about this crime, Sheriff. All we need to know is who did it. Who found the bodies?"

"A cowboy coming along the trail looking for work. He came riding in like thunder and banged on my office door."

"The people on the coach related to anyone in the area?"

"The woman and her son. Her husband has

a small ranch out of town to the south along the Santiam. He had a cabin ready for them. They came over from Helena. The man on the stage was a hardware salesman, and we don't know anything about the young woman."

"The widower. Did he have any enemies who might do this?"

"Not possible. He's a quiet man, good natured, thrifty. No enemies as far as I know. It's simply a dead end. I don't know where to start."

"Doesn't look easy. I'll go talk with the widower. Do you have any bad apples in town? Anyone always looking for a fight? Maybe someone who has been losing too much gambling?"

"Not that I've heard about. When a newcomer rides into town it makes big news. We don't have a paper, and people tend to talk: We don't get many drifters. Nothing to come here for."

"So that means the robber and the killers must be people from right here in the community."

The sheriff walked back toward the trail where his buggy sat.

"I hadn't carried it that far, Mr. McCoy."

"Nothing else here I can see, let's get back to town. On the way I want you to tell me everything you know about the two big ranches. I don't see how they could fit in, but they might somehow. What are they, the Box H and Lazy L?"

The lawman told Spur the story of both ranches. The owner of the biggest was Henry Haworth, a large, tough man who came here twenty years ago and founded his empire. He bought land, and gambled for some more, and now the sheriff wasn't sure how much of the land he claimed that he actually owned.

"Haworth is something of a rascal, but he's never been in any real trouble with the law as I remember back near ten or twelve years. He and his wife have three grown sons. Must be 19 or 20 up to about 23. Abel, Cain and Lot. His wife is religious. The boys whoop it up in town now and then but no real problems. I'd say the youngest, Cain, is in town more than the other two.

"Two years ago we had a real dry summer and water got short in the Santiam. There was some talk about damming up the river and since Haworth is the ranch highest on the Santiam, he would get all the water. The ranchers down below talked about organizing and fighting for the water, but then along came three heavy rains about a week apart. and all the springs started running again and the problem was solved.

"I went out and checked out Haworth's place. He showed me the ditch he dug and where he would put some water if he needed to save it. Had a regular sluice gate built and put in so he could open it if he needed to. But that all blew over."

"Looks like it's been a dry summer here,"

44

Spur said. "Is the same problem coming up again?"

The sheriff frowned. "It might. But I'll have a ruling from the Territorial legislature before then."

"What about the other big rancher?"

"That would be Efrem Longley. Part of his Lazy L ranch is across the river from part of the Box H. Most of the Box H is north and upstream on the Santiam. Efrem is one of the nicest men I know. He's community minded. He's a smart, hard working rancher and a deacon in the town's only church. He's a good neighbor. Efrem and his wife have three daughters, about a year younger than the Haworth boys."

"Is Haworth overgrazing? Does he graze and control public lands out there?"

"Most big ranchers do. No law against grazing free range."

"But there is a law against controlling it, fencing it, running other people off it. Does Haworth do that?"

The sheriff sighed. "Indeed he does. We've had a complaint or two about homesteaders being run off. No real violence, but enough loud and angry talk so the peaceful kind move on. Haworth pushes the law as much as he can. I'm concerned now about the dry spell. It isn't as bad as it was two years ago, but the time is getting close. It's got to rain in the next two weeks or we're going to have trouble."

"Range war over water?"

"Some would call it that. It means big problems."

"I have enough work finding the killers of those six people."

They rode in silence for a while. The trail followed the Santiam the last half mile into town, and Spur saw that it was well below where the channel seemed to be. There was no "whitewater" now. The water moved slowly, and he could see rocks and water marks on the bank where the level once had been.

Spur couldn't help but ask the question that had been bothering him.

"Sheriff, I was wondering. You don't seem to like the law keeping end of the sheriff's job. Why did you run for the office?"

Sheriff Quigley chuckled. "I ask myself that same question every week or so. I'm a lawyer by trade. I figured it might help me get known if I got elected sheriff. Then after one term I'd open my law practice and be set. Only trouble is there isn't that much work in this little place for a lawyer, and there already was one here. Maybe I'm waiting for old Wilson to die. Then I like the little town, and just decided to say. Been elected four times now. Nothing much ever happens here. Not until now."

"Sheriff, we'll get this one solved and taken care of so High Prairie can go back to a quiet existence. I'll keep you informed of what I do and what I find out. We always work with the local lawmen whenever possible."

Spur could see appreciation in the small man's eyes.

"Thanks, Mr. McCoy, I am pleased you're here. I just don't have the first idea what to do or how to start finding them killers. I'm right proud you're helping."

At the livery, Spur put his rented horse away and hung up the saddle. The livery man had a message for the sheriff.

"Sheriff, Mr. Sullivan, the banker, said you should come and see him just as soon as you got back. He said it was important."

Chapter Five

Spur listened to the excited message the livery stable man gave to Sheriff Quigley. The lawman looked up at Spur.

"You better come along, McCoy. This banker isn't the kind to get worked up about most anything. It could be important. Seems to me he had a shipment coming in on that stage."

When the two men walked into the bank on the corner of Main and Firist, Marshall Sullivan marched around the high counter the teller used and greeted them with a determined, grim smile.

"Sheriff, I think we have something that reflects on the stage coach robbery." He said it quietly so only the two men could hear. "If you would come into my office." When Spur moved with the sheriff, the banker looked at him sharply. "This is for the sheriff only."

"If it's about the stage robbery, Mr. McCoy here is a part of the investigation," the sheriff said.

The banker nodded and led them into his partitioned off office where they had privacy. He took an envelope from the top locked drawer of his desk and let two double eagles slide out.

"Gentlemen these are brand new 1873 Liberty Head twenty dollar gold pieces. Uncirculated. See how shiny they are, with no nicks or gouges of wear."

Spur looked at them closely. They were uncirculated.

"These coins were due to go into circulation the first of August. All banks and institutions were told to hold the coins until that time."

"You got these on the stage from Denver?" Spur asked.

"We were supposed to get them. Our shipment of two hundred of these coins was on the stage that was robbed, the massacre stage."

The sheriff took another look at the coins. "I hope you know who brought these into the bank, Marshall."

"So far we have it narrowed down to two depositors. Right now we're checking our records to see which one made a deposit yesterday. We should know in a half hour."

"You think these coins came from the stage robbery loot, and that one of the robbers spent them in town," Spur said.

"I know the bankers in Helena. They would not release the coins early. Unless we had a traveler from the east where some banker gave them out early . . ."

"I'd say the chances are good that you have

found our first lead to the robbery, Mr. Sullivan. My congratulations."

As Spur shook the banker's hand, the sheriff introduced them.

"Mr. McCoy is with the United States Secret Service, Marshall. They keep track of our currency among other things."

A clerk came in with a note and Marshall read it and beamed.

"We did have a deposit yesterday. We're ninety-five percent certain that these two double eagles came from the Pink Petticoat saloon deposit."

Spur looked at the sheriff.

"Far as I know the saloon is owned and run by a woman. She's honest and fair. Never much trouble in her place. She has the best bouncer in town, and he keeps the place straight. From what I hear of her I'd say she had no part of the robbery."

"A customer then," Spur said. "Not a lot of men would spend forty dollars in a saloon. That's two months' wages for most of them. Somebody there might remember a big spender."

"Let's take a walk, Mr. McCoy. I'm beginning to enjoy this kind of investigation work. Marshall, I'll take these coins as evidence, but you'll get them back."

They went across the street and down half a block. It was the only saloon in town Spur hadn't checked out the previous night. It was open but almost deserted. The time was a little before noon.

Through the swinging batwing doors, Spur saw the usual western saloon: long bar with a brass rail on one side. The rest of the first floor was taken up with small tables with four chairs around each and a deck of cards waiting. There were three faro tables, and one for throwing dice. Nobody was gambling. One man sat at the bar.

Toward the back was an open staircase that led sharply up to the second floor. Spur guesed the girls would be up there catching up on their sleep before the day's trade began coming in again about five that afternoon.

The barkeep looked up and nodded when he recognized the sheriff.

"Morning, Sheriff, haven't seen you in here for quite some time."

"This is official, Barry. The lady around?"

"In back, I'll tell her you're here. She don't like surprises. Got a minute?"

The sheriff nodded and they sat down at one of the poker tables. Spur picked up the cards and began dealing. He figured it would take any lady ten minutes to get presentable.

It took her twenty. They had played ten hands of seven card showdown poker, and the sheriff won seven of them.

"You should take up gambling," Spur said.

"My luck vanishes when there's money on the table," the small man said smiling.

She came around the end of the bar with a firm step in a business-like dress that any of the matrons in town might wear, tight around the throat, full over the bodice and

51

long sleeves. The lady was about thirty-five and still had a good figure. She was taller than Spur expected, maybe five-seven, and her black hair fell loosely around her shoulders.

Spur stood at once frowning, then he looked closer and began to smile. She was watching the sheriff as she came up and had given Spur only the briefest of glances.

"You always did say you wanted to own your own gambling saloon," Spur said as she stopped in front of them. She looked at him, her polite smile changing to a big grin.

"Spur McCoy! Where in hell did you come from?"

She took two steps and was in his arms, planting a big kiss on his cheek. He hugged her tightly, then let go and she stepped back.

"Spur, it must have been four years. Arizona. Oh, do I remember that last shoot-out! I still say you were lucky that I was along with my .44."

"I was lucky all right." He turned to the sheriff. "I knew this lady before," he said.

"I figured that," the sheriff said with a smile. "Miss Claudine, if you would sit down, I have some official business. Hate to interrupt a reunion, but duty calls."

"Yes, of course." She held Spur's hand as he led her to the chair and sheriff positioned for her. The men sat down and the sheriff took the envelope from his pocket. There was no one else in the saloon who could hear what they said.

"These two coins were deposited in the bank by your business. Oh, they are genuine, too genuine." He explained to her about the release date of the coins, and the possibility that they were stolen from the massacre stage coach.

"My god! You mean one of my customers might be the killer? The same one who shot those two women and that little boy?"

"It certainly looks that way, Claudine," Spur said. "As you might have figured out, I'm here to find the killers, and get the mail circulating again."

She was resilient, nodding slowly. "Yes, I understand. We do have a big poker game from time to time. Forty dollars. One of the girls might know, or Barry. Let me ask him."

"We need to keep this absolutely secret," Spur said. She nodded and came back a minute later.

"Barry says he can't remember any one person giving him two double eagles over the past two or three days. But he'll watch for those 1873 issue coins from now on. Right now he figures it could be any one of about thirty men."

The sheriff stood. "I need to get back to the office. We will work together on this robbery, won't we, Mr. McCoy?"

"Yes, absolutely."

"Fine." He waved his hat at Claudine, nodded to Spur and walked out the front door.

Claudine caught Spur's hand and they both

stood at the same time.

"I think it's time we had a small celebration. Reunions between old friends like this don't happen very often." She led him toward the back, down a hall and to a door marked PRIVATE. She took a key from a hidden pocket, opened the door and locked it as soon as they stepped inside.

The room was plush looking, like the inside of one of those luxury hotel rooms in New York. A thick rug covered the floor. The walls were decorated with pictures and drapes of expensive silk cloth. An overstuffed sofa sat to one side and a matching chair beside it. Both had been covered in an expensive silk material with fancy embroidery.

To one side sat a stylish writing desk that was open and a file folder and several envelopes near by.

In the center of the room hung a chandelier, one of the old cut glass types with holders for thirty candles.

She paused for a moment to allow him to examine the room, then pulled him forward.

"Wait until you see my bedroom. It is really something."

It was. For a moment Spur thought he had been magically transported into the Arabian Knights. The room looked like the inside of a sultan's tent. A four poster bed huddled at one side of the fifteen-foot square room. The bed was draped with silks and satins. The top of the bed over the four posts was a delicate combination of embroidered silks and swatches of fancy silk, loosely folded and braided into an intricate pattern.

A rug twice as thick as that in the living room spread from wall to wall. The floor was strewn with big harem pillows, and the walls were all covered in fabric, loose and swaying. The scent of incense burned filling the air. He noticed that there were six lamps situated around the room to provide light. That's when he realized the room did not have a window. Light came through a skylight that had been covered with glass. It gave the room a soft, filtered look that enhanced the atmosphere.

"Wow!" Spur said.

"Thanks, that was the nicest thing you could have said. Now do I get a real kiss?"

She flowed into his arms and Spur let the heat of her body's desire pour into him. It triggered memories of Arizona and the frantic, fantastic week they had spent together. As they kissed he picked her up and sat down on the bed.

"Now I think you're starting to get the idea," she said, her eyes still closed, her lips nibbling at his lips, then clamping firmly on his mouth again.

His hands found her breasts and he remembered the upthrust beauties in the buff, marvelously formed, sensitive to his touch. He caressed them and she moaned in delight, then she pulled away from him and spun around.

"Yes, my darling, wonderful Spur. But first I feed you. I remember how much stronger you are after a good meal. Will a half raw steak and a quart of beer suit you?"

He nodded and watched as she unbuttoned the dress and pulled it over her head. Under it she wore a pink chemise that came to her waist, with delicate straps over her shoulders, and her thrusting breasts unrestrained under it. Her petticoats were pink, and he could see at least three of them.

That was when he remembered that she loved to cook almost as much as to make love. And she was an expert at both.

She peeled off one of the petticoats to reveal another one beneath it. "Come on, big guy, let's go into my kitchen and get the steaks started. If you see anything you like, you can chew on it a little as an appetizer."

Her kitchen was eight feet square with a large kitchen range at one side fitted with a hot water coil and reservoir. At the other side she had an ice box that held a chunk of ice they must have cut during the winter and held over in an ice house with lots of straw. The ice bow kept food cool and cold without spoiling.

Claudine took an inch-thick steak ten inches across and put it in a frying pan. Then she stoked the fire and let the meat start to brown in the pan.

Spur reached around her from the back

and clamped one hand over a bare breast. He felt the warmth of the mound.

"Now here is what I like," he said. She twisted in his arms and kissed him, thrusting her tongue deep into his mouth as she did and then retreating. He lifted the chemise off over her head and her breasts swung out as if eager for action.

"Tits!" he said in awe. "Claudine, you have the best set of tits in the whole world!" He took one in his mouth, his tongue fighting with her nipple and Claudine groaned and sagged against him. Then she turned and with a free hand flipped the steak to the other side in the skillet.

"Brown on the outside, red and raw inside. Isn't that the way my man likes his meat?"

Spur laughed. "Steaks that way, but my woman I like as naked as the day she lost her virginity."

Claudine squealed in mock terror and stepped out of another petticoat. She danced away from him and quickly set a small table by a heavily curtained window. Then she came back with a slow wiggle with her hips that left Spur panting.

"Christ, what a decision, do I eat you first or the steak first?"

She danced toward him quickly, holding up one breast for his mouth. He bent and accepted it and she pushed against him again, her hand sneaking to his crotch and finding the hardness inside his pants. She rubbed it a dozen times, then pulled away and checked the steak. She moved the skillet back off the hottest part of the stove and put a lid on it.

"You have two minutes," she said.

"Plenty of time," Spur said. He jerked down the last petticoat and then her silk drawers. She stood naked in front of him, one foot at right angle to the other, her chest high and thrust forward, the glistening fur over her crotch dark black like her hair.

"If you see anything you like . . ."

He grabbed her and pushed her against the wall, spreading her legs with a sweep of one hand.

"Right here?" she asked surprised.

He nodded, his fuse burning shorter.

"Anytime you're ready, I'm ready, big lover!" she said. "The gate is wide open, come on inside."

He ripped open his fly and pulled out his shaft.

"Oh, my!" she said. "I had forgotten what a telegraph pole you keep in those britches. "Come on!"

He bent, positioned and thrust. He tried again and then she moved slightly and moaned as he slid into her, his sword into her scabbard as if they had never been apart.

"What do we do now?" she asked and laughed softly. It was an old joke between them.

He showed her. The unnatural position

compensated a little for his full head of steam. But still she began building before he did. When he sensed her almost over the edge he stopped his thrusting, and let her cool off. Then he punched upward again and again, until she was panting and almost ready. He stopped again, pushing fully into her hot enclosure, waiting for her to recover.

The third time she would not be denied. She surged past him and grunted and groaned as she tried to thrust down against him and at last the tremors drove through her again and again until she was spent and ruined for a time.

Her climax triggered his own pent-up desire and he plowed hard into her, lifting her frame off the floor and bringing her to a new rush of emotional release.

Spur thrust again and exploded into her, their pelvic bones grating against each other as he pressed her hard against the wall as his body gave the final spasms of desire.

Her arms came around him quickly.

"If you move for five minutes I'll kill you!" she said.

Both were panting now, with air gushing from them into the air. They heard the steak spitting and sizzling in the iron skillet, but neither could move to take it off the fire.

At last her arms loosened, and he bent his knees coming away from her. She walked to the bedroom and he moved the steak off the fire.

She was back in a minute, still naked, wearing the biggest smile he had seen in months.

"Sir, your woman and your steak are both ready."

Spur laughed softly. It was Arizona all over again. "I think I'll try the steak this time. But it couldn't be half as good as my woman."

Chapter Six

Spur McCoy put down his knife with his right hand and speared the choice bit of tender, blood red steak with the fork in his left hand and put it in his mouth. For just a moment he closed his eyes as his tastebuds luxuriated in the delicate flavor of the juices from the succulent meat.

"Chef Rene in New York's Savoy hotel could not have cooked it better," Spur said looking up at the deep brown eyes that watched him eating. Claudine was still naked, her breasts resting on top of the small table where she sat relishing every moment of his feast.

Her face showed three pleased expressions, then dancing eyes steadied. "As good as your woman?"

"Almost as good," he said. Spur reached over and kissed her and opened his mouth to share the bit of steak. She sucked some of it into her mouth and smiled as she chewed. There was only one man she would do that with. It was the most personal of all intimacies.

She nodded. "Almost as good."

They both laughed. He stood, as naked as she was. She moved beside him, her arms wrapped around his back her breasts pressing hard into his chest, her crotch pushing against his upper legs.

"Come. Remember in Arizona we ran out of new positions. Have you ever tried 'splitting the reed?'"

Spur shook his head.

"It's kind of wild. I'm on my back with one leg straight up in the air and you kind of upright with my leg on your shoulder and my other leg down flat."

"Show me," he said.

"I was really hoping you would say that."

They made soft sweet love three more times that afternoon, and Spur got to the printer in time to talk him into making up forty hand bills before he quit for the day. The posters were the usual size, twelve by twenty. They all said:

FEDERAL LAW OFFICER

Now in High Prairie to gather evidence for prosecution of killers of 6 persons on stage coach a week ago. Have definite proof on two killers, need more. Anyone spotting anyone riding into town July 15, contact me at Plainsman Hotel today from 1 to 5 P.M. Room 212. Full protection to all who testify.

He took the handbills and with a box of

thumb tacks posted them on forty of the most favorable walls and posts in town. It was just before dark when he got the last one put up. Already there was a lot of talk in town about the posters. He stopped in two of the saloons and heard all kinds of wild stories. No reward had been offered but he heard several men say they would testify anyway. Nobody should shoot down two women that way, especially the pretty one.

Spur nodded with the majority and went to his room up the back stairs. There was no one outside his door, but he expected company soon. He got into his room, jammed the chair under the door and then made a dummy and put it in his bed so in the darkness it appeared that a man was sleeping. He left the lamp burning on low wick and settled down on a blanket to one side of the window that opened onto a porch over Main Street.

He drifted off at once, but snapped awake. His Waterbury showed that it was slightly after midnight. He nodded again but came awake when the window near him slid up quietly. Spur picked up his already cocked .45 Eagle Butt Peacemaker and waited. A moment later hands appeared, then a head and shoulders as someone came through the window.

The intruder squirmed into the room over the sill, landing on his hands on the floor two feet below the opening. He brought in his feet and stared at the bed. As silently as death his hand brought up a six-inch knife and he held it like a sabre. Clearly the man had used a knife before. He checked the door, then moved on silent feet toward the bed.

He thrust the first time with all the power of his body behind it, striking what he thought was a broad back. The knife went in and he pulled it out and jabbed it twice more into the dummy on the bed. Spur shot him in the right leg and kicked the knife from his hand.

When the booming roar of the .45 faded in the room, Spur could hear the killer wailing.

"Help me! I'm bleeding to death. Stop the blood!"

Spur turned up the lamp, couldn't remember seeing the man around town, and shook his head.

"You tell me who hired you to kill me, and I'll stop the blood. Otherwise, you die right there on the floor in about five minutes."

"Oh, Christ! Don't do that. I can't tell. He said he'd kill me. Oh, Christ, no!"

The would-be killer was a head shorter than Spur, unshaven, dirty, wearing torn range pants and a tattered blue shirt.

"How much did he pay you?" Spur asked.

"Forty dollars. Then forty more when they find you dead in the morning."

"Double Eagles?"

"Yeah."

"Give them to me."

The man swore and handed them over. In

the light Spur could read the date: 1873.

"Eight dollars to kill a man? I must not be very tough."

"Stop the blood!

"Who set me up!"

"I don't know. It was dark, in back of the livery. Guy said to do it and come right back tonight and he would give me the other forty tonight and I could ride out of town."

"If you had gone back there he would have killed you," Spur said.

It was a chance, but all he had. He bent and tied the man's hands behind his neck, put a bandage on the leg wound, stopping the flow of blood. Then Spur tied the ambusher's feet together and cinched up his ankles to his hands, pulling them up tight behind his back.

"Stay there," Spur said. He took the man's hat and his knife and went out the hotel room into the hall. Only one man was there looking down the hall.

"Gun went off when I was cleaning the damn thing," Spur said. The man grunted in sympathy and went back to bed.

It took Spur ten minutes to move from shadow to shadow to the back of the livery stable. There was a chance this second man was also hired, but it was a risk he had to take.

He went into the blackness behind the livery and just this side of the big corral. Nothing. He paused and waited, every one of his thousands of pores and nerve endings reaching for some kind of signal. Nothing.

He moved to the far side of the darkness and crouched, waiting, with his pistol cocked and ready and six rounds in the chamber.

Twenty minutes later he saw movement at the side of the livery. Someone staggered around the corner into the blackness waving a bottle. Then came the sound of breaking glass and the man swore. He sang a dirty little song and then fell against the wall.

Two minutes later a voice sober and cautious whispered.

"Are you there?"

"Yeah," Spur whispered. "I done it."

"Good, come on over here."

Spur could almost see the man snaking the gun out of his belt.

"You come over here," Spur said and rolled silently six feet away from the barn.

The twin flashes of gunpowder around the cylinder and out the muzzle of a six-gun showered the darkness with small streaks of light that were gone almost before the eye could record them.

Spur was ready with his iron up. He tracked in one the flashes, shooting just below them and slightly to the right, giving allowances for a right-hander. He fired twice. The sound of a bullet hitting flesh was unlike any Spur had ever heard, something between a thonk on a watermelon and the sound of the same round hitting water. Both rounds struck home.

"Oh my god! I'm dying!" The man screamed, then he fell.

Spur waited almost five minutes before he moved. No one had come to investigate the shots or the screams. The other man had not moved. Spur went across the open ten yards in a rush and found the body where he thought it would be. There were two rounds near the heart. The man was sprawled backward on his side. Spur found two more double eagles in his pocket. He took them for checking later, but he was sure they would be 1873 double eagles. Wearily he went to find a deputy and show him where the body was.

The deputy on duty nodded as he looked at the man.

"Gus Talmage, a rummy who does odd jobs. He's never rated high enough to be a bushwhacker before. He must have been moving up in the world."

"This is as far as he goes," Spur said. "Tomorrow he goes down, six feet down."

Spur filled out a sudden death statement and said he would check with the sheriff in the morning. As he sat there he flipped two double eagles in the air and caught them. Both were 1873, uncirculated. Now the killer had spent six of them.

Back at Spur's hotel room the deputy took charge of the attempted murder suspect and called Doc Varner out of bed to patch up his thigh. The sawbones was unhappy at the wake-up call and did not treat the prisoner with tenderness.

"Next time you try to kill somebody, young feller, you do a better job of it, then you won't get shot and I won't have to come dig out the damned bullet."

Before Doc was done probing the drunk had stopped screaming, but only because he had passed out.

It was after two in the morning when Spur went back to the hotel, hired another room under a phony name and slept until eight in the morning.

His mouth felt like somebody had slept in it. He had three cups of coffee, a breakfast steak and hashbrown potatoes and an apple, and still he was hungry. Missing sleep always made him hungry. At least his wanted poster had stirred up some comment. He didn't expect much more from it. The real killer had struck and shown his hand. But Spur knew he should be back to check out the locals this afternoon, just in case. That would leave him time to make the ride out of the widower's place and to the Lazy L ranch on the way back. Time, that is, unless he ran into unexpected problems. The sheriff would want to talk about the dead man last night as well as the wounded man Spur dumped in his office after Doc Varner had finished with him.

Chapter Seven

Spur picked up directions to the widower's ranch at the sheriff's office. It was a six mile ride south of town, and close to the banks of the Santiam, the life blood of this region. The man's name was Ivan Johnson, he was forty-two years old and the sheriff said he was devastated by the loss of his family. He had left them in Helena so they would be safe and have it easier during the winter until he could get a proper house raised for them.

It was one of those visits Spur knew he had to make. From what everyone said it would be totally non-productive, but it was his job, and he was going to do it. The ride out to the ranch was pleasant. The sun played tag with a few high scattered clouds but none of them spelled rain. Spur could see how the size of the little river did not grow as he moved downstream. It barely held its own, and in places looked to be on the verge of drying up. Then new springs would bring it back to life.

The drought was worse than he had thought.

No one answered Spur's knock on the Johnson place door just before ten o'clock that morning. He went out to the barn and found no one. He saw a few cattle in a pasture another mile south and rode down.

A man in overalls and a railroad cap sat on the bank of the stream throwing rocks in the water.

"Sir, could you help me find Ivan Johnson?"

"Me," he said without looking up.

Spur got down from his horse and introduced himself. The man looked older than forty-two. He was gaunt, unshaven but not with a beard. His eyes were red and his hair was tangled under an old hat.

"Mr. Johnson. It's my job to help find the men who killed your family and robbed the stage. I'm going to find them before I leave the county. Do you know of anything that might help me?"

Johnson shook his head, then threw a stone in the water.

"Was someone trying to hurt you by attacking your family?"

"No. Nobody cares that much about us. We're new here."

Spur pressed on, asking the questions he had to, and in the end came up with exactly nothing to help the case. He thanked the man for his help, mounted up and rode north again. He had seen a sign pointing to the Lazy L ranch, just out of town, but noticed that it pointed north of the village instead of south. So he would have to retrace his steps to find the Longley clan. This was not going to be his best day.

Spur pushed the roan and came into the Lazy L about 12:30. With any luck they would not have finished dinner yet and invite him to take a plate. He was surprised to hear the dinner bell ring as he came into the ranch yard.

It was impressive, with three barns, several outbuildings, and a big ranchhouse, a separate cookshack and dining hall for the hands. Two bunkhouses flanked the dining hall.

A hand rode to meet him as he entered the building area.

"Howdy. You're that detective guy I heard about in town," the hand said. "Reckon you want to talk to the boss man. Tie up over yonder and I'll take you up to the big house."

Spur tied his horse and went up to the house. He had put on his formal range wear, a pair of brown pants, a brown lightweight jacket, white shirt and string tie. Now he was glad he had.

Someone stood behind the screen, at the back door waiting. The man was about five-ten, with silver-gray hair that had been black, and a still black moustache and goatee. His eyes crinkled as he smiled and held out his hand.

"I'm Efrem Longley, you must be that detective guy."

Spur took the offered hand, felt the

71

hardness of the skin and healed blisters, and smiled.

"Yes, sir, Mr. Longley. I'm Spur McCoy. Could I have a word or two with you?"

"Dinner time, young man. Us Longley's don't talk much when we eat. Welcome to sit down to the table with us. Be a treat for everybody. Come right in. You can use the vestibule there to wash the dust off your hands, you want to."

Spur said he would and found a table with a bucket of water and a crockery wash basin, dipper, mirror and a line-up of six towels. He washed his hands, combed his moustache and hair and dried on the first towel. Outside the open door he saw a flash of skirt and then it was gone.

Longley met him at the door.

"Right this way and I'll introduce you."

Spur was not ready for what he saw. In the kitchen around the big varnished plank table were four pretty women. One of them had to be the mother, but he was hard pressed for a moment to pick her out. Longley rescued him by introducing her and then naming his daughters.

"The first filly there on the left is Delilah. She's eighteen, and a mite shy. Next is Mary, who is nineteen and wants to be a schoolmarm or some such. My eldest is Bathsheba who we all call Bee, and she can ride and rope better than I can." The girls were all pretty, but Delilah was going to be the beauty.

72

Mary was a little aloof and cool, and Bee had a glint in her eye he had seen before. His place was between Bee and Delilah and Mary was just as happy.

"We're having a party next month, Mr. McCoy, a coming out party for the girls, just like they have back east. I'm inviting all the girls eighteen to twenty-one in the county to be my guests and we'll have an all night dance and announce to the whole country that these lovelies are now ready for marriage."

"Daddy, that's not what it's supposed to be," Mary said. "In New York they have the coming out party to introduce the young ladies to formal society."

"Society, hell. We don't have one here, just the business of getting my daughters married off proper. I told you, the one who claims the best son-in-law will be the one to take over the Lazy L spread."

Mrs. Longley nodded to Spur, and he had a feeling she was used to being left out of things, and that she didn't mind one whit.

Spur soon got the conversation shifted to the weather and the dry land. They ate enough food for an evening meal, roast chicken, corn on the cob, fresh peas and potatoes, and even some early tomatoes and big slabs of fresh baked bread and currant jelly. And pots of coffee.

"What happens if the river dries up, Mr. Longley?" Spur asked.

"If the river goes, I lose all my cattle. Them critters got to drink. Each one needs twenty gallons of water a day. That's a lot of water for five or six thousand head. Course, they all ain't right here. But if the river dries up, the only reason will be because that criminal upstream, Haworth, has shut it off. You heard about the sluice gate he's got? He could change the course of the river anytime he wants to, make it all flow over his land, and I couldn't get a drop of water."

"Mr. Longley, I don't think he would do that. There are laws about rivers. Under normal conditions the upper owner on the river may not deprive the lower owner his fair share of the water for drinking by man and his animals. Each owner along the length of the river is guaranteed enough water for his cattle."

"What happens if it does dry up?"

"That would be called an act of God, and every owner would suffer his losses. But one man can't take all the water and leave the downstream ranchers with none."

"Damn right, I been telling that no good Haworth that for two years. He says what he's got, is his."

"Now, Mr. Longley, you know that this means you have to respect the rights of the ranchers below you. Even if you have to let some of your stock die from thirst, you have to allow enough water through so each rancher below can save the same percentage of his herd that you are saving."

"This is going to get damn difficult. But if there's trouble it will be that damn Haworth. We had a run-in the first day I homesteaded here, and we been clawing at each other ever since."

Longley finished his meal and leaned back. "Glad we got that settled. Now, about the important matters. Which of my darling daughters do you cotton to? All of them are available. Why not pick out one right now before the rush of courting starts?"

"Father, really!" Mary said.

Bee, the oldest, winked at Spur and her father roared. "That's Bee, she'd be a handful for any man. By jingles, I know what we can do! Why don't you have a little courting session with each of my girls right now? Fifteen, twenty minutes in the parlor. Even close the door! See which one you like the best. Sure, I know, you're busy. But you brought such good news about the law and the water, I want to make it up to you."

Spur laughed at the discomfort Mary showed. "We could make it a kind of training. Your girls could practice on me, knowing it doesn't count. How would that be, Mr. Longley?"

"Hell, yes! Mother, you get the cold apple cider and put it out in the parlor, and some of those little cakes. We'll go in order—Bee first before she pops her britches!"

Spur thought Mary was going to bolt out of the room, but she sat and waited her turn. Bee was up and waiting for him. She linked her arm though his and walked him into the parlor.

The heavily varnished door shut with a loud click behind them and Spur had a sense that the parlor was kept closed off most of the time, and used only for special occasions. It smelled a little musty and cool. Bee was neither. She led him to a small love seat with room for two that faced the side wall. The back was to the only door and he helped her sit down, then sat beside her.

At once she leaned in and kissed him, a hot, demanding kiss that soon led to her tongue darting into his mouth. She came away smiling.

"Does that surprise you?"

"A little."

"Papa thinks I'm still a virgin," she said softly and caught one of his hands and put it over her breasts. "Pet them," she said. "Pet them or I'll scream and get you in trouble."

His hand moved over her breasts.

"No, inside!" she said, unbuttoning two of the fasteners.

Her hand slid in with his and pulled aside a garment and his hand closed around her left breast.

Bathsheba sucked in a long breath and shivered in a small climax that froze her face in glory for a moment. Her hands touched his crotch.

"You don't mind if I feel around, do you?" she said and before he could answer she had opened his fly buttons and her hand wormed through his underwear to his stiff manhood.

"Oh, yes, he's so ready! I wish we could do it right here! Right now!"

"No! I don't want to get shot."

She nodded. "Daddy might." She pressed his hand against her breasts again as she wiggled and a tremor swept through her. Then she took his hand out of her blouse, fastened the buttons and pushed his hand under her skirt. "I almost never wear drawers. See!"

His hand found her soft, bare inner thigh and she pushed it higher. "I have an idea," she said. "Do you have a long finger?" He nodded.

"Go ahead, poke me with that!" Then she worked at his crotch and soon had his penis out and standing tall. "If you hear the door jiggle or the latch turn, you pull me up, all right?"

Spur looked at her in surprise, then she bent down and took his erection in her mouth.

"Now I'll really be shot!" Spur said, trying to lift her up. She wouldn't budge, but kept working her mouth up and down on his manhood. She pushed his hand farther under her skirt and Spur found the wetness and drove his finger into her a dozen times, then came out, lifted her away from his throbbing, purple erection and pushed it roughly back into his pants. He buttoned up his fly just

77

before the door rattled, and Mr. Longley strode into the room.

They both looked at him over the back of the padded loveseat.

"Well, I hope you two got to know each other a little. Time is up. Mary is next."

"Good luck, she won't even touch you," Bee whispered. "Just talk, but watch out for little sister, she's getting hot panties again."

Bathsheba stood. Spur stood. He took her hand, thanked her for the enjoyable talk, and she walked out past her father.

Spur felt a touch of sweat on his forehead, and realized how close he had come to filling a newly dug grave.

Mary whispered with her father for a moment, then came in with a scowl.

Spur let her sit down and he stood.

"Mary, I realize this is awkward for you. Why don't you tell me what you want to do with your life? Your father mentioned teaching school. Would you like that?"

She brightened. "Oh, yes! Of course I would need a year of normal school over at Helena, but then I'd be fully qualified. We haven't had a qualified teacher at High Prairie ever. I want to help this country grow, and the best way is to educate our people. I've got lots of books and I read all the time."

Spur let her talk for five minutes, then he sat down beside her. "When I talk with your father, I'll suggest that he send you to normal school. Every town needs a good teacher."

"Oh, would you? I would be ever so grateful." She surged toward him, kissed his cheek and half fell against him pushing her breasts on his chest, then realizing what she had done, she eased back a little. She stayed close to him. "Mr. McCoy, you may kiss me if you wish." She turned her lips to him and he kissed her gently, then moved her away from him.

She still had her eyes closed.

"Mary . . . Mary," he called softly.

Her eyes popped open. "Oh my, that felt so nice! You are the first man I've ever kissed. I did like it. Now I see what Bathsheba is always talking about." She blinked. "But you said you would talk to Father about my going to school. I would be ever so grateful."

Soon the knob rattled and Mr. Longley came in with his youngest, the beauty, Delilah. The girls were all dressed much the same, in modest, but tightly fitting print dresses with long sleeves and high buttoned necks. And they all were clean, sweet smelling and big busted girls. Delilah sat down beside him and smiled.

"Would you like to kiss me?" she said softly.

"No," he said.

She scowled. "Lots of boys want to kiss me. I told them to ask Papa." She turned back smiling. "But you can kiss me if you want to."

Spur leaned in toward her but she leaned away.

"But not until after we talk. Are you staying here long? Have you ever been married? Where did you go to school? How did you turn out to be so handsome?"

He laughed softly at her. "You're scared to pieces, aren't you, Delilah? You don't know what might happen if I kiss you. So just relax. Mary wants to be a teacher. What do you want to do?"

"Get married, I guess. That's what most girls do. Get married and have babies and get fat and get old and die. It does all seem a little pointless, doesn't it?"

"Depends. A lot of wonderful, beautiful, amusing, exciting things can happen almost every day of your life, if you let them happen, if you look for them, watch for opportunities. Like right now. Have you ever been kissed?"

"No. Mama says I should wait and let the boy I'm going to marry kiss me."

"But wouldn't it be exciting, right now?"

Her eyes widened. "Right here? With Papa right out there listening?"

"Kisses are usually rather quiet."

"I don't know."

"Think about it. Now close your eyes." The second she closed her eyes, Spur leaned in and kissed her lips gently, just a brush and moved back.

She opened her eyes. "Was that a kiss?"

"One kind of a kiss."

"Oh! There are different kinds?"

"Yes. Keep your eyes open." He leaned in again and kissed her lips harder this time, and put his arm around her and pulled her tightly against his chest until he could feel her breasts flatten as he held her close. Then slowly he let go of her and eased away from her lips.

"That was a more serious kind of kiss."

"Oh!" Her face was blank. Then she smiled. "I really liked the last one. Could we do that agin?"

The door rattled and opened and they swayed apart as her father came into the room. Spur saw that Delilah was a little flushed, but she stood easily, nodded to her father and walked out of the room.

"Well, well. My little ladies all seemed impressed with you, Mr. McCoy. Remember, you can come courting any of them, at any time."

Spur made his thanks and thanked Mrs. Longley for the dinner and then walked out to the hitching rack with the rancher.

"You go see old Haworth. Tell him about my legal right to water for my stock, and make sure he understands. That way maybe we won't have any trouble. You seen how that water level has been dropping. We need some rain, and damn soon."

Spur told the rancher he would go visit with the other big rancher just as soon as he figured out the murders.

81

Then he paused. "I hope you consider letting Mary go to Helena to go to normal school. She·says the only thing she wants to do is be a teacher. It's an honorable and much needed profession. Consider it." They shook hands and Spur rode back to town. It had been quite a noon time. His watch showed that it was only a little past 1:30. He would have time to talk to some of the people in his room who answered his broadsides . . . if anyone did. Somebody would respond, even if it was a person with no help for him. He rode faster.

Chapter Eight

Two men and a woman waited outside his room when Spur walked down the hall at the Plainsman Hotel. None of them looked dangerous.

"Are you folks here about the stage coach massacre?"

They all nodded.

"Are you together?"

"No," the woman said.

Spur unlocked the door and invited her inside. He left the door open. She looked at it to make sure it stayed open, then sat down in the chair he provided her.

Five minutes later he was sure she knew nothing about the robbery. He thanked her and she left, smiling.

The first man had seen three men riding into town. One of them was draped over his saddle.

"Was that the hunting accident?"

"What he claimed. Knew that boy. Never did like to hunt. I don't think he was hunting at all. Them ones he was with is kind of nocounts themselves. I'd damn sure check out the three of them. Three could rob a stage."

"But then ride into town with a dead man? That doesn't sound logical." Spur watched the informant closely.

"Hell, yes it does." the man said. He was about forty. Spur had seen him in one of the taverns. "Had me a sheriff's job once down Texas way. Learned what some of these outlaws do, how they think. See, if they come right into town, and claim they got shot hunting, nobody would think a thing. Got to cover up the man getting gut shot and killed somehow. Makes sense."

Spur nodded. "Damned if it don't. What is your name?"

"Udell. Ty Udell. I ain't had work in a spell."

Spur nodded. "Maybe you could work for me for a bit."

"Detective work? Damn sure!"

"Stand over there by the window while I talk to this next man. Keep a watch out to the street and see if anybody is interested in this room."

"Yes sir!"

The last man in the line was drunk. He apparently had been that way for some time.

"Sure, I had a drink, but I know what I saw. Day of the massacre, I saw me one kid come hightailing it into town. He damn near killed his horse. It was all lathered up and he didn't even walk it out. He came up the alley and almost run me down. Didn't even bother to look at me. Jumped off his horse and boiled

84

into the back door of the Pink Petticoat. That's how the gents get up to the girls when they don't want everybody to see them. I had the job of walking out his damn horse, and when he came back he didn't even give me a nickel. Told him I walked the nag, and he kicked at me and walked up Main Street."

"Who was the kid?"

"Don't recall, but I might know in the morning."

"You have a good sleep and try to remember. You think on it, it could be worth a dollar to you."

"A whole dollar? I ain't seen one of them for a spell."

Spur showed him out and sat looking at the wall. He had heard about the hunting death. He'd have a talk with the sheriff about it. Then he had to take a ride on up north and see the Haworth clan. Another busy work project. But he had to do it, to relax the situation if he could. If thirty guns at both ranches started a range war he never would find out who slaughtered those stage coach people.

Spur gave Ty Udell five dollars and told him to go get a good meal and to watch around town for the two men he had seen before.

Five minutes later Sheriff Quigley had the paper in his hands.

"Yes, this is the report on the hunting death. They claim their friend shot himself when he dropped his pistol and it went off."

"That sounds a little strange. Most men carry their six-guns on an empty chamber so that sort of thing can't happen."

"True. They were so open about it that day and so shook up that I believed what they said without question. Of course, that was before we knew about the massacre." He studied the three names on the paper. "Jim Darlow was one of them, the other one was Zack Kinsey. He's the one who is dead. The third man is Roger Olsen.

"As I remember they were drinking buddies. Hang around the saloons on Saturday and by Saturday night they get into some kind of a fracas. Never anything to get arrested for."

"They work anywhere?"

"Kinsey was a hand at the Box H Haworth ranch. I think Olsen worked for the blacksmith here in town. And Darlow is out of work. Had been with one of the smaller ranches but they had to let him go. He didn't hook up with another outfit yet. Said he was looking."

"Let's just suppose, Sheriff. Just suppose the three were on that robbery, and Zack gets himself gut shot by a couple of pistol rounds. The other two go crazy and shoot everyone dead and then get their senses back. Wouldn't it be smart to bring Zack right into your office and say he was killed hunting? No cover-up on him because he's damn well dead. Could have happened that way."

"Could have, but I don't think these two have the guts or the brains to do it. I'll watch them and keep looking."

"Good. I talked with Efrem Longley this morning. The river is getting damn low and he's worried. Thought I'd ride up to see Haworth and remind him about basic water rights of downstream landowners."

"Good, we don't need a range war."

Spur waved and got back to his horse. He had stopped for a cold beer at the Pink Petticoat, but Claudine wasn't working yet.

An hour later he rode along the river on the far side, which should be the Box H land. He was looking for the sluice gate and the water works that would let Haworth capture a whole river. That would take some engineering.

He found it two miles above the end of the Longley range. The small stream took a sharp bend around a rocky point and the current swept entirely to the near side of the bank. Posts had been driven into the riverbed and a crude but effective baffling wall of three-inch thick planks had been built out over the twenty foot wide main course of the water. Over the wall was the sluice gate. It was simply another twenty foot wall of planks that cold be dropped straight down into the water and effectively block off ninety percent of the river's flow. He looked at the side of the stream and saw where a ditch had been dug. It was ten feet wide and three feet deep. The channel side was reinforced with cut logs.

It would be an effective way of diverting most of the water. Ahead along the ditch he saw what had once been a lake. Now the area was only damp with a few water plants and reeds growing. The lake could hold a large amount of water since it was in a natural catch basin that could be filled sixty or eighty feet deep.

Spur turned his horse along the ditch when a rifle bullet spanged off a rock ahead of him and whined off into the sky.

"Hold it, Buster. Right there. Not another step!"

Spur saw a horse and rider come out of the brush fifteen yards to his side, a rifle tracking him.

"Who the hell are you and what do you want?" the cowboy demanded.

Spur hadn't seen him before.

"My name is Spur McCoy. I'm a federal law officer and I want to see your boss, Henry Haworth. Now put down that weapon before I charge you with aggravated assault and throw you in the territorial prison."

The rifle lowered.

"Federal? A U.S. Marshall?"

"No. A lot higher up than that. Now take me to your ramrod wherever he is."

The rider wavered. Then nodded. "Can't take you, but I'll show you." He gave directions and Spur turned and rode north again along the valley and then up a small hill and down the other side to where a huge spread nestled next to the sparkling Santiam. There seemed to be more water in the river up here than lower down.

From this vantage point the home place of the Box H looked half again as big as Longley's. More barns, more corrals, more bunkhouses. The ranchhouse was massive, built of native stone and logs. It looked like it could stand for two hundred years. He was a mile from the spread when a cowhand rode up and asked who he was and what he wanted.

When he told him the hand called Spur "sir," and led him up to the ranchhouse and Henry Haworth. The rancher was almost as tall as Spur, but not as solid. He was fence rail thin, with deepset, brooding dark eyes, scraggles of dark hair on his mostly bald head, and clean shaven. He wore brown pants with suspenders and an undershirt with a brown sweater over it. He coughed as he looked up at Spur when his wife brought him to the study door.

"Who the hell is he?" Haworth asked his woman.

"His name is Spur McCoy, he's a federal law enforcement man and he wants to talk to you."

"Talk, about what?" Haworth said looking at Spur. The ranch owner remained seated behind a battered desk with a fancy lamp burning over it.

"Water."

"I was here first, I can use all the damn water out of the Santiam I want to."

"Not in this territory, Mr. Haworth. In the absence of any territorial water rights laws, federal law prevails."

"Who the hell says so?"

"The U.S. Constitution, the U.S. Supreme Court, and the Federal Judiciary. Do you want to fight all of them?"

Haworth looked at his wife, a small gray haired woman gone to fat years ago, and she scuttered out of the room.

"No water problems," Haworth said. "Nobody got any cattle dying of thirst."

"Not yet. But the flow of the Santiam is low, as you know, and the springs are drying up which means it's going to get lower. While I'm in the area, I want to be sure you understand the riparian rights of the land owners bordering the same flowing stream."

"Don't need to know. I do what I got to do and let the lawyers worry about it later. I let a thousand head of cattle die and then go to the law? Not a chance. I keep my beef alive whichever way I can. Then if the law comes, it comes. Dead beef don't help nobody."

"And a lot of your beef will be dead if you wind up in the federal prison for five years. Let me refresh your memory on water rights law. You have eleven ranchers downstream. Each of those ranchers has as much right to the water of the Santiam as you do. Each rancher has a right to drinking water for his cattle and his hands. If there isn't enough for everyone, for every cow, then each rancher must lose the same percentage of his herd. If that doesn't happen in a crisis situation, triple damages plus punitive damages will be assessed by the courts."

"You don't say."

"No, *I* don't say. The United States Government and the Territorial authorities say. These riparian rights are basic to our nation's welfare, and the United States Supreme Court has upheld them. What it comes down to is that sluiceway you have set up. When there is plenty of water you can use it all you want. When there isn't enough, your use of that gate will put you in direct violation of the law."

Spur was aware of others coming into the room. When he turned around, three large men stood behind him. They were as tall as their father but fifty pounds sturdier. It was plain they were the man's sons, they had his unmistakable brand.

"Hear that, boys. We got to share our river with them upstarts downstream. Like hell we will."

The oldest of the trio frowned. "We better go easy on taking that water, Pa. The law is the law, no way we can beat it."

"That's my eldest, Abel. Got a streak of logic in him that I'm trying to break. Other two boys are Lot and Cain. My wife had a religious streak when she named them. Me, I just got a mean feeling. I take care of my own up here on the Box H. Anybody got any complaints they best come well heeled to talk to me about it. Right, boys?"

Cain grinned and patted the .44 on his hip. Lot said nothing and Abel frowned.

"Mr. Haworth. Let me tell you about one case in Wyoming. The court calls it a precedent, and lots of times they base their cases on past ones. Ranchers damned up a small river, cutting off all water to those below. The first drought year more than 50,000 head of cattle downstream from him died for lack of water. The rancher was fined $40 a head for the cattle, that's $200,000, and was sentenced to ten years in the federal penitentiary. He had to sell his ranch and everything he owned to pay the fine. He'll be out in five more years. Gives a body something to think about, doesn't it?"

"Get off my land, McCoy."

"Your land? I understand there is some question about how much of the Box H you really own. That's what I'll be checking into next. You have a pleasant day now."

Spur turned his back on the still seated rancher and his three sons and walked out of the room. As Spur mounted up, he saw another horseman coming toward him. He was the eldest son, Abel.

"Thought I'd ride with you out toward the gate," Abel said.

"Good. I'd hate to get accidentally shot by a falling six-gun." Spur watched the man but saw no reaction.

Halfway to the big gate over the entrance to the ranch, Abel said what he had come to say.

"Don't take for gospel what Pa says. He gets riled up real easy, but he don't really want trouble. He's just had to push so long to keep the place together that he's still pushing."

"I understand. But if that sluice gate drops, all the Haworths are in trouble. You remember that."

"Do my best, Mr. McCoy. Do my best."

Spur waved and rode away toward town. He should get there before suppertime, and he was hungry enough to eat half a hog.

Chapter Nine

After his supper at the hotel, Spur went over to the Pink Petticoat to talk to Claudine. She was at the bar telling stories and waved when Spur came in. She had finished a tale about a bear and an Indian and moved down the bar to a spot beside the federal lawman.

"Nice of you to stop by again so quickly," she said, that angry smile on her face that he remembered from Arizona.

"I came and you were busy. No need for us to fight. You know my work always has first call."

She sighed, the angry smile faded and she touched his arm. "Damnit, I know. Why aren't you a saloon bouncer? I could offer you a job."

"Tried it, I didn't like it. Met both the Longleys and the Haworth families today."

"High society. Highest we got hereabouts."

"Has the weather been as dry around here as it looks?"

"Drier. We have a fist fight a week over the water rights when the river runs dry. Hope we don't have one tonight. Three of the down river ranchers are here, and then there's Cain

Haworth. That's the terrible mix. I must be a bad hostess to include them all on the same guest list. Cain's not blessed with a good temper."

"Who are the down river ranchers?"

She pointed them out to him. They were in the same poker game with six other players at a double table. Their names were Westcheski, Tsalles and Rudolf.

"They don't get into town often, but when they do, things can start to happen."

"Why?"

"They hate the big ranchers because they are small fry and the big ones are big. Lot of that going around."

"Old timers tell me this is as dry as it was three years ago," Spur said.

"They also say if it doesn't rain good and hard within a week, the Santiam will be a sandbox for the kids to play in."

"That soon?"

"They say so." She smiled. "I have to stay moving, and try to keep the beasts happy. You going to be busy later?"

"Never turn down an invitation. About midnight?" She nodded and moved down to a white-haired man at a poker table and kissed his bald head. Everyone at the table broke up laughing. Claudine knew how to keep her clients happy.

Spur walked toward the poker game with the three ranchers and saw it breaking up. The men had evidently lost a few dollars.

They moved to another table and ordered beers and sat talking. The tallest, Westcheski, was already more than a little drunk. His voice rose.

"Hell, I don't care if the little fart hears me. I still say we got just as much right to water out of the Santiam as his big outfit does."

"Yeah, sure, we agree. We just come in tonight for a good time, remember?"

"What's a good time? Hell, for me that's heading up stream with about two cases of them new fangled dynamite sticks and blow his sluice gate to old Billy hell!"

"Can't do that. Illegal." They all laughed.

Spur saw someone stand up at a poker table, then sit down when it was his turn to bid. The man was Cain Haworth and he looked mad.

Rudolph, the smallest of the three, lifted his mug of beer.

"Toast, toast to the damn weather. May it rain today, hail tonight, and wash us all into the gullies by morning!"

"Hear, hear!" somebody else shouted.

"I'll drink to that!" another voice said.

The three downed a swallow, and Tsalles stood.

"A toast to rain, and let it fall on everyone else but the Box H ranch!"

The three ranchers cheered and lifted glasses and drank. Then they roared with laughter.

Spur saw Cain start to rise, then sit down.

"I still say we should ride up there tonight, blow them guards away from that damn sluice gate and blast it to hell!" Westcheski shouted. He turned to the other men.

"Hey any of you guys with me? Who wants to get some powder and go up the river and blow up that damn sluice gate? Just dynamite it into Lincoln County!"

A dozen liquored voices rang out in the affirmative. It was the same group who would cheer if it were announced that every man who yelled loud would get his balls cut off. Spur knew the group; more important to him was Cain Haworth's reaction.

Cain pushed his chair back slowly, stood, adjusted his six-gun and walked toward the three men at the table.

"I'll go," he said. "I'll even show you where it is—then I'll blow your goddamned brains out!" Before any of the three could move, Cain's six-gun flashed into his hand and covered them.

"Now, what was this big talk about blowing up something?"

The men looked at each other. At last Westcheski pushed his chair back, stood and started to turn, then threw the chair with surprising speed at the gunman. The heavy chair caught Cain on the side as he turned away from it. It staggered him, but he kept his feet and the gun.

"You're Westcheski, the dumbassed white Russian. You run maybe two hundred head and don't know your balls from little green onions. What else you got to say?"

Spur didn't see her move. But all at once Claudine was behind Cain with a two barreled .45 deringer in his back. He felt the pressure and looked over his shoulder.

"No gunplay in here, Cain," Claudine said. "I keep telling you that. You want to stay here or ever come back, you hand your iron to the closest man. Otherwise you walk carefully out the front door and don't ever walk in here again. I can put both slugs right through your spine before you can get a shot off, and you'll be dead before you break in half. Do it now, Cain, now!"

There was a fire in her voice that Spur had never heard. Cain folded like a naughty boy, handing the .44 over his shoulder barrel first. She took it and nodded.

Cain stepped aside. She stared at Westcheski. "Rancher man, you broke up a three dollar chair. Pay up, now."

She took two steps toward him to keep him away from Cain, accepted the three silver dollars and slipped the handy little deringer back in the pocket of her flouncing skirt.

"Excitement is over, men," she said. "Back to the good stuff like drinking and playing poker."

"And women!" somebody called out.

"The best girls in the west, right upstairs," Claudine trilled, and every laughed.

Not quite everyone.

Cain Haworth glared at Westcheski. Then he charged. He caught the big Russian just as the man looked up, clamped his arms around his chest and blasted Westcheski across the table and into the next one. The jolt of the landing broke Cain's grip and he came up swinging. A right fist into the older man's gut, then one on his nose. By that time the rancher was tuned to the game.

The Russian hammered Cain's face twice, one blow on his cheek, the second one smashing his nose and bringing a gout of blood spattering the floor.

Cain bellowed in rage and bent to his boot. He pulled a six-inch knife from a boot sheath and held it in his right hand in front of him.

Spur darted in from the side, shouted at Cain, and when he turned, the agent kicked with his right foot. Leather met wrist and loosened the knife which fell to the floor. Spur stepped on the blade and stood there. He had pulled the force of the kick so it would not break Cain's wrist.

"You started it with fists, youngsters," Spur said. "You want to finish it, you do it the same way."

Cain glared at Spur, then the savage, wild gleam faded from his eyes. He shook his head and nodded.

"Yeah, sure. I'll go outside if he wants to."

The older man shook his head. "We've both been drinking too much. Maybe some other day, just you and me, kid."

"I'll be ready, anytime, old man."

Cain turned, picked up his hat and his six-gun from Claudine and marched up the stairway.

"Some poor pussy is gonna get a workout tonight!" a wag called out and everyone roared.

Westcheski looked at Spur, waved and sat back down at the straightened table. The three talked quietly, then the short rancher walked up to Spur.

"We thank you. We don't fight with knives. We all could have been cut up right bad."

"Fair is fair," Spur said. He watched the small man. "And I should warn you, I'm a federal peace officer. I don't want to hear any more talk about dynamiting any property that isn't your own."

The small man smiled. "Mr. McCoy, your work is known. We would not think of talking any more about blowing up the sluiceway or the gate. You know we have rights to the water. The next you hear from us we will already have blown up the gate, but you will not be able to prove it." He turned and went back to his friends. A few moments later they left the saloon. Spur guessed they would be on their way back south to their ranches. Dynamite wasn't for sale at night, even in High Prairie.

Claudine tapped his arm.

"Thanks. I don't like knife fights in my place either."

"You could have handled it. I was just closer."

She smiled. "I might have at that. You had supper?"

"Yep. But the right kind of snack would be interesting."

"You'll have to wait for that. Play some poker, lose some money, your public will like that."

Spur found an empty chair at a four hand table where none of the participants wore a tie. In three hours he lost four dollars, and made three friends. It was a worthwhile tradeoff.

By twelve-thirty the drinkers and gamblers had gone home, and only four of the girls upstairs were working. Spur helped Claudine and Barry the barman close up. They left one light on the back stairs for the late night leavers, and went into Claudine's apartment.

"How long did it take you to fix it up this way?" Spur asked.

"About a year. I've been here for almost three. Want to hear how I went from dancehall girl to saloon owner?"

'If it's a short story."

"Short and expensive. I landed in Tucson after we parted in Arizona and met a man I liked and he didn't care who or what I was, he wanted to marry me. So he did, and we stayed in town and he worked his mine and had just got it on a paying basis when he took sick. The lead poisoning came from the six-gun of a rival for the same vein a hundred feet underground. Either my husband or the other man had his tunnel dug crooked. Will died a week after he was shot underground. Nobody ever knew who pulled the trigger.

"I had some friends there after six months, and they arranged a sale of the holdings. I got forty-three thousand dollars for it. More money than I thought even banks had.

"I bought some clothes, got a trunk and started hunting for a situation, a town, and a place where nobody knew me. Here I am. I am the widow of a saloon owner. That's how I learned the business. The nice ladies of the town won't talk to me. They cross the street when I come by, leave the store, but half of them have husbands who patronize the girls upstairs once a week. So I maintain my smile and my good nature, and hope and pray that Spur McCoy will find me. Damnit, an answered prayer. What the hell am I supposed to do now?"

Spur laughed softly and kissed her. "If you have any good wine and some cheese, we could try some. I hear that's all the rage in Washington and New York."

"Let's try it."

They did.

When the wine had been sampled and the cheese cut and tasted she kissed him and sat back on the edge of the big bed.

"Do you think we should make love before,

or after the bottle of wine is gone?"

"Both," Spur said.

They did.

Chapter Ten

Barry the barkeep at the Pink Petticoat told Spur about it at 8:30 the next morning. He had just finished the breakfast Claudine had cooked for him and came into the saloon to head for the sheriff's office.

"Some Jasper rode in this morning half dead and burned bad. Doc fixed him up. He told the sheriff that some wild men had burned him out last night. Guy's name is Young and he's a rancher out about four miles north."

Spur asked Barry to tell Claudine that he would be at the sheriff's office and hurried to the little courthouse. Sheriff Quigley was almost ready to leave.

"Don't see how this has anything to do with the massacre, so I wasn't going to look you up. Welcome to come along if you want. We're leaving now. Young is still getting patched up, but he said he saw a red glow in the sky to the east of his spread. Might be a second rancher burned out last night. I don't figure where we're going I can make it by buggy, so I'm on this damn horse."

Spur ran for the livery stable and saddled

up the same horse he had used before. He caught them a mile out of town. The sheriff knew little else.

"Young said he woke up when he smelled smoke. Half the house was on fire and the barns were both almost burned down. At least he drove the horses outside and didn't lose any of the stock. He's got a wife and three kids, but they are all unhurt. He went back into the house to get a strong box with all of his cash in it. Saved it, but burned both his hands, his face and his legs. That's about it?"

"Haworth?"

"Could always be Haworth. Both these ranchers are just below the land he claims. He could be wanting to move in on them and buy them out cheap, or just run them off. Hard telling with a man like Haworth."

"That would make two fewer ranchers needing water out of the Santiam."

The sheriff nodded.

They had ridden at a trot most of the way. A quarter horse can cover six miles in an hour at that pace, and they got to the ranch a little after 9:30.

A woman rushed out from a small building near the well, her face a mask of fear.

"Is he all right? My husband got into town didn't he?"

"Yes, Mrs. Young, he's fine. Doc Varner is taking good care of him. He'll be along later with some supplies in a wagon, and some help."

Spur rode around the still smoldering, charred remains of the house, two barns and a shed. There was no way anyone could prove they had been torched. No kerosene cans, not witnesses, but there was no doubt in his mind how it had happened. He got off his horse and checked for horseshoe prints. He found several around each of the buildings, which wasn't unusual. It would make it too simple if he could find a broken shoe, or some strange markings, but there were none. Half the horses in Montana could have made the prints.

Back at the well house he talked to Mrs. Young.

"We didn't hear a thing but the fire. Woke us up and we ran out of the house. Then my husband went back in for the strong box. He was afraid the paper money and our homestead certificate would burn up even though it was in the metal box."

"He was right, it would have," Spur said. "This was a hot fire. You didn't hear or see anyone? You didn't hear any hoofbeats of horses riding away?"

"No. Must have been three or four of Haworth's men out there, but didn't see them."

"Why do you say Haworth's men?"

"He done it. My husband says so. And he's threatened us twice. Said sell to him or move out. That was it. Sell to him or move out or we'd be sorry we didn't."

"When did he threaten you?" Sheriff Quigley asked.

"Spring, when we was rounding up our strays over on the edge of his land. Said he owned the land all the way into town. My husband said we had proved up on our homestead, we owned it. He threatened us, and shot over our men's heads."

The sheriff was making notes on a pad of paper.

"Mr. Young said he thought he saw a glow to the east," the sheriff said. "Could that be over by the Foland's spread?"

"Husband said he thought it was. Good Lord, I pray that none of them got hurt." She reached her arms around the three children who huddled near her. They were from six to eight years old. "Her younguns are much smaller than ours."

Spur and the sheriff rode toward the Foland spread a half hour later. They had salvaged one bed from the remains of the house and set it up in the little well house. The kitchen stove would be salvageable after it cooled off a little more. The oldest boy had been looking for food they could still use from the root cellar and the pantry. They could eat for a few days and by then Spur was determined to have help for them.

They paused at a little rise and looked down into a feeder stream to the Santiam. The John Foland spread was smaller than the

Young place. It might run three hundred head of cattle and had a stand of corn growing in a fertile valley stretched out near the stream. Spur could see how some of the water from the creek had been diverted to feed the corn which was tall and green and starting to tassel out.

The ugly black scars showed plainly. The barn and house were charcoal and charred timbers. They could see a lean-to that had been built of partly burned boards under a tree near a windmill.

As they rode up a man came running out and fired a shot into the air.

"Hold it right there!" the man bellowed.

"John, it's Sheriff Quigley. We've come to help you."

The man put the rifle down and sank to the ground. When they came close enough they saw he was crying, tears dripping down his cheeks, his shoulders shaking with sobs.

"Jody died," the man said.

"John, is Jody your son?" the sheriff asked.

A woman came from the lean-to. She still had black smudges on her face and arms. Her skirt had been blue, now it was charcoal black. She walked up quickly and looked at her husband sitting in the dirt, the rifle leaning upward on his shoulder. He was crying, looking at the ground.

"He's been that way since Jody . . . passed on. We tried to find Jody in the dark last night. But the fire was roaring and he must have got scared and crawled under his bed. Just couldn't find him. Last few seconds John dragged me out of the room and then the roof fell in. John saved my life last night."

Spur motioned for the woman to come to one side where her husband couldn't hear.

"Might be best to bury the boy, right now. Help your husband get over his grief. Lots of times that helps the survivors."

"Yes. The Sheriff is here so it will be official. We'll do it. I'll tell John, then get little Jody ready. He was just four years old."

Spur spent the next half hour digging a grave near an apple tree. Jody had loved the apple tree his mother said. Spur jammed and slashed at the dirt, taking his anger out on it as he dug the three-foot deep hole. It didn't have to be very long.

John Foland seemed to rouse himself and take more interest as the little service began. Nicole, his wife, spoke some memorized passages from the Bible, including the Twenty-third Psalm. Spur started to lay the boy in the grave, but John shook his head and put the sheet wrapped body gently into the hole. Then as his wife prayed, he filled it in, not allowing Spur to help. He nailed together a wooden cross and mounded the dirt and pushed it in. Then John Foland blew his nose, wiped the tears from his eyes and walked over to the sheriff.

"I know who killed my boy, Sheriff. I saw them. Last night I had to get up and go to the privy. I was just coming back when I saw the barn start to burn. I ran out there and saw two men getting on horses. The horses both had Box H brands on their hips, and I'd recognize the men. They didn't know I seen them.

"I tried to put out the barn, and while I was out there they set the house on fire. Damn them! Time I got back to the house Nicole was up and waking the kids. We got four and they a handful sometimes.

"But then we couldn't find . . . I know the men, Sheriff. I can point them out in a crowd."

"Good, John. Good. We'll get things settled down here. You have a fine lean-to over there. We'll put some sides on it and see what kind of food you have left. Then we'll ride on out to the Haworth place."

They stayed there two hours. Spur found more boards and he got two sides on the lean-to. They salvaged a few blankets from the house. Soon it would be cool enough to find pots and pans. Even with the handles burned off they could be used.

Spur dug out tools and a few implements that had lasted. They could eat the sweet corn in another few weeks and had a big garden near the stream.

"Leastwise we still have the cattle," Foland said. "Tomorrow I'll drive three head in and see if I can sell them in town. I can butcher them out right there. Maybe keep one in the ice house for a while."

Spur watched Foland. He was a man back from the grave. He had suffered the ultimate torture, the death of his small son, and had mourned his heart out. Now he was healing, and while he would never be whole again, he was coming back, thinking ahead, making plans. He would survive.

They had to ride west to the Santiam, then only a half mile to the guard near the big gate. The guard scowled at the sheriff but let them through. He fired two shots into the air with his rifle to let the home place know company was on the way.

Spur had made sure that Foland did not have a gun. The odds were high that Foland would shoot first and talk later. The three rode the last half mile up to the ranchhouse and tied up their horses at the rail. As they did Haworth and one of his sons came out a side door and walked toward them.

"Sheriff, this is a pleasure. You don't get out this way much." Haworth didn't sound as if he meant it.

"Harry, you know Foland and McCoy, here."

"Yes." The rancher's eyes lingered on McCoy a minute, then moved to Foland. "Thought I saw a red glow down your way last night."

"My barn burned to the ground," Foland said.

"That's too bad."

"Thanks for sending someone over to help as soon as you saw the fire," Foland spat back at him. "Nice and neighborly."

"Wasn't sure it was your place. All my men were sleeping."

"Two of them wasn't. I was up late last night, Haworth. I saw two of your men set fire to my barn. While I tried to put that out they set fire to my house."

"Can't be true, none of my men would do that."

"Not unless you ordered them to."

"We tracked the two arsonists right here to your place," Spur said. "You've got some explaining to do."

"It's all a lie. This man has hated me for years."

"From what I hear, he has cause. We want to see all of your hands, Haworth. Those here at the place right now. Call them together."

"Afraid I can't do that. These men have work to do."

"So do I, Haworth," Spur said, drawing his Colt and training it on the two Haworths. The youth beside his father was Lot, the undecided. "You'll round up your men within five minutes, or you will be coming to town in shackles under arrest."

"You've got no jurisdiction . . ."

"The hell I haven't!" Spur thundered. "The whole damn *nation* is my jurisdiction. Lot, get the men rounded up in the mess hall. Right now."

Lot never looked at his father, he turned and walked toward the barns.

"Lot! You come back here!" Haworth thundered. Lot never broke stride.

Ten minutes later fourteen hands were in the mess hall, talking and laughing about the break in the day's work. Spur quieted them.

"The first three men, right here, stand up and move against the wall by the door and face forward."

"What the hell for?" one man asked. He was small and wiry, face burned brown but with a white forehead where his hat came. He was an outdoors cowboy.

"Because if you don't I'll knock you down and kick the shit out of you!" Spur shot back. The three man moved against the wall. Foland sat on a bench by one of the tables looking hard at the men.

"Now turn to your right, all three." The men did.

Foland shook his head. Three more men moved into position and did the same thing.

When the third group lined up Foland grabbed a tableware knife off the bench and lunged forward at the center man in the line. Spur caught him and took the knife away.

"That's one of them," Foland said. "Let me go! I'll kill the fucking bastard!"

Bolan held Foland and shook his head. "Let the law take care of it." He looked at the man. "You, step over here and sit down. You move a foot off that bench and I'll put a pair of .45 slugs right through your left eyeball. Understand?"

The man nodded, his bravado suddenly gone.

The other men were cleared by Foland. Spur turned to Haworth. "Where are the rest of your men? We need to screen them too."

"What about Gallagher? You charging him with arson?"

"Yes, and he'll also be charged with murder. Jody Foland died in the fire."

Haworth's eyes closed, then he squared his shoulders. "My man didn't have anything to do with that fire. We have witnesses who will swear he was here."

Spur scowled and the anger seeped out of his pores. "I bet you will, Haworth. You can buy witnesses to say any damn thing you want to. They are prejudiced and we'll prove it. Gallagher and the man he rode with are going to hang for killing that boy. He was only four! What would you have done if somebody killed one of your boys when he was four years old?"

Haworth turned and walked slowly toward the ranchhouse. The farther he got from them, the lower his shoulders sagged.

Lot came up and said they could ride down to the south pasture one ridge over where most of the other hands were branding late spring calves.

Sheriff Quigley moaned, then shrugged and got on his horse. He said he would be saddle sore for a month.

At the next valley, they found the branding

fire smoke and homed in on it. Ten men were finishing the branding. A rough corral had been built that held fifty head of calves, some of them still bawling for their mothers. A hundred head of cows bawled and stomped around the enclosure.

One by one the calves were hauled from the pen, thrown and held on one side as the Box H iron, red hot from the fire, seared the burn mark through hair and into cowhide. The bawling calf jumped up and ran into the herd of cows, hunting its mother.

Lot rode ahead and talked to the men. They stopped the branding and gathered near a water bucket. Foland rode past the men, turned his mount and came back. Halfway down the line he jumped off his bay on one of the cowboys. Foland clawed at the man's eyes, then slammed a hard fist into his nose twice before Spur got there and pulled him away.

The cowboy sat on the dirt, his chaps sprinkled with blood, his face surprised.

"That one?" Spur asked.

Foland could only nod. He kicked out viciously slamming his boot into the cowboy's leg. "That one!" Foland said. "He's the one who torched the barn."

Spur took the man out of earshot and glared at him. "I'm a federal law officer. I need to ask you a few questions. Answer them as truthfully as you can." The cowboy nodded.

"What's your name?"

"Ewald, Ed Ewald."

"How long have you worked for Haworth?"

"Near four years now."

"You good at obeying orders?"

"Long as they make sense."

"Where were you last night?"

A frown touched the man's face. He shrugged. "Playing poker with the boys. Lost two dollars at penny ante."

"Were you at the Foland ranch last night?"

"Hell no."

"That's enough for now, Ewald. You're under arrest for the murder of Jody Foland."

"That's crazy. I never even seen the guy."

"He's a child, Ewald. Four years old. He died in the fire last night when you torched the Foland's house."

"Died?"

"Right, as in dead." Spur tied the man's wrists behind his back, put him on his cattle pony and led him back to the Haworth ranch.

Lot went into the house.

Five minutes later Lot came out, said he would ride into town to arrange for a lawyer. Both the suspects were tied to their mounts and the small party rode off.

Spur talked to Foland where he turned off to his place.

"We'll have some help out to your ranch tomorrow morning. Don't worry, Haworth is paying for everything, he just doesn't know it yet."

116

Tears welled up in John Foland's eyes, but he kept them from spilling over.

"Thanks, McCoy. Thanks for not letting me kill either one of them murderers. That'd make me just like them. I don't want that. I got a wife and three more kids. Responsibilities. Lots of work I got to do. First got to get a house for them."

"That's what we'll help with tomorrow," Spur said.

"Much obliged, McCoy. I mean that. High time somebody put the running iron to Henry Haworth's high handed ways. He burned out one outfit north of him three years ago. Nothing was ever done. Now Haworth is grazing that land, using the pens, and the water."

"He's not getting away with it this time."

Foland nodded. A glint came in his eyes. "Damn right he ain't! Don't worry about me. I won't touch him. We got some law here now to handle him."

Spur turned and caught up with the rest hoping he could make good on John Foland's expectation.

Chapter Eleven

Halfway to town from the Box H spread, Spur McCoy pulled the small troop to a halt and glanced over at the sheriff.

"Make a bet with you, Sheriff. I wager that both of these Jaspers are going to be shouting their heads off about how they were just following orders, that Henry Haworth is just as guilty as they are, that he ORDERED them to burn out both those ranches."

"What odds?" the sheriff asked, picking up on the ploy.

"Give you five to one."

"Fine odds, you know something I don't?"

"Peers as how, Sheriff. We got ourselves two killers, here. One would be enough. What would happen if one of these Jaspers got shot up trying to escape?"

Gallagher and Ewald looked at each other.

"Hell, you won't do that. You're a federal lawman." Ewald said it.

"Who would know?" Spur asked softly. "You might not have meant to kill that boy, but he's still just as dead. We take you into town and you got maybe one chance in ten of getting off scott free. Depending on how good

118

a lawyer Lot here can hire. Damn, I don't like them odds."

"Which one?" the sheriff asked.

Spur shrugged. "Don't matter none to me. We could untie both of them and let the one who ran fastest get away, for a spell."

"I'd think maybe a flip of a coin," the sheriff said.

Lot Haworth frowned at both lawmen, uncertain what was going on. He had a six-gun on his hip. Neither official looked at him.

"Ewald, who told you to burn down those two ranches?"

"Nobody, damn it."

"You did it on your own? Why would you do that?"

"No, not on our own. We didn't do it."

"Think the guy who ordered a killing should have to stand trial with his bush-whackers who murdered a man on the trail?" Spur asked Gallagher.

He shrugged. "Guess so."

"Then shouldn't Henry Haworth be here beside you, getting taken to jail, charged with murder too?"

"Hell, I don't know. He just said burn them out, not kill anybody. He told us . . ."

"Gallagher, you asshole!" Ewald shouted.

"Go on, Gallagher, what else did Haworth tell you?"

The cowhand stared at his boots. "Hell, he said they were taking up space and he might have to let two hands go if the places didn't

119

get wiped out so we could get more stock in there. He said too, the water was getting shorter every day."

"So you and Ewald went out last night and torched the two ranches?" Spur asked.

"Yeah. Both."

"Which one first?" Sheriff Quigley asked.

"Young. Hell, we didn't know the kid would get hurt. We didn't mean to kill anybody! You can't charge us with murder!"

"Gallagher you slow witted cow shit!" Ewald shouted. He spurred his horse into Gallagher's mount and Gallagher fell to one side, slipped around the horse where he was tied until he hung upside down.

Spur dismounted and lifted Gallagher. As he did, Ewald took off, his horse in a hard gallop goaded on by the sharp spurs.

Lot lifted his six-gun and fired twice over Ewald's head. The cowboy stopped spurring and let the horse come to a halt. Lot rode out and brought him back.

Spur got them ready to move again. He had a confession by one man which implicated the second one. It should be enough for a conviction. Now he had to figure out how to play it against Henry Haworth. He still had a choice of charges, and he might do a little horsetrading with Haworth for a confession.

They continued on into town. Spur was still helping the sheriff book the two new prisoners, when Henry Haworth walked into the sheriff's office.

He was grim. He wore the same clothes he had on before, but now he did not have a six-gun.

Spur put down his pen and stared at the rancher.

"Your men have confessed to setting the fires. We can charge them with arson or murder. Whichever one they are charged with, you will be charged with as well. They also confessed that you ordered them to do the torchings."

Haworth took a deep breath. He pulled his hat off and slumped in a chair.

"Damnit! Nobody should get hurt in a little fire like that. I ain't admitting a thing. Fact is they could have done it themselves because I told my men I might have to lay off some hands."

"Possible," Spur said. "The government would look a lot more kindly on you, Haworth, if we knew that you had done everything you could to help those ranchers rebuild."

"How?"

"Tomorrow morning you should have two wagons loaded with food staples, blankets, clothes, kitchen gear, anything you can think of that those families might need. You send them out first thing, and you follow them up with wagons from the lumber yard taking our beams and two by fours and sheeting enough to put up two good houses.

"Could have a house raising out there

tomorrow, if we pass the word. And the Box H is going to supply all the lumber and nails and roofing and whatever they need. Right?"

The old man nodded. "Yeah, right. I ain't saying we did nothing wrong, but a neighbor got to help out. The Box H will do its part. You spread the word about two house raisings tomorrow. We need carpenters. My men don't know beans about building a house."

Spur nodded. "Can do. Now you get arrrangements made with the stores in town."

When Haworth left, Spur went up the steps to the county clerk's office and checked the deed files and the land map. He took down the descriptions based on landmarks, and then drew a crude map. From first impressions it looked as if the Box H owned about half the land they currently claimed. He would take that up with Mr. Haworth at an opportune moment.

The moment came sooner than Spur thought it would. He was in the Plainsman Hotel restaurant when Haworth came in, searched the tables until he found the Secret Service agent and walked directly to his table.

"It's done, McCoy. I gave the store instructions to put whatever they want on the wagons. One for each place. Cost me a thousand dollars before it's over. The lumber wagons will move out tomorrow and all of my hands will be split between the places to help work. You should be satisfied."

"Isn't me who's trying to be pleased. I think you're trying to talk yourself into doing a good deed." Spur paused. "You checked your holdings lately with the county clerk? The land map doesn't reflect your current boundary markers at the Box H. From what I saw you own about a third of the land you have posted as yours."

"Damn lie. I own the whole thing. Bought it fair and square. Got the papers to show it."

"Did you file them with the county? Doesn't mean a thing until the paper shows up in the county clerk's office." Spur gave him the rough map. "You better take a look in your safe out at the ranch. Peers your legal ownership papers are on the shy side."

Haworth glared at Spur. "You got any more tricks up your damned sleeve? You come in here snorting and raring like a wild boar, disrupting everything."

"I didn't set any houses on fire, Haworth. I'll see you at the two house raisings tomorrow."

The gaunt, thin man turned and walked away. Something was different about him. Then Spur figured it out. His face was clean shaven.

McCoy finished his dinner and went back to the sheriff's office. The banker had found no more of the new coins. Whoever had been spending them had stopped. For a moment McCoy knew he was putting in too much time on the river war and the burnouts, but somehow it all tied together. He didn't know how, but he was going to push both ends of it. The two men who came in with their dead friend still interested him. He would talk to Claudine about them. There was a chance there might be more in the group, another one or two who hung out together, who gambled and got drunk together. It was a chance. The sheriff said he had nothing more on either Jim Darlow or Roger Olsen, but he was watching both of them.

Spur stopped at the General Store, and found them busy laying out survival gear, equipment and food for the two families. The store owner said it was the biggest order he had ever put up, but he was glad it was going to folks who needed help.

Spur began to spread the word about a pair of house raisings the next day. All able bodied men were invited to help, and their ladies could bring food for everyone. Spur hoped he could get twenty men at each site. If so they could have the houses put up and livable before darkness the next day.

He found Claudine at the bar at her saloon. He had worked all the others making the announcement about helping the burned out families. He talked about it here and heard some assurances that the men would go out. Claudine said she would take a big bunch of sandwiches, fresh fruit, and cold beer. Four more men decided to go.

Claudine led Spur to an empty poker table. "I hope you never find the killers of those stage coach people," she said softly.

"Why?"

"Then maybe you'll stay around for a couple of years looking for them."

"Might at that. Could be I won't find them."

"Promises, promises."

"What do you know about a young man named Jim Darlow?"

"Jerky Jim," that's what my girls call him. Some quaint little movements he makes in the throes of love. I don't know much more. He's around the saloon now and then. Has a few weird friends, but then don't we all? That's about it."

"He get into fights, get thrown out, rough stuff?"

"No, not any more than some loud talk. He's a big talker when he gets sloshed. You on the other hand get quiet as a bunny rabbit and exhibit certain other traits of the same species."

"Never alone."

"Never?"

"Well, almost never." He squeezed her hand. "I've got to dig up my potato patch and see what I can find. Some of the old field work. I still have a killer to find. Maybe more than one."

"I think's it wonderful what you're doing for the two families that were burned out.

Just beautiful. And I know it's you behind it. When it happened before our glorious sheriff just sniffed a little, said wasn't it a shame and did nothing."

"One hand washes the other."

"I've heard that, what does it mean?"

'I don't know what it means, I just use it." He touched her shoulder, winked and walked out into the blackness of the night.

Main Street was a dark tunnel. Only the lights from the four saloons and the hotel made any indentation in the liquid black. The rest of the stores were locked up tightly. The big Seth Thomas on the saloon wall indicated it was only a little after nine P.M.

Spur moved toward the next saloon half a block down. He had forgotten the name now and couldn't read the sign. At the alley he stepped off the boardwalk into the inch-thick dust the hooves and wagon and buggy wheels had churned since the last rain. When the next rain did come a man would be ankle deep in mud.

He was just ready to step up on the boardwalk on the other side of the alley, when a pistol in the darkness to his right fired twice. Spur felt the slug take him high in the chest, somewhere under his collar bone, and he went down and rolled, crying out when he rolled over the wounded side. His right fist was full of hardware, but he had no target.

Footsteps pounded down the alley. The Secret Service agent was on his feet at once, running after them. There was no pain in his shoulder now—not yet. Just the sudden hammer blow and then nothing. He put his right hand up and felt his shirt front.

Wet! With his blood.

He ran faster. The alley ended at the next block where there were mainly houses. He saw three lights on. Spur stopped and held his breath. Shuffling steps sounded to his left, in the side yard of the first house. He held his position and the steps came again. Spur couldn't see a thing.

Slowly his eyes adjusted and a tree took shape and beside it, staring around, stood a man. He had a pistol up. Spur leveled in and took one shot. He missed. But it flushed the man out. He ran down the dirt street between the houses. There were no boardwalks here, nor fancy curbs as in the East. Just a dirt track between the small homes.

Spur chased him, the first tinges of pain coming in his chest. The bushwhacker was not a running expert. Spur gained on him easily. The man must have known it. Suddenly he stopped, turned, held the gun with both hands and fired.

There was no time to return the fire. Spur was less than twenty feet from the gun, he did the only thing he could. The agent dove for the ground, hit on his right shoulder as he always did ready to do a neat forward roll back to his feet and keep running.

As he hit on his shoulder and his body

crushed sideways, he screeched in agony from the wound in his other shoulder. Spur couldn't complete the roll. He went down in a sprawl, lost his gun and lay there panting to stave off the light headedness he felt. He knew he was five seconds from passing out. If he did the gunman would walk up and kill him. He fought it back, took deep breaths and sat up, reaching around for his Eagle Butt Peacemaker.

Ahead he saw the gunman moving his arm, tracking Spur with the handgun. Spur moved to one side, felt the blood rush away from his head and ducked low. The shot went over his head. With his head down blood flowed back into it.

His right hand closed over the mother-of-pearl handgrips of his .45 and he whirled it around and fired. The bushwacker jumped in surprise. Spur had not even aimed. He couldn't afford the time. He was letting the man know he had his gun back. The man turned and ran.

This time Spur had trouble keeping up with him. Every step, every jolt of his feet sent small needles stabbing through his shoulder. They went down a block, cut back toward Main Street and then he saw the man was silhouetted against the lights of a saloon. Spur stopped, held the .45 in both hands and fired the last two shots in the cylinder. The second one hit the man in the leg and he toppled. He tried to stand, fell and then began dragging himself toward the alley.

Spur walked as fast as he could toward the ambusher. Two drunks came out of the bar singing to their "doggies." They turned away from the man in the dirt. Another man came out walking more steadily.

"Stop that man!" Spur shouted. "The man on the ground is a killer, stop him!" The man looked Spur's way, but could see nothing. He drew his weapon and moved cautiously toward the man who now lay still in the middle of the street.

It took what to Spur seemed like ten minutes to walk the half block to the street. Three men stood near the man in the dirt.

"Broken leg," one man said.

"Know who this Jasper is?" another asked.

"He fainted, ain't that odd?" a third voice said.

Spur came reeling up to the group and put his hand on one man's shoulder for support.

"Hey. It's that federal lawman. He's been shot!"

Spur let himself down to the ground and turned over the man who lay there.

"Who is he?" Spur asked, his head feeling light again.

"Hell, that's Jim Darlow. He's losing blood fast." The man put his kerchief over the upper leg wound.

"Better get Doc, both of you could see him."

"Darlow. Jim Darlow is under arrest,"

Spur said, then he fell backward into the arms of the man behind him and the darkness of rest closed over him.

Chapter Twelve

Spur McCoy awoke in a small plain room. He was in bed and felt like somebody had run over him with a twelve mule team freight wagon. When he moved his left arm, pain gouged a dark hole in his brain and he groaned. Then he remembered: he had been shot.

A form appeared in the lighted doorway. He wore a white shirt with rolled up sleeves. Dark spots of blood showed on the front of the shirt. The man came into the room nodding.

"Good, glad you came back to life. Thought I'd lost you for a while there. How much blood do you think you can spread around town and still have enough to live on?" The form came closer. "I'm Doc Varner, the resident sawbones. Welcome back."

"Glad to be here. Bullet miss my lung?"

"Barely, but you bled like a stuck shoat. Your prisoner is in better condition, just a broken leg. I set it and he's over in Sheriff Quigley's boarding house."

"I hope that's a jail cell."

"It is. Quig said he wanted to see you, if you

made it. He's outside."

"He wanted my Eagle Butt Peacemaker," Spur said feeling a little woozy. He couldn't take time out to be shot. He still had lots of work to do.

Sheriff Quigley came in. "I hear you're tired of working with me," he said a wry little smile sneaking around the corners of his face.

"Hell yes," Spur said, stopped and took a deep breath.

"Jim Darlow said you shot him for no reason. Thought I better check your version."

Spur told him in short sentences, with pauses between.

"Check the alley over there, should be a blood trail down it."

"No reason to. I went to Darlow's boarding house and went through his things. He was one of the men who brought in that dead friend the day of the massacre. Under his bed, back in the corner where his landlady couldn't reach, I found a tin box. Inside were forty-six double eagles, 1873 mint date."

"Good. So he's one of them. You figure the other guy, Olsen and their dead buddy did the job?"

"Possible. Only trouble is I checked out Olsen's room here at the hotel. Nothing, not a single twenty dollar gold piece in the place. He evidently was smarter hiding them, or he wasn't involved."

Spur tried to think it through. Something

was out of place, but his head kept spinning. He tried to sit up and came within a second of passing out. At last he got the words said.

"That accidental death. They said Zack Kinsey dropped his six-gun. it went off and killed him. Did you check with the undertaker to find out if the body had just one bullet wound?"

"No, but I sure will. You take it easy. Looks like this thing is starting to wind down."

"Wish it was, but we have a lot of problems yet. You going to the house raising tomorrow?"

"Yes, in my buggy. Half the county is going to be out at those two places."

"Good. Hope I can make it." Spur wanted to say more but his eyes were too heavy and they closed before he knew it and he fell asleep.

The sheriff closed the door quietly, and talked to Doc Varner.

"Not a chance," Varner said. "McCoy is damn lucky to be alive. Another inch lower and his lung would have been hit and he'd have a lung fill up with blood where it isn't supposed to. He isn't moving out of that bed for at least three days."

Sheriff Quigley smiled. "If that's what you want, you better have some rope to tie him in. I got to pay a call on our undertaker. Seems strange going down there without a body for him to work on."

Spur woke up hungry. He forgot for a moment where he was and threw back the light cover and groaned as his left side chattered in pain.

The door popped open and Claudine bustled in.

"We thought you were going to sleep all day. Here it is after eight A.M." She stopped and a soft, gentle smile replaced the frown as she hurried to the bed and kissed his forehead.

"A fever. Doc said you would run one for three days. He had a devil of a time finding that slug and getting it out. He says we almost lost you."

"I'm too mean to die."

"Hush. I brought you some breakfast. Doc says anything, and the more the better, but no booze. Can you stand that for three days?"

"Have to."

He tried to sit up, but the waves of pain, nausea and light headedness came back. Claudine fed him with his head propped up just a little. She had brought a stack of hot cakes, hot maple syrup, two fried eggs. three slices of toast and strawberry jam, and a bowl of applesauce. He ate most of it.

"Did they get out of town on the house raising?"

"Half of town pulled out bright and early."

"I need to go."

"It's a long way to crawl. You can't ride."

"You have a buggy?"

She laughed. "Come on, Spur. You got the project started moving. They know how to do it. Heard one old timer say he hadn't seen a house raising like this in the county in thirty years."

"It's a good thing to get started again."

Spur took several deep breaths. "Yeah, that didn't hurt. Now I'm going to sit up. That breakfast helped." He wouldn't let her touch him as he edged higher and higher in the bed until he was sitting against the headboard.

"You get feeling any friskier and I'll jump right in there beside you," Claudine said.

"Don't tempt me. Where are my pants?"

Claudine lifted the covers and peeked under. "You're not wearing them, I can tell."

"Funny, Claudine, cute, strange. Find my damn pants."

"My, you *are* feeling better." She frowned slightly as she found his clothes on a chair below the bed.

By stages Spur was testing himself. He began by leaning away from the headboard. He almost fell off the bed. Again and again he tried until he could do it. He looked down at the bandage on his chest. It was high and taped in place.

After a half hour of work he could sit up without help and then began working on moving his legs over the side. That was easier.

An hour after breakfast he could walk with Claudine's help.

"Have you taken those sandwiches and beer out to the ranches yet?" he asked her.

"No. I've leaving about ten."

"I'll ride with you. Get Doc in here to wrap this damn hole in me again. I think it bled some."

When Doc Varner came in he was angry. "Tarnation! What in hell are you doing, man? Trying to kill yourself?"

"Got work to do, Doc. I remember a major in the war got a bullet through a lung. Next day he was back on the front lines directing a company of infantry. Depends on how much *want to* a man's got. Mine's pretty high right now. Bandage this hole up so it don't leak no more. I got to take a buggy ride out to the house raisings."

"Can't do it. Won't do it. You could start bleeding . . ." Doc Varner raised his brows and sighed. "What the hell, you're probably tougher than anybody I ever worked on. Sit down and take off your shirt. I ain't gonna help a strong man like you do a simple thing like remove his shirt."

"Atta boy, Doc," Spur said. The shirt was the hardest thing to take off. He left his left sleeve in and motioned for the sawbones to get busy.

When Claudine's buggy stopped in front of the doctor's office a half hour later, Spur was sitting in a chair in the sun waiting for her. Standing and getting up into the buggy tested his determination over pain. But he made it.

136

A line of sweat popped out on his forehead, but quickly evaporated. It was another hot, dry day, with not a hint of a cloud in the sky. And the river was lower again.

Claudine drove. She knew the way. The first half mile was murder on his shoulder. Then Spur began to exercise his mind-over-pain system. He tried to shut off the nerves that sent him the pain signals, and after a half hour of concentration, he had the pain dampened down to a slow rolling throb. He settled for that.

Claudine kept up a line of chatter all the way, evidently hoping to take his mind off his hurt. When they came over the last little rise and saw the Young place below, she shivered.

"Those two black things used to be a house and a barn?"

"Two days ago. Fire has a way of putting an end to lots of things."

Even from the distance they could see the activity below. It looked like a bumblebee nest. Teams of horses were dragging charred timbers away from the foundation. Wagons were loaded with the charred wreckage and hauled away. What looked like fifty or sixty people milled around, evidently working with some plan in mind.

The foundations were uncovered and the floor studs had been hammered into place by the time Claudine drove in.

It was a whirlwind of activity. Teams of men framed up stud walls. Others built triangular roof beams that would be lifted in place. There was a friendly, happy spirit everywhere. A dozen women had set up makeshift tables of boards over sawhorses, and had laid out a feast of fried chicken, potato salad, stews, meatloaf, and a dozen green salads, bowls of fruit, and the specialty dishes of half of the women in town.

One man came up and shook Spur's hand.

"I ain't seen nothing like this since back in the thirties," he said. "That was in Michigan and we had a barn raising one Sunday. We didn't have nowhere this many people. Does a body good to see this kind of outpouring of being a good neighbor."

He went back to pounding nails in the braces between the studs.

There was a whoop of excitement as the first stud wall was lifted into place. Two by four braces held it upright as the plate was nailed to the floor that had been rapidly laid over the joyce. Soon the second, longer wall was ready and hoisted up, nailed down and anchored firmly to the first one.

Before noon the four stud walls were up and the first of the framed-in rafter triangles were lifted up.

Men ate in shifts at the table, some working, others eating. Even before the final rafters were in place a team began pounding on the siding, starting at the bottom with the overlapping shiplap and working up to the top, allowing space for the men who had been framing in the doors and windows.

Spur had been walking around the yard cautiously. Claudine was next to him and now and then he had to touch her hand for support. Everyone knew he had been shot and marveled that he was out of bed.

Out near where the barn had been, Spur saw another crew at work. The plank corral had been burned, too. The half next to the barn was gone. Four men worked there, using salvaged lumber from the burned house and barn to reconstruct the enclosure.

When Spur walked in that direction he saw the ramrod on the project was Lot Haworth. Spur noticed Abel Haworth with his shirt off digging a post hole. Spur took Lot's hand in a silent greeting. Spur knew that if and when their dad moved on, the Box H would be in much better hands.

A rider came in from the Foland ranch. He reported work there was going well. They were about an hour behind the work being done at the Young place. He said they had sixty people, men, women and kids working there.

Spur tried to count. He gave up but figured there were over sixty at work here.

The cold beer, kept wrapped in burlap sacks filled with crushed ice from the community icehouse, was the hit of the house raising.

By two o'clock Spur had returned to the buggy and sat watching the roofing. There had not been enough sawed or split shingles in the lumberyard, so one side of the house was being shingled, and the other half covered with shiplap directly on the sheeting. It would hold for a year or two, but would be replaced with shingles if they arrived before winter.

"Cowboy, I'm going to take you home," Claudine said. The stone and rock fireplace was rising over the end of the house as the masons worked. There would be no fire in the box below for three days to allow the mortar to cure naturally.

Spur nodded. "Yes, I do feel a little tired."

She had saved two cold beers for him and he drank both on the way back. She drove slowly, but at every bump Spur winced. When they got back in town she turned down the alley in back of the Pink Petticoat and stopped.

Barry came from the bar and helped Spur into Claudine's bed. He sank down gratefully in the featherbed, thanked Barry and dropped off to sleep at once.

Claudine had put down his protests when he saw where she was taking him. She told him he needed nursing care, he wasn't going to be able to climb those steps to his hotel room, she had a bed and wanted to take care of him, and if he didn't like it he could shoot her. He kissed her instead and left her quivering in delight.

Now she looked down at him. Her hand on his head showed that his fever was almost gone. Now all she had to do was feed him and keep him quiet and let his strong body recuperate.

She smiled. Claudine wouldn't care if it took him two weeks to get back on his feet. But she knew she was dreaming.

Chapter Thirteen

Spur could not get out of bed the next day. He woke up with the fever again and the doctor brought some pills he said should help bring down the temperature. He scolded Spur for going to the house raising the day before. Spur was so sick he didn't even want to talk about the case.

By evening he was feeling better and ate two steaks and had two bottles of beer. Sheriff Quigley came by just after supper with a note of optimism.

"We call our undertaker Digger here, just for fun. He doesn't seem to mind. Anyway, Digger told me this afternoon that he remembers that Zack Kinsey death. He keeps records on the cause of death, and he has it in his book as two gunshot wounds two inches apart in the lower belly slanting upward. Zack was probably on a horse and shot by someone on the ground."

"Like he was robbing a stagecoach," Spur said.

"That would be a good assumption, Mr. McCoy. At least we know the pair lied about the death. So they have to clear that up. And one of them had some of the stolen coins. So we have a definite linkup between Kinsey, Darlow and Olsen. It just depends how far we can push it. I'm hoping for a confession."

"Are you going to arrest Olsen?" Spur asked.

"Not yet. I want him to sweat a little. He knows we have Darlow. He's probably worried about what he's talking about all day long in the jail."

"Good. If he runs, he's almost signing his death warrant."

Spur offered the sheriff a bottle of cold beer and the lawman accepted. He relaxed a little and unbuttoned his vest.

"I still can't figure out why they shot all six on the coach," the sheriff said. "If one of the passengers shot up one of the robbers, why not just kill him and let the others go?"

"That's one we're going to have to ask Darlow and Olsen," Spur said.

They talked about the house raising. The sheriff had been at the Foland place, and said they got it up and closed in even to the windows and doors before dark. He said the Young house was done all except for the door and two men were going back today to hang them.

A half hour later the sheriff left and Claudine came back from showing him out the door. She stood and looked at Spur with her own brand of puzzled frown.

"You were talking about three men and the

stage. What about the fourth one?"

"What fourth one?" Spur asked. "We only know about the three who came back that day, two alive and one dead."

"Oh! I always think of them as the Big Gun Four, that's what my girls call them. These four guys run around together all the time. Or they used to before Zack got killed. They would come upstairs and have a contest for the most times in a row, say in an hour. Loser had to pay. The girls kept track."

"Weird. Who was the fourth man?"

She walked around the room. "Hell, I guess there aren't any professional ethics here. They do lots of things together, like go buck hunting, and antelope hunting. Yeah, I can tell you. The fourth man on the Big Gun Four is Cain Haworth."

Spur looked at her for a long moment. Then nodded. "He's the Jasper who tried to knife those ranchers the other night. I'd say he has a violent temper. What do the girls say?"

"He's a steady with one, Pauline. She does get black and blue now and then. It's a rule, they always have to tell me if a customer gets rough. Most of her bruises come from Cain. He's a no good bum as far as I can see. But his mother probably loves him!"

"That fits in nicely. Where was Cain the day of the massacre? That is the question we need to find out. Did Pauline get any bruises that day?"

"I keep records. I can damn well tell you."
She went to her desk in the other room and
came back with a small leather bound book.
"Fact is she did. Pauline said Cain was here
most of the day."

"The day? Your girls work during the
day?"

"Not usually. He could have been here. Let
me look up the cash pay records." She came
back with a red leather bound book. "I'll be
damned. It shows Pauline had a twenty dollar
customer for most of the day on July 22. That
was the same day as the massacre."

Something was pricking his memory.
Something about that same day. One of the
men who came in response to his posters
around town. Then he remembered. The
drunk who said some wild eyed man almost
rode him down in the alley. The man got off
his half dead horse and went in the back door
of the Pink Petticoat Saloon and whoring
place. That drunk, Spur had to find him. If he
could identify the person going into the
brothel and tie down the time, it could break
an alibi. If the kid who rode in so fast was
Cain Haworth.

"That might give us something. Can you
send out somebody to find Ty Udell?"

"Sure. I see him around now and then. Why
him?"

"He might be able to help us."

"Tonight?"

"Right now."

145

"See what I can do."

"Tell whoever you send it's worth a five dollar gold piece if he can bring Udell back with him tonight."

Claudine came back a few minutes later. "I sent out two men who need work. They'll find him if he's in town. What is this all about?"

Spur told her. "A man doesn't ride a good horse almost to the point of collapse and then let it stand around. Best way to kill a horse there is. A mount like that has to be walked out, cooled down gradually. Udell might know the name of the drunk who saw all this happen. If he does, we have a good strong nail in Cain Haworth's hanging scaffold."

Undell came to the door two hours later. Yes, he knew the name of the man with whom he had waited in the hall.

"Snuffy Norbert, that's the guy's name. I've shared a pint with him now and then."

"Can you find him?"

"Yeah, just left him at the joint down the street. Well we was kind of behind the joint down the street."

Spur flipped him a double eagle. "Go get him and bring him back here. Come in the back door. Then hang around out front and have a beer, but don't get sloshed. I might need you again."

Ten minutes later Spur looked at Snuffy. The man had been on a three day drunk. He could barely stand.

"Sorry," Snuffy said. "It was his five dollars."

"Get him into a room over at the hotel and dry him out. I want him to be talking and making sense by noon tomorrow. No booze, but all the food you can get in him. Now get him out of here. Snuffy . . . no more booze for you either," Spur told Udell.

"Right. For a month's pay I can go dry for a couple of days. He'll be dry, I can guarantee you."

"Let's have a talk with Pauline."

"She's working."

"And I'm her next customer, right here." He handed Claudine a five dollar gold piece.

"Don't spoil her, that's overpayment."

"Not for what I'm going to do. I want you to watch."

"Strange, but interesting."

Spur had Pauline sit in the chair beside his bed and he grilled her for an hour. She wouldn't change her story. Cain had been with her almost all day. He had come early in the morning. His friends had gone hunting, but he didn't feel so good and she sat with him and got some food for him. He was there when his two friends came back with the dead man. She knew because when he heard the commotion outside, he dressed and went out. She watched from the window.

"Pauline, if you're lying to protect him, I'm going to throw you in jail. You understand that?"

She nodded, biting her lower lip.

"Pauline, if you're lying, you won't be working here anymore, whether you go to jail

147

or not," Claudine said.

Pauline looked quickly at Claudine, then nodded again. "I know. That's what happened. Why would I lie?"

"Because Cain might kill you if you didn't," Spur said.

She snapped her head up, started to say something, then hurried out of the room.

"She's lying," Spur said. "I can feel it. I know it. We've got to get some proof to show her, to implicate Cain so she'll testify for us."

"Maybe Snuffy."

"I hope Snuffy."

That night after Claudine closed up she came into the bedroom and undressed slowly. Spur watched. She came and stood near the bed, naked, and touched his shoulder.

Spur shook his head. "Maybe tomorrow. I'm doing good just sitting up, let alone trying to get anything else up."

She laughed and slipped into bed beside him. She didn't touch him, and that took a lot of effort.

"Like we were married," she said. "Can't have sex every night. Kind of like we were married."

"Don't worry, I'll make up for this lack of response just as soon as I can." He reached over and kissed her lips gently, then went to sleep.

She lay there a long time watching him. Then smiling and thinking about the next night, she drifted off to sleep.

When Claudine woke up the next morning, Spur was no longer in the bed beside her. She heard him in her kitchen. By the time she got out there he was eating ham and eggs and fried potatoes with onions.

"Want some?" he asked.

She nodded and he served her enough for three men, then went back to eating.

"Remarkable recovery," she said.

"Two days, that's all I can afford to be sick. The two days are up, so I have to get back to work. I've already walked around the block to test myself. Breakfast, then over to Doc Varner for a look at my puncture and a nice quiet chat with Roger Olsen before he decides to leave town."

"And don't forget Snuffy."

"He won't be making sense until this afternoon. Then I might also come and see Pauline. Tell her not to leave town suddenly."

Spur finished the breakfast, gulped down the last of his coffee and kissed her cheek.

"Work calls. I'll be back for that postponed romp I owe you, or you owe me, whatever."

She waved, still a little in a daze by his activity.

Doc Varner had been up for only ten minutes when Spur pounded on his door. The sawbones was surprised at Spur's appearance. His fever was gone, his balance back, and the wound was staring to heal nicely. He put some ointment on it and bandaged it up again wrapping some of the strips around Spur's chest and back.

Spur checked his six-gun as he came out the doctor's door. It was in place and working right. Not much to go wrong with a six-gun. He walked to the hotel and asked the clerk which room Roger Olsen had, and went up to 216. He tried his key and found that like many poor quality locks, his key worked just as well in the other lock.

Spur nudged the door open slowly, then standing behind the wall, pushed the door fully open. Nothing happened. He peered around the door waist high, and saw a man sleeping in his bed, fully clothed, and a six-gun inches from his right hand.

McCoy stepped in soundlessly, picked up the weapon and punched the butt into the man's stomach.

He came awake with a start, his right hand scratching for the gun that wasn't there. Olsen sat up.

"What the hell is this?"

"Judgment day, Olsen. Are you right with your Maker?"

"McCoy, the hot shot federal lawman. Heard about you."

"So did Jim Darlow, and he's in jail talking about everything he can think of. He's probably making up some of it, but right now it sounds good."

"That's his problem."

"It's also your problem, Olsen. Get up, we're going for a ride, just you and me."

"Where? The jail? You got nothing to charge me with."

"We've got plenty. Remember Darlow is our witness now."

"That sonofabitch!"

"True, but he's *our* sonofabitch. Now get smart. I'd just as soon blow your head off right now. You want to live, you forget about trying to run for it, or push somebody in my way. I never miss at ten to twenty feet. Now walk."

When Spur first started his plunge back into normality, he wasn't sure he could make it. His legs were rubbery, his shoulder ached, and a headache kept zapping him behind his eyes. But the walk around the block had started his juices flowing, and now the mental lift of getting his sights on one of the suspects lifted his physical powers as well.

Downstairs Spur told Olsen to point out his mount at the small stable behind the hotel. Spur told him to walk the horse to the livery two blocks over where Spur called to the hand there to bring out a horse saddled and ready to move.

A half hour later they were across the Santiam and moving into the drier side of the river. Ahead long rolling hills seemed to vanish into a plain. They crossed several dry water courses and Spur swore at them softly.

He found the spot he wanted, far enough

away from everyone so a shot or two and a scream would not bring any curious or helpful.

"Get off your nag," Spur told Olsen. "Dismount, right here."

Olsen got down. Spur took the reins to his horse and rode off fifty yards and tied both mounts to a struggling limb of a brushy tree.

He walked back and told Olsen to put his hands behind his back. Spur tied them with a length of rawhide he had brought with him.

"Sit down anywhere, and make yourself comfortable. This might take a few minutes."

"What?"

"You're gonna be dying to find out."

Spur kicked around some outcropping rocks nearby and soon found a rattlesnake. The reptile skittered away from him, but McCoy found a forked stick and pressed the snake into the sand with the fork behind the triangular shaped head. Deftly, the Secret Service agent picked up the rattler, holding it just in back of the head so it was helpless.

A few kicks later he found a second rattler and captured it the same way.

Olsen had watched with interest. Now he stood up and backed away.

"Hey, them things can hurt a guy."

"True, but only if they get their fangs into your flesh. Come on."

Spur prodded Olsen forward by thrusting the angry snakes toward him. Twenty yards ahead there was a dry wash, three feet deep, with steep sides. Spur kicked dirt down from the side to form a two-foot high dike on one end. Then four feet away he did the same thing, forming a small box-like earth hole.

"You ever heard of the Apache justice system, Olsen?"

"Hell no, I ain't no Indian."

"Pretend. The Apaches say that an accused man has a right to prove he is innocent. First he is asked if he wishes to confess to the charge. If he says he is innocent he is put in a pit with from two to ten rattlesnakes, depending on the severity of the charges. If he is bitten by the snakes and lives, he is declared innocent. If he is not bitten by the snakes after an hour, he is declared totally innocent.

"On the other hand, if he is bitten and dies, he is guilty. Now isn't that a simple, efficient form of justice? No bother with a jury, or a judge or a gallows. I like it. Quick, clean."

"I said I ain't no Indian."

"Right now you are." Spur dropped both snakes into the makeshift pit and watched them. They could not climb out. When they tried, the side fell down on top of them. Spur spun Olsen around and tied his feet together. Then he picked up Olsen and moved him a few feet to the pit.

"Remember, if you live, you're innocent. The roundeye courts won't be able to charge you with anything."

"Innocent of what?' Olsen said, still not

believing he was going to be put in the pit.

"Innocent of the slaughter of six people on that July 22 stage. Anything you want to say first?"

"Hell no!"

One of the snakes tried to crawl up the side, but tumbled back down. It coiled at one end, its tail rattling a defiant warning.

Spur picked up Olsen and dropped him into the pit at the end where the snake had not coiled. The pit was only four feet long, and Olsen fell on his side, then pulled his feet partly under him and tried to stand.

"You stand up I'll blow you in half," Spur said, firing one round past Olsen's head.

He screamed. The wail came out loud and plaintive, a kind of defiant plea for help and sorrow and anger all in one.

Spur threw a rock at the coiled snake and it uncoiled and glided toward the new element that had entered the pit. The rattler slithered around Olsen's pants covered leg. The suspect shivered and screamed again.

"Get me out of here!" Olsen said at last. "Get me out!"

"Were you there at the stage massacre, July 22?"

"Yes, damnit, yes! Now get me out of here!"

"Did you kill any of the six persons that day?"

"No, damnit, no!"

"Did Jim Darlow do it?"

"Christ! What do you want? I was there. Darlow was there, Zack was there. None of us done it."

The snake tried to go up the wall but the loose dirt crumbled down again. It turned and slithered straight for Olsen's exposed knee. He shivered. The rattler's eyes glittered. It stopped a foot from the foreign thing and coiled. Its rattler beat a steady warning.

Olsen looked down and saw the growing dark wet stains on his pants. He shivered.

"Well, Olsen still wets his pants. I didn't know that. Wait until I tell the girls up at Claudine's place. Who killed the people, Olsen? Who was the fourth man?"

"He would kill me."

"So will the snakes, but they'll do it right now and it will hurt a lot more. I've heard it takes about six hours after the bite. Your arm swells up to twice its size, your head almost explodes. You get so hot you think you're going to melt, and then everything goes crazy, and you babble and scream and puke all over."

The first snake had nestled in Olsen's lap. The lower tie had come loose enough so he could cross his ankles and his knees splayed out on each side. His wrists were still fastened behind him. The rattler felt the warmth of his body and welcomed it like another sun.

Olsen looked at it and screamed. His cry of fate and death and protest carried across the high prairie for half a mile before it blended with a gentle west wind and faded into the past.

"Who was the fourth man, Olsen?"

The snake behind him was still coiled, beady eyes smarting from the sand, still angry at being captured. The rattle picked up in intensity. The snake struck. Its lightning like thrust hit Olsen's foot, one fang sinking in and sticking in the rubber heel, the other fang hanging in air. It was trapped.

Olsen screamed again, but the rattler on his legs didn't seem to notice.

"Who was the killer, Olsen?"

"Cain." The name was said so softly Spur almost missed it.

"Who?"

"Cain Haworth! He went crazy. The kid from the stage pulled down Cain's mask and the driver recognized him and blurted out his name, and right then he figured he had to kill them all. Cain was a madman, screaming and shouting. I never seen a man so much like an animal. Now get them snakes out of here!"

Spur shot the first one off Olsen's boot, killing it. The second one he held down with the forked stick, pushing it off Olsen's legs so he could hop out of the way, then he let the snake go.

"What else happened up there on the trail?" Spur said.

"The driver pulled a deringer and shot Zack, and that spurred Cain on with his rifle and six gun. Then he shot all the horses and burned up the wagon. We figured if we brought Zack back saying he got accidentally shot hunting it would work. Damn near did."

"You want to hang, Olsen? According to the law you're just as guilty as Cain. You were there, you were a robber, and the deaths were a result of that robbery."

"Christ no! I didn't kill anybody! We was just out for a little fun!"

"You write out completely what happened up there, and we might be able to get you off with, maybe five years. Cain will hang, no way around that."

Olsen worried it. Spur cut his feet free and he stood.

"Damn that wild-assed crazy Cain Haworth! Should have known better than to ride with him. Crazy! Crazy as loco weed." At last he looked across the prairie. "I sure as hell don't want to hang for something Cain did. I'll testify against him. Tell it all just the way it happened. But you got to keep Cain away from me."

"Easy," Spur said. "Now I have to find Cain and bring him in."

"That might be easier to say than to do," Olsen said.

The two men walked to their horses and Spur helped Olsen mount. He left the man's hands tied, to remind him he was a prisoner, and he would be for a long, long time.

Chapter Fourteen

Sheriff Quigley was not surprised when he found out who the fourth man on the robbery-murder was.

"Cain has been headed for the gallows for a couple of years. Thought he could do anything to anybody. Just the opposite of his two brothers."

"Sheriff, let's keep it quiet about picking up Olsen and his confession. Then we can go get Cain tomorrow. Hate to admit it but I feel a little tired."

"Tired. A normal man would be in bed recuperating. We'll get Olsen to write out exactly what he has to say and sign it. You said if he cooperated with us we would charge him just with the robbery?"

"Figured it was a good trade. If he tries to back out of it, you remind him that I will come around and rattle his head."

One short walk up the block and Spur climbed the stairs to his second floor room in the Plainsman. He unlocked the door, stepped to the side and pushed it open. Nothing happened. He went around the frame and inside.

A girl sat on his bed.

"Good morning, Mr. McCoy."

She was Bathsheba, Bee, the eldest daughter of Efrem Longley who had been so sexy in their short talk in the parlor at the Longley spread.

"I heard you were shot and I wanted to come be your nurse. I'm good at nursing."

"Yes, I bet you are."

"Come in and close the door, Mr. McCoy."

"I shouldn't do that, we're alone."

"Yes, at last!" She shrugged her shoulders and her blouse fell to the bed. Her ripe, pink tipped breasts thrust out at him invitingly. "Close the door and lock it, Spur, I need you."

"You shouldn't be doing this." He closed the door and leaned against it.

"I know. But I want to go all the way just once to know what it feels like. I told you I'd made love before. But I haven't. One of the men at the ranch teases me. Lets me play with him but he won't do it, you know, put it inside me. He says my father would kill him."

She slid off the bed and he saw she wore only drawers that had been cut off just below the crotch. She was slender, with good hips and beautiful legs. Her breasts bounced and jiggled as she walked toward him. Spur felt his hot blood surging. She touched his shoulders, then leaned against him, her beautiful breasts flattening against his chest, her arms around him.

159

He felt the heat of her body. Her long blonde hair tumbled around her shoulders, some falling down her chest. She looked up at him.

"Would it be asking too much if you could kiss me?"

He did. Spur was surprised by the fire, the need, the hotness of her kiss. He held it as long as she wanted him to and it burned and burned until his mouth opened and her tongue darted inside, swinging around searching for his.

When they came apart, Spur was rock hard and ready. Her hand found his erection and she squealed in joy.

"Oh, yes! This is going to be a glorious party! And nobody to worry about, and no straw poking me in the back."

Spur smiled. "The ranch hand had you in the haymow?"

"We tried, but people kept coming in the barn. I nearly died wanting him. All he did was play with my boobies."

She led Spur to the bed, sat him down.

"I know you were shot and still recuperating, so I'll be careful of you. I can be on top even."

She unbuttoned his shirt and took it off, her eyes wide at the bandage around his chest.

"Does it hurt a lot?"

"Not now." His hands touched her breasts and she gasped, then smiled.

"Yes! It seems so natural. It feels good."

"It's supposed to. There's nothing unnatural about sex between a man and a woman."

"Show me!"

"We have lots of time. Aren't you afraid of getting pregnant?"

"No. I just finished my . . . my bleeding. A friend of mine says a girl can't get pregnant the day after she stops. That's why I came to find you today."

He reached out where she stood over him and kissed one rosy tipped tit. She shivered. He kissed it again and then nibbled on the morsel before pulling it into his mouth.

Bee moaned and fell on the bed on her back. Her knees drew up and spread and her hips pounded up and down as she shivered and trembled and a series of six hard spasms shot through her frame, distorting her pretty face, as she gasped for breath and tightened her small hands into fists.

The climax passed and she lay there panting.

"Good lord! I've never had one like that before. My friend rubbed me one night when we stayed together, but it wasn't that fine!"

She laughed softly. "I have an idea it's just going to get better and better!"

She unbuttoned Spur's fly and then pulled off his boots and his pants. She saw his short underpants and started to pull them down, but stopped. She jumped on the bed and lay and motioned for him to follow.

Spur lay down with some pain in his chest, then she was leaning over him, her breasts dangling delightfully above him.

He pulled her forward and let one tit drop into his mouth. Bee giggled, then her color rose and she nearly climaxed again.

"Oh, god but that feels good!" She was panting again.

"Take my shorts off," Spur said.

"Yes, I want to see all of you." She knelt beside him and slowly worked the garment down his hips until his hard penis swung upward.

"Oh! Oh! My, it's so big! How could that ever go in . . ." She sat there on her feet staring. Her hand came out and touched it and it jerked. She laughed and grabbed the shaft. "So hard! Like a stick."

"The better to enter you. Mother Nature thought of the problem. You've seen horses and dogs mate."

"Yes, but not up close. So hard!"

She stripped the shorts down and was fascinated by his scrotum.

"I've never really looked . . ."

Spur waited and let her explore. When she was satisfied, he pulled her over him on his right side and kissed her. She leaned back and stared at him.

"Gosh, but you are handsome! I'll always remember my very first time!"

"You sure you should? That you want to do it?"

"Yes! I've waited too long. My friend Betty says she's glad she finally did. Now she does, every once in a while, well, every month. She has a steady boyfriend and they get away. Once out in the woods that she said was just beautiful. They were naked in the grass and the sun shining down, then they played in the stream."

"I can't give you sunshine or a river."

"I don't need that. I want this bed and you!"

He put his hand on her round bottom and massaged it. She still had on the cut off drawers. His hand worked around and lower until he was massaging between her cheeks.

"Maybe we should take off the rest of your clothes."

"Maybe."

"You can always back out."

She sat up at once and stripped off her drawers, then turned and straddled his stomach. He was staring at her blonde thatched crotch.

"I don't want to back out."

Spur helped her lay beside him. He smothered her breasts with kisses and worked down slowly toward her pubic hair. She gasped, climaxed once quickly, then spread her legs as she realized where he was going.

"Oh, my, do you want to do that?"

"Yes," he said.

"Oh!"

He worked past her brush of blonde curls

and kissed the pinkness of her outer labia, and she boiled into a sudden and long climax that brought sweet smelling juices seeping out of her.

Bee squirmed under his ministrations.

"Lordy, I've never in my life felt anything so delicious! That was absolutely remarkable. Great!"

"Sweetheart, you haven't even started feeling good. The best is yet to come."

He thrust a finger into her vagina, and she screeched in surprise and wonder. There was no barrier there. He thrust again and reamed her, spreading her juices. Then he kissed her softly.

"Are you sure you want me to enter you, to make love with you?"

"Oh, darling yes! If you don't I'll scream and claim that you raped me."

"What choice do I have?"

Her legs parted more, he lifted her knees up and slid between them, his chest wound forgotten. She whimpered as he probed.

"Now, Bee, this may hurt a little, but it's just a stretching. Remember when you're a mother a baby's head will come out this same slot, it can stretch that large, so this is just a little bit of enlargement. It might hurt for a minute, but not much."

As he talked he probed, found the right spot and pressed harder and harder until the lubrication worked and the muscles relaxed and stretched and he slipped into her.

"Oh, Lordy! Oh, Christ! That . . . that . . . that didn't really hurt. Oh, glorious! You're inside of me! You broke through and you're fucking me!"

Spur laughed softly, then began his movements, slowly, letting her get the whole effect. She began to hum a soft little tune as her own hips began to work against his.

"Isn't it amazing that nobody has to teach a couple how to make love?" Spur said. "It's one of the few basic instincts left in man."

She didn't reply, just lay there smiling, her eyes closed, humming a little tune and working her hips against him.

Spur was in no hurry. "Do you like that?"

"Oh, Lordy, yes! I could lay here all day. Can I lift my legs?"

"Yes, it will feel different."

She put her legs up and locked them over his back, and she moaned as his erection probed a different track, touched new nerve endings and penetrated deeper.

"Oh, Lordy but that is delicious!"

Suddenly she climaxed. It was more intense this time, a rolling, surging kind that made her moan and yelp and left her so limp she couldn't say a word.

Spur waited for her, not moving for a few minutes. She roused and smiled at him.

"So wonderful! Is that what I've been telling boys I didn't want to do for the past four years? What a ninny! It is so glorious, so marvelous. I could lay here for a year!"

"It's also dangerous. Every exposure means you could get pregnant. And then the fun is over and the work begins. It means for every bit of joy and glory, there is some pain and some work ahead."

"Not if I don't get pregnant. I can watch my bleeding and only make love the day after I finish."

"Your father wants you to get married."

"Enough time for that, or when I find the right man. Oh, you're still hard inside me. You didn't yet?"

"No."

"Billy aways shot that white stuff out whenever I touched him. Sometimes he would do it three times."

"Once will be enough for me in my weakened condition."

He began to move again, and this time he punched hard and fast and left her panting. He knew she was building again, and before he climaxed she came again, the rolling, yelping, and moaning kind. He kept pounding at her, lifting her legs to his shoulders and thrusting as deep as he could reach with every stroke until he felt the flood gates open and the rush began that brought a groan from him, a surge of delight and excitement as he climaxed and panted. She had finished as well and he slumped on her. Her arms came around him when she lowered her legs, and they lay there panting, trying to recover.

"Darling do it again," she said.

He shook his head. "I couldn't for half hour, and I shouldn't. My chest is aching again. What did you tell your father about coming into town?"

"To see Betty, my friend. I come in once a week, and we talk and sew and gossip. She'll say I was there all day. I'll stop by before I go back home." She kissed him tenderly. "Once more?"

"I better not."

"You could kiss me again."

He did, a long, leisurely, exploratory kiss with mouths open and temperatures rising. He broke it off.

"You're trying to get me excited again."

"That certainly got me excited!" She rubbed her breasts against his bare chest below the bandage, then wiggled until he turned over on his back and she lowered one, then the other breast into his mouth for chewing.

"Delightful! When can we do this again?"

"Next month after your bleeding."

She laughed. "And you will be gone by next month. Daddy said you wouldn't be here long. Unless you want to stay and marry me. Then we wouldn't have to worry."

"Tempting, but I'm not ready to settle down yet either."

"But you never will get pregnant and have to."

"Hopefully."

They both laughed.

He pushed her up, felt a twinge in his chest and sat up and began dressing. She sat there naked, her blonde hair falling down her chest, covering her breasts. She stroked her hair.

"You sure about not wanting to get married? It would really please me. And you would be getting a fantastic ranch to help run, and take over when Pa can't do it anymore. A nice little dowry I'm offering."

He bent and kissed her lips, then each pointed breast.

"You make a remarkably tempting offer, even without the ranch. But I have a job to do. I travel all over the western states and territories. To California and to Washington state. What would you do sitting home alone?"

"I thought . . ."

"I know. Sex can't do it all. People participate in sex maybe three hours a week, young married people say. Three hours out of 168 a week, that's less than two percent of your time is spent getting sexy. There has to be a lot more."

He bent and petted her breasts and she reached up for a quick kiss.

"Now you better get dressed and then you can go have lunch with Betty, and tell her about your first time getting fucked."

Bee laughed. "I can't say that word unless I'm feeling real sexy." She paused for a moment, then picked up her clothes and dressed. Spur watched and she didn't mind. When she was ready for the street, Spur checked the hall, then kissed her nose and let her out.

"Maybe I can see you again," she said as she went out the door, then she walked into the hall and toward the stairs.

Spur closed the door, took a deep breath and felt his chest respond. The morning hadn't set back his recovery too much.

He would have a quick dinner in the dining room, and then see if Tyler Udell had dried out Snuffy enough to get him to talk. One witness was fine, but if they had two who could place Cain just coming into town after the massacre, they would be a lot more sure of a conviction.

Chapter Fifteen

Spur found Tyler Udell and Snuffy in a room at the hotel and saw that Snuffy was sober enough to talk. The problem was would he remember what happened that day over a week ago.

Spur used the "cold shower" technique of questioning, pouncing on the subject and whipsawing him before he knew what happened so he had to rely on instinct and recall.

When Snuffy looked up at Spur he saw cold green eyes you could strike a match on and a steel-hard angry face.

"Snuffy, you asshole! I need to know where you were the day that stage massacre took place. I need to know right now!"

Snuffy shrank back on the bed and pulled a blanket up to his chin.

"Christ! Let me think. Yeah, that was the same day I walked out that horse. Kept the nag from foundering. And the bastard that owned her never even came back for her. Don't know where he got to. Thought for sure he'd give me a dollar for saving his horse. Christ, I learned me a lesson there."

"Shut up, Snuffy! Just answer the damn

questions. I don't need a whole long story about it! Now, who owned the horse? Who rode that nag until he almost killed her?"

"Hell, easy. Cain Haworth."

"What time of day was it?"

Snuffy laughed. "Don't got no Waterbury. Don't hold much to keeping time, 'cepting when it gets dark and light. Good enough for me."

Spur cuffed him along the side of the head and Snuffy sat up on the bed, eyes angry.

"I didn't sober you up to find out about your philosophy of life, asshole! What time was it? Morning, afternoon, dusk?"

Snuffy took a deep breath, winced and held his side, then nodded. "Yeah, all right. It was after dinner time 'cause I got throwed out of a saloon 'cause they were serving noon meal at some tables. Must have been two, three hours after that. I'd say had to be three o'clock."

Spur's attitude changed. He reached down and shook Snuffy's hand. "We might need you to testify in court about that. Can you do that? We'll give you enough notice to get sober, and get a shave and a bath. Could you stand that?"

Snuffy drew back. "You ain't gonna pop me again?"

"Nope."

"Good. Ty said might be a half a pint in it for me if I remembered what happened that day."

"True. You tell Barry over at the Petticoat that you have a tab. You get a pint a day on me for the next two weeks." Spur flipped a twenty dollar gold piece in the air and caught it. "Or would you rather have this twenty?"

Snuffy reached for it, then shook his head. "Nope. I been a drunk too long. I'd buy three pints and get skunk-drunk and somebody would steal the rest of that twenty. I'll take the pint a day."

"And get a bath, a shave and a haircut and a clean pair of pants and shirt. Otherwise Barry won't give you a pint. Ty will help you." Spur handed Ty a five dollar gold piece. He went to the door and waved, then walked out the door and headed to the Petticoat to give Barry the word.

He was back in the street when a rider came in at a gallop.

"The Santiam's dried up! Not a drop coming through her! Dry as a sandbox in August!"

Spur went to the livery barn and got a horse. He took a rifle and his six-gun and rode out of town a half mile to where the Santiam curled past.

She was bleached bone dry.

He swore softly and turned upstream. It had to be that sluice gate he had seen. Nothing else would cut the flow to nothing. What little water got under the sluice gate would vanish into the river bed long before it got to town. He rode to the Young place and found the rancher gone. His wife said six men had ridden up that morning and talked, and her husband got his rifle and two boxes of rounds for it and ridden north with the men. She wasn't sure, but she thought she recognized Mr. Longley with them.

Spur thanked her and rode up the dry river on the trail north. He hoped he wasn't too late to prevent this from blowing up into a water rights range war.

He was.

Spur heard the rifle shots while he was still a mile away from the sluice gate. Two shots sounded and a seven or eight shot burst replied. Then sporadic fire came as he rode faster.

He stopped on a small rise where he could see both sides of the stream ahead. The sluice gate had been dropped. He could see water above it, and almost none below.

Puffs of smoke showed on the rise behind the gate on the Box H land, showing where the riflemen were. On the other side of the stream there was a heavily timbered hill where the firing sounds came from. The brush and woods were too thick to spot individual blue smoke from the black powder in the rounds.

For a moment it felt as if he were back in the infantry with a blue uniform on evaluating a Rebel strongpoint. The situation was clear. Nobody was going to win. From what he could see the Haworth men had dug in, with a breastwork of logs that had firing slots cut out of them. They could hold off a company from the front.

The attackers lay just behind a stretch of nearly a hundred yards that was open land, with no cover of any kind. They would be picked off like ducks in a rain barrel if they tried an assault.

Spur turned his mount and rode at right angles to the river to the open range side, heading for the woods and the finger ridge where the attackers must be. He came down the slope quietly, heard the firings and one or two whining incoming slugs, before he tied his horse and moved cautiously toward the combatants.

McCoy had no idea what he was going to do. Stop the attack was first, but beyond that, he didn't know. If no one had been killed yet, he had a chance.

He saw the first man behind a large Douglas fir. Closer to the front of the woods nestled under Engelmann spruce were two more men. Behind an old fallen log he saw the white-haired Efrem Longley. Spur worked his way down silently toward the first man and called to him sharply from behind.

"Don't turn around, you're covered. I'm friendly, I want to talk to Longley."

The man started to turn, then nodded. "Yeah. Fine. Sounds like that federal guy. Come on past." He called ahead so the others would know Spur was coming in and Longley sat down behind the log.

"What you doing up here?"

"Trying to keep your wife from being a widow. What the hell you trying to do, get this whole county into a range war?"

"Better war than to see my cattle all die of thirst."

"We can work out something better. Any of your people been hit yet?"

"No."

"Then tell them to stop shooting and let me talk to the men across the river."

"Can't do that. We have four ranches represented here."

"Then take a vote. Somebody gets killed out here, I can guarantee you that whoever pulled the trigger is going to hang. Now is this important enough to eget killed over?"

Longley sighed. His years were slowing him down and he hated it. "We're right, McCoy. You know that we're right."

"A lot of folks who were right also are dead. You want to be one of them then you jump out of the woods and storm across that hundred yards of open space and find out for yourself."

"Nobody is going to charge them. Just want them to know we're here. We got a plan."

"I bet." Spur looked at the river from over the log. The firing had died out as the others on this side watched Longley, who was clearly their leader. Spur could see the river and the way it surged against the gate. Some flotsam had built up there already. As he watched he noticed something floating down the now sluggish current. He stared at it closer. It was a wooden box lashed to two short logs.

The shape of the box looked familiar, and then he remembered where he had seen boxes like that before.

Dynamite!

The box would hold fifty to a hundred sticks, he couldn't remember which. More than enough to blow the gate into kindling. They would let it float down to the sluice gate where it would catch against it in the jam of small brush and limbs, and then one of the men on this side would shoot into the box until the dynamite exploded.

The new gelatin explosive wasn't as stable as black powder. Even a pistol bullet would set off a stick of it.

"Don't do it, Longley."

"Do what?"

"The box of dynamite."

"Too late now, but nice try."

As they talked the current quickened and the box lodged against the gate, caught there in the limbs and trash. At once six rifles fired at the container. Spur saw the slugs slam into the gate, into the logs holding the box afloat.

Maybe the dynamite was too stable to explode.

"Tell them to stop, Longley!"

Just as the rancher stopped shooting and looked at Spur, the river in front of them erupted in a gigantic fountain as the fifty sticks of dynamite exploded in an ear shattering, crunching roar.

The wooden sluice gate dam splintered and rose in great chunks hurtling into the sky downstream. Water geysered a hundred feet in the air and mud and rocks began coming down on both sides of the river as the explosion propelled them in all directions with equal force.

A great blue cloud of smoke hung over the area for a moment, then a slapping wave of sound and rushing air slammed into the trees and whistled around them until it played out on the slopes behind.

Now all was quiet. The gate and the posts were gone. The stream lay as it had been with the exception of a ten foot deep hole in the riverbed which rapidly filled with water from upstream. It overflowed and the water swept on down the main flood plain of the river's normal course. Even the ditch that had channeled water to the Haworth lake was covered and filled by the dirt and rocks from the explosion.

In a matter of five seconds the problem had been solved and as far as Spur knew nobody wounded. But the problem wasn't solved. Only the immediate flashpoint cause had been put out of business.

Suddenly the firing from across the stream began again, and the men ducked behind trees and logs.

"Bastards!" someone shouted from the other side. "I'll kill you all for that!"

"Sounds like Cain Haworth himself," Longley said. "He never was one with a slow temper."

"If anybody comes storming across that open spot, I don't want anyone to shoot them!" Spur said during a lull in the firing from across the way. "If they come, we shoot over their heads to turn them back."

As he said it three men jumped from the brush and waded the stream.

"Wait until they get fifty yards from the trees, then on my signal, everyone fire, BUT OVER THEIR HEADS. Anyone gets killed out there, somebody in here hangs!"

Spur waited. When the three men were at the point he had selected he shouted, "Fire!"

Thirty rounds whistled and snapped over the three men's heads in the open. One turned at once and ran back to the stream. A second soon followed. The third shook his fist at the woods, fired his rifle three times, then turned and ran back to the brush on the far side of the stream.

The Longley team lay in the grass for an hour waiting. There was no response from across the way.

"I think they have given up the fight," Spur said. "Now is the time you soldiers go home, and Longley and I go pay a social call on Henry Haworth."

Two of the other ranchers grumbled, but at last nodded and found their horses deeper in the woods and rode out. Longley watched Spur and nodded.

"Damn but you would make me a good son-in-law. Sure you don't cotton to one of my daughters?"

Spur swung up into his saddle and nodded. "Matter of fact, Longley, I cotton to all three of them. Three fine ladies. One of them is going to be a school marm, I hope. The oldest one is sassy and nice and the youngest is the beauty. But I'm not a good marriage risk. I'll be gone in a week. Now, let's swing south and come up the regular trail into the Box H ranch."

"Are you going to arrest him?" Longley said after they had the ranch in sight.

"Why?"

"He has violated our water rights."

"True. But what if he didn't order the sluice gate closed?"

"Who, then?"

"We'll have to wait and see."

Spur knew there had to be a confrontation with Haworth. It had to come now, but he had no idea of the outcome. This would make three felonies he could charge Haworth with if he had ordered the water diverted. He also had to pick up Cain Haworth and charge him with the killings.

The sentry at the first gate frowned when he saw them.

"Mr. Haworth told me not to let anyone past," the cowhand said. The rifle was held loosely in his hands pointing at the ground.

Spur's six-gun came up quickly, covering the man.

"Doesn't matter, this is official law enforcement business. If you have any objection to that you ride ahead of us with both hands on the saddle horn."

"You that federal lawman?" the guard asked.

"That's right, Spur McCoy, United States Secret Service."

"That's good enough for me. I'll tell them that someone is coming."

He started to lift the rifle.

"No," Spur said. He motioned for Longley to ride near the man and take the rifle and his pistol. "Let's ride up and see the man of the house."

Henry Haworth was on the front porch waiting for them when they rode in. From the looks of his face, Spur figured that he knew about the sluice gate, the dynamite, and the small war. His face was haggard, his eyes sunken and red. His scraggly sparse hair in disarray. Haworth leaned heavily on a gold headed cane.

"Reckon you know about the river."

"Yes. Did you order the gate closed?"

"No."

"Who did?"

"Cain. He took four men and went out just before dark last night. Didn't tell me. We still got plenty of water. It was a mistake that you corrected."

"Where is your son, Cain, Mr. Haworth?"

"Left. Soon as the explosion happened, he rode home fast and charged out of here with two horses. He headed for town."

"You mind if we confirm that with some of your hands?"

"No. Anything else?"

Spur saw that the old rancher was about to collapse. Lot came out and put his arm around his father, supporting him. Lot looked at Spur and nodded.

"I saw Cain ride out, Mr. McCoy. He had two rifles with him, and lots of ammunition. He took his two hand guns too. Said Darlow and Olsen were not going to get him in trouble. What did he mean by that?"

"We'll have to find out, Lot. If you say Cain left, I'll take your word for it. Thanks for the help of the Box H crew for the work on the two houses."

Lot nodded. "Least we can do. The barns will be next, the middle of August. We'll get it planned ahead of time."

Spur tipped his hat and walked with Longley back toward where the horses were tied at the rail. Longley gave the guard his weapons, and the two men mounted and rode toward town.

"So Cain is running," Longley said. "It doesn't seem reasonable for him to light out because of the sluice gate thing."

"He's running from more that that. He's the one who killed those six people on that stage."

Longley sighed. "It figures. Never have had much use for the boy. And he's been trying to come courting Bee for three or four months now. She told me not to let him."

Spur reset his low crowned gray hat. "I think we better move along a little faster. I got me a bad feeling about this Cain Haworth."

Chapter Sixteen

As soon as the two riders came into town Spur knew there was trouble. Groups of men and women talked on street corners. There was a knot of men around the sheriff's office. People in the street seemed to be waiting for something. Spur and Longley rode to the little court house and tied up their horses.

"It's her father!" somebody in the crowd said.

Mrs. Longley came bursting from the group of people near the sheriff's office and threw herself into her husband's arms. She was sobbing. He looked at her curiously, patting her back and talking quietly. Then he listened carefully to what she told him.

"Efrem, somebody took Bee! He stopped our buggy and looked at us and then told Bee to get out. It was awful. He had his guns!" She shivered and sobbed against his shoulder. Then went on.

"Bee wouldn't get down from our buggy. The man on the horse with the gun was Cain Haworth, and she's told me several times that he has bothered her and she doesn't like him. Then he rode up and grabbed her and pulled her onto his horse. I screamed at him and hit him with the buggy whip. He fired two shots over my head and then rode out of town to the east."

Longley headed for the sheriff's office. Quigley met them at the boardwalk.

"It was Cain Haworth," Quigley said. "We have two witnesses who identified him. Our posse is almost ready and we'd like you to come."

"I want to go along, too," Spur said. The sheriff nodded.

It was almost three o'clock that afternoon before they knew for sure where Cain and his heavily loaded horse were headed. He had started east, then circled around to the south and was on a honey-bee streak for the Longley ranch. The posse rode faster then, not bothering to track more than every half mile or so.

The group consisted of two deputies, and three townsmen who were reliable, sturdy and good shots. The sheriff had recruited them as special posse members for emergencies. This was no rag tag mob out for blood. Rather it was a trained unit, used to working together and all willing to obey the sheriff's orders.

"He's gonna burn down my buildings," Efrem Longley said as he charged along at the head of the posse.

Spur figured Cain was looking for a pair of

fresh horses. He would know he couldn't stay ahead of a mounted posse for long double loaded. There would be little time for anything other than saddling new mounts and making sure the girl didn't run away.

When they came within sight of the Longley ranchhouse, they saw it was still standing. Nothing had been burned. Both girls and three of the hands were in the front yard. The hands had been tied to a tree and were still trying to get lose. The girls were solemn and Mary had red eyes from crying.

Delilah told them what happened.

"This man came riding up with Bee, shot at one of our hands and made him tie up the other two, then dragged Bee to the barn and pretty soon they rode out the side door, both on fresh horses. They went south."

"Did he hurt you?" Longley demanded. Both girls shook their heads. Longley ran inside and came back with two boxes of shells for his rifle and headed south. The posse followed.

A half mile below the buildings, Cain evidently had ridden into the shallows of the Santiam. The group had to split, working both sides of the river to find out where he came out. At the current low level of the river, he could ride along it for miles and leave no prints.

That's what he did. The sun was staring to go down and still the posse was split across the river.

"He'll come out sooner or later," Sheriff Quigley said. "He can't camp overnight in the water."

An hour later it was dark and they still had not found the tracks leaving the water.

Spur had been holding his side as he rode. It hurt, but not enough to make him stay behind. He studied the river and the gently rolling plain. Cain was no more than an hour ahead of them. How had he stayed out of sight? Now he could leave the water and ride all night. He could walk the horses and still cover four miles an hour. From dawn to dusk he could put forty miles between him and the searchers.

Quigley looked at his seven men. "Can't do much until it gets light," he said.

Spur shook his head. "He wants us to stop, Sheriff. Put yourself in his shoes, what would you do?"

"I don't know."

Longley spoke up. "What I would do is slow us down, like he did with the ride in the water, then when the sun went down, I'd get back on land and move as fast as I could for as long as the horses would hold out, then find some thick brush and hide."

"That's good, Longley," Spur said. About the way I'd play it, Sheriff, this is your command, but could I make a suggestion?"

"Yes."

"Let me take Longley and two men and move out along the river. We probably won't

find any tracks, but odds are he will move on
down the river route because it's flat and
easy going beside it. What we might find is a
campfire, or hear some sound. Anything is
better than all of us sitting here. We will have
you and your men here as a background in
case he tries to double back."

"You find anything fire three shots and
we'll catch up," the sheriff said.

Spur nodded and Longley took one of the
men the sheriff designated and moved across
the hock deep water. Spur and the other
deputy moved down this side of the stream.
They agreed to keep in contact with each
other by lighting a match every mile or so.

Spur gave up trying to read the ground for
any sign. Even with the partly cloudly moonlight, it was impossible. They would move
slowly, watching for fires and listening. Spur
hoped he wouldn't hear any screams.

Spur figured by the location of the big
dipper that it was nearly midnight. He had
just seen the flare of a match across the
stream, and gave an answering one. When he
looked south again he saw a glow in the sky.
Fire!

"Longley!" Spur shouted. "See that fire
ahead? Is there a ranch down that way?"

"Yeah, Iverson. He's on your side of the
river. We better ride!"

By the time they covered the two miles to
the Iverson ranch, the barn was burned
down. Iverson sat on the steps of his house

watching. He had a bullet in his shoulder.

"Damn Cain Haworth!" he told them. "Pranced in here and demanded two fresh horses. I said no. He shot me. No warning, just blew me into the ground. Then he took two horses, changed the saddles, took your daughter, Longley, and rode out south."

"How was Bee? Had he hurt her? Was he forcing her to go along with him?"

"Damn right he was forcing her. She tried to talk to me and he told her to shut up. He almost hit her. That kid had a wild look in his eye."

"She was . . . was still dressed proper?"

"Yes. I don't think he'd had time to do anything. Efrem, I'd like to ride with you, but I couldn't help much."

"You stay put, Bill," Longley said. "Come daylight you get into town and have Doc Varner look at that shoulder. We better be moving on."

"How long ago did they leave, Mr. Iverson?" Spur asked.

"Not more than an hour, maybe less. Good luck."

"We'll leave these two men here in case he comes back and tries to burn your house. The deputies will signal the sheriff to come down and wait with you. We'll move out and try to trail Cain. You tell the sheriff what happened when he comes."

They rode.

The best route south was along a county

road that passed near the ranch house and wound to south and east, away from the river. Spur rode for a quarter of a mile, then stopped, lit a stinker match and a handful of dead grass and checked the dusty roadway. There were tracks of two horses, both moving fast. There were no night insect tracks over the hoof prints as there were on those made earlier in the day. These were the right tracks.

They rode for another hour. The moon came out brightly. Every half mile they stopped and checked the trail, which had turned into something of a wagon road. The same pair of prints were there.

Spur felt they were gaining on the killer. He had no good evidence, he simply sensed it. They came to a spot of woods near a feeder stream where the trail forded across under an archway of a dark tunnel. Spur slowed. It looked dangerous.

The pair of rifle shots came like a booming death knell in the dark silence of the Montana night. Spur bent low on the far side of his horse. He heard a cry and saw Longley slump in the saddle and bring his mount to a stop.

Spur tugged at the reins and brought his mount around to grab Longley's horse. He led it to the side of the trail and dismounted on the wrong side catching Efrem as he tumbled from the saddle.

"Where are you hit?"

"Thigh. Hurts like hell. Think it broke my leg."

Spur helped him die down in the grass. Another rifle round slammed over their heads. It came from across the trail and twenty yards down.

Longley nodded and bent to bind up his leg.

Spur darted across the road, running low and hard. The hidden rifle spoke again, but the lead missed. McCoy slid into the brush quietly, not making a sound and listened. If Cain was the gunman, Bee had to be there too. He listened. At first he could only hear the crickets and a night hawk. It was probably a North American goatsucker. An owl hooted down the trail.

Then he heard movement. Man movement. A twig cracked, leaves rustled. To the left and going away from him. Spur knew he couldn't fire while the girl was with Cain. He moved in the direction of the pair, testing each step, careful not to make a sound.

After ten steps he paused. The sounds came from ahead of him, but closer.

A horse nickered somewhere beyond.

Someone yelped in pain.

Whispers followed, all ahead.

Spur moved faster, testing steps, checking as far as he could see in the darkness of the brushy area.

"No!" a woman's voice said indignantly.

A hand hit flesh with a slapping sound.

Spur rushed forward, his pistol out, his

face a mask of anger. Suddenly he broke out of the woods. Ahead two dark shapes showed in the moonlight as horses. He fired his pistol into the air and dove to one side.

"No, no! I won't. Help me whoever you are!"

Spur fired again, over the heads of the horses.

There was a scream. Then a man cursed, and Spur heard saddle leather creaking. Spur leaped up and charged toward the first horse. The one behind it wheeled away and rode.

"He's getting away!" Bee Longley shouted.

Spur was sure then, he emptied his six-gun at the fading black blob in the dark night, then called softly.

"Bee, where are you?"

"Over here. He tied me to some bush."

Spur found her, cut the rope and told her where her father was and that he was wounded.

"Go through the woods here and call to him. Help tie up his leg. You could get a fire going too, after I'm gone. I'll take your horse, it's fresher than mine."

She clung to him, then reached up and kissed him. "Good luck, wonderful man," she said.

Spur stepped into the saddle and swung the horse down the trail south. Now the fugitive had less of a head start, and he had lost his trump card. Now they would play the game according to Spur's rules, which meant there were no rules, it was kill or be killed.

Spur began by riding down the road at full gallop for a quarter of a mile. Then he took the Spencer and fired seven shots down the road and at slight angles to it. Spur pulled off the road into a patch of woods and wiped down his horse, staked it out where it could graze and lay down with his head against a tree trunk and his right hand closed around his six-gun.

Spur was aching tired. His side hurt again. He needed some rest. He had been up for almost twenty hours. As he thought about Cain, he decided this was the second night Cain had not had any sleep. The night before he had been closing down the sluice gate, and tonight he was running. A few rifle rounds over his head would convince him he had to keep right on running. Spur would be up at the first signs of light and start tracking him. He should have three hours of sleep.

Morning came slowly. The sun was hidden by a light overcast, and as Spur jumped up and checked his weapons, he was afraid that it might rain and wash out Cain's tracks. On the other hand the land needed a good soaking.

He was in the saddle a few moments later, checked the road and found the hoofprints that showed no oddity, and worked down the road. He rode in hundred yard spurts, then paused and studied the ground from the back of the roan he had borrowed from Bee. Cain's trail was still straight down the road, and the marks showed that he was pushing the horse. If he foundered on him out here he would be in deep trouble.

Two miles farther along the wagon road, Spur noticed that the horseshoe prints were lighter now, without so much toe thrown dirt. The mount had slowed almost to a walk.

The next time he checked the horse was wandering from side to side on the road, as though either the rider was sleeping, or the horse was in the first stages of giving out.

Spur came to a small rise and studied the land ahead of him. The light overcast had burned off and the sun shone brightly again. There would be no rain today. He could see five miles south, half that to the east and west. No smoke showed. He saw no ranches or houses. Nor could he see Cain ahead on the straight road.

He rode half a mile this time before he checked the tracks. They were more erratic than before. It was the horse now, Spur had seen the signs many times before. There were uneven hoof marks, side to side motion, and here and there dark streaks on the dirt that could only be unintentional urination.

He walked his mount now, watching the trail carefully. On a hunch he moved off the road, angled a quarter of a mile into the plains and rode hard south again just out of sight of the trail, then worked back to the road through a copse of brush and small willow and cottonwood trees. Nobody near the roadway could see him come.

On this new stretch of roadway, he could find no evidence that Cain's horse had passed over this section. Spur tied his mount in some brush and worked through fringes of high grass and trees north near the edge of the trail.

Ahead lay more of the light brush. A short distance beyond lay a swale with the dry course of a creek surrounded by dozens of small trees. There were no evergreens.

Spur remembered when he had burned out one killer with a grass fire, but that wouldn't work here. He squirmed forward through the grass and shrubs, working toward the heaviest part of the hardwood trees. He found a fist-sized rock and threw it thirty yards in the brush. The stone hit a tree bounced off through dry leaves and cracked when it hit another rock on the ground.

Twin shots thundered into the spot from somewhere to the left. Spur watched but saw only tendrils of blue smoke drifting up through the thick growth.

He angled toward the smoke, moving as cautiously and quietly as he could. Cain must be awake, or partly awake to hear the rock hit. But after being without any real sleep for going on fifty-two hours, he also must be bleary eyed, jumpy, his nerves raw bands stretched drum tight.

Spur worked through the grass and light brush on his belly, pulling the Spencer with him, holding his Eagle Butt Peacemaker in his right fist.

He worked another six feet forward and a ruffled grouse took off a foot ahead of him in a wing flapping thunder that sounded twice as loud because of the surprise. Spur rolled four feet to his right just as two slugs zipped through the grass where he had been. Grouse don't panic unless someone is right on top of them, and Cain would know that.

Spur waited for five minutes, listening, watching. He heard nothing. Perhaps his quarry was sleeping.

He worked forward again, came to an open place and stared out from behind a heavily leafed shrub. Under a large cottonwood tree he saw a black hulk. A horse was tied deeper in the shadows. As his eyes probed the hulk again, he realized it was a lean-to of sorts. Boards had been pushed against the trunk of the tree forming a dark cave.

Spur couldn't see inside it. As he looked past the lean-to he decided that if Cain had been here, he had a clear view of the trail less than twenty yards away. An easy bushwhacking murder.

Nothing moved in the dimness of the lean-to. Spur put three slugs through the opening and rolled to his left. There was no response.

He fired again, and rushed the small shelter. Just as he came up to it he smelled the smoke, then heard the sputtering of a fuse.

Dynamite fuse!

He leaped away from the opening, trying to shield himself behind the thick tree trunk.

The explosion thundered through the morning light, splattering the boards of the shelter backwards in a froth of splinters and dirt, sending a cloud of smoke into the sky, and blinding Spur with dust from the explosion.

Spur rolled, feeling the pain in his chest from the old wound, then came up with his pistol cocked and ready. From across the clearing a rifle barked and a round dug into the ground an inch from Spur's knee. He realized that was all of him the shooter could see around the tree.

McCoy stood up quickly for total protection behind the cottonwood, and looked behind him. He had no other cover to run to. He was cut off, and the man ahead of him carried a rifle.

Chapter Seventeen

Spur bent low and peered quickly around the base of the big tree at knee height. He saw only a rifle poked over the lip of the small creek where it had cut deeply into the soil. The rifle spoke and a round thudded into the big tree.

After drawing back for a moment Spur reached around tree and put a round into the dirt directly beside the rifle barrel. He couldn't rush forward. It was a long time until darkness. He had no dynamite bombs. He took a quick look around the other side of the tree head high. Yes, the ground slanted downward to the river. By crawling straight away from the tree, Spur would be out of the direct line of sight of Haworth. It was worth a try. He checked the angle, bellied down into the grass and crawled away from the big tree seeing that the land slanted down on this side of the tree as well. After thirty feet he got to his knees and bent over double he raced for the fringe of brush again and its protecting cover.

Once there, Spur checked his rifle, which he had been dragging behind him, and made sure it was ready to fire. Then he worked his way around to the side of the big tree, moving without sound, searching for the wanted man's horse. Or did he have a horse? Spur had thought he saw one tied in the woods, but it couldn't be in any shape to ride.

His own horse!

Spur reversed his direction and ran flat out, not worrying about the noise now. He got to a spot where he could see his horse and lay down in the brush, hidden from view and waited.

It was less than two minutes later when he saw Cain working through the woods toward the mount. Spur let him get almost to the horse, then slammed a .52 caliber round from the Spencer through Cain's right leg. He went down in a heap, spun and fired three times with his pistol.

"Give it up, Cain. Your horse is gone, you're wounded, and the posse is less than an hour behind us. You don't have a chance."

"What kind of a chance do you think I have against a jury in High Prairie?" He fired twice more, then began crawling away. A moment later he was out of sight.

Spur worked forward carefully. He had the advantage now, he didn't want to lose it. He was just beyond his horse when Cain's rifle spoke sharply. The round missed Spur by a dozen feet, but he knew he wasn't the target when the borrowed horse behind him screamed in mortal pain and went down, legs kicking in fury, the sickening scream of the dying animal coming again and again, until at last the legs were stilled and so was the death cry.

Spur worked forward again, crouching in the brush, eyeing the way ahead. What if he was wrong? If Cain's horse was still sound, the man would be gone for good.

McCoy lifted up now and ran from brush clump to clump, not knowing where Cain was, but gambling that he was well away from this part of the woods. Spur circled and found the spot where he thought he had seen the horse. It was there lying on its side. As he watched he could see no movement.

He had to know.

The Secret Service man pushed closer, then took another chance and dashed the last ten yards across open ground and touched the animal. Already it had started to stiffen. The beast had been ridden to death.

Spur ran back the way he had come, worked up to the spot where he had wounded Cain and looked for blood stains. He found them on leaves and blades of grass.

Slowly he began to track Cain Haworth. The young man was clever and knew the country. McCoy worked down the dry stream, running after rounding bends in the shallow draw when he knew he was out of sight, working more slowly when he would be in Cain's firing view.

Within half an hour the dry water course

had emptied its sand into the Santiam. Despite the low water above, this downstream section had picked up enough feeder creeks to make it a worthwhile small river again. Spur checked up and down the water, but could see no wounded man. Every few steps in the sand he had found small damp spots where a drop of blood had soaked into the dryness.

The Santiam was not deep enough to allow a man to float down it on a log yet. At least that choice was not allowed the fugitive.

Spur's nose twitched. Smoke! A light wind blew up the small valley he was in. He had seen no buildings. The smoke meant an Indian camp, a homesteader, or a traveler's campfire. He was sure that Cain had not stopped to build a fire. Cain still ran ahead of him. The droplets of blood indicated that he might be slowing down a little. As the chase slowed, and Spur relaxed somewhat, the nagging pain in his upper left chest came pounding back at him. He fought it down, deliberately thought of something else, and moved back into the brush along the creek as he went downstream.

The fugitive would be at the fire, wherever it was.

Spur found it twenty minutes later. The homesteader's cabin was minimal to meet the requirements to "improve" the one hundred and sixty acres. The owner had "cultivated" a half acre to match that need, and had built three pens out of poles for his cows. He would be a rancher, not a farmer.

He would be if he survived today.

The cabin was twenty yards beyond the stream, made of logs hauled in from the timbered slopes, chinked and mortared. A clothes line behind the cabin showed a woman's petticoats and a man's work pants and shirts. No children's clothes.

Spur knew at once that he could not show himself. With all the caution at his command, Spur moved forward in the woods, until he could see the front door of the cabin. There was also a well there, a bucket and windlass with a ratchet and a rope to reach the water.

A small barn at the far side was now only a shed, with the promise of more later. Twenty head of calves bawled in the pens, and it seemed that this rancher was just getting his start the hard way.

A pistol shot echoed through the morning air. Spur wondered if it were still morning. He hadn't thought about the time. He waited, that was all he could do now. McCoy wondered if the man of the house were dead or wounded. As he thought about it, the heavy door opened, and Cain came out with a woman held in front of him as a shield.

"Spur McCoy! I know you're out there, you bastard. I know you. You tracked me. You just caused this homesteader in here to die. It's all your fault. You want this pretty woman to die too? Answer me or I'll slit her throat right now!"

Chances are he wouldn't. The woman was his only bargaining chip, he wouldn't kill her, Spur decided.

Cain shouted at him for five minutes, holding the woman. Cain could see now that she was bare above the waist. Small breasts showed over Cain's arm that viced around her stomach.

Then Cain changed his tactics. His right hand came out with a knife, and he held the woman and made a slice across her right breast.

She screamed, a wailing protest of fear and anger and pain and suffering. Spur sighted in with the rifle. He was eighty yards away. An easy shot. But he wasn't sure if the weapon had been sighted in or not. An inch one way or the other and the wrong person could die. He looked at legs, but the woman was big enough to cover Cain completely.

Spur bit his lip and waited for the woman's screams to die out.

"It's all your fault, McCoy. She wouldn't be suffering this way if you threw out your weapons. I'll let you walk away from here free. I'll take the horse and you can go your way." He laughed when Spur didn't respond.

McCoy fired. The rifle round went precisely where Spur had aimed it, maybe a half inch to the left. Now he knew where the rifle would fire. The bullet smashed into the door jamb and splintered wood fragments into the pair but neither one was hurt.

Cain screamed at him. Spur was sure the man's eyes were wild with fear and anger, the way they had been in the saloon that night. He touched the tip sight on the end of the rifle with his wet finger, then sighted in again. This time when Cain reached around to cut the woman again, Spur aimed and fired rapidly, the slug slashing through Cain's lower arm, breaking both bones, driving him back inside the cabin. He slammed the door but for several minutes Spur could hear the man wailing in pain and anger.

As soon as the door shut Spur ran. He circled the clearing looking for horses. He found two behind the shed, which housed two milk cows. The shed could not be seen from the side window of the house. Quickly Spur put halters on the two horses and led them directly away from the shed into the woods, then ran with them a half mile down the small valley through the trees, and tied them to brush where they could graze.

By the time he got back to the cabin, it seemed to be much the way it had been before. Spur went to the side of the house with no window and ran the twenty yards to the log cabin. He pressed against the cabin, panting. As his breath came back, he fisted his six-gun and worked around to the corner, checked to be sure no one was on the other side, then edged up to the window with four, foot-square panes of glass, and peered inside.

It was a one room cabin. On the far wall he saw a small fireplace and cooking gear on the hearth. There was no stove. On the wall to the right stood a homemade bed with a mattress of straw and grass, Spur guessed. Lying face down on the blanket was a man in rough work clothes. A large red stain of blood thickened beneath his head.

Spur ducked down and went to the other side of the window to look at the other half of the house. He saw the woman had been tied to a chair. She was naked. Her legs had been spread and Cain sat in front of her laughing. Spur lifted the Peacemaker and sighted through the window. It was an angle. Would that make the bullet deflect? Probably. Cain sat with his side to Spur and his pants were around his knees. Spur aimed just below Cain's arm at his side, and fired.

The bullet hit the glass pane, and deflected enough to miss Cain, but slashed through the upper outside of the woman's thigh.

Cain reacted with the first sound of breaking glass, rolling toward the window and out of range. Three shots blasted through the other window panes, and Spur ran around the house to the door and tried to open it. Locked, or braced shut. He kicked it. It gave a little. Three more kicks with all his weight behind it and the door gave way.

Spur had reloaded as he ran, now he swung the six-gun into the house and darted inside.

Cain was gone. The wood frame of the window had been lifted out and Cain had gone through it. Spur looked out, saw a form running into the far woods. He paused only long enough to cut the woman free, told her he would be back to help her, and rushed out of the house.

Spur peered cautiously around the end of the big logs that formed the first row of the structure. Cain would be lying in wait up there, ready to pick him off with the rifle the moment he moved out across the open spot. Spur had to go the long way. He went to the front of the house, and ran directly ahead for the woods. He made it without attracting any shots. Once in the cover of the trees, he ran to the right, to circle the short side of the clearing to the point where Cain had escaped.

As he ran Spur felt his energy and his desire weakening. He was still wounded, he had been up for two days with almost no sleep, and he was so tired he could barely stand.

Then he thought of Cain. He had been up almost three days without sleep. He was wounded twice in the leg and arm, and he was the one running.

Spur snorted, made sure his weapons were both ready to fire, and hurried along the plain and easy to follow trail. Now he had to think the way the hunted man would. What would he do? What would he try?

Cain's first priority would be to kill Spur.

If not kill him, disable him. That meant a trap, an ambush. Spur knew he was in better physical condition than Cain who had a serious leg wound, a broken arm, and had to be still losing blood from it. Spur paused and listened.

They were in heavier timber again, with a few Douglas firs and Engelmann spruce dotting the hard woods. Cain could hide behind any of the big conifers and pick him off with the rifle.

Spur heard nothing. Then a scream came from somewhere ahead. Was it a trap, a trick? Had Cain simply fallen on his wounded arm, or tripped and hurt his leg? Spur had to find out. He took a calculated risk and ran up the slope to the ridgeline fifty feet above.

Spur heard the roar and looked to his right. Through the thin brush and conifers he saw a grizzly bear rear up on its hind feet and tower eight feet in the air. The beast made a swiping motion at something and a pistol fired. Just ahead of the advancing king of the northwoods, Spur saw a flash of Cain going down. He wasn't sure if the grizzly had hit Cain or if he dove to escape the mighty paw. If the swing had connected it was powerful enough to tear off an arm, or a head.

Another pistol shot fired and Spur saw now that Cain was under the bear, and five or six hundred pound beast was growling and roaring in fury. Cain edged backward, scuffling along on his hands and feet, his back to the ground, his eyes watching the animal hovering over him.

Spur made the decision without considering the circumstances. A man simply does not let a human being be mauled and devoured by a grizzly bear.

The Spencer roared three times, as fast as Spur could pull the lever to eject the spent cartridge and pump in a new one. There was no desire to kill the magnificent beast. All the shots hit the bear in the left shoulder and it roared in pain and turned toward its new enemy.

Cain jumped up and raced into the heavy timber, and Spur saw that he carried only his pistol, the rifle lost somewhere in his surprise by the grizzly.

Spur realized the big animal could run faster and farther than he could if he were unhurt. But the bear had three .52 caliber slugs in one shoulder and that would slow him down.

The Secret Service Agent charged downhill, through the light brush in the same direction Cain had gone. In a way he now regretted his humane act. The grizzly would have killed the pistol wielding puny little man. Then it would have been over. Perhaps the terror of being torn apart by a grizzly would have been a fit punishment for the crime.

Spur kept running. He could hear Cain crashing through brush ahead. There was no attempt at stealth now, only for survival, and that meant putting as much distance as physically possible between themselves and the infuriated grizzly.

The course carried Spur past the side of the low valley and up the side of a slope. He saw Cain for a moment as he vanished over the ridgeline. The fugitive was moving slower now. Spur turned and ran thirty yards parallel so he would come to the ridge in a different area.

Moving up slowly in a new position may have saved McCoy's life. He peered cautiously over the ridge, the bear forgotten now, the enemy with a deadly weapon became important again. Just across the ridge and near the point he had crossed, Cain lay beside a tree, his pistol up and ready.

Spur could see only the edge of his face and a hand with a six-gun. McCoy had no shot, not even with the rifle. Silently Spur edged back across the ridgeline and hurried ten yards toward the ambush point. When he peered over the ridge again past a heavy growth of grass, he saw that Cain had left.

Ahead Spur heard the man running again. There couldn't be much energy left in Cain. He would hole up soon. Cain was hunting a defensive position, and he knew the territory.

It was slow going for a while, as McCoy tracked the quarry running through the brushy woods. More Douglas fir showed now and Ponderosa pine and a sprinkling of

Western larch. None of the trees had been harvested, it was sparse but virgin timber land.

The trail led to a valley, and then turned up a small flowing stream a yard wide. The gurgling water became a drinking fountain for Spur who didn't realize how thirsty he was. His canteen was on his dead horse.

To Spur's surprise he saw a thin column of smoke coming from the canyon. He was sure Cain's tracks led in that direction. There could be only one reason for the smoke: it was a trap. Spur worked into heavier woods beside the stream and moved up cautiously. He had less than a hundred yards to go.

Spur's mind and every nerve ending in his body were alert to the slightest detail that might be out of place or dangerous. He saw nothing, no trip wires, no deadfalls, no snare that would lift him high in the air after catching one foot. Nothing.

Spur made the final thrust toward the smoke. He could smell it now, see tendrils lifting through the trees. Then he spotted the source. The fire had been built in the mouth of a small cave that became a dark circle in the far bank of the stream. A cave, a fortress. The perfect defensive position.

McCoy stared at the cave and knew the chase was not over.

Chapter Eighteen

Spur lay in the woods and watched the hole. Slowly he realized it was more than a cave. It was a tunnel, a mine tunnel that must have been there for years. The remains of tailings showed on both sides of the small creek that ran down and into the Santiam.

What was left of a wagon road could be seen on the far side of the stream. Young fir and larch trees had grown up and brush covered part of the old tracks. A mine, not just a cave. That presented a whole new problem. Sometimes mines had more than one entrance.

At once he made an assumption that this one probably didn't. It would have had to be extensive and successful for that kind of a tunnel and shaft system.

Maybe Spur could wait for Cain to put more fuel on the fire and nail him with a round at the mouth of the tunnel. Just then some branches came out of the darkness and landed on the fire. It was too late to shoot by the time Spur brought up the Spencer.

A voice boomed from the cave, distorted and faint, but Spur could hear it.

"McCoy. You must be out there by now. You've had an hour to find the smoke. Come on and get me, bastard! Come and find me. I used to work in this mine. I know every square foot of it and I can run you around for months in here."

Spur did not respond. Cain wouldn't know if he were outside the tunnel mouth yet or not. When the monologue finished, Spur moved slowly, working closer to the cave. He crossed the stream and ran toward the tunnel. The agent was well to one side and out of sight. If Cain came close enough to call out again, Spur would act.

Time didn't matter now. It was permanently midnight in the mine. There must be some torches. Enough of that for later. He hoped he could finish the chase near the entrance.

It was almost an hour later when Spur heard movement inside the tunnel. Spur had worked up soundlessly until he now stood just outside the square set framing of the tunnel mouth. The agent could hear the foot-steps, saw sparks fly as the unseen man tossed wood on the fire, then the voice came.

"McCoy, you might as well come get me, I'm never going . . ."

The rest of the words were blasted by sound as Spur leaped in front of the tunnel and fired six times with his six-gun and then jumped back. He pushed the rifle around the timbers and fired five more times into the hole.

When the echoes of the barrage faded into the distance, Spur heard a sullen laugh.

"Close, but no prize, lawman. A good tactic, but not good enough. Now come and get me!"

Spur pushed the spent rounds from his pistol and pushed new ones in. He checked his pockets. He had fresh packets of stinkers, the cardboard matchsticks with sulphur and salt peter on the ends that could be struck on the bottom and lighted. He reloaded the Spencer so it had seven rounds in the tubular magazine that slid in through the stock. The Spencer 1860 7-shot repeating rifle had half the range of the new army Springfield .45 caliber rifle. But he preferred it for short work.

His ears had been straining, but he had heard nothing from the tunnel. There had been no shots. Perhaps Cain was getting short on rounds for his pistol. Perhaps he was out of ammunition.

Spur knew he would backlight himself the moment he started into the tunnel. He would do it quickly, from this side of the front of the tunnel to the far side just inside. A running, diving roll would do it. He pressed at the bandage high on his chest and hoped it would hold for one more diving roll.

He waited another five minutes, then turned, ran forward, dove at the front of the timbers and rolled inside, coming to his feet and pressing against the rough rock wall.

There had been no shots, no attack. He let his eyes widen to accustom himself to the dim light. Torches, there should be some close at hand. Or had they all been used up by wandering explorers?

He stared hard at the walls near the front and found a torch. It was a two foot fir branch. The end had been injured when still on the tree and it grew a thick pad of "pitch" around the wound. The pitch was solid turpentine, and burned with a brilliant flame. Pitch sticks would start on fire even when soaking wet because the water could not penetrate the cells of the heavy pitch wood.

Spur carried the stick, slung the rifle over his back on the strap, and put the Peacemaker in his right hand. He moved forward slowly.

There had not been rails in the tunnel, or if there had they were gone now. The dirt floor was cluttered with fallen rocks and dirt and stones from the ceiling and walls. Here there was no framing, just a naked tunnel cut through the rock and earth. The rock had been firm enough to hold the ceiling. The tunnel was seven feet high and most of the opening was six feet wide.

Spur walked softly for twenty feet and realized that he could see no more than two or three feet in front of him, and that distance was becoming shorter. He had to use the torch, and maybe become a target, or he had to turn around.

He knelt down and took out the stinkers. Hope more than logic told him that Cain was down to his last three or four shots in the pistol. He would use them carefully, use them to kill, not on a wild long shot.

Spur struck match to the fir pitch and saw it catch at once. He couldn't have had a better torch if he had soaked a gunny sack in coal oil and wired it to a stick.

The pitch blazed up brighter and brighter, and Spur held the branch at arm's distance in front of him and hurried along the tunnel.

Twenty feet farther in he came to a drift, a side tunnel that hd been cut in exploring for, or removing, ore. He checked it and found it was only a dozen feet deep, but it had been dug out fifteen feet high. There was a long iron rod with a sharp point on one end that had been dulled, and a round ball on the other that had been slammed repeatedly with a sledge. It was a slow, cheap kind of hand drill, that would be held by one man, pounded by another, and turned with every blow.

Spur went back to the main tunnel and listened.

Nothing.

He worked down the path faster now, cleared three more drifts to each side and came soon to a wider, higher place where timbers were positioned in the center and bolted in place. When he looked closer with

214

the torch he saw it was a shaft that went straight down. Spur dropped a rock down and listened for it to hit the bottom. It went down a long way before he heard the sound of bottom. There was a tattered remains of a two-inch rope hanging six feet into the shaft.

Cain wasn't down there, unless he was dead at the bottom.

Spur moved around the vault-like room and found four more tunnels leading off. He guessed now that this must have been a producing mine of some sort, that had been long abandoned.

He looked up when he heard the sound. The light from the torch did not carry far enough for him to find the source. It seemed to be coming from one of the tunnels that went out like spokes. Then he saw the rails on the center tunnel and he jumped off the thin steel rails that extended into the darkness.

A moment later an ore car eight feet long and weighing hundreds of pounds thundered down the rails and slammed into the foot thick timbers at the dump point. When the sound faded, Spur heard laughter up the track.

Now he had a direction.

The pine knot burned brightly, but he caught another one and carried it with him. There were more of the torches up this way. Here there was evidence that the mine had been worked more recently. Piles of ore showed on the floor at the end of some of the drifts. He found a shovel and a pick in one of the drifts where they had been left by some weary miner.

The ceiling of the main tunnel was lower here. In some spots Spur had to bend over to get under. Here and there he saw square sets of timbers that roofed up what must be soft spots in the ceiling.

Once when he looked ahead into the darkness he saw the glimmer of a torch. He fired at it, only to have his eardrums assaulted by the thunderous explosion of the .45 in the confined space of the tunnel, where the sound slammed from one close wall to the other, and reverberated through the whole mine, the vibrations causing sifts of sand and dirt to pour down from the ceiling, and in some cases small rockfalls came down.

He moved ahead faster now, not checking the side drifts until he came to the point where he figured the torch had been.

He saw the light well before he got there. It was another "room" dug out where they must have found a large deposit of ore. The area was twenty feet high and twice that wide. Six torches had been lighted and put in holders around the walls. The black oily smoke lifted to the roof where it hung in blue waves.

Spur saw at once that four more tunnels led out of the room. He marked the one he left by knocking a pair of fresh chips off the blue-gray rock by the entrance. Spur could see no one in the enclosure. Cain had to be in one of the other tunnels, waiting for an easy shot.

"You might as well surrender, Cain. You have nowhere to go. This is the end of the line. We can starve you out if nothing else. We don't have to wade in there and trade .45 rounds with you. You're a dead man if you stay here. You have a chance with a judge and a jury."

"No chance at all, you know that!" Cain shot back at him. The voice was high, strange, wild.

"Yes, a chance. Tell them you went crazy. You didn't know what you were doing. There always is a chance with a good lawyer and a jury of twelve men. It's better than dead."

"How do you know, McCoy? You've never been dead."

"True, but the dead people I've seen don't look like they are having one hell of a good time." Neither of them spoke for a moment.

"You know anybody who died?" Spur asked.

"Yes! That shit-assed little boy on the stage. He pulled my mask down. The robberies were just exciting games for the four of us. Hell, we made a few dollars and nobody got hurt."

"What about the mail that didn't get delivered?"

"That's all in my dresser out at the ranch.

Hey! I wouldn't mess around with the U.S. mail! Man can get in trouble doing that!"

"Come on out, Cain. It's over. The game is over. Time to pay up on your bet. You bet and you lost, now you pay. Simple."

"Yeah, right. True. Only when they collect they stretch my neck. I'm not that crazy. I kill you and I can get out and away."

"What about the rest of the posse? They are right behind me, exxept for Efrem Longley. You hit him in the thigh, hurt him bad."

"Good! Longley caused all our trouble!"

"Not so, Cain. You caused all of your trouble. We know you were with them at the stage. You, Jim Darlow, Zack Kinsey, and Roger Olsen. We know you went crazy and killed everybody, even the horses. Why the horses, Cain?"

"They saw me. They heard my name. They could have testified against me too. I had to kill them."

"I understand."

Spur knew where he was now, at the entrance to the middle tunnel. Spur eased away from his spot and moved around the circle putting the ore car between him and Cain. The other man couldn't see Spur move.

"So, throw out your pistol, Cain. I think you're out of ammunition anyway. You never were much good with guns."

The answer came with three shots, thundering into the cavern. When the sound

218

soaked into the rocks, Spur heard the six-gun being triggered again and again, but each time the firing pin fell on a used chamber.

Spur peered over the ore car. Cain lay in the mouth of the tunnel, looking out, pulling the trigger at regular intervals, with the weapon clicking. Spur darted around the car and jumped on top of the fugitive.

Cain dropped his gun, laughed at Spur and picked up a second pistol Spur didn't know he had. He aimed it at Spur who had holstered his own weapon.

"Now, you're going to find out how much fun it is to be dead, Spur McCoy, United States Secret Service Agent. My friends tell me it ain't no fun at all."

Spur's hand eased toward his own leather.

"Don't move it another inch, and get off me. Sit up in the dirt, then lay down, face down, right there."

Spur had no choice. He lay down. Cain reached in carefully and snatched the Peacemaker from the leather and laughed. He threw away the weapon he had been holding on Spur.

"It was empty!" Cain said. He laughed, howling in a wild kind of joy that consumed him. Spur jumped up but heard the laughter cut off and the muzzle of his own six-gun press against his forehead.

"Down, boy, down!"

Cain sat in the dirt across the six foot tunnel from Spur and stared at him. "Hell, guess you ain't such a bad sort. I just don't take to you. Don't matter. We'll both be dead in sight of twenty four hours. That is if them posse guys is any good back there."

He laughed, looked at the eagles carved into the mother-of-pearl grips on the Peacemaker. "Damn nice. Yeah, lawman. Yeah, I killed them, I had to. They would have told on me and my old pappy would have beat hell out of me. So I shot them all. I had to. I'll show you just how I did it."

He aimed the .45 at Spur and then said, "Pow, pow!" Cain laughed. Then he began to cry. Spur edged forward. Cain didn't seem to notice. Spur moved another foot.

"I see you coming," Cain said. "Shit, I can't do nothing right! Maybe this will be right!"

Cain Haworth put the muzzle of the .45 in his mouth and pulled the trigger. The big .45 slug bored through the roof of his mouth, stormed through his shattered brain and burst out of the top of his skull peeling back a four-inch chunk of bone and brains and splattered them against the top of the tunnel.

A half hour later, Spur McCoy sat outisde the old mine. Sheriff Quigley had sent two deputies into the tunnel to bring out the body. As they waited the sheriff checked Spur's wounded chest.

"Least it isn't bleeding anymore. Doc Varner's going to chew you out right good when we get back."

"I guess. How is Longley?"

"We patched him up, and told him we'd have Doc Varner come by first thing tomorrow. He'll be good as new in a month."

The sheriff waited with Spur, then looked at him. "Did Cain kill that rancher back a few miles?"

"Claims he did. I heard a shot."

"Widow said he did. She wants to thank you for . . ."

Spur waved. "She's got problems enough."

"The boys helped her bury her man. She'll be going into town until she can get some help."

Spur nodded and found that he almost went to sleep before he could stop.

When the deputies came out of the mine they put the body down and one told the sheriff they couldn't find the top of his skull.

Sheriff Quigley shook his head. "Don't matter, tie him on a horse and let's get moving. I'd just as soon walk anyway, and we're going to be at least one horse short."

Spur McCoy went to sleep three times as they rode slowly back to the Longely ranch. Efrem wouldn't let Spur leave.

"I need that man around here," Longley kept saying. He waved at his eldest daughter. "Go talk some sense into Spur."

Bee tried, but Spur could barely understand her. He let her kiss his cheek, then they rode again for town, and a bed and Spur hoped for at least twenty-four hours of sleep.

Chapter Nineteen

Someone pounded on Spur McCoy's hotel room door at ten A.M. but he mumbled something and went back to sleep.

Doc Varner arrived about four that afternoon to inquire about his chest wound and Spur told him to go feed himself some pills.

At eight P.M., twenty-six hours after he took to his bed, Spur's feet hit the floor. He couldn't sleep anymore.

Now all he wanted was food. In the lobby he found Bee Longley waiting for him. She had been there all day. She smiled at him and his three days growth of beard, his unkempt hair and the wrinkled clothes he hadn't bothered to change after sleeping in them.

"You're beautiful!" she said.

Spur blinked. He should know who she was. Slowly the image of upthrust, hot bare breasts and pumping hips came back to him and he nodded.

"Bee . . ."

"I bet you're hungry. I tried to take you dinner once, and you threw me out. I never got into your room but you shouted some terrible things at me through the door. I

222

think you were alseep all the time. I know you sure were mad."

He nodded and walked into the dining room. She smiled and trailed after him.

Spur sat down at a table, waved for a whole pot of coffee and drank two cups down without more than blinking at Bee who sat opposite him.

When the second cup of coffee hit bottom, he shook his head, wiped the stringy hair out of his eyes, found a comb in his pocket and combed it back, then he wiped his eyes with the white cloth napkin he had been given, and realized he wasn't really blind. He blinked the film away from his eyes and saw Bee smiling at him.

"Gorgeous!" he said, feeling the first pangs of humanity. He waved at the young girl who came to wait on him. "Just bring me some of everything, a big steak, and potatoes and half a loaf of bread and a quart of milk, lots of vegetables, and chicken if you have any. Oh, got any roasts or stew?" The girl grinned and ran for the kitchen.

Spur turned back to Bee. He sighed, shook his head again and put his chin on his fists. "Little Bee. How is your father?"

"Doc Varner said he'll live. The bullet went clean through his leg, missed the bone. I tied it up tight so he didn't lose too much blood. I . . . I never got a chance to thank you for saving my life."

"He wouldn't have killed you."

"He would . . . afterward. He told me that. Said how good I was depended how long I lived. He wasn't a nice man."

"No."

"Have you seen Doc yet?"

"No."

"I'll go find him and have him come see you just as soon as you finish eating!" She was up and gone before he could protest. Spur had another cup of coffee and the fried chicken and roast and potatoes and brown gravy and vegetables came. There were six dishes with food on larger than normal plates. The waitress said his steak was coming, did he want it seared on the outside and raw in the middle as usual? He nodded and went back to eating.

Sheriff Quigley stopped by at his table.

"Rip Van Winkle, you woke up."

"Nearly."

"Before you go to sleep again, how do you want me to charge the two surviving stage coach robbers?"

"With stage robbery. Olsen gets a break on his sentence if he gives evidence against Darlow and pleads guilty."

"And the two arsonists?"

"How did Haworth take the confession and suicide of his son?"

"Hard. Lot and Abel had to help him walk to the funeral this morning. He's aged twenty years this week. Abel says he's running the ranch now. He's assured me he'll pay for materials to rebuild the barns at the two ranches, and that there won't be any more trouble."

"Let's charge the two arsonists with arson, stiffest kind possible according to Wyoming Territorial law, and forget about Henry Haworth. He's paid enough." Spur paused and cut a big chunk off the two-inch thick T-Bone steak. "That is unless you want to handle the cases some other way. This is your primary jurisdiction."

"No, no I like your suggestion. I'll get the papers drawn up in the morning. If you stop by I do have some other papers I need you to sign. Concerning the suicide, the confession, and the death of the rancher."

"Right. About ten or eleven. I may sleep in again."

"Don't blame you." Quigley watched Spur finish another drumstick and break a huge piece of bread off the loaf. "Are you sure you're getting enough to eat? I understand they have some great apple pie here served with a wedge of the sharpest cheese in the country."

Spur nodded. "Good. I hadn't even thought of dessert."

When he finished the food, he felt ten pounds heavier, but the great chalky empty spot in his chest had been filled and he felt better. He headed back upstairs, noticing his clothes for the first time. He could also use a bath.

The moment he came into his room he saw Bee testing a tub of bathwater. Steam rose from a bucket of hot water beside the tub. A chair held two towels and a bar of soap.

"I . . . I thought you might want a nice relaxing bath."

"Sounds good."

"I get to wash you."

Spur smiled. "That also sounds good. But what would your daddy say?"

"He already has approved. When us Longleys want something, we go after it. I told him I was going to hound you until you married me, even if I had to bed you first."

Spur chuckled. "I bet he swatted you for that."

"No, he just looked me up and down, and said to go to it. He said if I couldn't do it, then it couldn't be done . . . get you to tie the knot."

"Sounds like a challenge."

"It will be fun to try." She began unbuttoning his shirt, and he caught her hands and kissed her, then let her continue.

A short time later Spur settled in the tub, his knees sticking out. It felt good to get a backscrub again. She was careful not to get the bandage wet.

"Doc Varner was out at a ranch welcoming a baby to the world. His wife said you should come see him tomorrow."

Spur nodded. Bee was still fully dressed. She had hardly hesitated when she pulled his pants and under drawers off, but now as she washed lower and lower he saw her begin to get excited.

"Should I wash . . . everything?" she asked. Spur nodded.

"Oh!" She frowned. "Then, you'll have to stand up."

Spur did and she giggled as she soaped his flaccid penis and his heavy scrotum. She washed his legs quickly and came back to his crotch.

"You figure there's any way we could get him to take a little interest in the bath giver?" Spur asked.

"We could try," she said flashing him a smile. Quickly she washed the soap off his crotch then reached in and held him and kissed the limp head. She yelped as it pulsed and lifted slightly. She laughed and kissed it again, then fondled him and in a minute he was straight and bold and hard.

"Now that is more like it!" Bee said. She unbuttoned her dress and opened the bodice. Bee caught his hand and put it inside the opening and under her chemise.

"My that feels good!" she said. "All kind of warm and soft, and . . . just nice!"

Spur stepped from the tub and picked her up, holding her fast to his still wet body and carried her to the bed.

"So you told your old dad you might bed me did you?"

"I told you, I go after what I want!"

He dropped her on the bed and sat down

beside her.

"Fair is fair. We had a fling a few days ago, right? No promises, no strings, no demands."

"Yes, and it was beautiful."

"So I must be fair with you. I can't marry you. I can't stay here. I can't take you with me. I'm a roving man, that's my job. I'm in a different town almost every week. I'm not the man for you."

Bee bit her lip. "And . . . and my letting you have me all night isn't going to change your mind?"

"Right. That's what I'm telling you. A girl has to think about her reputation."

Tears squeezed out of protesting eyelids. "Damnit! I want you so bad! Why can't it be different?"

"It will be for you, some day, with someone. Now, before I touch you again, you can button up your dress and comb your hair and get in the buggy and I'll have a reliable man drive you back to your ranch, or you can go stay overnight with Betty and her parents."

"Oh, damn!" She sat up and leaned in and kissed him hard, then she bounced off the bed and quickly lifted the dress over her head, then three petticoats until she had on only a thin chemise and her knee length drawers.

"No. I want to stay here with you . . . all night, if you'll have me. I want to make love with you a dozen times, and have you show me all the tender ways to love a man and tell you how I feel and I want you to tell me how you feel and pretend just for one night that I am married to you." She stopped and sat on his lap and kissed his lips hungrily. She watched him closely for his reaction.

He nodded.

Her face blossomed with a beautiful smile, the frown gone.

"Then if I never do meet that perfect man and love and marry him, I'll have a powerful memory to help me get through the days, and I can always dream about what might have been."

She pushed back off his lap into the bed, and lifted the chemise over her head and lay there waiting.

Spur lay beside her, leaned over her and kissed both her breasts and smiled down at her. "Bathsheba Longley, you are one hell of a lot of woman. You are young and eager and so sexy it makes me leap to attention. I'm passing up a beautiful woman here by not taking you with me. But it just couldn't work."

She sighed. "You know for sure, because you've had this same problem before."

"Somewhat the same. But never such a beautiful, beguiling, sexy, marvelous problem."

She blinked rapidly and a single tear seeped out of one eye and ran down her cheek.

"You know just the right thing to say. Now quickly make love to me gently and all night and let me fill up a storehouse of sweet memories to last as long as I need them."

He kissed her and lay gently over her.

"Bee, I'm going to have a stack of wonderful memories to keep me going, too."

It began gently, with soft, tender passion, and before it was over the first time had grown into a furious, fire-filled rampage of every emotion they had ever felt, and ended with a clawing, scratching, wailing pair of climaxes that came together in a performance they knew would be hard to top. But they would try.

They had nothing to eat or drink in the room, and by the time he thought of it, it was too late. For a while they sat side by side on the bed, talking quietly. She poured her soul out to him, telling him her deepest secrets, things she had never told anyone. She told him how Betty had played with her one night in bed and they both had become excited and rubbed each other into climaxes.

"Since then I do it myself once in a while. Is that so bad?"

"It's not bad at all. But a man should excite you more than that ever could."

Bee grinned and played with his limp lance.

"There is no problem there! I am simply floored by the way you get me so worked up I want to lay on my back for you. Will it be that way with me for some other man?''

"Yes. Making love, having sex, is a natural act. Mother Nature intended it that way. Everyone is good at sex, it's like saying someone is good at breathing. We all can do it. Sex is the same way. The trick is to find the right person to be with, to love, to marry.''

"Oh, I know, and I thought I had!''

"But it has to be right for BOTH people.''

"Yes, now I understand.'' She hesitated. "Would it hurt, I mean would it be all right if I was on top?''

Spur laughed and pulled her on top of him "No hurt of mine can be so bad that you can't lay on top of it.'' He grinned. "Especially when you are all beautiful and naked and sexy this way.''

They made love again, gently and they talked all the time, telling each other exactly how they felt, when the thrill came and how it felt, every tingle and breathlessness, every spasm and climax.

They slept after that and woke early in the morning before dawn for one last lingering lovemaking as the day began.

Spur sat on the edge of the bed and watched her dress.

"Will I ever see you again?''

"My business here will be done soon.'' He stopped and frowned, walked to the window and looked out the blind. A soft rain fell outside. The heavy clouds looked loaded with water vapor.

231

"It's raining!" he said.

"Oh, wonderful!"

"Looks like it's going to rain all day and all night, a real soaker. The drought may be over."

"See what wonderful luck you've brought us? Sure you won't stay? I've got a big ranch to offer you, and me." She threw her arms wide and pushed her breasts out.

Spur kissed her cheek and managed to miss the tub of bath water which still sat in the middle of the room.

"I think you better wait for a better offer. One of these days somebody around here is going to knock your socks off. Have you ever said hello to Lot or Abel Haworth?"

"Not on your life!"

"Things are going to be different now. Both are extremely fine young men. Make it a point to say hello the next time you 'just happen' to walk past them. It could prove interesting. And what a joint venture the two biggest ranches would make!"

A small smile began to play in Bee's eyes and around her delicate mouth as she thought about the handsome Haworth boys.

Spur kissed her mouth, then walked her to his door. She reached up and kissed him once more, then tied her sunbonnet on and headed for the desk to find out where they had put her buggy.

Spur smiled as the door shut. Then he dove back in bed and pulled the covers up over his head. Now maybe he could catch up on some of his sleep before he confronted Dr. Varner. Then the sheriff and finally Claudine over at the Pink Petticoat.

Chapter Twenty

Spur spent a half hour shaving, combing his hair and dressing. He put on his black suit, ruffled front white shirt with the big cufflinks, and a narrow string tie, then went to see Doc Varner. The sawbones pretended he didn't know him. At last he stared at Spur and scowled.

"Sonny, next time I tell you to stay in bed three days after you been shot up bad, you damn well stay in bed!"

"Yes sir," Spur said.

Doc grinned. "Damn glad you didn't this time. Most of the town was shocked by what Cain Haworth done. Everybody knew he was a little wild, but had no idea he was that crazy. Just never can tell about people. Me, I'm going into veterinary medicine. Patients never backtalk you."

"You want to take a look at me or not?" Spur said with an easy irreverence.

"Might as well now that you wasted this much of my time. Didn't have to dress up formal just to come see me."

"I always do."

Five minutes later, Doc Varner had the

wound examined, put on some more of his favorite ointment and wrapped it tightly again.

"I'd guess you're getting ready to travel. That bandage will do for a week, less you get too active. Healing up fine. Bother you any?"

"Only when I lose a wrestling match with a pretty woman."

"Serves you right."

Spur gave the doctor a twenty dollar gold piece. "That take care of my bill?"

"And then some."

"Put it down for one of your charity cases."

"Done." Doc looked up. "Where you heading from here?"

"To a telegraph to find out what kind of orders, directives and problems I have. It's a big country."

"True. And I think I've got twins coming. If I can tear myself away from your sparkling wit and conversation."

Spur laughed, waved goodbye and went out the door heading for the sheriff's office.

Sheriff Quigley was in and waiting. He had the papers all drawn up in his secretary's best printing waiting for Spur's signature. Two were complaints, two sets of charges, and an account of how Cain had shot himself as Spur had told it to the sheriff. Spur made one small change and signed it. The last document dealt with the death of the rancher who had been shot by Cain. Spur signed it as well.

"Ever find the rest of the double gold

eagles that belong to Marshall Sullivan over at the bank?" Spur asked.

"All of them but one. Cain had a hundred of them in that same drawer with the mail. A lot of folks are breathing easier now that the mail has been delivered. All sorts of important papers in those packs. At least that boy didn't burn the mail."

"Small favors," Spur said. There was nothing else to be said. Spur reminded the sheriff he wouldn't be around for the trials, but they had more than enough evidence to convict all four men on the arson and robbery charges.

"Stop by and see us anytime," Sheriff Quigley said.

"Don't wait up for me," Spur said, grinned and walked out the door.

Next stop for Spur was the Pink Petticoat. He waved at Barry behind the bar and went back to Claudine's private quarters. He knocked and then opened the door. She sat at her little kitchen table with a long black cigar in her mouth and a cup of coffee beside her.

"Don't say a word," Spur said. "I'm basking in the glory of being your local hero, and now I want a little peace and quiet and some slow easy loving as I recuperate for a few days from being shot, trampled and put upon."

Claudine chuckled softly and waved her hand toward the bedroom.

"Yes, oh lord and master, what would you desire first?"

"A little rest, a bunch of good food and a lot of loving."

"In that order?"

"In any damn order you want," he said. He was tired. Suddenly tired of running and watching over his shoulder. Tired of being shot at and punched and kicked and trampled and always having to be right.

Claudine would understand. She would put up with his guff for a few days. It was a reaction. He often got this way after a tough case. It passed. At least so far it had. He sat down and pointed to her coffee cup. She poured and he realized he hadn't had any breakfast.

"Food," he said, and bent over, putting his head on his crossed arms on the table. He relaxed and was asleep. As he slept the dream came again, the dream of someone chasing him, and he wasn't sure if they would catch him or not. Just as the evil looking man with the big gun closed in on him, someone shook his shoulder.

"Bacon and eggs, hashbrown potatoes, fresh biscuits, coffee and blackberry jam. Will that do?"

Spur came out of the dream and grinned.

"Yeah, that's going to do. Just don't tell anyone where I'm at, not for at least three days."

Spur began eating his breakfast and Claudine watched him, a patient, knowing expression on her face as the tip of her tongue moistened her lips.